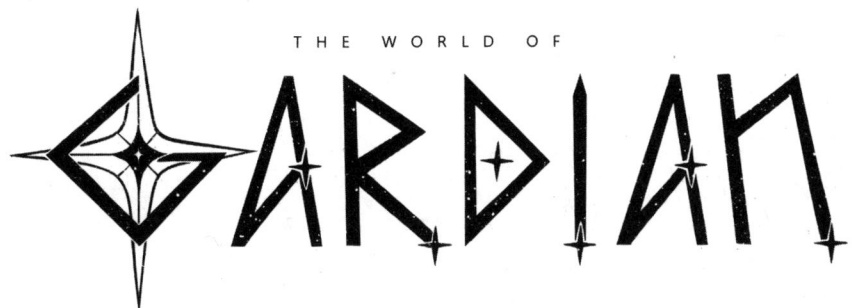

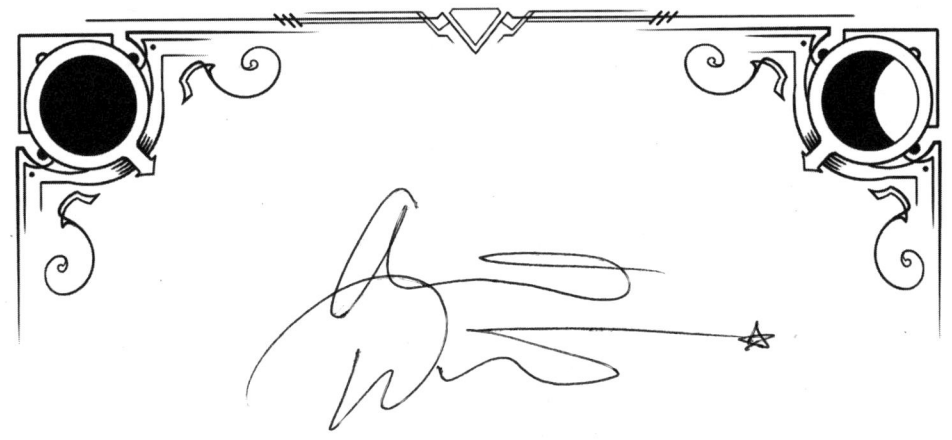

THE WORLD OF GARDIAN

Written by
Audra Winter

The World Of Gardian, LLC.

Copyright 2025 by Audra Winter
All rights Reserved

Limited Edition Dust Jacket Illustration By - Elrose Balan
Cover Art By - Amanda Jean
Interior Illustrations By - Elrose Balan, Martha Heloiza Santana Da Silva, Martin Bruno, and Joseph J Ramirez
End Page Illustration By Daniel Hernandez
Logos By - Brian Joshua Arnedo Magbojos
Cover Designed By - Karen Yu
Book Designed by - Joseph J Ramirez

Published by The World of Gardian, LLC.

All characters and events in this book are fictitious.
Any resemblance to persons living or dead is strictly coincidental.

The scanning, uploading and distribution of this book via the internet or any other means without the permission of the publisher is illegal and punishable by law. Please purchase only authorized electronic editions and do not participate in or encourage electronic piracy of copyrighted materials. Your support of the author's rights is appreciated.

ISBN 979-8-9989524-3-2

First Edition, June 2025
Printed in Canada
10 9 8 7 6 5 4 3 2 1

TABLE OF CONTENTS

World Map	6		Chapter 23	228
Chapter 1	11		Chapter 24	238
Chapter 2	18		Chapter 25	247
Chapter 3	29		Chapter 26	256
Chapter 4	40		Chapter 27	264
Chapter 5	52		Chapter 28	270
Chapter 6	61		Chapter 29	278
Chapter 7	77		Chapter 30	288
Chapter 8	86		Chapter 31	298
Chapter 9	98		Chapter 32	304
Chapter 10	106		Chapter 33	313
Chapter 11	118		Chapter 34	318
Chapter 12	130		Chapter 35	325
Chapter 13	139		Chapter 36	340
Chapter 14	145		Chapter 37	351
Chapter 15	154		Chapter 38	362
Chapter 16	162		Chapter 39	370
Chapter 17	172		Government Systems	378
Chapter 18	181		Glossary Terms	379
Chapter 19	190			
Chapter 20	200			
Chapter 21	209			
Chapter 22	218			

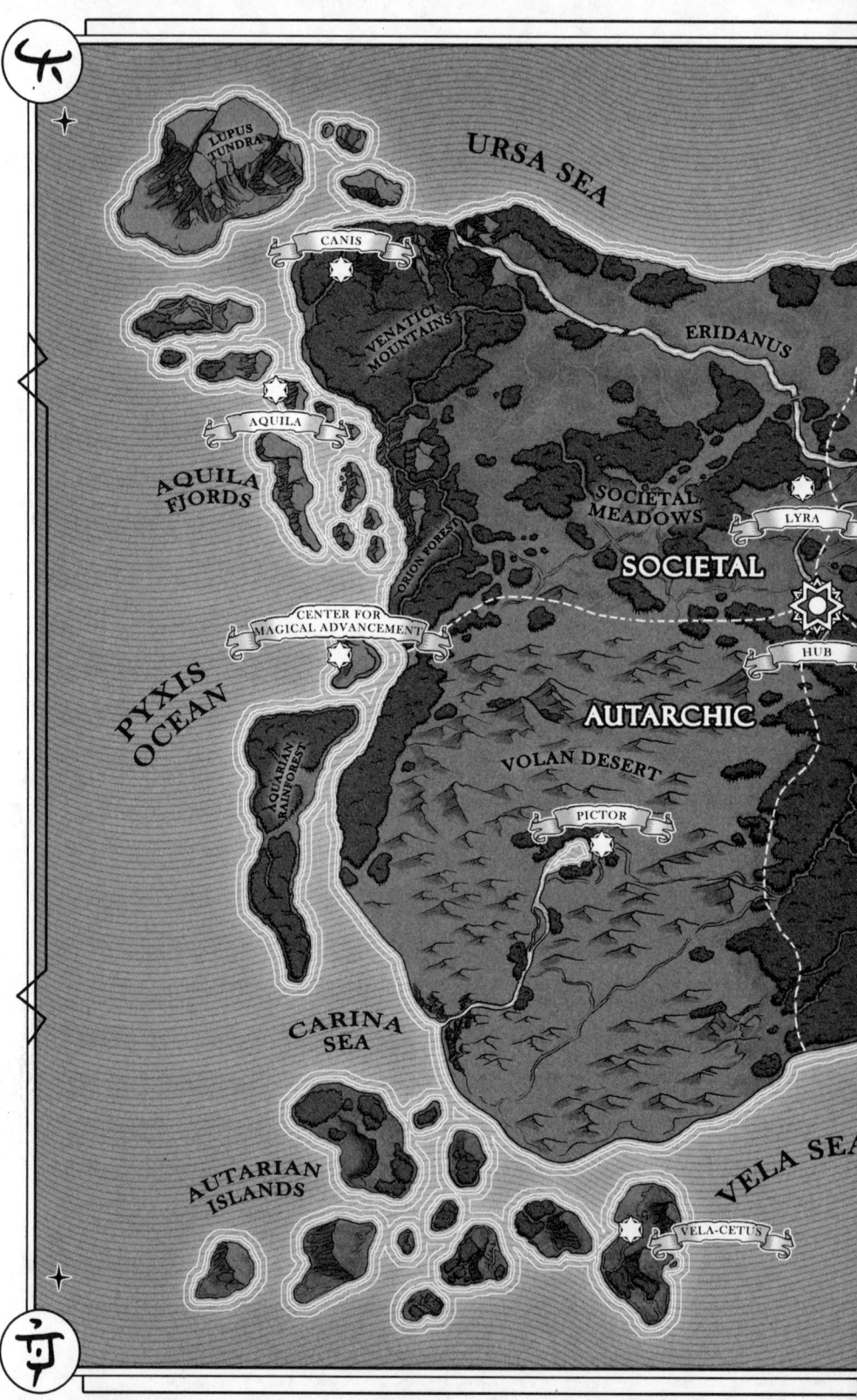

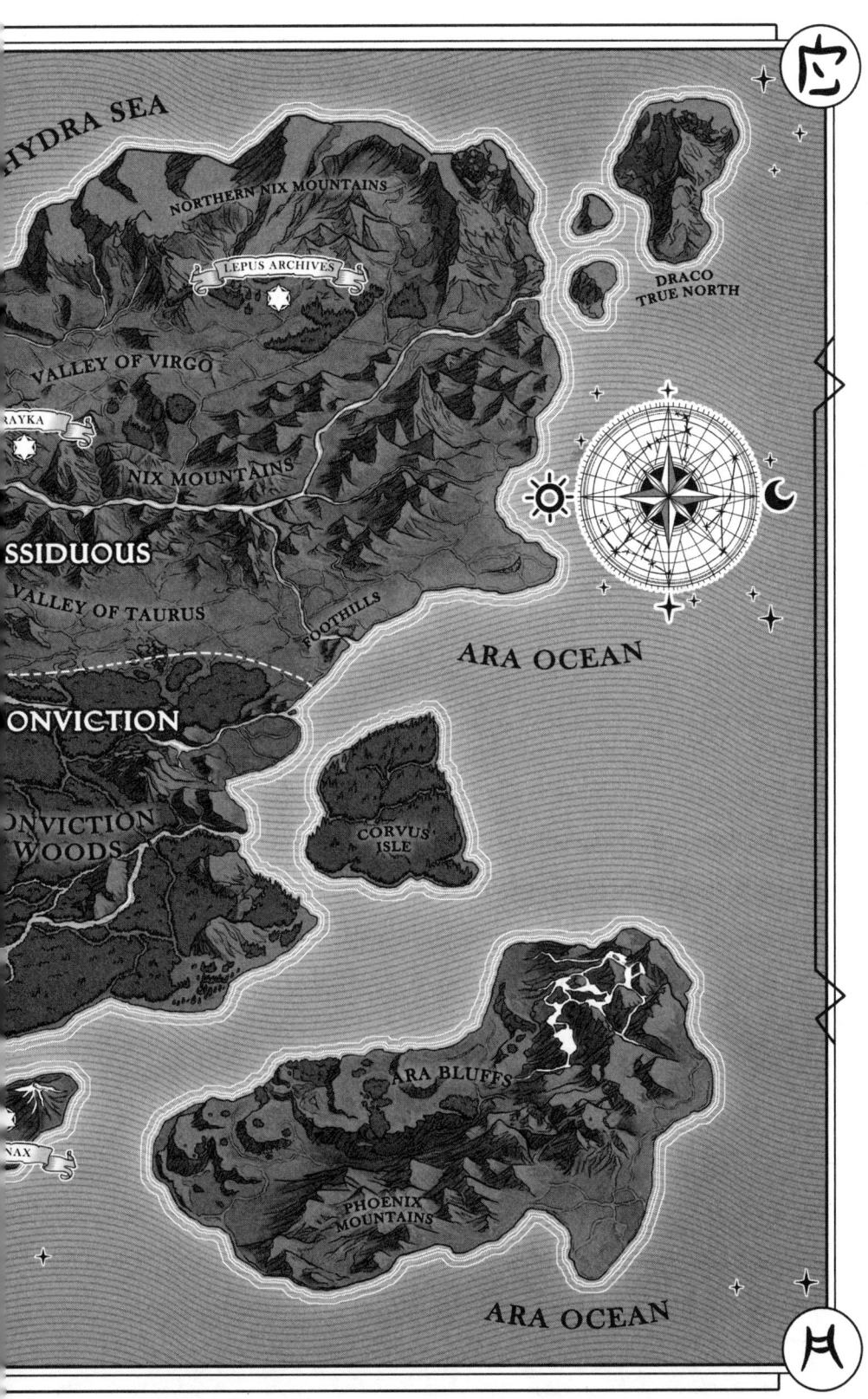

We blurred the line between humans and machines, and it burned Earth alive. It started with the angry oceans and burning forests, then came the earthquakes, eruptions, and extinctions. All we knew was lost in the destruction, but all we know was formed on the central continent. Humanity, we're known for surviving, and survive we did. Clusters of humans from all corners of the world prevailed through the disasters, and with the fall of each homeland, we sought anew. The central continent welcomed us. We deemed it the guardian land for humanity: Gardian.

In our darkest hours, the Cosmos remained unchanged. The Sun and Moon continued their chase through the sky and the Stars told us tales of those before us. When we couldn't understand our neighbor's language, we spoke the universal language of the stars. We found ourselves intricately woven together by the fates we couldn't see, like the invisible lines connecting the constellations. We paid our respects; we asked what they wished us to do, and they responded.

"Do not create machines when the stars above have always been within."

As we shared the stories of the stars, the Cosmos connected energy to magic and magic to body. It began with the three archpowers of the Sun, Moon, and Stars: Libran Healing (Libra), Spirit Walking (Cancer), and Zodiac Turning (Scorpio). The archpowers, attached to date of birth, were genetically transferred from one generation to the next, evolving into numerous magic systems throughout all 12 signs. Magic became rampant as society rebuilt and progressed alongside respect for the sacred lands and ecosystems of Gardian.

We advanced through the sharing of skill and story from the stars. We divided to function as one society: CONVICTION for leadership, fire, and law (Scorpio, Aries, Libra), ASSIDUOUS for sustenance, knowledge, and protection (Taurus, Virgo, Capricorn), AUTARCHIC for water, healing, and travel (Cancer, Pisces, Sagittarius), and SOCIETAL for light, magic, and art (Leo, Aquarius, Gemini).

Welcome to the World of Gardian.

CHAPTER 1

Someone had rewritten the history of Conviction Woods, the cursed forest I called home. Despite all the texts describing Conviction Woods as eternally inhabitable, there were hundreds of wartime artifacts scattered amongst the forest's grounds. The records had been altered to hide the truth of Gardian's last war, a truth that allowed the Woods to protect those mysteriously meant to survive beyond its boundaries.

I lingered on the edge of the farthest northern reach of Conviction Woods. Before me stood a crumbled and dilapidated stone arch, old runic etched across its surface, worn away by the structure returning to the earth. A few fallen stones lay scattered across the surrounding ground, freezing into the dirt as ancient remnants conjoined with snow and soil. Beyond the arch's gaping mouth laid Assiduous's barren territory.

Assiduous's barren territory, and its occupants who didn't want me meandering on their land. It was too late for me to trace the rest of the runic on the arch. I'd only recorded the lower carvings, my arms too short to reach the tallest stones. I let my eyes linger on the writing to try to memorize the patterns. The clock ticked as enemies neared, and while my feet drew me away from the arch, my mind bent around the writing.

The arch's inscriptions must've been centuries old. I'd never, in any of my studies, seen a combination of Union languages on an artifact. Mixing two Union languages was almost unfathomable to modern-day society; besides our common tongue, Gardian prioritized the separation of the four Unions—Conviction, Assiduous, Autarchic, Societal—in their own societies and territories. Even more intriguing, the arch dated back to a war where Conviction and Assiduous were enemies; a combination of the two languages was further proof that Gardian's recorded history was wrong.

I had spent months scouring over records, libraries, and books to pinpoint the location of the arch as soon as I spotted it mentioned in a 300-year-old document. My research eventually revealed that the arch was placed in Assidian territory on the edges of the Woods at the border, though that could've spanned hundreds of miles from the eastern part of the Hub, Gardian's shared centralized city, to the coastline of the continent. To trace the steps of ancient battles to the coordinates of the arch was a tedious process requiring my nose to be stuck in at least two dozen scrolls within the past couple of months.

Deciphering the runic on the arch was my next step to decoding the true history of Conviction Woods, and the moment I finally found it, an Assidian border patrol just had to be there—of course.

There was no doubt about it. The two of them had spotted me. I'd stepped past the 10-foot-wide path into Assidian territory where the arch stood, and they were headed straight toward me.

I backed up to Conviction Woods, safely passing beyond the aura of protection set on the trees. A faint shimmering aura of gold, green, and silver light flickered and shifted around the lanterns as I settled into Conviction's territory on the opposite side of the trail. Although it was a remarkably visible barrier, many Assidians, especially new recruits, were stupid enough to break through it, no matter how many times their Stellarium higher-ups warned them.

The two patrollers were approaching, both wearing thick winter cloaks with fur hoods. The man wore a forest green embroidered with the Assidian emblem and Taurus glyph, while the woman flaunted an umber coat with the Virgo glyph.

"You saw her, didn't you?" said the Taurus man. "At the arch?"

"Yes," the Virgo woman responded. "She wouldn't have had time to run north or south on the East Trail."

"So... she went into Conviction Woods?"

"Not a chance. She wouldn't survive."

"Are you sure you saw a red cloak?"

"I'm certain, and I'm tired of you doubting my every word."

They couldn't have been older than twenty-five. Young and inexperienced was what the Assidian Stellarium looked to employ, an easy job that made a steady income, enough to provide a young adult enough to live. Conviction hired guards for the same purpose, though our border patrols were less necessary along the trails, as outsiders from different Unions would rarely volunteer themselves to wander into Conviction Woods.

"You're sure she went in there?" the Taurus asked again.

"Yes." She rolled her eyes. "Where else do you suppose she disappeared to?"

The two of them stood in front of the Woods, curiously staring at what they saw as a forest empty of occupants. I wasn't visible past the aura that shielded and hid any entity who could survive beyond the boundaries.

"She wouldn't survive," he repeated.

The Virgo crossed her arms. "I still think they made it up."

"Who? What?" He raised his brows. "Who made what up?"

"The Conviction Stellarium. They made up the whole 'Conviction Woods is deadly' thing to keep us out. Have you ever talked to someone who has actually seen a beast?"

"No, and that's because they don't survive when they see one." He shivered and took a step back. "I say we leave it. She's gone. We can hang out here for a bit in case she comes back."

"They trained us to stay out of Conviction Woods, but they never told us why. The border patrol trainers mentioned nothing about what the Woods are like. All they said is that they're dangerous."

"This isn't worth it for a raise. It's one girl. Even if we catch her, we probably won't get much from it."

"Not if she's a Scorpio. Her capture would cover us for months." Her determined eyes were set on the space where I stood. "I didn't hear any screams. We would've heard if she was attacked."

"This is absurd. I'm *not* going in there." The Taurus took another step back. "No way. Absolutely not. Even they won't go in there. Good luck, you're on your own."

"You're a coward. I won't go far."

They, as in Convictionists. The guy wasn't wrong—normally, the Woods didn't make exceptions for anyone, regardless of Union, despite being part of Conviction's territory.

But my family was proof that there were exceptions, somehow, someway, and I would find out why.

I stepped farther back into the Woods, ducking behind the trunk of a massive pine. Its deep sepia bark shimmered gold when my hand fell atop its body. Sunlight filtered in green from the reflection of pine needles above, the forest floor covered in moss and shed cones from the hemlocks. Moisture clung to my skin with the humidity of the temperate rainforest.

Behind a nearby pine, a wolf laid idle, basking in a patch of cozy moss. Its nose twitched when it caught my scent, looking up to ensure I was familiar. Once I was approved, it rested its head back down on its paws, turning over on its side to warm its belly in the sunlight. I, too, enjoyed the peaceful hush of the Woods, the company of the unbothered creatures acquainted to my presence.

To anyone else, the Woods were a living hell amidst the land of Gardian.

The woman took a step beyond the lanterns, breaking through the aurora boundary. She met my eyes with a smile, her hand resting on a belt as she unsheathed a dagger.

My fingers traced over the half-moon necklace resting above my cloak. I snapped it off and shook the necklace, causing its transformation spell to activate. With a flash of pale blue light, it shifted into a short broadsword. Its deep ebony metal flared in the sunlight as I faced it toward her, grasping the red and gold handle.

Her eyes darted around, observing the tranquil forest around her. "So, it was all a lie."

I smiled, and she shook her head in bewilderment at the expressed emotion from a Scorpio. I wasn't concerned. She'd never dare to talk about what the Woods were about to unleash upon her, let alone try to return.

I waved at her. "Good luck. Hope you can run fast."

The sunlight waned. Shadows crept along the trees in tendrils and swallowed the golden hues. A sharp wind hushed the birdsong, brushing

along my shoulders. The inviting greens contorted, vines swallowing the forest floor in a sea of mossy sludge, while a fog curled around trunks.

The wolf stood as a shadow seeped into its body. Its yellow eyes blinked scarlet, a stare that was said to slice your soul in half, devouring you from the metaphysical before the physical. It stalked past me; the vines on the forest floor didn't tie themselves around my ankles; the shadows avoided my skin.

Blood oozed from the beast's maw when it unleashed a hungry snarl, its body reeking of putrid, rotting limbs. Panic flooded over the woman's face, and she looked to me with wide eyes, as if I could do anything about it.

"If I were you," I said, shaking my sword to reverse it back to my pendant, "I would turn back now."

In any other circumstance, she would've disregarded a Scorpio's warning. Some part of me found satisfaction in seeing the Assidians listen to my instruction when they stepped beyond the boundary of the Woods.

She turned her back to the beast and scrambled to the lanterns as the creature leapt forward, snapping at her leg. It merely missed as she broke through the aura and slammed against the dirt of the East Trail. The beast didn't follow her out, instead watching her with its piercing red eyes in case she crossed back over. For a few moments, both remained in a standstill, until the forest recognized the departure of its threat. The shadows sunk into the ground, golden hues washing over the trees in a glimmering wave.

The black fog melted off the wolf. It glanced back at my direction, and after determining that the Woods were clear of intruders, it trotted over to me. I knelt and stroked between its ears as it curiously gave me a sniff-spection. It wagged its tail before it returned to the bed of moss, flopping back over. I must've been approved again.

Beyond the boundary, the Taurus was screaming at his colleague. Her dagger had been thrown aside. She sobbed, begging him to believe what she'd seen.

With a satisfied, guilty smile, I turned away from the East Trail, walking deeper into the Woods; there was no use in letting the day waste by attempting to wait for the Assidians to recover. The wolf, catching my movement, perked its ears and bounded after me to guide me home.

The forest understood how to defend me, and I was on the verge of rewriting its history.

Chapter 2

By the time I made it home, the Sun was lingering above the west horizon. Between the trees sat our house in a sandy clearing where trunks and foliage bent away from the old A-frame cabin. The wood logs were sun-stained, crumbling and barely held together by an aged enchantment set upon the foundations of the house years ago. Moss blanketed its walls and gave the entire clearing its earthy smell; though midwinter raged throughout the rest of Gardian, Conviction Woods kept its humid warmth year-round. Our parents found and restored the abandoned house in the Woods before Avia—my half-sister—and I were born. All four of us were immune to the Woods, and not a single one of us had any clue why.

Avia was on the porch, lying back with her legs dangling off the side of the platform. I rolled my eyes at the fact that she was wearing my black pants again. Similar to the Assidian guards, Avia had a border patrol crest embroidered next to her Aries glyph on her orange coat, symbolizing her loyalty to guarding the Conviction-Assiduous border.

"Rieka." She glanced up with a smile, looking down at her watch. "Three hours late. What was it this time?"

"Ten miles out into the forest to the Assidian border. I had the pleasure of watching a Virgo border guard get chased out of the Woods by a beast."

I climbed the stairs to the door with a missing lock, each step creaking in its own tone. Without giving her time to respond, I kicked open the door to immediately look at the coatrack against the wall. My eyes caught to Dad's blue and tan Autarian long coat with a gold Cancer symbol—I smiled. He'd made it home in time. Dad's formal attire had taken my spot on the rack, so I ripped my cloak off my shoulders and threw it on the dusty couch that sat right next to the door.

"You walked twenty miles? Today, of all days?" Avia said as she followed me in. "What time did you get up?"

"Maybe if you didn't sleep like a rock, you would've heard me sneak out at 3 AM." I threw my bag down beside the pile of mud-smeared shoes and boots. "I'm perfectly fine. It's flat. I had a plan, and I've done way more."

There was barely a temperature change from the Woods to inside the house; though midwinter raged throughout the rest of Gardian, Conviction Woods kept its humid warmth all year long. Most houses in Gardian had an enchantment cast by ice mages to keep them cool in the summer; we never even needed one. Avia and I had grown up alongside the temperate humidity, and I was a little bit convinced that the moisture had seeped into my skin over the years.

"One of these days, they're actually going to catch you, and no one will be there to bail you." Avia followed me in, her voice carrying through the hallway like an echo chamber—loud, distinctive, and most importantly, my sister's voice.

"They haven't yet. You look inviting." I nodded at her black clothing underneath her cloak, and her blonde hair plastered across her glistening forehead. "We have the Ceremony in a couple of hours, and you haven't even started to get ready. Something exciting must've happened at work, and you just have to tell your sister, right?"

"You look and smell like you jumped in a stagnant pond. You're lucky that Dad gave us water in this house, and you're even more lucky that I'll let you shower first." She smacked me on the arm. "Also, the contract says I'm not supposed to tell anyone about my work day, *including family*."

"When have you ever listened to rules? It's almost like you were waiting for me to get home to tell me."

"How many laws have *you* broken today? And hello? The Code?" She gestured toward her face, then over at mine. "You're smiling."

"Yeah, okay. I'm not watching my emotions with you. Never have, never will. I don't care how close we are to the Ceremony."

"That's not what the law says."

The Scorpio Code recited itself in my head: *never show emotions, never befriend others, and never fall in love.*

After a moment of hesitation, I scoffed. "As if you're listening to the law more than I am."

Avia slumped over the table in the small, empty dining room near our front door, her head hung over the table as she rubbed her face. Underneath her hands were eyes downcast with concern that she was trying to smother. Aries, the warrior, the fighter, taught to not show fear. Though not showing fear wasn't an official Code that the Aries Stellarium issued, it was held above Avia's shoulders with societal pressure. In that moment, for the first time in years, I saw the irresistible worry in the tears at the edges of her eyes. She wouldn't dare let them fall.

A guilt crept through me. If only I could listen and obey my Code as much as Avia inherently rarely feared. I had to break the silence before either of us cried.

"I found it, Avia."

She looked up quickly. "The arch? The *right* one?"

"The *right* one."

I reached down to unbutton my bag, pulling out a wrinkled map of Conviction Woods. Dad, Avia's father and my adoptive father, had drawn it for me years ago. The ink was fading from the sunlight it'd been exposed to while I explored the Woods. I placed it down on the table and slid it in front of Avia, tracing my index finger alongside the dotted border of Conviction and Assiduous, resting my finger on top of a mark I'd made.

"I thought it was going to be around here. That's where I was a couple of days ago." I barely moved my finger south. "But it was here. The writing across it was a combination of Driksaal and Rurian. It was different from the writing on the other arches I've seen."

"The fact that you found it is proof of your insanity," Avia said. "I've never been placed on the border around there. Most of the arches look the same to me anyway."

I tried to ignore her lack of excitement. Dad would've been much more enthusiastic about the discovery. "Where's he?"

"Dad? Probably at the Ceremony location already. Mom left a note on the door this morning. Did you..." She paused before she finished the sentence to rub her face.

"What?"

"Did you even notice the note?"

I pursed my lips. "It was dark."

"Notes are there for you to read, Rieka." Avia paused, narrowing her eyes at me, contemplating whether or not to tell me about her day. I shut my mouth and stared at her. "Fine. The Aries Leader visited the border today."

"An Arctura was at the border?"

"Yes, weird stuff," she continued. "I feel like he should have more important things to do, like sitting in a fancy office or something."

The Aries Leader was a big deal, and she was trying to act nonchalant about it. Atlas Fulbright was one of the two Arcturas leading Gardian's entire Stellarium. He was perhaps the most influential governmental figure in Gardian, leading with the other Arctura, the Scorpio Leader.

Seconds after she spilled her secret, Avia's face burned with shame. Her body was quick to follow. I could feel her heat radiating from where I was sitting. As a fire mage, her skin burned at a higher temperature than the average human, fluctuating with the intensity of her emotions. Over the years, we'd paid for multiple pieces of furniture and clothing to be enchanted with fireproofing, just in case.

I focused back on my map, running my index finger across it. The only details were in the sections of Conviction Woods, and even then, there were many blank spots where my legs could not reach in a day or two. The other three-fourths of my map had the names of other territories written out—Societal, Assiduous, and Autarchic. Soon, I'd be able to detail the big mysterious splotches of untouched paper. Dad had left them blank when I was young so I could expand the map as I grew older.

Avia tapped her fingers against the tabletop. "Can you shapeshift my dress for tonight?"

"I don't think you're going to give me a choice." I rose from the table with a sigh and made my way down the hallway. "I'm tired."

"Whose fault is that?" Avia sprang from her chair and bolted past me to my room. She opened the door, but hesitated before stepping in, and for good reason. "Oh, god, it's *literally* a warzone."

I'd accidentally left out some rusty wartime arrows. Polished and restored blades hung on twine covered the wall next to the door, a larger shield in the corner of the room. Scrolls littered the floor with historical accounts of all ages, runes and symbols I'd copied from books, overdue texts I probably should've returned to the library weeks ago, papers with scribbled charcoal symbols I'd traced or sketched from locations in the Woods. Stacks of books lined the walls. Most I'd read over the years, a few I hadn't gotten to yet. My most recent fixation was sitting in the circle of my mess on top of a wolf-fur rug in the middle of the room, papers detailing one of the locations in the War of the Rebalancing where a battle had taken place on the Conviction-Assiduous border near an ancient arch; the *right* arch.

A wooden box in the corner was full of smaller trinkets I found on the boundaries of the Woods and had to return to the Stellarium to keep my job as a training historian. Every Stellarium, regardless of the Union or sign, was hungry for any information to reverse the curse on the Woods. I only gave them the less-interesting items I found on the outer boundaries of the Woods. I was worlds ahead of their knowledge base on the forest; most of my artifacts were from within the Woods themselves, and they'd never know I had them—to their understanding, no one lived in the forest that was supposed to kill anyone who stepped foot in it.

A few paper lanterns hung from the ceiling, lit with an undying enchanted flame. Spoken, enchanted words could extinguish them at night, but I enjoyed sleeping with the luminescence. There were many times I didn't fall asleep in or on my bed, but instead on the comfort of the fur carpet or the cool wood floor. I liked the floor.

"You're so much more of a mess than I am, and that's an impressive feat," Avia said. "How did you make this wreck of an organizational system worse than when I saw it two days ago?"

I shrugged. "I've got a specific order for things, and it works."

"I know, Rieka, trust me on that one."

"Look." I stepped over a pile of books to my circle, reaching for the scroll from the library. I handed it to Avia. "It detailed the battle on the border and recorded the arch in the records. Someone died underneath the arch in a skirmish, but hours later, their body had vanished, and they were found alive in the Hub. Said to have similar healing properties found on their wound to the healing pine sap collected from the trees leaning over the boundary of Conviction Woods."

"Some days, I'm convinced you're losing your mind."

"The next step is tracing the writing across the arch and seeing if I've seen the same writing anywhere else." I reached down to shuffle through papers to find a couple of my sketches of combinations of languages I couldn't read. "The fact that there's a mix of languages on the arch—it's older, much older than the other arches on the borders. Those all have Driksaal or Rurain, not a combination of the two."

"That's cool. I still need you to shapeshift my clothes."

I didn't acknowledge her, swallowing my irritation, and stepped over a couple of stacks of books to reach the closet stocked with black dresses and shirts. We'd learned early on it would be easier and cheaper to buy low-quality clothing and have me shapeshift it into something of higher quality. I swung the door open, barely missing a pile of papers. I pulled out two worn dresses and threw them on top of my bed.

Avia didn't dare to step beyond the doorframe and into the mess of my disorganized order. "I want something mostly red, but with yellow swirls."

"I would've designed it just like that," I snapped, but then breathed in to remind myself that my mess of interests were mine, not hers, and I could only have her attention for so long until she wanted something from me.

I closed my eyes and focused all my power on the dress in front of me. I pictured what she wanted, exactly how she told me. It didn't take much for me to shapeshift the dress; I was used to the process. The shapeshifting light pooled from my hands, enclosing the fabric in a white glow until all traces of the black were gone. Red and yellow spread across the glow like the flow of a stream, and with one last bright glow, it was finished. I took a minute to regain my composure, leaning over my bed as my heart raced. My hands burned from the magic. With a shaky breath, I threw the dress toward her.

"Thanks. Don't exhaust yourself for yours." She caught it and left the room. "And for my sake, go take a shower after you're done with it."

I shooed her out focusing on the other black dress, using the same process of magic on it, but with far less effort. When I opened my eyes, my simple ombre black and red dress was in front of me, Scorpio's colors. I gasped this time, sitting down on my bed as my vision crackled and blackened.

Shapeshifting had never been easy for me. Compared to Avia's fire magic, my power was harmless and somewhat weak. I had a few substances I'd learned how to morph over the years. Fabric, sand, and metal were the textures I could—barely—change. It still managed to save us the effort of buying more clothes, especially with Mom's shapeshifting, too.

I slipped into my travel clothes again, draping my enchanted necklace over my head. On the way out of my room, I tripped on a book and, to avoid falling onto rusty arrows, crashed into the wall instead. I threw my hands out to stabilize myself as I came nose-to-nose with the collection of sharpened knives on the wall. In the reflection of a blade, my one red, one gold eye returned my gaze. The longer dagger underneath it directly aligned with the scar across the middle of my neck, a wound without an origin, a mark of a blade I couldn't remember being cut by. I gently brushed my thumb against the fully healed wound.

"I have been telling you for *days* that this is unsafe, Rieka," Avia snapped as she leaned against the doorframe. I flinched at her loud voice. "And right before the Ceremony, too? Imagine if you showed up with a fresh cut in your neck. They would think that you'd just been punished for breaking the Code. On the same day they start seriously holding the Code against you."

I couldn't look her in the eyes. "I'm fine, Avia."

"You almost weren't. Get out of this battlefield and go take a shower. Now."

"How much time do I have?"

"The Ceremony isn't actually that far away. Mom told me yesterday that it's at the stage near the outskirts of the Hub, the one that's slightly down the East Trail. The weird location," she said. "It's the one that you go twenty minutes or so south on the Trail from the Hub. We've both passed it before."

"The part of the East Trail that curves around the Hub a bit?"

"Yup, that one. Another Convictionist is attending."

I carefully stepped back to avoid the arrows on the floor. "Must live in the southern Convictionist regions of the Hub?"

"A guy and his family." She held her forehead as if she was trying to remember the facts. "That's what I was told by a couple of other Aries. Rumor goes around. Heard he's a year older than me. Libra."

"He's a year older?" I raised my brows. "Yeah, right. You already tested the system by delaying your own Ceremony, you were 'busy' with work, I'd doubt that someone gets away with it for two years. Did your friends tell you this?"

"They were serious, I promise." She grinned. "Aries, we always tell the truth."

Not even a week ago, Avia's fellow guards had lied and tricked her into walking into a Pisces-owned clothing shop in the Hub while she was wearing her mud-covered border guard uniform. It hadn't gone well.

"I guess we'll find out who's right," I said. "It all sounds suspicious to me."

"Ah, yes, Rieka-the-Investigator-of-all-things."

"Do you blame me for questioning what your friends tell you?"

Avia pointed toward the bathroom to avoid answering. "Rieka. Shower. Go."

I grumbled at her, avoiding obstacles on my way to the hallway. I paused to glance back at Avia when she didn't snap back at my complaining noises.

Her smile faltered for a second as she gestured toward her face. "Don't do anything stupid with the emotions. Remember the Code."

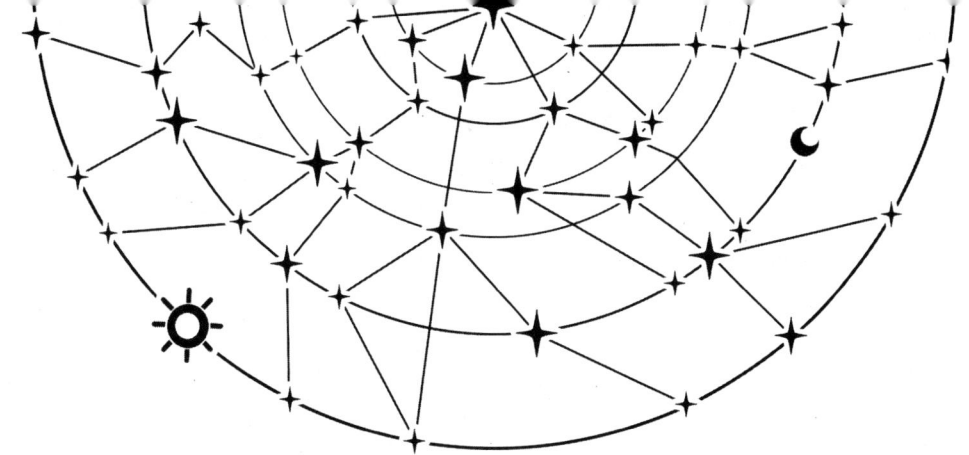

Chapter 3

"Aries, the farthest right. Your right, not mine. Libra in the middle. Scorpio, left."

Avia and I ended up standing for over an hour in awkward silence with the Libra Ceremony Master. On top of the dead grass in the clearing, chairs were set for an audience, the pines of Conviction Woods surrounding us. We didn't encounter any issues traveling the lengthy walk through Conviction Woods to the East Trail near the Hub, though my legs were certainly aching.

The other attendee had finally arrived—late, but still present. He hurried on stage while the man I assumed to be his father disappeared into the audience. As he straightened his back and settled between me and Avia, I took a slight step aside to avoid feeling shadowed by him. For being a Libra, he had a surprisingly muscular frame and intimidating height, though gentled by the white suit complementing his brunet hair and bright amber eyes. I could've sworn his gaze caught a golden hue in the sunlight when he glanced over at me. He gave me a friendly smile.

The Ceremony Master stepped forward to the middle of the stage. Behind her sat the audience, which was a lot more of Avia's friends than I expected; I would not get involved in that mess on my way home. In front of them, our parents sat in the front. Dad was wearing a white polo with a gold rim, signature to Libra's colors, despite the fact that he was a Cancer. Mom must've shifted his clothing to disguise him so he could still attend our Ceremony. Dad was not supposed to be anywhere near Conviction Woods. In fact, Dad living in Conviction territory as an Autarian was equally as dangerous as me breaking the Code. Though he mostly used the house in the Woods as his safe haven from the law, he traveled in between Autarian and Conviction territory to support us using his skills as a water mage with the Autarian Stellarium.

Mom, a Scorpio in all black, sat next to him, perfectly still, careful to avoid showing any sign of connection to him. Mom and Dad's relationship directly broke the Union Law, a law consistent across all Unions to only marry within your Union, said to keep the order within Gardian and maintain responsibility between the signs and their contribution to the functioning of the world. The Union Law was older than the Scorpio Code, in place for the entirety of Gardian's history. Dad got around that one by spending copious amounts of time in Autarian territory when he wasn't with us.

The most peculiar member of the audience was a woman sitting in the back, cloaked in all black. A hood covered her face, and her hands lay neatly folded atop her lap. She sat with a spine made of iron as she stared at the three of us. Perhaps someone from the Scorpio Stellarium to keep tabs on me and make sure I didn't break the Code.

"Attention!" the Ceremony Master called out. We straightened. She looked down at her script. "Today we gather to induct these three individuals into their rightful positions as official members of Gardian. They have become honorable members through their training, education, and careers to learn their sign's place in our society. Upon completion of the Ceremony, they will become fully subject to any law governed by all sectors of the Stellarium."

She paused to glance around as each of us acknowledged and looked back down as she prepared her monotonous tone for the script again.

"Following the banishment of the archpowers three centuries ago, the Ceremony was founded to expose inductees with the magic systems of Zodiac Turning or Libran Healing. In the era of the War of the Rebalancing, archpowered individuals were revealed when forced to perform motions of activating the archpowers. We are to honor this tradition of the Balancing Ceremony to symbolize the strength in the structure of our world, and to celebrate the peace found in the absence of the archpowers. For this reason, Libra and Scorpio both hold special addendums to the Balancing Ceremony to follow the earliest tradition of screening for the archpowers."

The Ceremony Master finally looked up from her podium. Each of us acknowledged.

"We will begin with Aries. State your name, occupation, relationship status, and place of residence."

I silently begged Avia to be cautious about how she said her residency status. For a year, we'd worked together on the wording of the statement until we could perfect it. Mom technically had a house in the Hub where she claimed I lived while we grew up, but that left Avia without a technical residence—because of the Code, she couldn't live with our Scorpio mother, only I could. I didn't know who our parents paid, but there were fake official documents that stated Avia was in adolescent Aries' community housing; children were forced to live in community housing if their parents were not in the same Union or were Scorpios. But that was only up until 18 years of age when the Ceremony was meant to take place, and Avia had aged out of adolescent housing a year prior. We were "living" together at Mom's fake address in the Hub.

Avia cleared her throat. "Avia Phelan. I am a border guard, single with no outer relationships to any non-Convictionist. In the last year, I have been living with my sister in the south corner of the Hub. She is trying to find proper housing after switching her job with the Stellarium."

"It is against Scorpio's law for any sign to be living with a Scorpio, no matter the familial ties," the Ceremony Master interjected. "You will need to separate. I will contact the Scorpio Stellarium to find your sister accommodation. As neither of you had participated in the Ceremony up to this point, we will excuse the break of the law just this once."

I couldn't show any sign of fear, forcing myself to stare forward and conceal any emotions, despite my face paling.

"Continuing," the Ceremony Master stated, "Libra."

"Chase Marin. I'm a messenger working and living at the Conviction-Autarchic Exchange Center. I am single with no ties outside of my Union."

The Ceremony Master walked toward him, pulling a knife from her belt. Once standing before him, she put its blade to her palm, slicing a tiny nick into her hand. When blood drew, she held her hand to him.

He bowed, placing his hand atop hers as a dim, slightly yellowish magic gathered in his hand. He focused intensely on it, as if he was afraid of making a mistake with the weak light. The touch remained for a few moments. With my proximity to him, I noticed his hand shaking. When the Ceremony Master pulled her hand back, she held it up to show the blood and wound remaining on her palm.

"Dreamseeking," the Libra said. I caught the long breath he let out. "Thank you."

The Ceremony Master nodded at him with a pleased smile before shifting her attention to me. Her gaze went cold when she met my eyes. "Scorpio."

"Rieka Spring," I said. "I am a historian reporting to the Stellarium. I reside with Avia Phelan. I am single, without personal acquaintances."

"Magic."

"I am a shapeshifter."

I bowed just as the Libra attendee did, lifting my hand. From my studies, I'd read about Turning dozens, if not hundreds, of times. Scorpio was expected to understand history enough to perform the action at the Ceremony; I'd known the position of activation years ago, the way Zodiac Turners would punch their fist out and focus their magic into a wheel of light. Without a moment of hesitation, I repeated the action, striking my fist out before me.

There, in the flare of the fast movement, there was a tiny ache in my arm, a mere rush in my head. In one second, a white light blinded me, and in the next, it was gone. The warmth of magic gathered at my fingertips, hidden in my palm, invisible to anyone who couldn't pry open my curled fingers. It was insignificant enough for me to dismiss it as a quick activation of my shapeshifting in the abrupt motion of moving my arm.

Her eyes scanned over my face as I stood frozen. Her fingers tightened around the podium as she searched for something to call me out on, anything, for an uncomfortable amount of time. I swallowed, ignoring the fading warmth in my hand. I had shown no signs of the flash that rushed through my body.

Instead, she turned to pick up a yellow cloak behind her, embroidered with the Aries glyph and Avia's name. She walked to Avia, and I let my shoulders ease. Avia dipped her head as the Ceremony Master wrapped the cloak around her shoulders. She repeated the process for the Libra with a white cloak.

When she approached me with a crimson cloak embroidered with my name, she tilted her chin up, meeting my eyes for a split second before refusing to make eye contact. There was something about the look she gave me that I wouldn't ever be able to erase from my memory. Pure hatred and disgust spread throughout her amber irises. I didn't react; I couldn't.

"The last thing Gardian needs," she whispered, narrowing her eyes at me, "is another one of your kind."

Even within our own Union, Libra was one of the signs who disliked Scorpio's emotionless reign over Gardian. They held the extra burden of monitoring the Scorpio Code as mediators, and they did not like the decisions they had to make for Scorpios who broke the law.

She backed away and headed to her podium to read her script again. "With the gift of these cloaks made from the hands of the people of your sign, you are required to wear them in all public locations to be recognized and identified as your respective signs. Thank you for your cooperation and strict path of knowledge. Serve your Union and sign well as you continue to build upon the skills in which your sign contributes to our society. This concludes the official Ceremony. You are now permitted to sit at the feasting table."

I could barely keep my attention on her finishing lines, more distracted with the peculiar woman in the back of the audience. She hadn't budged. She shifted her pose ever so slightly to reassure me she wasn't just a statue placed in the chair. The dying sunlight caught a revealed piece of metal on her hip. A dagger.

The crowd clapped for us as the Ceremony Master left the stage. I shook my head quickly to clear my mind and hurried to Avia's side as she rushed to Mom and Dad. Dad greeted us with a smile, Mom expressionless for her safety.

"You two are excellent daughters," Mom said quietly, careful to keep her voice down so the officials couldn't hear her slip out of Scorpio's formal speech. Mom was a tall, middle-aged woman with long, wavy black hair and gray eyes that could barely stay on us as she made sure the Ceremony Master didn't see her face or mine. Yet, she kept her facial expressions hauntingly still, far more efficient and effective than I could ever be. Though with years of practice maintaining her composure, even she despised the Code for what it stripped her of.

I'd learned to understand the hidden love in Mom's still face. Although she pursed her lips and kept a blank expression, her gaze revealed both fear and pride. She was terrified of the Stellarium and always had been. She'd told me of how she was taught the law when she was a child, trying to find any way to escape from those in control until she discovered the comfort of Conviction Woods and its protection from the Stellarium entering. Secretly, she might've loathed the Scorpio Code far more than I did—she worried both for herself and her daughter.

"Dad are you..."

Avia cut herself off as Dad hushed her. Avia wrinkled her nose; a man normally dressed in ocean blues looked like a foreigner in white and gold.

"Rieka. No." Mom tapped her foot to mine to stop my amused smile before it even occurred. I resisted a sigh. "Rowan is a coworker of mine. He is a Libra."

"Right now, he is," Avia said quietly, trying to evoke emotion out of our mother. Dad—Rowan—gave her a look. "Sorry."

"I think I pulled it off." He reached to his collar and snapped it back with a grin. "It's undeniable."

"Okay." A twinge of amusement sparkled in Mom's eyes. "Rieka, Avia, I apologize for your separation."

Avia shrugged. "Won't keep us apart."

"Hush! Stop speaking for your sister," Dad scolded her. "You know better. Go eat. We'll talk after dinner."

Avia smiled at me. She was my voice and had always been. Together, we walked to the table away from the seats in front of the stage. The Libra sat in silence, hands neatly folded in his lap and back straight as he waited for us. A platter of food for each of us was set on the table. Avia sat down first, and I followed her, adjusting myself in my chair.

"Hi!" Avia greeted him immediately, holding out her hand. "My name's Avia."

"I gathered. Chase." He shook her hand across the table, giving his palm a weird look when he pulled it away. "Your hand is warm."

"That's normal, don't worry."

"And you?" he said to me.

GARDIAN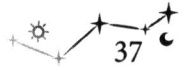

"Rieka's a learning historian. Oh, I mean, her name's Rieka. She's a Scorpio. I'm a border guard."

I resisted the urge to rub my face. Avia could never go into a public-speaking job.

"I can introduce myself, Avia," I said. The Libra—Chase—looked up from his plate of food. I straightened my facial expressions. I loathed the straightforward sentence structure I forced myself to switch to. "You are a messenger?"

"Yeah, I run scrolls and stuff back and forth between conference rooms. It's boring. They let me live there."

"Forced to separate." Avia derailed the conversation. "Damn."

"Do you need a room to stay in?" Chase asked, nodding at me. Was he flirting with me, or just being friendly? Or flat-out stupid for not hearing the Ceremony Master say I couldn't live with anyone else? I couldn't tell. Regardless, I didn't like any of the options. "I'm sure I can work something out to get you an arrangement for at least a couple of nights, knowing you technically work for them, yeah?"

I hesitated, but my sword was resting hidden on my neck, and he was just a Dreamseeker. I *could* wander back into the Woods after walking some distance from the Ceremony, but I would risk being spotted by the Stellarium. Let alone, I did not want to walk more distance for no good reason.

A shift in the background caught my attention as I drifted out of my thoughts. The woman wearing black rested her hand on her dagger. A shaky feeling accumulated in the pits of my stomach, a quick pain spreading across my head before vanishing. I put my hand to my forehead to erase the nervousness. She turned in my direction, then walked toward the exit of the clearing toward the East Trail.

"Yes, that would be ideal," I said to Chase, eyes tearing away from her as she exited. The Stellarium wouldn't let me go unsupervised. I gave him a half-smile, still partially distracted, and his face lit up with surprise at the expressed emotion.

Shit. I'd slipped again, unsure of what to say, so I quickly looked down at my plate. On it was a bounty of exotic and bright fish with scales still intact, likely caught in somewhere around the Ara Bluffs where many Convictionists resided, a delicacy enjoyed only from the volcanic island. I was starting to get sick of seafood—fish from Dad's work with Autarchic, fish from the creeks within Conviction Woods... I would've done anything for a change in diet.

"Well," Avia started again, "we can survive away from each other. I'd like to see how I manage on my own. A change will be nice."

She nudged me jokingly. Managing on her own meant no little sister supervision. I'd stopped her from starting fires in the house many, many times over the years, and she'd spoken over me in public to save me from getting reprimanded. It wasn't a great idea for the two of us to spend more than a day or two apart.

I continued eating to distract myself from my own thoughts. When Avia and I were close to finished, Dad approached us with a warm smile.

He placed his hand on Avia's shoulder. "Avia, you can stay with me if you need to."

Avia gave him a look. Never in a million years would Avia go to Autarian territory with the Cancer water mages. Not to mention, she had a thing against Pisces, and a vendetta against Sagittarius for making her job difficult by being where they weren't supposed to be.

"I will be okay," I said. "I am traveling to the Exchange Center to inquire about a room as I work for them. Avia and I will meet in the Hub later in the week."

"M'kay, Rieka, be safe. You've got someone to walk with to the Hub in case it gets dark?"

"It's easy enough to follow the East Trail to the Exchange Center," Chase reassured him. "I'll be walking with her."

Dad took a moment to look at him. Seeming to trust Chase, he shrugged and gave him a smile. "Thank you, young man."

Turning away from Chase, Dad lightly touched his neck with his hand. I nodded. He barely motioned to Chase, knowing I had my hidden weapon on me. He'd taught me long ago how to fend for myself.

"I'll let you finish your meals," Dad said. "I'll talk to you girls soon, alright?"

Avia flashed him a smile and turned to me. "Rieka, meet up tomorrow?"

"Location of the fountain?"

"You got it. We'll figure something out."

Chapter 4

Thankfully, the location of the Ceremony wasn't too far from the Hub. The officials carefully watched me exit the Ceremony, but didn't seem to question when I left at the same time as Chase. I wasn't breaking the Scorpio Code by simply traveling with another sign, and it wasn't like I was friends with him. In my defense, the only other place I could go was the Hub.

Chase was treading carefully, remaining a few feet away from me as we walked. I kept my eyes fixed forward, my mouth shut, emotions still. My legs burned as I fought through sheer exhaustion. I couldn't complain, as it was entirely my fault for walking too many miles to count after waking up at 3 in the morning.

"Have you taken this path recently?" Chase said, finally caving into his urge to break the awkward silence. "The East Trail, I mean."

"Yes."

"Where do you live?"

"Miles north in proximity to the southern corner of the Hub. There are numerous clearings protected from the cursed boundaries of Conviction Woods. I accompanied my sister in our accommodation within a community of border guards."

It was a total lie I came up with on the spot, aligning with what Avia had told the Ceremony Master. I bit my tongue to stop myself from telling him to leave me alone. It was late, I'd woken up at 3 AM, and the last thing I wanted to be doing was faking my speech to a stranger.

"Not *in* the Hub? That seems awfully inconvenient."

"And you?" I avoided his question.

"Currently, the Exchange Center."

"I apologize for my misspeak. Where was your residence prior to the Exchange Center?"

I bit my tongue. Each day, my resentment for being forced to speak that way grew stronger.

"Similar story, with the outskirts, close to the Hub." He had his hands tucked into his pockets, unbothered.

There weren't any clearings with residences for at least twenty miles south on the East Trail. There were areas similar to the stage for Ceremonies, or small vendors, but certainly not housing. He'd repeated my lie.

Though I wanted to question him, exhaustion slowed my thoughts and care for the subject. The last thing I wanted to do was be on the East Trail with a random dude from the Balancing Ceremony and come up with a clever way to interrogate him over his lie. My thoughts kept drifting off to the shimmering boundary of Conviction Woods, my hand hovering over my necklace. Though Chase appeared to be fairly harmless, I would've been safer walking to the Hub if I were to travel through Conviction Woods. We were getting closer to the city, only a 20-minute walk or so, and the only pleasant resolution to the night would've been my house nested amidst the comforting forest.

"Sorry to interrupt your staring match with the creepy forest. Do you guys have to talk like that?"

"What?" I almost lost my composure for a moment. "Pardon?"

"I just figured, I've never really asked one of you, and the long walk, you know…" he trailed off before gesturing to his face with a smile. "I mean, with the whole Code. Does fun exist in your vocabulary?"

"Perhaps. I explore."

"You explore what? Is exploring fun for you?"

Oh my god, if only he could shut up. "I traverse and study the regions surrounding the Trail."

"So formal. It sounds like it *could* be fun." He huffed. "I do messenger work, and I think it's fun sometimes."

"It does not sound fun."

"Neither does aimlessly walking around alone on the Trail."

"I occasionally discover intriguing objects." I looked over at him when he perked up at my answer, though not sure why I was humoring him. He was far too friendly for my sleep-deprived state. "I investigate clearings and the outskirts of Conviction Woods. I humbly return my findings to the Stellarium for the progression of Scorpio society."

"Like, what kind of findings?"

"I located an arch." I kept my emotions still while explaining. He was lucky I wasn't often asked about what I found and that I'd take any opportunity to talk about my research. "My travels comprised 20 miles in search of the historical arch, if you will."

"The historical arch, got it. You've been looking for it. You did that today?"

"Affirmative."

"That sounds like a lot. And you're still walking? Props to you. I also look for those kinds of things when I'm walking on the Trail... out of boredom, though. But I guess that's what you said you do for fun. Never mind, disregard that."

I suppressed a sigh at his small talk. The Hub was only a few minutes ahead. The light of the city was beginning to beam through the trees and glow on the horizon of the path. It was my beacon of hope to escape from the nightmare that was a bored Libra.

I let my mind wander to the arch to brainstorm a solution to my missing runic. I was missing half of the etchings, and I would be bored out of my mind in an unfamiliar room. The Hub placed me closer to the arch than our house in Conviction Woods; it was a great opportunity to make multiple attempts to sneak past the Assidians to finish my task. I had to come up with a way to reach the upper runes. Dad was heading to Autarchic territory for a few days, and Avia was a couple inches shorter than I was.

"I hate how the Hub blocks out the dark skies," Chase rambled on, reaching his arm out—his long arm out—to pretend to trace the Stars with his index finger. He was tall. Conveniently tall. 6'4", maybe 6'5". With arms that looked like they could reach the top of the arch.

"How many arches have you passed in your times on the Trail?"

His eyes lit up at my question. "Not too many. At least, not many *historical* arches, if you will."

I barely stopped myself from snapping back at him. "It is the largest arch I have charted thus far. If you are inquisitive, I would greatly appreciate your time and company in the following days for the duration of my travel."

"Did you just invite me to explore with you? That's a change," he said with a smile. "To answer your very ominous question, sure. I work tomorrow, but the day after, I'm off, and I don't have any plans."

Success.

Before we could continue our conversation, and most importantly, before I had time to accidentally break my emotionless state, we stepped out of the boundaries of the East Trail and into the start of the Hub's cobblestone streets.

After the Sun set, I particularly enjoyed the ambience of the Hub as it transformed into a mystical display of light and warmth. A fountain sat before us, welcoming us with shimmers of candlelight on water. The shops and buildings—constructed of mostly wood, stone, and metal—flickered with the glow of fireplaces reflecting off panes of windows. A gust of cool wind brushed astray sign banners, accenting the creak of wood with soft fabric against stone. My eyes caught to a combination of light magic and torches radiated a gold luminance upon the buildings, shops, and wanderers of the night, while a few colorful light specs buzzed around from enchantment magic. Castle structures sat on the horizon, miles upon miles away, in the vast expanse of the city. It never failed to stun me.

I was intensely familiar with the southern part of the Hub and understood the route to the Exchange Center, following each turn and curve in the streets where buildings squeezed against each other in the populated city. North, west, then northwest. The solitude of the eve enhanced the sounds of distant chatter and the quiet hum of enchantment magic. I would've enjoyed it even more if Chase hadn't been with me.

Relief washed over me when I caught sight of the Conviction-Autarchic Exchange Center, placed on the farthest southern edge of the wide expanse of Gardian's capital. I stopped to admire the building in the dark. The Autarchic blue, white, and silver flags—representing Cancer, Sagittarius, and Pisces—draped at its sides. Conviction's red, gold, and black conflicted with the Autarian color scheme, but the duo of Unions represented an alliance critical to Gardian's functionality. The Exchange Center, one of many buildings to coordinate between the Unions, had been established near the outskirts of Conviction's part of the Hub as a center for Autarians who needed to visit with Convictionists for communication purposes.

When we entered, I exhaled in relief at the unusually peaceful environment. It was devoid of activity, shaded from the moonlight filtering in from the massive blue and gold-stained glass windows. The ceiling stretched far above us, arching three stories high, painted with a mural depicting a battle in the War of the Rebalancing where Convictionists and Autarians fought together. The only others in the open space of the lobby were two boys lounging behind the reception desk, chattering away. They sat up straight when we approached. One boy wore white and blue with fiery accents, Sagittarius, and the other a lighter and darker navy, Cancer.

My head spun. I'd almost forgotten that it wasn't the first time I'd noticed the Sagittarian wandering the Exchange Center. I recalled seeing a group of Aries sneering at him a couple weeks prior. Sagittarians were mocked, atypical to see in civilization. Most of them lived on the seas off the southern coasts, enjoying the destruction of every possible thing in their path. Sometimes, they'd wander on land where they weren't supposed to be. According to Avia, it made her life miserable. I thought that was a bit of an exaggeration.

"What can I help you with?" the Sagittarius asked, his brown eyes awake with attention. They complimented his dark hair and olive skin. He brightened when Chase leaned over the counter. "How are you, Chase? Haven't seen you up this late in a bit."

"I'm well, thanks. The Ceremony was irritatingly late." He bowed his head in gratitude and motioned toward me. "I could use your help."

"I participated in a Balancing Ceremony this eve and was ordered to remove myself from my household to avoid residing with my Aries sister," I explained. The Cancer rolled his eyes at my formality, muttering something underneath his breath and turning away. I continued. "Is there a vacancy? I am employed at this location as a learning historian."

He glanced down at some papers while Chase peered over the counter to watch. The Sagittarius looked back up to me with a smile. He was suspiciously friendly, compared to his Cancer friend, who clearly wasn't in the mood to put up with a Scorpio.

"I have a Taurus brother. They separated us, too, when they found out I lived in Assidian territory. I miss the mountains," he said with a sigh before glancing around to make sure the lobby was empty. "We have a room that'll be open for some time. I can squeeze you into it since you work here, and it's an emergency. It's on the fifth floor where the rest of us stay."

"I thank you for your cooperation."

"Robin," he introduced himself, despite my dull attitude. "Explorer. You must've met Chase at the Balancing Ceremony?"

"Correct."

"You'll enjoy it here. Kinda rare to see a Scorpio as a historian. Feel free to stay as long as you need." He stood up, reaching for a set of keys behind the desk. "I've got your back. I know how it is."

The Cancer shook his head at his friend and mouthed something ugly to me. I ignored it and hurried after Robin as he made his way down a hallway. He turned to a flight of stairs, and we followed him up. Turning to stride down a windowless hallway on the fifth floor, my exhaustion slowed me from keeping up like I normally would. We halted in front of a room without a name on the door.

"Here we are." Robin tossed me the key. "519."

Chase waved at him. "I'll see you around, man."

Robin patted his shoulder. "Don't cause trouble."

He left the conversation to return to a different room down the hallway. I shifted my attention and unlocked the door to 519, swinging it open and making my way in.

"Oh, so no thank you for my Sagittarius friend? Or a goodbye?"

I paused before I closed my door. "I thank you for your help and will meet with you soon."

He grinned. "Alright, if that's how it is. I'll see you in a couple of days."

I closed my door with a long sigh, leaning against it to let myself ease, though was quickly disappointed at the lifeless setting of the room, stone walls and a white-blanketed bed with a single wooden table accompanied by a poorly cushioned chair that looked like it would hurt my back after 10 minutes. It was too tidy, too empty of life, too much of a reminder of the blank personality I was meant to adopt by my Stellarium. I tore off my clothes and collapsed in bed.

The Hub had transformed with the exchange of the Moon for the Sun. The entire color spectrum washed over the gray and brown of structures from all 12 signs. People in shops and stands shouted out to grab a passerby's attention, although most walking by ignored them. Somewhere in the distance, there was an echo of a violin, and the smell of fresh baked goods lingered in the air from a nearby cafe.

I sat against the stone wall of the fountain while pulling my new cloak closer to myself. Even with the parka I'd shifted my dress into—which also caused me to faint on top of my bed—the midwinter freeze was creeping into my skin. I tucked my hands in between my thighs and hunched over until I spotted Avia in the distance. I stood up and stretched, tucking my hands into my pockets.

"No injuries?" I said as she approached.

She breathed heavily, catching her breath before she could respond, holding up a finger while she recovered. Avia had a funny habit of walking faster than she should without realizing it.

"No trouble?" she finally got out. "And yes, no injuries. You look cold."

"Oh, sorry, I've been waiting out here for someone who showed up an hour late." I glanced around to make sure no one was within earshot of us. I'd perfected the art of keeping my emotions still but my tone informal when I was sure no one would overhear me. "Are you doing okay?"

She transferred my pack from her back to mine. I momentarily enjoyed the warmth radiating from it. "Are you doing okay? I'm not the one who had to follow a strange guy into the Exchange Center."

"I'm fine." I watched my breath billow into the frosty air. "I got a free room. Chase has been helpful so far. Annoying, though. Dude wouldn't shut up."

She wrinkled her nose. "Libra."

"He's not too bad. He didn't attack me, so that's a plus."

"I know, I just don't trust Libras. They're always so perfect. Suspiciously perfect."

"I get it."

"You know," she leaned closer to me, "did you notice how absolutely ripped that guy was? I thought they weren't supposed to be intimidating for their mediation stuff?"

I snorted. "You think he's that intimidating?"

She crossed her arms. "You know that's not what I meant, Rieka."

Before we could continue gossiping, a shout stole our conversation. Both of us whirled around. An older teenage boy burst out of a shop not too far from us. Two officials sprinted after him, one of them lurching forward and grabbing his arm. They threw him to the ground.

I sensed the danger as soon as I spotted their unmistakable black attire. Avia instantly moved away from me to the other side of the fountain. The two officials hadn't looked in our direction yet, distracted by their target.

The boy had a Scorpio glyph on his red cloak. My heart fell. The Scorpio's cloak was marked officially, given to him at his Ceremony. He retaliated against the Stellarium's grasp, but both officials were tall, with broad upper bodies. They trapped him with ease, their firm grip solidifying on each of his arms.

Another teenager ran out of the shop, dressed in Gemini uniform. He reached out to the Scorpio, who yelled as their fingertips brushed. The Gemini slipped underneath one of the official's arms and pressed his lips to the Scorpio's. One of the officials almost impulsively shoved him away before recognizing that they'd be in trouble if they hurt a Societalist. They instead yanked the Scorpio from him.

"Let him go!" the Gemini pleaded. "*Please!*"

The Stellarium maintained their unforgiving expressions.

The Gemini buckled to the street, sobbing. He tried to reach out for his lover as the Stellarium forced him away. The Gemini's scream gurgled with horror when one of the officials lashed out at the Scorpio's chest. Avia ran to comfort his Gemini companion, fallen on the street.

As the Stellarium dragged their victim past me, I kept my emotions utterly still. The boy's face was full of despair and fury, flickering with a consuming rage that spread through every inch of his expression, a rage that reminded me of my own. The fire burning in his eyes was familiar, shared, against the Code that told him he couldn't love, yet he had anyway. In the split second where our gazes met, his face flooded with recognition. He kicked back at one of the officials as he passed me.

"Rieka," he said as tears streamed down his face, "thank you."

Rieka.

He knew my name, but I didn't know his.

I let each of his words individually strike me, waking me up, alerting me to reality; I wasn't alone. The familiarity of his stare followed me as he maintained eye contact, although I couldn't remember where I recognized him from. Somehow, someway, I knew I was supposed to understand why he was familiar. Words were stuck in the back of my throat, choking me, my tongue twisting with so many things I wanted to ask him. I couldn't push a single sentence out.

He smiled at me with a nod, as if forgiving my silence.

He accepted his fate, turning compliant with defeat as the Stellarium led him to his demise. I wanted to process what I'd seen, but that was nearly impossible with the gazes of other signs watching me, expecting me to do something, say anything. After a few moments of my shocked stillness and blank face, they instead dispersed, uninterested in a typical sight of the Scorpio Stellarium's wrath. I cautiously approached Avia and the Gemini. He was mumbling something to Avia, his words jumbled and coarse as he struggled to breathe through his panic.

"Rieka," she said quietly, refusing to look up at me, "leave."

"He'll make it back," the Gemini choked out. "I'll find him."

Avia threw her hand in my direction. "*Leave*, Rieka."

I backed up, turning my back to the scene before I could fail to hide my fear. The Stellarium would have him dead before the Gemini could even begin to search, and I'd be next if they caught me with Avia again.

Chapter 5

After losing sleep over trying to remember how the Scorpio boy had known my name, I'd only been met with confusion. I sat alone the next morning in the lobby of the Exchange Center, holding the bridge of my nose to ease my headache. A flurry of snow outside hung a serene haze over the space and reduced voices to whispers. I silently watched as others arrived for their shifts at the Exchange Center, entertained by the mundane interactions between Convictionists and Autarians brushing fresh snow off their hair and cloaks. For the most part, the Convictionists appeared unbothered by our usual harsh central winter in the Hub, while southern-coastal Autarians shivered and mumbled complaints about the weather.

When I finally stepped out of the Exchange Center to start my trek to the arch, my feet sunk into a few inches of fresh snow. Though annoying to shuffle through, it cast a hush over the normally bustling chaos of the Hub's streets. The colorful sign banners on buildings were like splashes of paint on a white canvas of a winter storm. I occasionally wandered by a residence, possibly Stellarium officials with luxury homes situated in between

merchants.

As I passed the fountain, the scene of the Scorpio Stellarium's brutality rang through my consciousness as a warning bell. Mom was right—they were getting worse, more strict, more aggressive. Black cloaked individuals lurked around corners and in the shadows of buildings, waiting to snag their next victim. And, for some reason, one of those victims knew my name.

I distracted myself by observing a post in front of a Stellarium building. The board listed all twelve signs in order of power: Scorpio, Aries, Libra, Cancer, Gemini, Aquarius, Pisces, Virgo, Taurus, Leo, Capricorn, then Sagittarius. Scorpio and Aries had reigned their Arctura status over Gardian for as long as I'd lived. The Arcturas held the most power over introducing and influencing new laws with their Leader vote counting as two instead of one.

I curled my lip. The post was simply another reminder of how our identities were shaped through an energetic connection between birthday and magic as soon as we entered this world. It laid out our future within seconds, determining where we'd live and who we could love. With our sign came our power, certain types more common among different signs, determined by the magic of our parents and how common it was in our sign.

A shiver traveled up my spine after leaving the post behind me. I scanned the white atmosphere as snowflakes drifted from the sky. Some distance away, a woman in black skulked around the corner of a building. The bright red Scorpio glyph stuck out like fresh blood on her cloak. I drew a deep breath in, and kept on my way, trying to ignore the nagging sense that she was watching me.

I glanced over my shoulder while hurrying through the accumulating storm. Though she hadn't advanced, she held a dagger in her hands as she looked directly at me. My blood rushed to my face, but I had no reason to be afraid of the Stellarium attacking me. I was allowed to meet and talk to other signs, just not befriend them. Whatever the hell that was supposed to mean. The Code was vague enough so the Scorpio Stellarium could manipulate it to their will.

I crossed onto the East Trail and let my shoulders ease when the Stellarium member didn't follow me. I kept a close eye on my surroundings for danger, but the snow was a blessing in disguise, reducing the amount of border patrols necessary with the lack of travelers. The Stellariums must've assumed they wouldn't have much activity on the Conviction-Assiduous border when it was so cold out.

They were wrong, at least in my case, and at least in Chase's. He stood patiently near the start of the East Trail, flashing me a smile when I approached him. The day prior, we'd talked in the hall to coordinate where to meet.

"You're late." He glanced up at the cloud-smothered sky. "I was here before the Sun rose."

Biting my tongue to hold back a sharp response, I walked past him to put distance between us. "I apologize."

"Can you stop that? The 'I apologize' and 'I thank you'? Seriously."

"I apologize. I thank you for bringing it to my attention."

"Very funny." He glared at me, hurrying to catch up to my pace. "Did you notice how many Scorpio Stellarium officials were out in the Hub today?"

"Yes, the Hub has many brave officials to protect our people."

"I wonder why that is?" he said, dismissing my fake loyalty. "There were so many of them. Seems like they've been everywhere recently."

"Scorpio is trained under moral and strict law to prepare our youth for greatness. We begin learning the Scorpio Code at age 5."

"Oh my god, I'm over that, please stop. I know you probably hate them. Everyone does. Did you have any friends in school that ended up working for the Stellarium?"

I didn't respond. He was a comfortable distance behind me. I didn't bother looking back.

"Oh. Right. No friends allowed."

"Correct, *never befriend*."

"Ridiculous, that you guys have rules so strict. You know, my father, he doesn't like the Code, either, and he doesn't talk like you do when he's with me," Chase said. "I kinda assumed all Scorpios were like that. Maybe you all loathe it secretly, but have to follow it, anyway."

"Your father is a Scorpio?" I hadn't caught that at the Ceremony, but I was way too distracted with everything else to see where he disappeared to in the audience. "The Scorpio Code prohibits him from residing with you."

"Yeah, it's complicated."

"And you trust me to retain that information?"

"I saw you smile at the Ceremony. I can tell you love your sister, too. I'm not *stupid*. You've given me more than enough context clues."

I slowed down to let him catch up. He should've outpaced me with his long legs, but he needed to actually use them. He was too busy talking. It would be too rude of me to tell him to shut up, especially when I needed him to listen to me to trace the upper runes.

"What do you think of the Code?" he pushed, tilting his head with curiosity. "Honest answer, please."

Though I wasn't one to trust easily, he was convincing me that he really was just a talkative, bored Libra trying to find a way to fill his time. He'd told me his Scorpio father had broken the Code, and I genuinely believed that he was oblivious enough to tell me that.

"The Code enforces Scorpio's place of power. It is a holy law, initially enacted during the War of the Rebalancing to obey the will of the Gods. If that reason remains true today, I do not see it observed." I stepped over a fallen pine. "Are you educated on the noble history of the Scorpio Code?"

"Something to do with the War, holy instructions on obeying the Code?"

"That is correct. As a historian, it is my duty to report a truthful history of Gardian. I have tirelessly studied dozens of scrolls and texts regarding our great Scorpio history, and as of recently, I have begun to doubt the legitimacy of the Code's establishment."

His mouth hung open. "That is a bold statement against the Scorpio Code."

"Don't you dare repea—"

"I won't," he answered before I could even finish. He paused for a moment. I somehow knew exactly what was about to come out of his mouth. "I thank you for your trust."

After another few hours, we had trekked down the East Trail enough to see the arch in the distance. The trail was still barren on the snowy day—out of all seven miles of our expedition, we hadn't seen one other group of people, not even border guards.

Chase was wheezing from the walk, and when I stopped, he held his knees with a long breath. I, for one, didn't think the seven-mile walk was too strenuous. There was no incline, and the Trail was far less snowy than the Hub. I'd already recovered from my long distance walking a couple of days prior.

After taking another look around to make sure the Assidian border patrols were nowhere near, I hurried to the arch. Chase, with an emphasized, exhausted sigh, followed me.

I set my bag down, unbuckling it to grab pieces of thin paper and charcoal. I pressed the paper to the lowest runes, brushing the charcoal stick over them. My fingers trembled in the cold air, too stiff to be precise. My heart was pulled to the Woods behind me. I would've preferred to travel through the warmth of the forest.

In the end, having a tall person who could trace the top runes made it all worth it. Chase brushed his fingers along the aged stone brick, his index finger tracing each carved rune. He paused at a couple of the upper runes, narrowing his eyes.

"Are you observing something interesting?" I readjusted my grip on the charcoal slab and blew on the paper to brush away the sprinkles of black marking.

"Yeah, actually, I am seeing something weird."

I glanced up.

"Some of these runes, I saw them yesterday on the sixth floor of the Exchange Center. I was sent up there to retrieve a weapon for the Aries Arctura." His face was close to the stone as he examined it. "I'd never been up there before yesterday."

"Excellent, we are investigating the sixth floor next," I decided for him, grabbing another paper to reach up the arch.

"It's classified, and you didn't ask me if I wanted to go with you to the sixth floor, but okay." He paused. "Rieka, can you read this Driksaal?"

"I cannot."

"I *can*. I didn't try to read it yesterday in the Exchange Center, but now that I look at it..."

I froze. "Are you speaking the truth?"

"Yeah, I can't read the Rurian, but I can definitely understand the Driksaal," he said casually.

"Sorry, how do you know how to read ancient Driksaal? There are no translation guides to ancient Driksaal."

"That's the thing. To my knowledge, I don't speak or read ancient Driksaal." He took the paper from my hands when I couldn't reach any higher to trace the runic for me. "I can barely speak modern Driksaal."

I stared at him blankly. He was making absolutely no sense.

"Looks like some kind of incantation." He paused again at the top of the arch on an enlarged brick with a unique rune separated from the repetition of the others. **"Restore and revive, by the balance of the blood, call upon the cause of the Callexus.'**

When he removed the paper to touch the stone, a faint gold shimmer rippled over the symbol. A combination of a low-frequency whistle and buzz crackled from the activated magic. He yanked his hand away, almost dropping the paper into the snow. I dove forward to catch it, throwing myself into the powder. Cold sliced against my cheeks as snow puffed across my black clothing. It took everything in me to resist the urge to glare at him.

"Sorry," he said quickly, reaching down to pick up the paper and finish tracing the upper runes. "I got startled."

I couldn't hold my frustration back. "What made you think it was a good idea to speak a suspected incantation—that you're not supposed to be able to read in the first place—when it mentions a notoriously cursed object?"

Legend said the Callexus, a mythical sword of immortality, cursed anyone it touched with immortality. It belonged to a tale taught in early education meant to demonstrate the necessity of magical balance: Mathias Merek, a man sent by the God of the Sun, saved Gardian by transferring the all-too-powerful magic of immortality into the Callexus. When Mathias's son, Silas, fell into temptation and touched the tip of the sword, the Gods cursed him to suffer through a lonely, infinite life, a punishment for ignoring holy orders and neglecting magical balance.

"Oh, that's what it took for you to drop the formality? As if you wouldn't have demanded me to read it, anyway." He crossed his arms as he looked down at me. "Chill. It's a myth that came from the time of the War. You said this arch was mentioned in wartime documents, right? Makes enough sense to me."

"That does not explain why you activated a rune." I barely kept my composure, trying to breathe slowly. He was way too casual about being able to read an ancient language that I'd been attempting to translate my entire life. "How did you translate the Driksaal?"

"I told you; I have no clue. I've never learned how to read any kind of Driksaal. Libra learns Kaelin for mediation and communication with the other Unions." He shrugged. "Your guess is as good as mine. You're welcome."

When he diverted his attention, I rolled my eyes and stood up. We finished tracing the runes on multiple pieces of paper, folded them carefully to not smear the charcoal while numbering them. I tied them together in a scroll of papers with a string and placed them back into my bag, hurrying over to the East Trail. Chase slowly followed me, his gaze lingering on the top of the arch.

"What's the rush?"

"We are trespassing on Assidian territory."

His eyes widened as we stepped back to the dirt path. "And you didn't tell me?"

"You would not have agreed if I warned you." I fastened my bag over my shoulders. "I invite you to correct me if I am wrong."

He crossed his arms, narrowing his eyes. "That's highly illegal, you know that?"

"You and I trespassed. If I am reported, we will both face the consequences."

He shut his mouth.

"Exactly. Let's go."

He didn't start walking until I was a few paces ahead. I stole one last glance toward the worn arch. It was almost as if I could see a low glow of gold over the area, a hue sparkling against the white. If it wasn't for the snow, the faint aura wouldn't have been visible. The air smelled of a peculiar combination of metallic blood and the sweet pine sap from the trees deeper in the Woods. A mimic of an article I'd read—the smell of a golden healing magic saving a Convictionist 300 years ago, hauntingly similar to the look and smell of Libran Healing.

Conviction Woods hadn't lost its magic, and neither had the arches attached to its ancient ties.

CHAPTER 6

When we made it back to the Exchange Center, Chase sent me up to my room while he attempted to convince Robin to give him the classified sixth floor access key. I sat against my door in silence, trying to contain my frustration at the fact I spent my whole life attempting to translate historical documents only for a random Libra to automatically understand ancient Driksaal. Chase finally knocked, and I jumped to my feet, swinging the door open. I considered shutting it again when I caught the smug look on his face. He dangled the keys in front of me with a grin, and I snatched them from his hand.

"You're welcome." He stepped aside and beckoned with his arm toward the floor access sign in front of the door to the stairs. "The only reason I'm agreeing to this is because I have no idea why I could read that stuff."

"How did you obtain access to the key?" I asked as we stepped into the stairwell.

He stole a glance down the stairs to make sure we weren't being followed. "Told Robin that my boss needed me to grab a special text for the Libra Stellarium."

"He believed your lie, after you received access to the sixth floor for the first time yesterday?"

Chase glanced over at me with another cheeky look on his face as we reached the top of the stairs. "I have my ways."

I pushed open the stairwell door to the sixth floor. The hallway sent an eerie sense through me, starting in the twitch of my nose, traveling down to the pit of my stomach. There were only two lanterns strung across the ceiling, casting the passage with a foreboding shadow, worn brick and stone covering the walls. There were fewer doors than on the other floors, many of them with cautionary no-trespassing signs. Not a single room had a glow at the crack of the door from a light inside. The floor was completely vacant.

Chase was right—etched runic spread sporadically across the walls. I walked a few steps into the hallway, kneeling to brush my fingers over one of the larger runes. Just in case, I stole an unnecessary glance around, my hand hovering over the flap of my pack. When the coast seemed clear, I pulled my references to hold them next to the runes on the walls; the writing was an exact match.

The discovery would've taken me many years and copious amounts of luck without his help. I didn't understand how, or why, there was a connection between the ancient arch and the Conviction-Autarchic Exchange Center. Something wasn't adding up.

"I was right, yeah?"

I flinched at the sound of Chase's voice, ducking away as he leaned over me.

"These are the smaller runes across the lower arch that you could reach," Chase said as he walked down the hallway, running his hand along the wall. "But I don't see the big rune that was at the top of the arch. Maybe

I'm just missing it, though."

Before we could continue our conversation, the sound of a door opening and closing bounced off the walls from down the hallway, where the light tapered off. Behind us, the door we'd entered from echoed with the same petrifying sound.

There was another entryway—one we couldn't see, one we didn't know of. Likewise, at least one more set of keys to the sixth floor existed. Either Chase had lied to me, or they'd lied to Chase.

The lanterns barely flickered when the airflow shifted. A sickly, knotting dread grew in the pit of my stomach. The flames were disturbed again. Shadows shifted positions. I couldn't turn around; I was too afraid to—Chase's eyes were stuck to whoever was behind me.

The shape of another person slithered out of the darkness of the hallway I faced. Their shadow, disguising them with the shield of the hallway's darkness, morphed into the shape of a figure cloaked in black. The dimming glow of the lanterns flashed on a blade in their hand. They pulled their hood down, revealing the stone-cold face of a middle-aged man.

His cloak bore the Scorpio Stellarium emblem.

Within the flash of a moment, the man behind Chase sprinted forward, his knife in hand as he dove toward me. I tore my dagger out of my pocket and ducked away from him. Swinging a longsword in a dark hallway would've been a terrible idea. A burst of magic flew past my head. It slammed into the wall where I previously stood and exploded into a flurry of screaming light particles. A lantern floating on a string above flickered out with a puff of smoke.

I didn't get a second to recover as another ball of light flew toward me while the man with the knife readied himself again. Chase moved behind him, and without hesitation, he wrapped his elbow around the older man's throat. With ease, he threw the official to the ground. The mage met my eyes as another shot of magic grew in his hands.

"What did I do wrong?"

He didn't answer, returning my question with a blank, lifeless stare.

Chase drove his fist into my attacker's chin, and I struck my blade into his arm while he struggled to recover from Chase's hit. The other man on the floor threw his knife toward my leg. When it narrowly missed, he grabbed my leg and sent me crashing to the ground.

My body went limp at the impact. I temporarily lost sight of the scene, unable to move, unable to breathe. Amongst the fizzling static consuming my sight, a dim glow illuminated from one of the lowest stones on the wall. Its humming magic whispered next to my shoulder; it was the same symbol on the center of the arch that lit up gold when Chase touched it.

Pressed against my skin, the rune now throbbed with a pale red light. It emanated a low, gentle chime, vibrating against me. Spewing out from the magic was a fragrance that made anything I'd ever smelled before pale in comparison—it was somewhat of a mix between the strongest-smelling pine I'd ever found in Conviction Woods, acrid fresh blood, barely sulfuric, with notes of a strangely sweet and unrecognizable floral. I leaned away from it. It paused its humming. The smell gentled.

I didn't have time to ponder. I slammed my hand into the runic stone while kicking the light mage away. As I pushed the glowing stone into the wall, a thrown knife pierced my thigh. I gasped in agony as a tiny *click* resounded from an empty room behind the stone wall. A rectangular space shimmered to expose a room full of bookshelves, and my hand slipped through the glimmering red portal. I rolled into it.

The light mage threw an arm after me. Instead of following me through the aura, his hand slammed against a solid wall. It sent him reeling back with a pained shout and a confused, wild stare, as if I had completely disappeared. As if the wall was still stone. As if it wasn't a portal to a new room.

Chase's gaze stuck to the rectangular opening I'd activated. His eyes met mine. Though I was vulnerably sprawled on the floor, I was safe on the other side of a door only we could see. He stepped a few feet forward before snatching up my bag. When the light mage jumped toward him, Chase stepped aside into the invisible doorway. It shimmered gold. The man's body hit solid rock.

Chase and I were in a room only visible to us.

Both of the men stared at the space we'd disappeared into. One was bruised and broken, the other bleeding out. They exchanged a glance. Shock spread across their faces when they thought they couldn't see us.

"What the hell?" the man with a busted jaw said, looking at his counterpart mage, speaking language highly forbidden to a Scorpio.

"We need to leave." The other pointed to the stairwell. "Now. Tell everyone you know to notify Arctura Verena."

Notify the Arctura. *Notify the Arctura.* In five minutes, all of my previous attempts at hiding from the Stellarium were negated.

The doorway shimmered and disappeared again as Chase stepped further into the room, shrouding us in complete darkness. I tensed, sucking in a deep breath and fighting the nausea from my pain. My leg was bleeding out.

"A torch," I forced out, "is there a torch near you?"

"The room could be trapped. I got this."

A golden light illuminated the room, sourcing from Chase's hands. It pooled in his palms, spreading up his body through his veins. His entire self throbbed with golden magic. His amber eyes flashed with the same glow; I wasn't crazy for thinking I saw his eyes catch gold in the Sun. The brilliant luminescence was nothing like the pale yellow magic he'd used at the Balancing Ceremony.

A drop of light fell from his hands and splattered to the ground.

The single particle burst across the room in a blinding explosion of light, torches flaring to life and restoring what was previously an abandoned room. The activated magic sought my knife wound as the aura crawled up my leg. With a warm buzz, the knife clattered to the stone floor, the wound disappeared, and the room was alive. I'd never seen, nor felt, anything like it.

But I'd certainly read about Libran Healers.

"Pardon me," I started, "if I recall correctly—no, never mind, fuck formality. I thought you said you were a Dreamseeker!"

"Oh." He glanced down at his hands instead. "I am. You know, to get into other people's dreams, we summon the light..."

"Is Dreamseeking similar to Libran Healing?" I accused him, keeping our interlocked gaze until he was visibly uncomfortable. "Because, as far as I know, Dreamseeking isn't a damn archpower."

He opened his mouth, searching for words. "I wouldn't know?"

"You're a terrible liar," I muttered underneath my breath.

"What?"

"Nothing!" I snapped.

I stood up quickly to move away from the blood on the floor. He had no idea I'd seen my wound heal, and if he knew, he'd try to cover it up with another lie. It was all over the horrible attempts to hide his fear and guilt. I would question him later when we weren't in an intriguing secret space.

He turned around in a circle to take in the room. Old bookshelves lined the room's walls, drooling with astray papers and jutting-out spines of literature, artifacts smothered in dust. The room was thick with a combination of smells from a bloody metallic magic and archaic, musty pages. A desk leaning on a cracked leg rested against the wall across from us, vials of dry ink amongst curled scrolls stacked on its shelves.

I carefully inched toward the desk. Any previous hesitation toward Chase and his suspicious magic were hushed by my curiosity. "Looks like an Archive to me."

"The Scorpio officials must've been guarding it," Chase said. "Two officials guard each Archive. It's the Scorpio Archive."

We couldn't have been luckier. The Archives contained critical or sensitive documents that the Sign Leaders designated to secure. Of each of the twelve Archives hidden throughout Gardian, we happened across *my* Archive—in other words, paradise.

"Okay, so what does the arch have to do with this?" Chase rubbed his forehead, as if he was thinking too hard. He probably was. "I just don't understand why we could enter, and they couldn't."

"Here's a start: all the Archives are centuries old. And, I don't know, it would make sense that you could read an ancient language if you have a form of ancient magic, and that you could use said ancient magic to get us into an ancient Archive."

"Didn't *you* activate the portal?"

"Nice way to dodge the question. Are you done playing dumb yet?"

I wanted to believe he truly had no idea what I was talking about, but everything in me knew he was lying for his own safety.

"You know what I'd appreciate? A thank you. Not an 'I thank you,' a 'thank you, Chase, for saving my life.' I didn't have to defend you out there. I could've left you to die," he spat. "Also, your formal speech is *bullshit*, and I cannot stand another minute of it. It stops now, Rieka."

I took a step back at the use of my name. I knew he was right. He'd taken a massive risk for me, and I'd returned it with a cold demeanor. He was genuinely trying to understand, a grace that was rarely granted to me as a Scorpio, the first outsider to treat me with kindness when I couldn't return it. I'd waited my entire life to be given a chance to show myself. The opportunity was placed right into my grasp.

"Thank you," I said, letting the tension in my shoulders ease. "Why are you being nice to me?"

Chase barely smiled. "Look, Rieka, if you can act genuine and put the rest of the ugly Scorpio attitude behind, I won't have a problem. I could tell you were resisting the urge to break the disguise, and I thought, 'Well, maybe she just needs someone to listen.' I felt bad for you. You were protecting yourself, and I've seen my father do the same.."

I'd almost forgotten Libra's skill in reading a room. If anyone were to read me like a book, it would be a Libra who regularly interacted with a Scorpio. He'd disarmed our argument in minutes.

"I'll be genuine," I finally agreed. "If I'm going down, you're going down with me."

"And I'll remind you; I didn't sign up for that."

"I know. I'm sorry."

"Don't be. What normal person gets to see an Archive in their lifetime?"

Instead of continuing, he started examining the bookshelves while I stood before the desk. Next to a pile of aged papers, an untouched, pristine scroll sat idle. At my touch, a quick red shimmer rippled across the exposed text. I rolled it open as Chase skimmed the books to find an old letter written in Kaelin. The edges of the scroll were burnt, as if someone had tried to destroy it. I narrowed my eyes at the signature.

"No way." I held the aged yellow paper up to the light. "No way."

Chase looked over curiously. "Look at you go. That's a lot of emotion coming from a Scorpio."

"That's a lot of sass coming from a liar," I retorted. He rolled his eyes at the lost progress, muttering something underneath his breath. "It's a letter from the War of the Rebalancing."

"How do you know?"

"The Code doesn't make me illiterate, Chase."

"Just making sure." He set a book back on the shelf and peered over my shoulder at the paper. His face stilled in shock as he read the words. A moment of silence passed between us. I could practically feel the horror emanating off him as he read the scroll with me.

To the Autarian Hellarium,

I am writing to document the unpreventable injustice internally occurring within the Conviction Hellarium. We are experiencing a violation of human rights through the weaponization of religion. The gods will not be pleased.

Blaine has fabricated and enacted a law

underneath the title of "the Scorpio Code." The Scorpio Code contains three tenets: never show emotion, never befriend, and never fall in love. Blaine claims to have located the scripture concealed within the Scorpio Archive. His status as an adjunct to the Scorpio Hellarium allows him to establish validity in the "discovery" of this "holy oath." Following Blaine's attribution of the lack of the Code to the imbalance of Zodiac Turners, the majority of Scorpio's population has accepted the Code. This law strips the right of choice from Scorpio Individuals and thus encourages them to join the Hellarium. Despite losing the war, the Scorpio Hellarium will maintain their governmental influence and dictation of the economy.

Furthermore, I regret to inform you that Blaine inflicted himself with the blade of the Callexus. I predict he will manipulate the truth of the Callexus and its existence to preserve his power for an undeterminable amount of time. I have since regained possession of the Callexus, and it has been returned to the Nix Mountains to prevent further damage to Gardian's magic system.

Sincerely,
Silas Merek

I'd been taught that the Mereks were a manmade myth, the Scorpio Code a holy truth. In my hands, I held proof of the opposite—Silas Merek was still alive, and the Scorpio Code was a weaponized lie.

"Oh, okay, that's not confusing at all." Chase leaned against the wall. "The Callexus is real and has to do with the Code. I'm reading this correctly, right?"

"We were taught immortality wasn't any more than a children's tale." I set the scroll down as my heart raced. "Because the Code was created—and likely still enforced—by an immortal."

Chase picked up the scroll. "And we know this is real, between the arch's inscription of the Callexus, and we are undoubtedly in the Scorpio Archive."

"Right." I met his eyes. "The Arctura knows this exists and is choosing to keep this knowledge hidden in the Archive."

"Well, yeah, if the Code is a lie, so is the Scorpio Stellarium's power." Chase handed it back to me to look at the rest of the scattered papers on the desk. He picked up a neatly folded white note that stuck out amongst crinkled and yellowed papers. His eyes widened as he read it. I immediately snatched the paper from his hand. "Rieka—"

"Oh my god."

It was a note addressed to *us,* written in fresh modern runic, with a translation guide to ancient Rurian numbers. Someone had signed it off, *"you're welcome."*

Chase and I looked up at each other.

"Did we..." Chase held his hand over his mouth as he tried to make sense of any of it. "Did we get set up?"

"How?" I took a step back from him. "I have been searching for that specific arch for months now."

"Yeah, and I got sent up to the sixth floor for the first time yesterday. I wouldn't have recognized the runic if I hadn't been up here. The arch had an incantation about the Callexus. This scroll is about the Callexus. We'll need to go back to the arch to use that translation guide. There's something over there that we missed."

"Who sent you to the sixth floor yesterday?"

"My boss. Random Libra guy. Don't know him all that well."

"That doesn't help." I paced, thinking through each of the steps. "I would've hit a dead end if you weren't with me to visit the arch. Someone knew that I needed you to be able to read the ancient Driksaal on the arch and recognize it on this floor to get into the Scorpio Archive."

"I'm telling the truth when I say I wasn't taught ancient Driksaal. I have no clue why I can read it. That's an entirely new fact about me I only learned today," Chase said, shaking his head. "Whoever led us to the Archive knew something about me that I didn't even know."

"And if they knew where the Scorpio Archive is, let alone the existence of that scroll, they've got authority. Someone of status who is against the Scorpio Stellarium."

None of it connected, none of it made sense. The pressure set in. Within hours, the Arctura would know we'd broken into the Archive. They'd seen Chase defend me in the hallway. Breaking the Code meant death. Discovering the location of the Archive meant death. Knowing the truth to dismantle the Scorpio Stellarium's power definitely meant death. And yet, we'd been set up to find that same truth.

Fear coursed through my body.

"The Callexus," I said, "is our only way of escaping death. The Stellarium can't say we faked this letter if we hold the sword mentioned in it. Proving the existence of the Callexus exposes the Code as a lie."

"Does that negate the fact that we just broke into an Archive? If the

Callexus doesn't exist, and this scroll is lying, we're dead."

"And if we do nothing about it, we're dead within days instead." I rolled the scroll up. "Someone sent us into here."

"The Hub isn't safe for us," Chase warned me, his voice lowering. "When do you talk to your sister next?"

"Tomorrow morning."

"Okay. The Exchange Center has plenty of travel supplies from visiting Autarians. We need to get things put together and depart tomorrow without the intention of returning to the Hub. Can your sister deal with leaving on a short notice?"

"She'll get over it. Is it a risk that our names are attached to our rooms?"

"Yeah, it's the Stellarium we're talking about. They obviously know more about us than we know about ourselves. Here's the plan," Chase started as I stuffed the scroll into my backpack. "We make sure the coast is clear and sprint down the stairs. Robin was off work in his room when we got the key from him. We bang on his door until he answers and demand a different room."

"Okay, but just to be clear, I'm not sleeping with you."

"You are *not* my type."

"Glad we're on the same page. I'll take the floor."

I followed him as he approached the area of the portal activation. I pressed my hand to it, and it shuddered with a red light. The hall was silent, a haunting scene of our inevitable demise, blood splattered on the floor reflecting the flicker of a single lantern left on the wall. After both of us swallowed our panic, we sprinted out of the room. Chase almost fell into the door to the sixth floor, yanking it open.

I tripped over the first step, flinging myself around the corner, while Chase grabbed the rail and hoisted himself over to jump ahead on the next set of stairs. When we somehow made it to the fifth floor without injury, I leaned against the door to the hallway, listening for any indication of activity. Silence. I ripped open the door and Chase led the way to room 512.

Chase frantically banged on Robin's door. "Robin! Let me in, *now*."

"Hold *on*, Chase, give me a second to put on my damn boxers." Shuffling sounds came from inside of the room. "Chill out. I just took a shower."

"Right now, boxers can wait!"

"I thought we had a conclusion about—"

"This isn't about that. Ego check yourself!" Chase's face looked like someone had set it on fire. I burst out laughing. "You are risking my life right now, Robin!"

I was trying to be quiet but failing horribly. Chase gave me a nasty glare. I opened my mouth for a snarky remark, but Robin swung the door open before I could tease him. His mouth dropped as soon as he saw us. I could only imagine the sight—bloodstained shirts, Chase with a bruise on his jaw, and half my pant leg torn open from a knife.

Robin moved aside to let us in. "Now, what the *fuck*, man?"

We stumbled in and Chase shut the door, leaning against it and sliding down to sit on the ground in defeat. He shuffled in his pocket for the key to the sixth floor and wordlessly tossed it to Robin. I held my knees to take in deep breaths before I started laughing harder than I'd ever laughed before. Robin looked at me like I was completely insane. He might've been right.

"It's life or death right now. We need a room," Chase pleaded.

"Please."

"God, Chase, I knew you were desperate, but not *this* desperate."

"*Robin*," he snapped. "Stop, I'm not joking about this."

"Well, yeah, no kidding, you've got a Scorpio woman this time—"

"No. I'm done. To make it abundantly clear, I am not trying to bang her, or you, or anyone else. I am trying to stay alive!" Chase stood up quickly. He towered over Robin, who finally shut his mouth. "Listen to me. She is a friend. A friend who is also in a life-or-death situation. On the sixth floor, we found—"

"Nope," Robin interrupted him. "I am not responsible for you. Either of you! Don't you dare tell me why she's breaking the Code, or whatever is up there, or anything illegal."

"Okay, fine, but if an official from Scorpio or Libra spots either of us, it's going to cost us our life. And we need you to lie about what room we're in," Chase said. "Please, Robin, I'll do anything."

Robin crossed his arms. "Really?"

"He's not lying," I spoke up. "I won't drag you into this, but we're in danger. Genuinely, please help."

"You've got emotions, I believe you." Robin walked to the other side of his room, to a door to a connecting room. He opened it. "If Kinder finds out about a Scorpio in his room, you're dead anyway."

That must've been the Cancer boy I'd met a couple of nights ago. Blue sheets were on his bed, coordinated with the beautiful paintings of the ocean and sea-faring creatures spread across the walls and ceiling.

"He left unexpectedly because of illness. You have two days. If anyone asks, I'll tell them you left. They won't think about checking Kinder's room," Robin said. "Also, if Chase chooses to be a whore, I'll hear it and kill him myself."

"I'd also kill him, don't worry," I added.

Chase turned his back to me and walked into the dark room attached to Robin's, slamming the door. I waited for a moment to hear the bathroom door open and close in the next room over. I turned back to Robin, opening my mouth, and then closing it. The next thought I had was despicable, but it would protect our backs.

"Go ahead, say anything you want about him," Robin said.

I took a step closer to Robin to make sure Chase didn't hear me. "If anyone without the intention to immediately murder us asks, we're sleeping together with no attachments, because that's more legal than being his friend. I'm not breaking the Scorpio Code, and you *didn't* just hear me laugh."

"You're funny, I like you. I've got your back. I know how it is for people like us." He held out a fist to me, and I matched it. Sagittarius was just as stigmatized as Scorpio. "Chase is a good friend. I just enjoy poking fun at him. Rest well."

I nodded, and with that, I opened the door and stepped into the dark room to find Chase had spread blankets across the floor for me, and was curled up on the mattress without cover, his back to me. I smiled.

Chapter 7

"Rieka. Open your eyes."

I gasped in a panicked breath and jumped to my feet at the sound of Dad's voice. As I was thrown into the familiar sights of Conviction Woods at night, I stumbled backward at the weightless feel of my body. The movement of each of my limbs was slowed and miscalculated, as if I'd stepped into a different realm where gravity had a delayed reaction.

"Breathe. You're in a dream." Dad grabbed each of my arms to stabilize me before I lost my footing. "Look around and take in where you are."

I peered up the massive trunks of the cedars and their peeling bark, the earthy smell of wet soil and recent rain. The mossy ground was soft against my bare feet and shifted as I stood amongst an open clearing in the forest I called home. The warm, humid night was familiar as golden magic and fireflies danced around me. A gentle hum hid underneath the wind's whisper.

"I don't think I've ever been in this part of the Woods, but it's beautiful."

"You have. I'm pulling from your memory," Dad explained, and I focused back on him. His eyes barely illuminated with a sapphire light. He took a step back from me, his hands sliding off my arms. A blue aura quickly passed over his skin, tiny constellations sparkling up his body from his wrists. "Where are you, Rieka?"

"Is this real?" I asked in place of a response, looking down at my hands. The longer I adjusted to the dream, the more it felt like I was awake. My eyes caught to another ripple of the strange starry magic rushing over Dad's skin. "That's not your magic. I'm imagining this."

"It's real. I'm using magic to step into your dreams by accessing a safe setting in your memory," Dad explained. I stared at him, attempting to figure out if my brain was making it all up. Dreams were rare for me. "I sensed your fear at a level I've never felt it before. What happened?"

"You sensed my fear? This can't be real. You're a water mage." I shook my head to clear my mind. "Not a Dreamseeker."

"It's okay, Rieka, I'm both a water mage and Dreamseeker," he urgently reassured me. He *did* sound like himself. "I don't have time right now to explain more. I promise I'll tell you all about it later. Right now, I just need to know if you're safe."

I caught the frantic panic hidden underneath the calm façade he was trying to uphold to soothe me. His breaths were unsteady, rapid, his pupils enlarged. Another fast flash of blue light rippled over his skin. Something was wrong with him.

"Are you okay?" I took a hesitant step forward. "You're not dying, are you?"

"No! No, I'm not," he said with a raspy laugh, shaking his head. "I'm fine. That's the last thing you need to worry about. Are you safe?"

"I think so. Maybe not. I'm at the Conviction-Autarchic Exchange Center. I don't know what's going on, Dad. I somehow got into the Scorpio Archive and found a scroll that proves the Code is a lie. The Code was made up during the War, the whole story about the Callexus is real, the Scorpio Stellarium attacked me—"

"Rieka, it's okay, I believe you," he interrupted me with a warm smile, despite pulling in a deep, rattling breath. "You don't need to explain further. You found evidence against the Code. I'm so proud of you, kid."

His tone of voice, the way he looked at me, how he tried to hide whatever pain he was experiencing to make me feel better—I knew he was being honest about Dreamseeking me. It was real. I broke into tears, and he reached forward, pulling me into his embrace. A wave of emotion swallowed me, breaking into shivers at the anxiety that hit me all at once. His hand rubbed against my back to comfort me. The tension in my shoulders barely eased.

"I don't know what's going on. Someone led us into the Archive. I'm scared," I said, tripping over my words through my panic. "They're going to try to kill me."

"You're with Chase? Right now?"

"In the same room, yes." I paused. I hadn't told him Chase's name, nor that I was with him in the first place. "How'd you know?"

"He's the safest person you can be with right now." His chest slowly fell as he breathed out in relief. I pulled back to give him a look of confusion. "I'm sending Avia to the start of the East Trail. Meet her there instead of the fountain and get out of the Hub."

"Dad, what's happening?"

"It'll be okay, Rieka, I promise. Everything that's happening to you is a good thing. Trust it." He gasped in a breath, as if he was on the verge of fainting. A brighter blue aura surrounded him, blurring his shape. "I love you, kid."

I was thrown out of the dream, my eyes wide as I desperately absorbed the sight of a calm blue room in the Exchange Center. I gasped in a breath, sitting up to frantically cough. Chase lurched forward at the sound of my wheezing.

"*God*, okay, good morning. Are you okay?" Chase asked, swinging his legs over the side of the bed. "What happened?"

"My dad just visited my dreams," I said, my voice hoarse. "I didn't know he was a Dreamseeker. He said he could sense my fear, and that he was sending Avia to the East Trail so we can get out of the Hub."

"That's lovely."

"No?"

"Sarcasm." He stood up to walk to the bathroom. "What do you mean, you didn't know he was a Dreamseeker? Didn't you say he's a Cancer? I'd think he would want to tell you that, considering he's going to and from territories."

"Yeah." I pulled my knees into my chest, hugging my legs. "He's a water mage."

"Are you sure that was him Dreamseeking you?" Chase's voice echoed from the open bathroom door.

I sighed. "I'm sure."

"How're you feeling?"

"What?"

He leaned out of the bathroom to look at me. "I asked how you're feeling?"

"Okay, I guess." I stared at him blankly. "Why?"

"Um, just trying to be a decent person." He shook his head and disappeared again. "You were saying yesterday how we're both dead if we don't find the Callexus, and your dad visited your dreams. It's a lot to process, especially for someone who has been taught the opposite of emotional regulation skills."

"Oh. Yeah. I have a lot on my mind. We need to get out of here. I'm nervous about being in broad daylight."

"Why don't you take a moment to relax and organize yourself? I'll gather some travel supplies from downstairs so we can get ready to backpack. Better that I go anyway. The Stellarium's used to seeing me here." He closed the bathroom door behind himself, grabbing his golden-trimmed white cloak from where he'd thrown it over Kinder's desk chair. "Assuming that your sister will already have everything prepped for herself?"

"Dad wouldn't send her out missing anything. He travels enough to have a method for packing." I laid back down on my back, staring at the murals of the ocean across the ceiling. I clasped my hands together to ease their shaking. "You'll be fast?"

"As fast as I can be." He smiled as he readjusted his cloak on his broad shoulders, stepping toward the door. "You seem like someone who would enjoy making lists. Maybe work on that to keep yourself busy."

"Could you take the rest of the stuff from my room while you're out there?" I leaned over to grab my cloak and dug into the pocket for the key. I tossed it to him, and he caught it with ease as he walked out of the room.

As soon as the door was shut, I curled into a ball and threw my blankets over my head to decompress. I was adjusted to spending hours upon hours by myself in my room, shuffling through stacks of scrolls and organizing artifacts, alone in my own world. The dark, warm space of the blankets calmed me down. I breathed out slowly to feel the rise and fall of my chest. I wasn't *uncomfortable* with Chase's presence, just overwhelmed by having another person around. Dad trusted him, so I knew I could trust him. I'd just never been particularly fond of spending time around men that weren't my dad.

I hadn't realized how much I needed the space to reset. I lost track of the time that went by, though it couldn't have been more than 30 minutes. The sound of the door opening and closing stopped me from dozing off, and I peeked out of my layers of blankets.

"Bad news." With a loud sigh, Chase threw down two large packs with supplies attached to them. I wasn't entirely sure how he carried all of it up the stairs. "Winter storm rolled in overnight. It's a white out, and this building is infested with the Scorpio Stellarium. We're lucky you didn't go with me to get the backpacking stuff."

I scrambled out of my cocoon of blanket warmth. "What?"

"Yeah. They're raiding the rooms on the second level right now." He opened the door to Robin's room before he started to quickly organize his things. "He's working at the desk. Go look out the window in his room."

I hurried into the attached room, shielding my eyes at the bright light filtering through the window from inches of snow. I let my vision adjust to the snowflakes flying past the window. There must've been at least six inches of snow on the ground. My heart dropped. I turned my back to the brightness of the winter storm. I immediately started to grab my stuff and shove it into the pack that Chase pushed toward me.

"The closer we get to Conviction Woods, the warmer it'll be," I said as I stepped into the bathroom to throw on the thermal layers he'd grabbed from downstairs. "Did you check the direction of the wind?"

"West. Conviction Woods is on the west side of the East Trail. If we can get there, it'll be much milder." His voice was muffled from the other side of the door. I stepped out of the bathroom a moment later as he pushed down on a sleeping bag in his backpack. "There's another back stairwell at the end of the hallway, so we don't need to pass through the lobby."

"Ever backpacked in the snow before?" I asked him as I scrambled to lace my boots. "It'll be cold."

"I'm not worried about it." He fastened his pack over his cloak. "I'm more concerned about the Stellarium making it to our floor before we're out. Let's go."

I quickly checked the room. "There'll be less Stellarium activity outside with the storm."

Chase didn't respond, looking out the door before he fully opened it. My vision blurred with adrenaline; a reminder of the terror we'd felt the night before running through the Exchange Center after finding the scroll. Chase yanked open a door at the end of the hallway, and when there wasn't any sound of activity in the stairwell, we ran down the flights as fast as possible. I burst out the exit door, taking in a restricted breath of cold air as the wind rocked my body. We both hurried away from the Exchange Center into the empty white space of the Hub. Though first panicked and hurrying from the building, we slowed when we were a safe distance. The normally bustling streets were empty with the snow decreasing visibility.

"Well, snow scared 'em away, at least. Surprising, they act colder than the temperature out here," Chase finally said after a few minutes of silence, his voice slightly strained from the effort it took to push through the snow. "How often do you travel in the winter?"

"Every once in a while," I said simply, avoiding the fact that I was used to traveling memorized paths through Conviction Woods across easy terrain and long distances. I ignored the burning in my thighs from the resistance created by the accumulating snow. I shielded my eyes to discern where we were going. A vast white expanse surrounded us.

"Have we passed the fountain yet?" he asked, raising his voice as a gust of wind struck us. "Are you navigating this?"

"The fountain's behind us." I kept trekking forward, though I was losing my line of sight. My doubt about pathfinding in a storm sank in. "I'm following the general shape of buildings."

I'd bite my words minutes later when we undoubtedly reached the fountain. I started to wonder if we'd taken a wrong turn. Snow pierced into my skin as the temperature dropped, the whistling wind deafening me. We'd made the silent mutual decision to take the risk of walking into the wrong building and try every door we could find, but each was snowed in or locked shut, every sign of life halting in the freeze. Critical minutes of time passed without another body in sight. I wasn't sure what part of the Hub we were in.

GARDIAN

When I pushed the back of my hand to my lips, they'd lost sensation. My fingertips burned, legs screaming as I struggled through building accumulation. The wind resisted me from every direction, battering my body until I forced myself to pause to try to recalculate my path. There were no footsteps to trace when the fresh snow disguised the time we'd surely spent going in circles as night fell. My world started to spin, distort.

My hands trembled as a response to the bitter cold. I yanked my cloak closer to my body. Underneath my gloves, I knew without looking that my fingertips were turning purple. My lungs burned and screamed at every breath I took. Black spots dotted my vision, my knees shaking before they gave out.

I collapsed.

Chapter 8

A golden light pierced through the darkness of the storm, so gold that it was all I could see. My heartbeat stabilized; its drumming amplified by the surge of magic. With a sharp ringing screaming through my head, I blinked, and I was back in my body.

Two hands rested on my wrist and arm as a golden light spread through my veins, a restoration unlike any kind of healing I'd ever felt before. A warm energy raced through my body in a shockwave. Through the haze of the snow, an abrupt smell of blood filled the air as I gasped in a breath. I turned my wrist, watching as the light searched for my blood through my vascular system. The frostbite at my fingertips was reversing, purple skin reverting as the power of healing touched it.

I looked up and remembered Chase was with me.

I knew it.

His entire body was alight with healing. I met his eyes, luminescent and glowing gold to match his magic. There wasn't a record of a Libran Healer in at least three hundred years. Shock made me rigid as I burst into shivers at the numbness washing over me. I kept the speculation of his potential archpower stashed in the back of my mind, but I hadn't believed my intuition as much as I should've.

  He slowly removed his hand from my arm, throwing his cloak over my shoulder. The warmth of his healing was dissipating, though he looked completely unfazed by the cold. I'd read before that Libran Healers were adept at surviving, stronger against illness and temperature. It was the very reason they were feared, a power so close to immortality.

  A shout cut through my thoughts. Both of us flinched. The fiery light of an undying lantern flared through the snow, a new figure kneeling before us. He grabbed Chase's arm and yanked him to his feet. A hand was extended to me, and I took it from the man wearing a distinctive orange cloak. He guided us through the snow, pushing us to a tiny building no more than a few dozen feet away. It took minutes to struggle through the snow. After fighting the heightening drift at the door, the man swung the door open and shoved Chase inside. He guided me in more gently, slamming the door behind us.

  I instantly relaxed in the tiny office; the perils of the blizzard were absent in the warm environment. We dropped our backpacks next to the door. I relaxed as my eyes adjusted to the gentle light, taking in slow and steady breaths. Chase held his knees for a moment while he wheezed in air, then shook the snow out of his hair.

  I slid my snowy cloak and coat off my shoulders, placing them on a rack next to the door. The office was quite small; a tan couch sat in the front of the room behind a coffee table, a bookshelf across from it. In the back of the room was a wooden desk and file cabinet hugging a door to another room. Nestled in the wall to the right of the desk crackled a lit fireplace. Magically lit paper lanterns, strung from the ceilings, accentuated the red, orange, and yellow colors on posters and paint decorating the cozy room. Off-white star maps spread across the walls, and above the couch was a map of Gardian written in older Conviction Driksaal. On the ceiling was a mural painted in a style similar to the art in the Exchange Center, depicting a scene from what must've been the War of the Rebalancing: Aries mages with fire bursting from their hands, one man standing over the body of another as a protective force. It was a curious choice, considering Conviction lost the War of the Rebalancing.

I narrowed my eyes at a nameplate on the wooden desk. *"Atlas Fulbright."*

My gaze ripped over to Chase as realization struck both of us in the same moment. Fear coursed through me, and I stepped back hesitantly, fixing the expressions on my face. I struggled to take the reins of the shock I was feeling.

Atlas Fulbright was the Aries Leader. The second-to-top Arctura.

He gestured toward a chair next to the couch. "Take a seat."

"Yes, sir." Chase immediately sat down, his hands trembling. I stood next to him, keeping my emotions absolutely still. "Sir, are you the Aries Leader?"

"I am." He gave Chase a warm smile and held out his hand. "Call me Atlas. Nice to meet you."

Chase shook it. "Chase Marin."

"Thanks, but I already knew your name." Atlas sat down in the chair at his desk and nodded at me. "Rieka. Relax. I can only try to fathom how overwhelmed you must be."

Chase and I instantly looked at each other.

"I'm sorry?" Chase said quietly when I returned his surprise with a blank stare. I couldn't break the Code in front of an Arctura. "Why do you know our names?"

"For one, you learned the Scorpio Stellarium's biggest secret, and everyone in the Conviction Stellarium knows." Atlas leaned back in his chair and threw his legs on his desk. He readjusted his round gold glasses as he examined the two of us, running his hand through his fluffy chestnut hair. He wore casual attire underneath his orange cloak, a long-sleeved black turtleneck and khakis—unusually casual for an *Arctura*, of all people. His striking eyes, amber and blue, stuck out against what he was wearing. "Also, I helped you find the Archive. You're welcome."

Chase must've caught the tiny sway in my body from the lightheadedness taking over. He stood up quickly, moving aside so I could sit down in his spot. I folded my legs close to myself, as if protecting my body, and all I could think about was how badly I wanted to be alone in my room in Conviction Woods. Chase sat down on the ground, his back against the front armrest of the chair to avoid getting too close to my legs. I appreciated how careful he was about my space.

"Alright, now that we're situated—" Atlas began, and Chase opened his mouth to say something. Atlas put his hand up. "Ah—nope, here, let's get the shock over with. I know she found the arch. I know you're a Libran Healer."

Chase and I stared at him in disbelief. There was no way it wasn't a trap.

"How?" Chase finally forced out. "How did you know that about me? I've only ever told my dad."

"I'm an Arctura. I just know these things." Atlas smiled and crossed his arms, dangerously close to tipping his chair over. "There's not much you can hide from the Stellarium. You're damn lucky I'm the part of the Stellarium who knows about your archpower."

"And you led us to the arch?" Chase followed up. "Aren't you supposed to be working alongside the Scorpio Arctura?"

"'Supposed' is the key word there." Atlas sighed heavily. "I'm not fond of Verena's leadership style."

Chase nodded slowly. "So you led us right to a scroll that disproves the law she swears by."

"Precisely. I despise the Scorpio Code. I have my reasons."

"Why us?"

"Ready for this?" Atlas rubbed his hands together. "The Aries Stellarium can't expose the scroll. That'd be pitting Aries against Scorpio, and we don't want another war on our hands. Ideally, the Scorpio Code gets reversed by Scorpio. Easy answer: a Scorpio historian who hates the Code and a Libran Healer who can read ancient Driksaal."

The realization visibly hit Chase. "Is *that* why I can read a language I was never taught?"

"Libran Healers can automatically read Driksaal. I'm quite surprised neither of you knew that." Atlas yawned. "How long were you out there?"

"We had no choice," Chase defended our choice to leave, ignoring the question to not embarrass the two of us. I made a note to myself to thank him later for carrying the conversation. "The Scorpio Stellarium was on the second floor."

"Did you not figure out that someone from the Stellarium helped you find the Scorpio Archive? And, if that person knew where the Archive was, wanted to show you that the Code was false, and knew your names, they probably would've kept you safe and hidden from Scorpio?"

Chase narrowed his eyes. "In our defense, there's no way we could've predicted that the Aries Arctura was on our side, and to be clear... you're part of the Stellarium, who is trying to murder us, and we walked into your office."

"I want you to trust me. Look, I'm here to protect you." Atlas continued. "You're two young folk I rescued in the storm, and most importantly, neither of you are Aries. All I did was save your lives. I don't have any obligation to say a thing about you."

He was either being genuine for reasons we didn't understand, or manipulatively charismatic. Knowing the Stellarium, it was probably the latter.

"I know things about you and her that I'm not supposed to know," Atlas said to Chase, "so let's get on equal ground, Libra, and I'll tell you something that I'm not typically allowed to share. Fair?"

"Why should we believe that you're not just going to turn us in?" Chase asked hesitantly.

"Because I despise Verena and the Scorpio Stellarium just as much as you do. I have my reasons." Atlas had no intention of disguising the disgust hidden in the tone of his voice when he spat out Verena's name. He swung his legs down to lean forward, his elbows on his desk, resting his chin on top of his folded hands. "I can't be responsible for dividing the Stellarium. By letting the two of you wreak chaos, you make my life significantly easier."

Chase pondered the offer. Atlas held out a hand. Chase looked back to see if I agreed, and with no other option in sight, I gave him a small nod. He reached forward and shook Atlas's hand.

"Now, Rieka, this involves you, too." He held a hand out to me.

"You don't tell my secret, and I won't tell yours. Sound good?"

I wasn't sure what else we had to lose, so I shook his hand.

He smiled. "The history of the Zodiac Turners. The magic was destroyed in the War of the Rebalancing. True or false?"

"True?" Chase answered slowly.

"False," Atlas corrected him. "It's still in Gardian. It's still here, like your healing. There are six known Zodiac Turners in Gardian. At least. We *think*."

"Six?" I echoed. "To my understanding, the only Zodiac Turner is the immortal Blaine, who, as told by the scroll's content, created the Scorpio Code."

"Knock it off with the formality. I already know you've broken it," Atlas told me. "Also, just because the scroll didn't list out the names of the Turners doesn't mean that Blaine's the only Zodiac Turner."

"You said at *least* six, and that you *thought*," Chase repeated. "So, there could potentially be more."

Atlas, holding onto a pencil that he was tapping in his hands, went quiet for a moment to inspect us. "If I were you, I'd focus on the number six."

I exchanged a glance with Chase again. The Scorpio Stellarium was already after me for breaking the Code. Atlas appeared to be on our side—*suspiciously* on our side—but more than anything else, I was intrigued.

"What direction should we go from here?" I asked.

Atlas's eyes lit up at the omittance of Scorpio formality. "You tell me."

"The arch. You gave us a translation guide to ancient Rurian."

"There you go." Atlas stood up and stretched. "We are right next to the East Trail, by the way. I'll give you that much with your blizzard navigation skills. I've got you for the night. I have a room in the back with a bed, if one of you would like to sleep there and the other on the floor."

"She can have it. I took the bed last time." Chase nodded at me. "I can sleep on the floor."

"That settles it." Atlas stood up and walked to the back door. "I'll be out here."

"Thank you," I said as Chase and I followed him, breathing out slowly at how nice it felt to speak normally.

"My pleasure." He opened the door. The bed was already made. "And pleasure to meet you both, as well."

"You too," Chase said awkwardly as Atlas closed the door on us. Chase leaned against the wall, holding his forehead. He listened to Atlas walking away before speaking. "Your sister will be on the East Trail tomorrow, too?"

"Definitely, I'm sure my dad told her how much risk there was going into the Hub." I narrowed my eyes at him. "You're a Libran Healer?"

"Yeah."

"Are you serious? 'Oh, I have ancient magic. It's not too big of a deal.' Oh my god."

"Now, it's my moral duty to tell you that I am trained to find a just and equal stance to this," Chase said. "I really don't know you that well. Was it my obligation to tell you?"

"I don't know, maybe when an entire room lit up with magic that was undeniably Libran Healing, you could've told me? That seemed like a good time."

"For the record, I *am* a Dreamseeker. It's just not my primary magic." He sat down on the floor. "I don't even understand why I'm a Healer, so why should I put the burden on you? According to my dad, my mother was an Aries fire mage, and he's a shapeshifter."

"So, what, you're the descendant of someone who managed to hide Libran Healing in the War?"

"That's my best guess. If you have any better ideas, I'm open to it, because I've spent years trying to figure this out."

"What about your grandparents?" I asked.

"Died when I was two. They were both Scorpio, not healers."

"Strange," I said. "You don't know much about your family, do you?"

"Any more than you do?"

I shut my mouth.

"You should actually get some sleep," he said. I laid down with a single nod, focusing my sight on the ceiling. "Rieka. Could you do me a favor and not tell anyone else about the archpower? I managed to keep it hidden for this long."

"I understand. It'll stay between us."

I woke up with a groan, my body still aching from the snowstorm. On the floor, Chase lay wide awake, staring at the ceiling. I yawned and rolled my neck.

"Finally." Chase sat up. "Good morning."

"What time is it?" I threw myself out of bed with a stumble, brushing myself off. "Avia is probably so confused. Is it still snowing?"

"10 AM. You needed to sleep while we had a safe place to stay." He looked amused. "The snow only started to slow down an hour or two ago, anyway."

We both got ourselves together before carefully walking into the empty main office. Two plates of breakfast had been set on the coffee table, the lit fireplace spreading a blanket of warmth into the office. Chase and I were both silent for a moment, looking at each other in wonder. Chase sat down on the couch, holding his head. He eventually picked up his plate of food, inspecting it closely to make sure it wasn't obviously poisoned, then hesitantly started eating. I sat down next to him.

"He just left us in here," Chase said slowly, "and trusts us in his office?"

"I'm just as confused as you are." I started eating the scrambled eggs, too hungry to ignore the worry of the food being tampered with. "I prefer this over being in a cold tent, though."

Chase shrugged, focusing on his plate of food. Both of us were quiet for a while as we ate, tense in anticipation for Atlas's return. Dozens of minutes passed as we waited, and eventually Chase set his plate down, leaning against the couch while his leg shook.

With a sigh, I stood up and started inspecting the room closer. I inched toward the desk with Atlas's name plate and peered around. Dozens of papers sprawled across the surface of his workspace, many written in common Kaelin runic by Atlas, a few signed by other Leaders. A freshly dipped quill sat beside a paper in the center of it all, where it seemed like Atlas had drawn a chart of a human sitting and a zodiac wheel on top of it. Around it was scribbles and notes of different powers associated with each sign. Another paper next to the drawing was a list of magic systems in Gardian. Tiny scraps across the table seemed to add stories to the different drawings, with arrows connecting back to the big chart he must've been creating.

I opened my mouth to point it out to Chase, but he was hyper-focused on staring at the door, watching my back to warn me before Atlas could catch me looking at things I probably shouldn't have been.

I moved to the bookshelves, stocked with fiction, a lot of mysteries, and a few books about miscellaneous magic. The book that caught my eye, though, was an outfacing cover with the title: ZODIAC TURNING. I narrowed my eyes, reaching toward it.

"Can you stop touching things for, like, a second?"

"He's got a book about Zodiac Turning faced outward."

"Okay, and? Should you be touching it?"

"I don't know, you tell me."

"The answer was supposed to be 'no.'"

As I picked up the book, the door opened. I instantly set it down as Atlas hurried in. I stepped aside from the desk, quickly tucking my hands behind my back. Atlas raised his brows at me.

"Reading my stories?" He walked over to his desk. Terror froze my body and mind. "You're quite a curious individual."

"I apologize." I stepped aside and fixed my emotions in an instant.

"Curiosity is good, no worries." He looked down at the book in my hand, then up at me. "You're welcome to keep that."

Out of respect, I carefully set it back down on the shelf. It had an embellished leather cover and seemed to be of value.

"I distracted them, by the way."

"Distracted who?" Chase asked.

"The Scorpio Stellarium." Atlas nodded at the front door. "I told them I had a report that you'd been seen on the other side of the Hub. You should've seen how fast they flocked over there. Best to keep moving. East Trail's about a five-minute walk. I'm sure you've passed this office before."

Chase lifted his backpack off the ground to adjust it on his shoulders. He gave me a small look, as if warning me to be cautious the second we walked out the door, in case Atlas was lying to us. I slipped my boots on when he sat back down at his desk, grabbing his pencil to resume his work on the drawing I'd examined. Chase watched him closely as we readied to walk back out into the Hub.

"Oh, Rieka—" Atlas said as I put my hand on the doorknob, "—Rowan wanted to give you this."

I had to act fast as Atlas tossed something at me. I caught the small bronze object. When I opened my palm, I examined the compass that he'd thrown at me. I tilted it in the warm light of the office, a blue ripple flashing over the glass panel protecting the cardinal directions. It had some sort of enchantment. I tilted my head and smiled to myself; I had a cheap compass I always carried with me, but the one that Atlas gifted to me seemed of much better quality.

Atlas gifted it to me. Because Rowan wanted me to have it. I instantly looked up. The Aries Arctura knew my dad's name.

"Go on now." Atlas nodded at the door with a smile. "Your sister's waiting for you on the East Trail. You're going to a place called Rayka. Autarian-Assidian town. Have fun."

CHAPTER 9

Atlas hadn't lied to us. In the short walk it took to find Avia, Chase and I hadn't seen a single member of the Stellarium pass by. With Avia, we'd traveled for a few hours on the East Trail, explaining everything we'd encountered—omitting the part about Chase's healing—and the strange encounter with the Aries Arctura. As we finally neared the arch, I slowed down, my heart jumping at the excitement of whatever we'd find next.

"I've never been over here." Avia pushed past me and hurried toward the arch, completely disregarding the fact she'd crossed into Autarian territory.

"Did she just walk over a border without a second thought?" Chase asked quietly as we followed her. "Is she always like this?"

"Aries. It's the no-fear thing. Welcome to hell."

I traced my fingers down the runic of the arch, discerning the two languages apart. I reached into my cloak pocket for my notebook, pencil, and the translation guide Atlas had left us for Rurian digits, handing it to

Chase. He stepped closer to the arch, carefully brushing away snowflakes to reveal the writing. Avia, who was more interested in the structure, left us to translate the digits on our own. After a few minutes of discerning worn-away inscriptions and matching them to the guide, we had a set of numbers.

"Check it out." Chase looked over my shoulder. "Latitude and longitude, right?"

I slid my backpack off my shoulders to pull one of my maps from the side pockets. A few years back, Dad had given me a world map with latitude and longitude he'd found in one of the Autarian markets as a birthday gift. I had yet to use it but always carried it with me in hopes that one day it would be useful. I smiled as I traced its lines, following the numbers from the arch's ancient Rurian. My index finger settled on a spot on the Assidian Nix Mountain Range where the Eridanus, Gardian's largest river, forked off into a dead end. I double checked, and for the second time, I found the same point. I circled it.

"Do you think that's where the Callexus might be?" Chase asked.

"How did either of you figure out anything from the mess of runic on this arch?" Avia reached for my map, and I moved it away from her heated hands. She grumbled at me.

"It's the best we've got," I said to Chase, ignoring Avia's comment. "We can't cross over the Eridanus. It's too big, and Assidian territory is desolate. It'll be best to go around the Hub and up to Lyra, then sail the Eridanus into the mountains."

Footsteps crunched the soft snow behind me. A twig snapped. I froze. Avia and Chase immediately shut their mouths. Our distraction had betrayed us.

"Rieka," Chase said quietly, unmoving, his eyes stuck on the space I had my back to. "Get up."

I shoved the map and translation into my bag before I spun around.

Approaching us was a young woman no older than us. Her stone-cold blue-gray eyes pierced into me. Lengthy, ghostly white hair draped over her shoulders and down her back, a striking difference from the full black uniform she wore. Open underneath her coat, she wore a tight long-sleeved shirt and high-waisted combat pants designed for fast and fluid movement. A longsword was strapped to her back.

As I met her eyes, I caught that her left eye was a paler blue than the right. She looked familiar, hauntingly familiar. Her deathly intense gaze wasn't new.

I could feel Avia's heat begin to burn as she pressed her hands together, preparing for attack. She glanced at the Woods, then mouthed something to me. Chase couldn't go into the Woods. We couldn't get out of this as easily as we normally could; we'd have to fight.

She didn't say a word until she stopped directly before us. Her longsword was still sheathed on her back, no magic in her palms. Her emotions were eerily still, a monotonous stare that felt angrier than the Scorpio Stellarium's cold expressions.

"State the object placed into your bag," she said in Scorpio formality as she approached us.

I desperately searched for words to piece together an excuse so she wouldn't demand the translated coordinates but came up with nothing. Neither Chase nor Avia responded to her, though Avia's hands were starting to burn red. Chase unhooked a dagger on his belt, one he'd started to wear the day before as a precaution following our sixth-floor ambush.

"I will repeat the command," she said, pausing before us, "state the object that you placed in your bag."

"A map gifted to me by my father." I rested my hand on my necklace. "Why must you inquire?"

"Hand over the map," she snapped, breaking her formality. "I know who you are, Rieka."

"It's rightfully mine. Why do you know my name?"

She readjusted her cloak. Underneath one of its folds sat the Scorpio Stellarium symbol.

Avia dove at her. I broke off my necklace and shifted it into my sword. Our attacker immediately summoned a pale blue magic in her hands, meeting Avia's fiery grip with her own. Avia screeched at the touch, reeling backward before even making an impact on her opponent's skin, as if the magic shocked her.

I rushed at the girl with my sword, and she unsheathed hers in return. The sound of clashing metal shrieked through the air as I shoved her backward toward Conviction Woods. I narrowly avoided her blade slashing my side, swiveling my body to parry with my sword. She tore off her coat and flung it away, allowing her faster movement while exposing a muscular upper body outlined by her tight sleeves. The sight of strong arms and shoulders, an indication of a well-trained swordswoman, sent terror through me.

There was no way I'd outmatch her.

She shoved me back with one push of her sword against mine. I let her advance, holding my sword in defense to shield from her attempts to impale me. She forced me closer and closer to the boundary of the Woods, and I pretended like she was winning. I only needed one deceptive move to throw her into the Woods and give us a victory by letting the beasts tear her apart. My vision blurred with instinct, my body acting before my mind.

Chase sprinted past us, his feet sliding on gravel as he narrowly missed the boundary of Conviction Woods. He grabbed the Stellarium member by her shoulders. Despite her intense strength that rendered my sword skills useless, Chase was still taller and broader than she was. His grip on her arm halted her movement and gave Avia time to react, sprinting at the attacker with a spark in her palms. The girl was outnumbered three-to-one. One-on-one, she would've easily killed me, but with Avia and Chase on the boundary of Conviction Woods, the skirmish was in our favor.

Chase yanked her toward the Woods. She threw her sword down when he retained his hold on her shoulders. Instead of shoving him away to protect herself from crossing the boundary of Conviction Woods, she returned his grasp, dragging him down beyond the lanterns. It shimmered as they tumbled into the Woods.

Avia and I froze. Both of them would be dead in moments. Chase saved my life in the halls. It was my turn to return the favor.

While Avia and I took off to the boundary, I flicked my sword to return my weapon to my neck as a pendant. We burst through the aura. Within the Woods, Chase was lying on the ground, heaving in breaths at the shock he must've endured from being thrown down. I immediately hooked my hands beneath his arms and attempted to drag him out. He shouted, slamming his legs against the earth to stop me.

"What the hell are you doing?" I shouted. Avia stood next to the boundary, ready to help him through. "You are going to *die* in here!"

"I'm not!" he yelled, "but *she* will!"

I tried pulling him back again, but he shoved my hands off him, digging his boots into the forest floor to stabilize himself.

It clicked. Enough time had passed for the Woods to react to foreign bodies. There were no shadows pulling Chase deeper into the forest, no beasts hunting the Stellarium girl. Conviction Woods remained peacefully still and neutral.

I looked at Chase with my mouth open, ready to shout at him to figure out why he could survive in the Woods, and he pointed at the new girl. She was frozen in place, eyes full of a sudden terror, a face full of regret. We were all at a standstill, trying to find anything to say about the anomaly we all were.

Avia was the only person out of the four of us who was functioning, and she took the opportunity. She lifted a hefty branch, stumbled down the slight hill, and, as hard as she could, whacked it into the girl's head. She was instantly knocked out, her limp body collapsing on the ground.

"What the hell is going on?" Chase demanded. "You survive here?"

"*You* survive here?" I echoed him.

"I've always survived here. I swear, I thought I was the only one," Chase sputtered, shaking his head. His eyes were wide, his hands trembling, his chest heaving with rapid breaths. "I grew up in Conviction Woods with my dad."

"So did we, with our parents," Avia said, setting the branch down and kneeling at the Stellarium girl's side.

"We've never seen anyone else survive in here." I stared at Chase, who sat on the ground in shock. "What makes you different?"

"Ask that question to yourself. I genuinely don't understand any more than you do. All I know is that the Woods don't try to kill me."

"That's all we know, too," I said. "What about her?"

"Rieka, seriously, do you want me to have an answer? I don't. I'm as lost as you are. I don't know how I survive here, or how you survive here, or how she survives here, or what just happened."

"Scorpio Stellarium emblem but check this out—she's not a Scorpio," Avia said, examining the unconscious girl's attire. Chase and I snapped our attention over to her. "She's got the Pisces-Aries glyph. She's a cusp, chosen Convictionist. The Scorpio Stellarium must've hired her."

"She was a terrible hire, then," Chase said.

"You weren't hit by her magic, and none of us expected the other to survive in the Woods. It was a matter of who came to their senses first. You're welcome." Avia looked back up at me. "Rieka. They sent an assassin after you. And we just knocked her out."

Horror rushed over me.

Avia made a motion toward Chase for the blade he'd drawn. "Give it to me. I'll take care of this."

"Absolutely not." Chase took a step back. "I'm not helping you kill her. If she's Pisces-Aries, she's being taken advantage of by the Scorpio Stellarium."

"She might try to kill us again," Avia continued, "and if she's one of their assassins, she made the choice to make money from Scorpio."

"No. She's no older than the three of us. She didn't get a choice if she was just a kid," Chase argued. "I cannot believe how fast you just resorted to wanting to kill someone. This doesn't make sense. A Pisces-Aries would not willingly choose to work for the Scorpio Stellarium."

"He's right." I nodded at Chase. Avia glared at me for not agreeing with her. "We took her down this fast. We could do it again, if necessary."

"I don't even want to leave her like this," Chase said. He bent down, reaching for her head. His hand ran over a bump underneath her hair where she was struck. "This shouldn't be lethal. She'll wake up, and if she survives in the Woods, she'll know the healing properties of the forest."

I stared at him. "What?"

"The sap in the trees, you can use it to heal," Chase repeated himself, stabbing the side of the nearest pine. When sliding the blade out of the trunk, a sticky sap with gold flecks clung to the metal. Chase knelt again to spread the sap across her head. "It'll kick in, give or take two hours."

"I could never figure out how to activate the magic of the sap I kept reading about," I said, my voice in a curious hush.

Chase ran his palm over the sap on her forehead. It lit up with a golden luminescence and a soft buzz, presumably activated by his healing. "Let's go. My house is not too far, maybe four miles northeast, closer to the Hub. My dad'll be home."

"Your dad survives in the Woods?"

"Your parents do too, yeah?" He met my eyes. "I'll answer any reasonable questions on the way, and I'll expect you to do the same."

Shivering from the shock and wonder, I could barely fasten my backpack to my shoulders again. Without another question, I let Chase lead the way to safety, leaving the Stellarium assassin asleep on the ground behind us.

CHAPTER 10

I couldn't decide if I was surprised or not that Chase was being truthful when he'd told us his house was not too far from the outskirts of the Hub, barely resting within the boundaries of Conviction Woods. It was an area of the Woods I hadn't bothered to explore, far past where Avia and I lived, and what I had deemed as desolate due to its tough-to-navigate terrain. Chase had a method of weaving in between unclear pathways through an area of the forest that was overgrown by vines and moss. His muscles were starting to make sense as he periodically moved hefty, rotting trunks or bent branches to allow us through the backcountry.

Chase's house, though not much bigger than our house, seemed to be much sturdier. It had a new-ish framework, sticking out from the mosses, ferns, and looming cedars, unlike the way our house seemed to rot into the earth it was slowly succumbing to.

Chase paused in front of the house, drawing in a deep breath before knocking on the door. It was opened moments later by an older man slightly shorter than Chase, who almost looked too young to be his father. The amber eyes matching Chase's immediately caught my attention; one was barely lighter than the other. He froze when he noticed his son wasn't alone.

I kept my emotions still, even after Chase insisted that his father rarely obeyed the Scorpio Code in the Woods. I partially expected his father to act like Mom, with a sturdy tone and hints of the Code's influence on her personality, but instead I was met with a bewildered expression written across his face.

"Excuse me?"

"*I know*," Chase said, pointing at us. "They live here, too. In Conviction Woods."

The man's eyes darted between Avia and me.

"They were at the Ceremony, remember?" Chase said, his voice faltering. "We were attacked for the second time, Dad. Help. Please."

Snapping out of his daze, the man ushered us into the house. It was quite cozy inside as we were first greeted with the living room, far more modern than our own, with a red woven carpet that appeared to be art by Gemini artisans underneath a hand-crafted wooden table. Chase's father sat down on the couch, gesturing at his son to join him. Chase sat next to him, already trembling with an uneasy glint in his eyes. Avia and I walked over to the adjacent couch.

Chase's father broke the silence. "Who's trying to kill you?"

Chase explained the situation with the Stellarium and the Archive, nodding at me. I drew the scroll from my bag, hesitantly handing it over to his father, who took it, and unrolled it. His eyes widened, and he set it down instantly.

"No way."

"The Aries Arctura may or may not have saved us from a blizzard in the Hub yesterday," Chase started blurting out, "because, apparently, he helped us to the Archive. And protected us last night. Not sure what that was about. The translation guide he gave us helped us to discern coordinates from the arch's Rurian."

"The Aries Arctura." His father leaned back, holding his head. *"No way."*

"I'm sorry, Dad," Chase apologized, "but a Scorpio Stellarium member also attacked us, who we assume to be a hired assassin, Pisces-Aries. Avia knocked her out, and we escaped."

"I'm not even sure what to say to you right now." The man slowly sat back, rubbing his face, eyes wide in shock. He looked over at the scroll again and handed it back to Chase before running his hands through his dark hair. "Hold on. Go back. The Aries Arctura led you to the Archive?"

"I was sent up to the sixth floor of the Exchange Center the day before I went to the arch. Atlas left a note for us with translations to ancient Rurian digits. We just found out from those that the Callexus is in the Nix Mountains. We're guessing." Chase said frantically, waving his shaking hands as he tried to explain the situation in the simplest way he could. "Finding the Callexus would change history and reverse the Code."

"Of course the Aries Arctura got involved." His dad leaned back with a deep sigh. "Why wouldn't the Aries Arctura get involved?"

I narrowed my eyes. I couldn't understand what he was trying to say.

"Sarcasm, Rieka," Avia said when she caught the confused look on my face. "He's saying it's absurd that the Aries Arctura got involved."

"Oh." I refocused. "Do you have any insight on Fulbright? He knew things about me and Chase that we'd never told anyone outside our families."

"He's an Arctura. The Stellarium learns secrets about us in so many ways you'd never even consider," he said. "Better question. How are you here?"

"How are *you* here?" I shot back.

"It doesn't matter. None of us know why we live in the Woods," Chase interrupted before I could continue pressing his dad. "The assassin passed right through the boundary, too. We're not safe."

"The only reason we survived the assassin was because all four of us were in shock in the Woods, and Avia happened to be the first person to come to her senses," I added.

"She had some kind of electrical magic that disarmed me fast," Avia said, gesturing to her hands. "We're magically outmatched, by far, and your son didn't let me kill her."

"Good for him. Where are your parents?" he responded. "At your house?"

Avia shrugged. "Probably. They were both there when I left this morning."

"Dad, we can't go back to the Hub, and hiding in the Woods would be a cowardly move when we have an object that could change what we understand about the War," Chase interrupted again. Libra had taught him well—he knew exactly the right moment to divert a conversation. "Where should we go? We assume we need to head to Lyra to take the Eridanus into the Nix Mountains."

"That sounds best. There isn't much in Assidian territory until the mountain range. You'd run out of resources without stopping halfway in Lyra."

Chase nervously pursed his lips. "I can Dreamseek you every night and keep you updated."

His father's shoulders eased. "Please."

Chase teared up. "I'm sorry."

"Don't overthink it. You're doing the right thing," he said. "You're lucky to have even stumbled across what you found. It's not something to brush over. You know how I feel about the Code."

I perked up. Chase's upbringing was peculiar, even further past the fact that he could also survive in the Woods. His father, a Scorpio, didn't question how I befriended his son, something he knew was against the Scorpio Code, nor even attempted to hide his emotions from me. How many more families like ours were out there, hiding in the parts of the Woods that I never reached?

"You should get some rest," Chase's dad suggested. "We have a guest bedroom down the hallway. I'll clean it up."

My hesitation and speculation grew at the mention of a guest bedroom in the Woods. Though it was suspicious, we had one, too, because our house had existed long before Mom and Dad moved in. My notion of isolation in the Woods was in shambles, between the strange magic I'd seen Chase use with the pine sap, to his Scorpio father who didn't believe in the Code. Yet, I was comforted by the idea of resting in a safe house amongst the familiarity of the Woods before being forced to camp in the cold for days, if not weeks.

The vivid warmth of a dream seeped into my skin in replacement of my burning magic. I soaked in my surroundings as a spectator, observing an uncontrollable development of a setting fleshing itself out in my subconscious.

I observed another version of myself, clothed in all black at a school desk when I was a child. Avia wasn't in the same class, as she was a grade older than me and more advanced at her magic than I was. My young body slumped over a wooden desk, my finger tracing along a textbook's words. My raven hair, longer than I kept it at my current age, fell over my shoulders and draped onto the desk. The horribly nostalgic smell of chalk and dried ink overwhelmed my senses.

A couple of Aries boys sat to the left and right of me, one of them sending a burst of fire magic at the other, then exploding into a fit of giggles when one of their papers almost caught fire. A Libra girl obediently watched the lecture in the closest desk to the chalkboard while an Aries boy next to her tried to flirt with her. I was the only Scorpio in the class, other than the teacher himself, who struck the board with a baton to draw attention to the lesson he'd written. The class was barely engaged. I couldn't recall what subject he taught.

"Spring!"

I snapped my head up at the mention of my last name. The teacher's face was stern, cold, lifeless. I slowly straightened myself and my quill, reaching for my paper that was supposed to have notes on it.

He struck the board with his wooden stick. "Are you paying attention, child?"

I read the words on the board rapidly. Zoning out, I'd become completely lost in the lecture. Even as a child, my attention span was little to none. Each and every distraction in the environment would lure me away from the important lessons. My mouth opened as I scrambled to come up with something, anything, to say to him to prove my worth in the classroom.

"Miss Spring." He cleared his throat. "You are showing fear."

"I apologize," I said with a stammer, blinking a few times to fight the tears welling up in my eyes. Mom wouldn't be happy with me if I got in trouble while Dad was in Autarian territory. "To uphold the value of truth among Scorpio, I admit I was not paying attention."

He tore his eyes away from mine, addressing the class that was hushing to await the announcement of my punishment.

"I am requesting your presence after class, Miss Spring."

All eyes were on me. I swallowed, unable to focus as I quivered in my seat. There was no amount of mental preparation I could do to withstand what awaited me the minute the class was let out. Mom had scolded me the night before to remember to conceal my emotions in school. My fingers trembled against the textbook; any hope of attention lost as I flipped pages mindlessly.

Time slowed as I anticipated the teacher to hold his hand to the door. The other students rushed out to get a break from his monotonous teaching. I bit my tongue and stared at my textbook as his shadow inched closer. He loomed over me, his hands neatly tucked behind his back as he cleared his throat. I forced myself to look up, pressing my palms together to stop their relentless shaking.

"I request you to remind me what you and I spoke about two days prior, Miss Spring," he asked, eyes unreflective of anything other than a ghost of a human. He wore a black suit, his gray hair and eyes complementing his empty style. The only color in his demeanor was a bright crimson Scorpio glyph on his suit jacket.

He reeked of musty smoke and ash, and as I spectated the memory in the consciousness of my eighteen-year-old self, I realized he had likely hooked up with an Aries the night before—Scorpio's sexual culture was meant to be our only pleasure in an obediently stale life. A snarl wanted to gather in my throat, but I was trapped in the body and memory of my younger self, who cowered in the shadow of authority.

He placed a hand on my desk. "I requested an answer."

"Do not show fear," I answered him quietly. "Do not show boredom. Pay attention and represent the drive of knowledge in forfeit of emotion."

"That is correct. Repeat to me what actions you chose today."

Tears dared to spill down my cheeks as my chest rose and fell rapidly. "I displayed fear, sir."

"Repeat to me your actions at this moment."

"I am displaying fear, sir."

"We show no emotion. I wish to hold higher expectations of you. The reign of our power relies on our youth, Miss Spring."

"I understand."

There was no empathy left in him, if there was any to start. "I suspect you do not understand."

He grabbed my arm, his face stone cold, and yanked me out of my chair. I stumbled after him as he dragged me out of the classroom and into the hall, leading me into an office. I couldn't control my instinctive fear. Tears streamed down my cheeks. The bruises on my back hadn't yet healed. I couldn't go home with more. I was too terrified to discern the surroundings as I was pulled to my inevitable punishment. The blurring of my vision prohibited any resemblance of clarity.

A door slammed shut behind me. Another Scorpio man sat at a

desk near the corner of the room while a girl my age slumped over in a chair.

"Miss Spring has chosen to repeat her disobedience." My teacher walked over to a cabinet, yanking a drawer open to reveal a small whip. I backed up against the wall, tears soaking my shirt as I was cornered. "Repeat our law."

"Do not show emotions."

The other girl looked up as he forced me to my knees with a shove of my shoulders. I sobbed as the whip struck against my back once, gasping in air and clawing at the stone floor for forgiveness and safety.

It struck again, sending a sickening crack through the air to leave itself ringing through my ears and deafening me. I silently cried as the stinging sensations sank in through the numbness my body attempted to weaponize against the punishment. The stench of metallic blood infiltrated my senses as I was blinded in the vision of a red terror. It struck again. Then again. And again. It happened three times a few days before when I smiled at a classmate's comment. Through my agony, I grappled for a sense of understanding of what I did wrong. I fell victim to my thoughts in their war against my instincts, obsessing over why I couldn't pick up the Code as easily as others my age.

"Stop! Oh my god, I hate you bastards so fucking much."

There was a pause before the next strike, surely a heavenly force to break me free of my suffering. Gasping in a breath of reality, I turned my head to find where the yell had come from. It was the girl, who was now standing. My attacker stepped back from me as I pressed my bleeding back against the wall.

From my present perspective, I could recognize the same face, the same blue eyes, the same lengthy white hair that belonged to the assassin the Stellarium had sent after me. She wore a white and red shirt with black slacks, far brighter and fitting to a Pisces-Aries compared to her modern all-black. She challenged the man's gaze with a defiant smile.

"I request you to inform me of your identity," the man with the whip said.

"Leave her alone," the girl responded with a snarl. Her hands lit up with light blue magic. "You better back your ass up *right* now."

"Narah." The Scorpio man sitting at the desk cleared his throat. "I am commanding you to sit down."

"No." Her electric light flickered from hand to hand as she held her defiant stare. The teacher with the whip took another steady step backward to avoid her magic. "Are you intimidated by a thirteen-year-old girl? Conceal your emotions."

"Narah," the man in the chair repeated. "I am commanding you to sit down. Now."

She spun around to glare at him, facing one of her palms out. "I said *no*. I don't fall under your control. Leave her alone, or I'll shock both of you. *Again*."

"Your disrespect will be reported to the Aries Stellarium," the teacher warned.

"Yeah? They won't do anything about it, I promise," she spat back, storming over to me. She gently wrapped her fingers around my arms, a touch of empathy amongst a hellish flashback. I flinched at the touch and ducked away from her as my instinct activated. She smiled, her hand sliding to my own instead. "Come on. What's your name? I'll get you out of here."

She didn't blink an eye or resemble a hint of fear as she guided me past both the men. She flipped them off as she backed out the door and into the hallway. Shock invaded my headspace and interrupted any thanks I could give her. I'd never seen anyone, let alone another child, stand up to them. My back burned and bled, but for the first time, there was a sense of safety in the back of my head, as if my pleas had been answered. Mom would be furious with me, Dad was out of town, and in a time when Dad's comfort wouldn't greet me, I would find any sense of comfort in a human that let me know I was no dog to be bent into obedience.

"Are you alright?" she paused to ask. "I'm Narah. Pisces-Aries."

"The bruises on your face." It was the only thing I could think of. "Did they hurt you, too?"

Her gaze cast aside. "No. Your name?"

"Rieka. Scorpio."

"You should go to a healer," she suggested, nodding at my back. "Let's go to the nurse. I won't let them chase you. They're done with you today."

"Why did you help me?"

"They were hurting you, and I hate them." Narah shrugged and gave me another warm smile. My hand was still in hers as she guided me through the hallway. "Like you can control how you feel. The nurse on this academic wing is a Pisces. Do they bring you to the South Wing when they're done with your punishments?"

"Yes, to the Scorpio healer."

She wrinkled her nose. "Fuck them. That can't be good. Come on, let's go to the North Wing."

Others were staring at us as we walked down the hallway. I wasn't sure how to process it as I limped.

"You should go home early, Rieka," she suggested. "Do you have a parent who's home?"

The memory paused in its tracks, freezing my younger self in time. Thirteen years old, hand in hers, I was uncovering a piece of my own self that had been smothered for unknown reasons. Unfamiliar emotions surged through me: confusion, hurt, pain, wonder, astonishment. Feelings of the past and present were merging as I experienced the duality of time and memory, learning a secret I'd kept from myself. Narah, the girl who was an assassin hired by the Scorpio Stellarium to kill me, was a savior in my subconscious, buried underneath layers of trauma.

I looked down at my hands, a ghost floating above my memory, magic surging through every part of me, my fingers becoming more realistic as they numbed with white light.

Gasping awake, I tore open my eyes to the darkness of a guest room in the Woods. Avia, on the floor in a sleeping bag, was out cold.

I sat up and drew in a deep breath, my eyes adjusting to the light emanating from my hands. I blinked a few times to understand if I was still in a dream, but the persistence of the luminescence told me otherwise. A gentle, prepared electric magic tingled my fingertips, emitting a barely audible hum.

The magic was unknown to my mind, but to my body, the burning sensation in my veins was familiar as it ebbed through my forearms. It seared, begging for some sort of release that I wasn't sure how to accomplish. The longer I breathed steadily, focusing on the hypnotizing glare of the light, the more it slowly eased. In minutes, it dissipated, disappearing into my skin and leaving its ghost as an ache in my arms.

Chapter 11

In the following two weeks, we'd traveled by foot around the Hub, careful to avoid border patrols on a neutral road meant for foot and horse traffic. The trading route to Lyra wove through the middle of Societal's expansive territory. The grassy plains were never ending, an up and down of browned hills for as long as I could see, speckled with fresh snowfall. I let my imagination wander to what it must've looked like in the summer, a green and luscious landscape blooming with wildflowers. The travel allowed me time to process the storm of events I'd experienced in less than a week following my Ceremony. I hadn't mentioned the dream or the magic I'd felt that night. I let it sit in the back of my head, pondering on why the simple interaction as a kid felt like it meant more, why it caused a spur of light to fiercely activate in my veins.

We were at last approaching Lyra. I'd heard the rumors about Societal's township, but nothing would compare to my first look of a new world with vibrant colors and chiming voices.

    Not one wall of the town was left untouched by art. Geometrical, rectangular-shaped buildings made of clay and stone were painted with blues, yellows, and reds, and murals spread across walls depicting creatures, humans, and magic alike. Crowds bustled through streets buzzing with magic, Societalists yelling and rushing around each other with a smile. Comparing the Hub to Lyra felt wrong—although alike in their marketing chaos as street vendors yelled out deals, the friendliness in Lyra was a virus spreading with each bump of a shoulder. The sidewalks were made of colorful stone bricks circumventing in various directions, spirals of weaving hues mimicking the flow of magic. The culture was alive and thriving at the heart of the Societal Union—Leo, Aquarius, and Gemini. In the distance was a lumbering castle, seemingly tiny from where we stood. Although hundreds of miles spanned in each direction of Societal's territory, Lyra remained in close proximity to the Hub for transportation of goods. Winter did not stop commerce in this part of the world.

    As we wandered through town to find the market, the culture and life of the city slowed in our presence, as if we were emanating an aura that erased the friendliness off strange faces. Every other Societalist we passed veered away from us as we followed a road through Lyra. I had never elicited the same reaction out of Societalists in the Hub.

    I couldn't shake the feeling, but I hadn't noticed Avia and Chase being affected by the phenomenon. Chase looked as if he wanted a nap, and Avia was far too distracted by the busy surroundings to notice anything astray. Aquarius, clothed in cool blues, would pause to stare. Surely, attention from Aquarius couldn't have been a good sign; Aquarius was the leading sign of Societal.

"Where to?" Chase asked, peering around at the streets.

"Do we look that weird?" Avia looked down at herself when a Gemini man deliberately bumped into her shoulder. "They're surely used to Convictionist travelers."

"I feel like they're staring at me," I said.

"No shit, people don't like Scorpio." Avia took the lead without hesitation. "Thought you would've figured that out by now."

I contained my frustration at her tone, forcing myself to follow in her steps before I lost her in the crowd. Chase shook his head at her, sticking next to me. He still hadn't adjusted to the interactions between two sisters; I was plenty used to Avia's sass.

Avia paused in front of an Aquarian man, waving at him. "Sir! Where's the best place to eat around here?"

The Aquarius gave her a friendly grin. "Just follow the red path to—"

He immediately stopped talking as he caught sight of me. He scowled, mouthed something foul at me in Tyak, Societal's language, and hurried off. Avia yelled a Driksaal curse back at him.

"What are you *thinking?*"

A jutting voice cut through the crowds behind us. A young woman veiled in a silk ombre blue cloak, no older than Chase, approached us, her eyes darting between the three of us. She grabbed Chase's arm and tugged him across the street to shove him into an old, vacant clay building. As she motioned to us, Avia and I ran in after her. The girl slammed the door behind us to a building that must've been an unused dining hall, a few unorganized, dusty tables and chairs thrown around in no particular order. Old paint and colorful glass shards covered the walls, chipping and flaking off in some areas with modern runic messages written across it. It might've been a mural at some point.

The girl who had pulled Chase aside quickly stole my attention. She was beautiful; black skin with a gold undertone, and bright, shining sapphire eyes. Thick hair somewhere between curly and wavy extended past her shoulders to the middle of her back, her hands soaked with either water or sweat. I couldn't tell.

"You are so damn lucky I pulled you in here. You can't be prancing around out there when you are a shining beacon of death."

Her voice, faintly Autarian-accented, caught me off-guard. She had a Cancer glyph on her cloak. Lyra was not her home.

"Who are you?" Avia immediately interrogated her. "Why'd you drag him in here?"

"Between the three of you, Libra was the least likely to retaliate against me, and I was right. Listen, the Scorpio Stellarium has been everywhere in this city for days, waiting to ambush you." She checked the lock of the door again before meeting my eyes. "Societal's angry that the Scorpio Stellarium infiltrated their space, and in my opinion, reasonably so."

I gave Avia a bewildered look.

"We haven't seen a single Stellarium member, though?" Chase questioned. "We've just gotten a lot of gross looks from Societalists."

"Where do you think would be the first place a traveler would go after traversing barren territory for days?"

"The market," Chase realized. "They were waiting to ambush us at the market."

She crossed her arms. "Yeah, you're welcome."

"Cancer. You're not a Societalist." Avia held a hand to her as a peace offering. "You're an outsider, too."

The Cancer was hesitant to take her hand. She stepped back, crossing her arms and lowering her shoulders. Unease reflected in her sapphire eyes. Her entire demeanor was fascinating for someone who grew up in a continental forest. She wore a necklace of seashells, contrasting with her dark tones. Underneath the necklace was a baby blue blouse and flowy oceanic skirt. Cancers were often sea folk, and she wasn't an exception. She almost intimidated me with how beautiful she was.

"Rieka." The girl said to me with a bow of her head, ignoring Avia. "Kaia. Water mage, Cancer."

I was about to introduce myself before I realized she'd said my name. Why did *everyone* know my name?

"Okay, now I don't trust you." Avia narrowed her eyes. "What's your reasoning for being in Lyra and knowing her name?"

Kaia hesitated, but instead of speaking to Avia, she once again redirected the conversation to me. "I was searching for you, actually."

"Me?" I pointed at myself. I couldn't stop the surprise from showing. "I'm sorry, what?"

"My Scorpio brother told me about how you protected him from the Stellarium a year ago," she explained, yet it made no sense to me. I'd never protected another Scorpio, as far as I knew; it would've been a straight track to getting beat up by an official. "I will say, I wasn't expecting to find you so *easily*, casually strolling around Lyra."

"But I..."

"They killed my brother before I could see him again."

I looked up sharply. Chase's face fell, and Avia looked away from the conversation. Fierce emotions reflected across Kaia's face, a contrast to her peaceful appearance. Her gaze pierced into me, as about as sharp as the dagger on her belt. She was armed.

"The Scorpio Stellarium killed him, you mean?" I asked quietly, holding out my hand. For a moment, I ignored the question at hand as to how she knew my name, and why she was claiming that I protected her brother. "I'm sorry."

She scanned my face with a look of surprise at my sympathy. Finally, she reached out and shook my hand; my suspicions about her gloves were right, damp to the touch. A rush of peace coursed through my body, my shoulders relaxing and pounding heart calming at the touch of the water. Like Avia's natural body heat from her magic, water mages had a calming demeanor they could spread to others with their magic. Dad had the same trait.

"I don't understand," I said. "I can't recall protecting another Scorpio a year ago."

"I know I didn't make a mistake." Kaia confidently met my gaze. "He told me about how you were the first person to defend him against the Stellarium—you and Narah. The two of you were the reason he finally agreed with me that he needed to escape Conviction territory before Scorpio killed him for his Gemini partner. I was going to them on a Sagittarian ship to give him an escape from the Code."

It hit me. The Scorpio boy in the Hub three weeks ago knew my name and thanked me as he was being dragged away from his Gemini partner. She was being honest.

"Who the hell is Narah?" Avia butted in.

The second realization struck me as I processed what Kaia had said. I had no memory of protecting Kaia's brother from the Stellarium, yet he'd thanked me as he was led away to his death. The only moment I could recall knowing Narah—the assassin—was the single flashback in my dream. But Kaia knew my name, and she knew Narah's.

I couldn't remember, but I couldn't forget. There was familiarity in Kaia's brother, in Narah's gaze, in the memory I'd experienced in my dreams—and the strange magic that had activated because of it.

I was missing something.

"You're being honest," I said slowly after I realized I'd been quiet for a moment, trying to piece together the facts that had to be true. "Can you explain to me what your brother told you?"

"A year ago, he was attacked in Conviction's part of the Hub by the Scorpio Stellarium when they found him breaking the Code with his boyfriend. He told me that you and Narah had masks to hide your identities from the Stellarium, and you did something to the officials to drive them away. You reassured my brother that it would be like the attack never happened, that the Stellarium would never mention him breaking the Code that day; and you were right. They appeared to forget. When he realized he wasn't alone in breaking the Code, he began to fight to escape Conviction. They didn't catch him with his boyfriend again until three weeks ago."

I remembered nothing of it, but somehow, I knew it was true from the spite against the Stellarium that rushed over me in an angry wave. Tears gathered in Kaia's eyes as her emotions contorted.

"Sorry, *who* is Narah?" Avia interrupted again.

"The assassin that attacked us a few weeks ago." I put my hand up to her to stop her from speaking again as I looked at Kaia. "Kaia. I know you're being honest. Avia and I saw him being taken by the Stellarium a few weeks ago, and he knew my name. But I don't remember any of this, I—"

"Rieka, no, wait, we're not moving past that. What the fuck do you mean, the assassin that attacked us? Why do you know her name?" Avia grabbed my arm to distract me, and I shoved her away. Chase stepped in between us, gently urging Avia away from me. "You need to explain. Right now."

"*I don't know,* Avia. Back off. I don't remember protecting her brother, and I *definitely* don't remember working with Narah. All I know is that the night we were in Chase's house, I had a nightmare about meeting Narah a few years back in school. She distracted the Stellarium while they were punishing me for breaking the Code. I didn't think it meant much, any more than just encountering her once. I figured I probably forgot about that moment because it was traumatic."

"Clearly not, if you have a random Autarian that knows your name, and knows your *assassin's* name," Avia snapped, shaking her head. "Why didn't you tell us you knew her? That feels like it's significant information!"

"Avia. Stop." Chase put his hand on her shoulder to distract her. "If it was a traumatic nightmare, she had no obligation to tell us about it. She had every reason to believe it was a one-off occasion that she forgot about because it was traumatic. It makes sense that she'd recall that flashback after finding Narah again as an assassin."

"I didn't tell you because I don't know her, Avia. All I know is that she's being truthful about this, and I'm missing something," I snapped, ignoring what Chase said. Something burned inside my arms, inside my chest, at the frustration toward my sister.

"Let's calm down for a moment," Chase said before Avia got angrier. He stood in front of her so we couldn't face each other. I looked up at him with a glare. "Just to be clear about what's happening—you had a nightmare about a memory where you met your assassin a few years back in school. But there's more you can't remember, because this girl knows your name and hers from her brother, who recently recognized you in the Hub."

"Yes, that's right." I slowly breathed out to release the tension. He gave me a gentle smile and stepped back from being in between Avia and I. "Thank you, Chase."

"What are we supposed to do with this information? Do you think you forgot because of trauma?" Avia asked, more calmly this time. Chase's tense shoulders eased at the diffusion of the argument. "As far as I know, there's no magic that can take away memories, is there?"

"Not that I know of. I guess trauma, maybe. But I feel like I'd remember something so significant."

"It's the Stellarium, and there's a lot of things we don't know they're capable of," Chase pointed out. "We can figure this out later. I don't want to hear either of you argue in front of a stranger. Hey—you said your name is Kaia, right? How did you know we were coming to Lyra?"

"My mother," Kaia continued, raising her chin, "is Rhea Moku, the Libra Leader. I didn't think she'd tell me where Rieka was; it would be a breach of confidentiality, if she even knew of Rieka's existence. She upholds the law, and if she's found breaking it, she's kicked out of the Stellarium. Not only did she immediately tell me you were traveling toward Lyra, but that you knew something about the Code, something that was taking you north."

Silence spread amongst the four of us. Chase and I looked at each other.

"This has to do with the Aries Arctura," Chase realized, keeping our gaze interlocked as both of us thought through all the implications. "He told the Libra Leader where we were going, who told Kaia, who…"

"Wants to see Verena rot for what she did to my brother," Kaia finished for him. "My mother wants to see the Scorpio Stellarium fall, but she can't do a damn thing about it. I can."

"The Scorpio Stellarium killed the Libra Leader's son for breaking the Scorpio Code," Chase connected, shaking his head slowly as he stared at Kaia. "The Libra Stellarium is on our side. Atlas sent us to reverse the Code, the Libra Leader sent you."

Kaia met his eyes. "Absolutely."

"Maybe I should've stayed in the Woods." Avia sighed and turned away from the conversation.

I ignored her, looking at Kaia and taking a step closer to her. Not too often in my life had empathy fought with my survival instinct, the same survival instinct that wanted to subconsciously listen to the Code tell me to hush my emotions. I let it go.

"I'm so, so sorry, Kaia," I said, leaning forward. "They're despicable, the Scorpio Stellarium. Your brother didn't deserve it. None of the fatalities from the Stellarium ever did or will."

"It's fine. I'll see the downfall of the Stellarium that killed him, and the Stellarium he hated so much." Kaia's face fell, her breathing unsteady, expressions tumultuous and angry with grief. "What do you know about the Code that Verena is trying to hide?"

"It's a long story. We have a scroll that we found in the Archive claiming the Callexus to be real, and the Code a lie. We're going into the Nix Mountains for the Callexus."

"I know how to get to the Nix Mountains from here. If you head southeast, you can reach the Societal River Port on the Eridanus," Kaia said quickly. "It's on the edge of Societal and Assiduous territory, and if you take a boat downstream, it goes directly into the Nix Mountains."

"We wanted to pass through Lyra on the way to gather some supplies and rest, though," Chase said.

"Let me help. I have the funds to pay someone off so we can have a safe place for the night." Kaia glanced at the door. "Traveling through the midst of Lyra in broad daylight as a Scorpio is asking to be killed."

"So we split up," Avia decided. "It'll be less obvious. Rieka is wearing red. She could get away with being mistaken as a Leo or Gemini. Chase is wearing white. He could also pass as a Gemini. Rieka shapeshifts the glyphs on cloaks to be those, and I'm sure Kaia and I can probably get away with walking through Lyra."

Chase laughed nervously. "Is that implying we have a bigger bounty on our heads?"

"You were the ones that broke into the Scorpio Archive." Avia snorted. "I thought we had that established on day one."

"Oh, it's Chase, by the way. Libra, if it wasn't obvious," Chase introduced himself to Kaia. "I'm sorry about your brother."

"Nice to meet you. If you let us go into the crowd first, I can lead you somewhere safe. There's an inn around the corner, straight out of this building and to the left on the main road. Give me and the Aries 20 minutes, and we'll be safe for the night. Trust me."

I met her eyes. There was a spark of sheer fury and determination shining in her irises. I could feel the drive of her anger, and I was drawn to it. She was a reflection of all that I held back growing up against the Stellarium, and my curiosity pushed me to know more about her story. She wanted revenge, and so did I.

"Avia won't hurt you," I said to her. "I promise. She acts all tough, but she's just protective."

Avia opened her mouth to snap back, but I reached toward Chase instead. He flinched and gave me a confused look as I placed my hand on his cloak, unprepared for the touch. He relaxed as I shapeshifted the symbol on his cloak to represent Gemini, and then my own into Leo.

It was still risky with the contrasting colors on our cloaks, especially considering white wasn't a primary color of Gemini's, but I couldn't waste my energy shapeshifting, as long as we were quick.

Chapter 12

Moments before I followed Chase out of the building, he abruptly turned around and shoved me back from the door.

I tensed when he grabbed my shoulders, tripping backward in shock. He held my arms and stabilized me before I fell by pushing me against the wall. He threw his hands away from me seconds later, and I shrunk down in his shadow as he leaned his shoulder on the wall, his arm hovering next to me, threatening to fall on my side.

Terror froze my body but allowed me enough time before aggressively retaliating to catch that he hadn't even looked down at me. His eyes were glued to the open door, watching something I couldn't see while completely unaware that he was practically pinning me to the wall. With a body twice my size, his focus was on shielding me. If someone glanced in, they'd see him, and not me.

It was an act of instinctual protection, but I didn't like it, not from a man. I pushed his arm away and backed up. He looked down at me, horror rushing across his face as he realized what he'd done. I kept a defensive position, revolted at the action, even though I knew it had nothing to do with ill intentions.

"Fuck, Rieka, I'm so sorry, there were two Scorpio officials passing right in front of us when I opened the door, and slamming the door shut would've brought attention to us," he said quickly. "I'm so sorry. I shouldn't have touched you without asking. That's my bad. I was just trying to—"

"It's okay," I interrupted, unable to look him in the eyes as I held my arms closer to myself. I was already trying to erase the event from my memories. "It surprised me, that's all."

"I didn't realize how close I was to you. I was just trying to block them from seeing you. I promise I wasn't—"

"It's fine. You saved us from a potential deadly encounter. I get it."

"I don't want you to interpret it in the wrong way." The guilt remained written all over his face. "I'm sorry, I have to make this clear: I don't have feelings for you but genuinely appreciate you as a friend."

"I feel the same. I figured that was assumed." I breathed out slowly. "I didn't think you were into me. I never got that impression."

"Yeah, but I just wanted to speak it out loud." His tense shoulders eased as he relaxed. "I don't want you, or anyone else, to interpret our interactions in the wrong way."

"Trust me when I say this, Chase, it's mutual."

Both of us went silent at the understanding—we'd had the same adverse reaction to a necessary protective act.

I trusted him. I wasn't sure if it was a good or bad thing. He knew exactly how to communicate with me when I'd never learned how to communicate. Perhaps it was the nature of a Libra to find even ground, or

perhaps it was genuine human care I'd never had from someone outside my family. My instincts wanted to run away, but the thought of losing him as a friend stirred a wrenching feeling deep within my chest.

Chase cleared his throat to break the silence. "Let's go before more of them show up."

He glanced out the doorway and nodded at me, and we both plunged ourselves into the crowd of color. With the signs of our cloaks changed and our hoods over our heads, the crowds weren't reacting like before.

Two women in black cloaks were hidden in the shadows of a tall blue building. They were facing away from us, and I weaved through the crowd with a curse underneath my breath as we followed Kaia's instructions to the inn. We didn't have much time. Another man wearing all black was walking our way.

Chase ducked closer to me. "Keep your head up. Don't look at him. He shouldn't question it with what we're wearing."

I did as he said. The man walked past us.

The old inn was in sight by the time my magic began to drain my energy. In less than five minutes, I was out of breath from traveling across the roads and through the crowds.

Kaia motioned toward us. She opened the door, leading us inside. As the Sun set, it shone through a large stained-glass window in the inn's lobby, casting an array of colors across the dimly lit room. The inside of the inn was contemporary, painted in colors matching the rest of Lyra. Pots and other ornaments were set as decoration around the space. If I hadn't been fearful of staying in Lyra, I would've stopped to admire the art and culture of Societalists.

The Societalist at the front desk turned his head away when we walked in, acting as if we were invisible when we walked directly in front of him. Kaia hadn't been joking about paying them off. She led us down a hallway with a set of keys in her hands. The three of us followed her up the stairs to the third floor. It was a relatively small and quiet inn, and if anything, it vaguely reminded me of the Exchange Center.

Kaia unlocked one of the rooms, beckoning the three of us in. Chase nervously clung to my side, and I told myself I'd antagonize him for it later, to make up for the awkward interaction. For someone so tall and intimidating, it was obvious how constantly nervous he was. I caught him holding his hands behind his back, barely glowing with a dim radiance—strange.

Avia took a chair, turned it around, and sat down. What was it with her inability to sit in a chair normally? With a sigh, I unloaded my gear and rolled my shoulders, finally resting on the single queen-sized bed in the room. Chase sat down next to me, hiding his hands behind his back. Contrary to my room in the Exchange Center, a couple of intricate paintings were mounted to the wall, and pottery pieces were arranged on a desk near the kitchen.

"So," Avia said, "to properly introduce myself, the name's Avia Phelan, Aries. Long story short, the Scorpio Stellarium wants Rieka dead."

"I want the Scorpio Stellarium dead," Kaia responded simply.

Oh, I liked her attitude.

"My brother and I, we grew up close; he was a Dreamseeker. He was close to our mother. He'd tell me about the number of deaths daily in Scorpio, the punishments." She paused again, moving the rim of her cloak aside. I recoiled at the sight of a Stellarium emblem. "I worked my way up into the Autarian Stellarium. For him. I was going to buy a ship and get him out of there. And now—"

She reached into her cloak pocket, pulling out a leather pouch. She dropped it on the table next to her, and the sound of coins jingled. A lot of coins. It was a hefty bag.

"Right, the Autarian Stellarium has *money*," Avia said. "And you're a water mage. They need you for water supply."

"And now, I have money that I want to spend on tearing apart the goddamn Scorpio Stellarium after they put my work to waste and took what mattered to me the most," she finished, turning her attention to me. "So, yeah, of course I went right for the first person who wasn't my brother to fight back against the Stellarium."

I could feel the anger radiating from her, the despise, the spitfire desire to see the downfall of a mutual enemy. For someone with an outwardly soft and elegant appearance, the way her voice spiked with resentment each time she spoke the Stellarium's name told an entirely different story of a fierce personality with a raging determination.

We continued to explain the situation with the scroll, Atlas, and the encounters with the Scorpio Stellarium. She listened, intently engaged in the whole story, leaning closer to us as the conversation drew on. We stopped the run-down at the moment we'd arrived in Lyra.

"Rieka, you're smart. I hope you know that, with everything you've figured out so far with reversing the Code." Kaia crossed her legs and raised her chin at me. "Though you don't remember, I have no doubt you were the reason he finally decided to fight for his love."

That was all I needed to want her with us. I didn't need Chase or Avia's approval.

"You're welcome to join us." I offered my hand to her. Avia pursed her lips. "If you want a change in pace, that is."

"Rieka," Avia said quietly, a threat.

I ignored my sister. It was *my* initiation of change I'd fought for my entire life. I knew what I wanted to hear and what energy I wanted with the people helping me to reverse the Code.

"I'd be honored to help you to the Callexus. The Eridanus is familiar to me," Kaia said, and shook my hand. "That river runs right into the Nix Mountains at the spot your map guides you to."

"Kaia, do you understand that the Scorpio Stellarium will go after you, too? We've learned they'll try to kill *anyone* who presents a threat to the Code, not just Scorpio," Chase warned her. "It's life or death if you're with us."

She laughed at him. "That's how I like it."

Chase smiled as he held his hand out to her. "Welcome aboard."

In their handshake, I caught something, something that no one else did. A split-second flare of gold rippled over Chase's hand, and a blue over Kaia's, dim enough to only be seen if someone was paying close attention. *Neither* of them noticed as they maintained eye contact while their hands pulled apart.

I stood up. "Can I talk to Chase for a few minutes?"

He opened his mouth to say something. Kaia gave me an understanding nod and headed toward the door while Avia glared at Chase and me for making the decision to welcome Kaia without her permission. Nevertheless, she stood up and followed Kaia outside, shutting the door behind herself.

I immediately turned to Chase. "What was that?"

"What was what?" He pulled his hands to the front of himself, looking down to notice his veins barely lit with magic. "Um? I don't know."

"When you shook her hand, there was a flare of gold. I thought I saw hers go blue. Did you not feel it?"

"No, I didn't feel anything." He let his palms glow. A golden light trickled down his skin, beginning as a liquid, but dissipating into sparkles of light as they fell into the air. He winced, leaning his head back as his fingers curled into his palms. "I've had excess magic the last few days. It's painful when I don't use it. It burns. It might've interacted with hers on accident."

"Has it ever activated before when shaking someone's hand?"

"Not that I can recall," he said, "but I haven't gone this long without using my healing."

"You mean, since you last used it on me in the blizzard? How did you survive before?"

"Yeah, it's been over a week, and normally I'll go out into the Woods and heal injured deer, elk, and other animals in Conviction Woods. I'm pretty sure my healing gets stronger with age, too."

"Is there anything I can do to help?"

"I don't think so, unless you're injured or sore."

"My lower back is sore from the weight of the pack, my calves hurt to stretch. Would that help?"

He nodded with a slow breath out. I offered my hand. He hesitated, his palm hovering above mine as he waited for my permission.

"It's okay," I said. "I trust you, go ahead."

His fingers brushed against my skin, and for a moment, lingered to pool with magic. I closed my eyes to fight the swell of discomfort. Every fiber in me told me to leave him alone, never touch him again, especially after being shoved against a wall earlier. I wanted to resist, but I didn't let myself.

His golden magic seeped into my hand, and I opened my eyes out of curiosity. The light curled around my arm through my veins, warmth rippling through me. I instantly relaxed at the sensation.

It was incomprehensibly gentle, feather-light and soft, a natural ease through the transfer of magic. It felt like I was lying in a clearing in Conviction Woods on a warm summer day, a canopy of cedar branches over my head casting a green refraction of sunlight upon my body. The feelings that accompanied the warmth of a forest clearing were strangely familiar. It was almost like I had a memory associated with the feeling of the healing, but not his healing—it was the emotion itself that the healing instilled in me as it ran its course through my body.

A pang struck my head, a low ringing spinning through my ears like tiny needles pricking my memory, but before I could wonder or ponder why, the strength of his healing washed away any remnants of the pain.

He drew his hand away, and the light faded from my body. A sense of comfort crackled in the air, a tracing effect from the healing. There was a slight lingering smell of blood again, but in seconds, it was gone, not nearly as overpowering as it was in the blizzard.

"Thank you." He stared down at his lap. "I really appreciate it."

"You know," I said, "I don't understand you. Why are you so nervous, if you're powerful both magically and physically?"

I instantly regretted asking. I had phrased it wrong, and it could've easily come off as an insult. But instead, he gave me a small smile, understanding my struggle with language and communication.

"Why are you afraid to express your emotions in public places?" he asked.

"Because the Scorpio Stellarium is trying to kill me."

"First of all, physical strength is a quality in Libran Healers. That's how our bodies regulate the transfer of blood and strength. I didn't have the choice. I was strong even as a child. Self-defense and strength can be interpreted as a lack of balance in the body. Perfection in the middle of strong and weak is where they want us to be. At some point in my life, I became obsessed with that perfection to make up for the judgment I received when I was a child. We're on opposite sides of the spectrum, Rieka, but in the end, we're afraid of the same thing."

The Scorpio Code repeated itself in my head again, but it wasn't worth it to obey it anymore.

"Thank you for listening to me. I'll let your sister in now. I'm sure she has things to say." Chase stood up to walk toward the door, then paused when his hand rested on the knob. He considered me, hesitating before he took a step back so his voice wouldn't carry. "Hold on, question. I swear to god, the new girl is the most beautiful person I have ever seen in my life. You agree, yes or no?"

"She's really pretty, but I don't know about the most beautiful. Sounds like a personal bias of yours," I said as an automatic response, rolling my shoulders. I paused when I caught onto what he'd said. "Why're you asking me?"

"I needed validation, and you're the right person to ask." He swung the door open. "You were staring."

Before I could defend myself, he grinned at me and opened the door to let the other two in.

CHAPTER 13

"No one from the Stellarium is down there. Lobby's completely empty," Kaia reported, ushering us out of our room to hurry to the lobby.

After the Sun rose, we'd prepared to leave Lyra after deciding we could make the walk to the Eridanus. According to Kaia, it wasn't too far away, at most a day's worth of travel. I was thankful that I was typically up way too early so I could hike long distances in the Woods. Avia, on the other hand, trailed slowly down the hallway. I walked behind her, encouraged her around the corner and into the lobby.

I immediately stopped. A man in all black stood in front of the front door leading out of the inn. Another leaned against the front desk, and when Kaia opened her mouth to say something to the Aquarius working it, the Stellarium official held a glowing hand toward him as a threat. The Aquarius shrank back, trembling in his seat, staring at us with terror flashing through his gaze.

"Miss Spring."

My head jerked up at the mention of my name as a woman stood up from a velvety pale blue couch. She wore a pitch-black tunic and tapered slacks matching her torso. A thin, scarlet-outlined raven cloak with gilded gold designs draped over her shoulders and cascaded to the floor, where her heels posed one over another. The glyph of Scorpio flared in gold on her cloak, complimenting her silvery, cold eyes. Long, straightened salt and pepper hair splayed down her back. The dim lighting accentuated her sharp facial features; another official with similar features stood behind her.

"We have been searching for you, Miss Spring," the woman said in an utterly-still tone. "What a delight it is to meet you. I am Verena Arke, the Scorpio Arctura. To my understanding, you have broken the Scorpio Code and trespassed upon Societal territory."

I looked my enemy in the eyes: the same person who'd given me a torturous childhood, the same person responsible for hundreds of thousands of deaths, the same person who knew that it wasn't justifiable.

"Lyra is considered Union-neutral ground," I said, raising my chin. "It is my moral and rightful duty to seek truthful knowledge of Scorpio's history."

"I regret to inform you that your occupation fails to place you above the law. There is no founded excuse to negate breaking the Scorpio Code."

"I am aware."

"Miss Spring, we request you to accompany us to the Hub."

My stomach knotted at her blank, empty stare, and her gaze piercing into me as if daring me to make a move. I swallowed the memories that flashed back to me at the feeling evoked from her expressionless face. Verena extended her hand to me; a neglect of a choice I didn't have in the eyes of the Stellarium. They were hunters salivating at the idea of my flight taking hold of my instinct. All my life, I had been a runner underneath the Scorpio Stellarium, a cowardly wolf backed into the walls of Conviction Woods with its tail tucked between its legs, whimpering underneath my breath from the wounds they'd inflicted.

"No. *No*, I won't follow you back into the Hub only for you to end my life and silence me with the same law I am fighting to overthrow. I'd rather die than follow the Code."

"Pardon me?" Verena adjusted her cloak. Her heels made a tiny clack against the inn's cobblestone floors as she walked toward us. "You will come with us."

Chase took a step closer to me, his demeanor completely changed as he stood tall with a fierce glare at Verena. In my peripheral, I saw Avia's hands glow red. Kaia's face contorted with fury at the sight of the Scorpio Arctura.

"First of all," I said, "don't call me by my last name. My name is Rieka."

Verena didn't answer me.

"As much as I appreciate your gracious request, I know how you treat those who disobey." I raised my chin, anger boiling in me. "And you do it for the power trip."

Verena calmly tilted her head at me. "Perhaps this pattern of outbursts has led to the becoming of a disloyal member of our people. You are not mentally sound."

"I'm more mentally sound than you, that's for sure. The Code was a lie made to torment Scorpio."

"How long has the Scorpio Stellarium known about the scroll?" Kaia yelled suddenly. "You murdered my brother and stopped my mom from communicating with me!"

Verena didn't even blink an eye at her, turning back to me. "May we meet in private to speak on this matter?"

I laughed at her. "Absolutely not."

A crowd had gathered from all the commotion we were causing. Societalists from different rooms in the inn hurried into the lobby to watch. The Stellarium had to act their best; hide their emotions. My job was to make them look horrid. A swallowing fury suffocated any remnants of fear.

"The scroll confirms the Scorpio Code was created in the War of the Rebalancing to manipulate and control Scorpio. The Scorpio Stellarium is aware of this and continuously ignores it to keep Scorpio in power. Anything else you'd like me to say to ruin your reputation?"

"You are insane, Miss Spring. Your scroll is simply fake."

"She is *not*!" Avia screamed. "Don't listen to them!"
"Here it is, Societalists. Here's your proof," I raised my voice for the new curious bystanders. "*We* are not *them*."

The crowd was entranced. The lobby had become a blur of bright colors from the dozens of Societalists. Faint murmuring rippled through the room. Any trace of emotion had completely vanished from Verena's and her officials' faces. Their statuesque trance was evidence of their manipulation.

"What are you going to do?" I stopped pacing, transforming my necklace into my sword. I held it up. "Fight me with magic? Be my guest."

Verena had her hands pressed together. None of the Leaders disclosed their power to the people of Gardian in the "name of equality." Both she and her official remained still.

Something deep inside of me burned.

I had been muzzled before, screams muffled by sandpaper stuffed into my mouth and raked over my wet eyes. I bled sorrow and fury infused into my veins from sentences I hadn't said. Words had been jammed into my jaw. Shut your mouth, stop complaining, you coward. Show no emotions, feel no love, silence your anger. I was a force of fighting and fury and fire, I was everything they feared.

My magic flared to life, an unfamiliar and repressed lost spark of fury. An ancient anger built itself inside of me, as if a funnel cloud was forming in the depths of my core. The imagery of lightning flared in my head as a burst of rage struck. My veins were bright and shining, rippling through my entire body. I held one of my palms up, twisting it around. An instinct engulfed my control, erasing any fear I'd had in the face of the system threatening my life.

I had been silenced for too long.

A man wearing black sprinted toward me. I threw myself out of the way, and the anticipatory crowd erupted into chaos within a split second. I hurled my sword on the ground toward Avia as she dashed past me. The man who jumped at me recovered.

I punched my attacker in the chest. The culminating magic in my veins shot out in a burst of a blinding flash. White light snapped through my fingers and manifested itself in a circle, throbbing through my entire body. The man was blasted backward into the wall as a zodiac wheel illuminated before him, quickly twisting from Scorpio to Sagittarius.

I breathed in for what felt like the first time in my life.

The crowd silenced as I stared down at my trembling hands, the light fading away while the zodiac wheel disappeared into a burst of chiming, glittering specks of light. The man was on the floor, either unconscious or dead; I wasn't sure.

Avia grabbed the hood of my cloak and yanked me forward. I snapped to my senses and sprinted out of the inn after Chase. Kaia, after screaming something at Verena, ran after us. The shouts of Verena and her official resonated behind me as the inn exploded with cheering. The four of us bolted down the streets of Lyra, careening away from vendors and between people. Behind us, blurs of the two women in black were in our pursuit.

"Kaia, where the hell are we going?" Avia shouted, throwing herself over a cart.

Chase shoved it aside, knocking a basket of apples to the ground next to a bright yellow building. Kaia ran to the front, shouldering two Aquarius girls away from her. I broke through a couple holding hands in front of me.

A blast of magic sent by an official whizzed past me and almost hit Chase in the back. He pushed another cart aside, narrowly avoiding a girl who leapt out of the way. We held an advantage over them, younger and faster, with someone who knew how to weave through the township to find the outskirts.

Kaia skidded to a halt in front of a cliff. She took Avia's shoulders before she could stumble over the edge, and I stopped, staring at the drop below. The Stellarium officials slowed to a halt behind us. All of us paused as we breathed heavily. Verena brushed herself off and fixed her cloak, looking up at us with a blank face.

"So," she began, "what is your choice?"

Kaia's water magic wrapped around our ankles and dragged us off the cliff, flinging us into midair.

Chapter 14

As we plummeted to the valley beneath us, I hit a wave of water so cold that my body convulsed midair.

My eyes snapped open as I gasped in the water. Kaia raced down the cliff with a wave at her feet, catching the three of us. It sat us down gently at the bottom of the cliff and washed back into a half-frozen creek nearby. Chase coughed wildly, sitting on the ground, and Avia groaned. Kaia landed on her two feet, brushing herself off as water dripped from her palms. The sting of water was fading from my mouth as my anger faded, a dim throb still in my veins.

"That was easier than it normally was," Kaia said as she looked at her hands, still glowing with a deep blue magic, then back up at the cliff. "I hate her."

"Yeah, that was enough for me." Chase laid down on dead grass, holding his hand to his chest. He slowly breathed in and out slowly to stop his coughing. I sat down next to him to let my body rest for a moment.

"You blasted a dude across the room with a zodiac wheel!" Avia yelled, bending over to rub her fist on the top of my head. I swatted her away. "And all this time, we've been antagonizing you for your shitty shape-shifting!"

All attention was on me. A burning sensation was still tearing through my body, my anger dwindling away, but echoing in bursts of energy and light. My veins pulsated, somewhat similar to when Chase's veins lit up with healing, except mine was a whitish-red electrical magic. My mouth went dry with shock.

"You're a Zodiac Turner?" Kaia asked.

"Not to my knowledge," I said.

"It's definitely to your knowledge now," Chase added. "There is absolutely nothing else that could've been. I can't even come up with a different name to call the magic I just saw you perform."

I paused, giving him a side-eye. Avia and Kaia were far enough to not hear it if I took a quiet jab, so I leaned closer to him. "Maybe I'd call it Dreamseeking."

He gave me a look, rubbing his face with his hands so they couldn't see his reaction. "Rieka, please."

"I don't understand." Avia shook her head at me. "Zodiac Turning hasn't existed for centuries. Why you?"

I pressed against my forehead with one of my palms, a dim headache beginning to set in. The exhaustion of the magic I'd used felt nothing like how I felt after using too much of my shapeshifting. Shapeshifting was only a secondary magic to a main archpower. "Better question. How did I go that long without noticing it?"

"Have you ever felt anger like that?" Chase asked. "Or let it release?"

"Not that I can recall."

"Well, there's part one of your answer. The Scorpio Code might've halted you from catching it earlier, if it's an emotion-based magic, and that's what it sounds like to me."

Libran Healing was an emotion-based magic, too. Chase knew it wasn't impossible, not when he also carried an archpower said to be completely absent from Gardian. There was a missing connection for both of us. Where, from my lineage, was there a Zodiac Turner? The answer felt like it should've been close, barely in reach, yet just out of my fingertips.

"How come you have the magic?" Avia asked, as if she'd read my mind. "Is there something you're not telling me?"

"Do you really think I know something you don't?" I snapped. "Neither of us saw a single clue about this growing up. We have the same parents, Avia. They would've told both of us if they knew anything about this."

"I mean, you do have a missing biological father. Maybe this is related to that. Just to be clear, Mom's never mentioned anything about your dad, even just to you?"

"No, she wouldn't talk to me for days every time I asked. But that's probably the closest hint to figuring out where my Zodiac Turning came from, because we know it's not Mom." I sighed, laying down next to Chase. It felt strange, claiming Zodiac Turning as my magic system, but Chase was right—there was nothing else that could've described what happened. "Atlas did say that there were six known Zodiac Turners."

"He said six, at least," Chase added. "He was talking like there were more than he knew about."

"Oh, you're right," Avia said. We'd explained to Avia everything Atlas had told us. "You're saying that a Zodiac Turner could have assaulted Mom?"

"Avia." I sat back up to glare at her. Kaia and Chase looked at each other to avoid what Avia said. "Not right now."

"But it's relevant. Her aversion to talking about it would make a little more sense, and that seems like the closest answer to why you've got the magic."

"How'd you do that, Rieka? Make the whole zodiac wheel thing light up?" Chase diverted the conversation.

"I'm not sure. I felt the strain in my veins, the light, the anger, and then it all exploded when I punched him." I slowed in what I was saying. "And yeah, you know, now that I think about it, that's how Zodiac Turners activate their magic. They roll their fingers into a fist and punch."

"You've never punched anything before?" Kaia asked.

"I've punched things before, but that never happened. Maybe it was the emotional aspect of the energy forming." It hit me. "Oh my god, I did feel something flare up when I made the motion at the Balancing Ceremony."

"Did you really? I didn't catch that," Chase said.

"No one did, and I brushed it off as my shapeshifting potentially activating with the sudden motion."

"What if you can't control it?" Avia suddenly asked.

The four of us went quiet. He was right; how was I supposed to control a notoriously powerful and uncontrollable archpower, when I never even had the motivation to try to practice my shapeshifting? I hadn't intended to blast a man into the wall with a zodiac wheel. I was no stranger to the tales of Zodiac Turners becoming unchecked weapons when taught improperly, or not at all.

"Let's get moving," Chase quickly diverted the conversation to diffuse the tension that had suddenly grown. "Verena is still up there and could potentially find a way to follow us down the cliff."

Avia stood up, wringing the water from her shirt. Chase stretched his back before climbing to his feet. Empathy reflected in his eyes when he looked down at me, offering a hand. Without hesitation, I took it, and he helped me to my feet.

"So, Kaia, off to the docks?" Avia said. "You know the way there?" She started ahead. "I do indeed."

Before us laid dead grasslands, muddy with melted snow. Rolling hills spread out as the morning Sun rose above the horizon, casting a fiery glow across the sky. A tangerine-golden haze veiled the meadows, the dormant stray trees creaking in the wind. Birds soaring above whistled their morning calls to the earth and sky. A few houses on the horizon were alight with the Sun. A cool breeze brushed the land. More of the same landscape we'd seen in the Societal Meadows.

With Avia and Kaia ahead, chatting about various things, Chase walked at my side. "How're you feeling?"

"A little tired," I admitted, "and exhausted."

"Mhm, we all are. That's okay. It won't be long until we get to the docks."

I nodded. He remained next to me for the rest of the day.

The Sun was setting when we walked into the harbor that separated Assidian and Societal territories. The town was made up of a few homes and shacks leading to a large collection of boats on the still water of the Eridanus, a river that expanded out as far as I could see, Gardian's most critical sailing route that ran through the northern region of the continent. The distant Nix Mountain Range appeared to be on fire in the lowering Sun's hues. Though I enjoyed the sound of our footsteps against the maze of wooden pathways and winding, I didn't exactly prefer smell of watery moss and decaying fish.

Throughout the all-day trek, we'd gone back and forth about the risky idea of stopping at the port for a night. I was more exhausted than typical, every muscle in my body aching with each step I took. Chase had seen me falling behind and tried to urge the others to rest for the night. He'd somehow convinced Kaia to agree with him over the course of a few hours. Avia couldn't have cared less either way. I was nervous about the Stellarium catching up, but my exhaustion triumphed over worry. We'd decided to look for an inn.

That was ruined quickly. When we turned a corner on the docks, Chase threw out his arm to stop me from walking forward. He looked up at a taller sailboat, narrowing his eyes—whatever he was seeing was far out of my line of vision. The shadows on the dock shifted in the setting Sun as a figure of a young woman stood up, wearing an all-black Scorpio Stellarium uniform that contrasted with the soft brown color pallet of the harbor.

With the setting Sun behind her, orange tinted Narah's white hair, beams of sunlight falling at each of her sides and outlining the shape of her body. Her fierce blue eyes met mine, piercing into me like a knife driven into my heart. Anger contorted her expressions, accented by the fiery hues covering her image. I struggled to look away.

"Rieka?" Avia said. "Just to remind you, that's your assassin you're staring at."

I was already trapped in the cycle of trying to decipher why she was angry at me, or how I knew her. She grasped the rail of the sailboat she was on, holding it with one hand as she swung down to the dock with ease and agility. She stretched out her hands, sparks of pale blue electricity crackling between her palms. The smile spreading across her face broke her emotionless persona.

Kaia did not waste a second, sprinting forward to pull the lines of the boat Narah previously stood on. Avia jumped forward to untie a knot, while Chase stood his ground next to me, though kept glancing at the boat heist that Narah did not seem to care about whatsoever. Her stare was caught in mine, as if she couldn't see beyond the unbreakable eye contact.

Something in my core strained, ached. I couldn't pinpoint why she felt even more familiar than before. A piercing pain shot through my head, my ears ringing, followed by an intense surge of magic rushing through my veins.

Pain engulfed me and I stumbled forward, granting Narah enough time to strike. She faced her palms forward as bolts of light shot out of them and connected with my skin. Electricity coursed through my body as the blinding light of my own magic consumed me, the voices of the others tapering to a whisper in the back of my mind. My veins throbbed as an aura of light expanded around me. I was choking on my own magic as it blurred all else but Narah, my surroundings slipping into a shadow, as if I was trapped in a forcefield with my assassin. I opened my mouth to speak, but I couldn't form a word.

Power raced through me as I convulsed from the remainder of her electricity. I met her eyes as my whole body illuminated, stronger than it had been when I sent the zodiac wheel into the man only hours before. Spikes of agony rippled up my body as her electricity continued to spark along my fingers. It was soaking into me; I was absorbing the energy. My own magic roared within me, stronger than anything I had ever felt.

"I know you."

Those three words were the only sounds I could force out of my mouth as Narah looked down at me. She was four, maybe five inches taller than me. She reached to my cheek, her fingers tracing along my jawline. There was a sickening disturbance about the interaction, something so wrong. Something that was causing me to choke on my own breath.

"Do you, Rieka?" She raised her head and circled me, her hand sliding down my shoulder, across my arm, to my palm. Electricity sparked between her fingers and my own. "Then tell me who I am."

I was left searching for words I couldn't form. What it felt like to be touched by her—it was familiar, known, but attached to an empty space in my mind that was meant to hold a memory. It wasn't fury that was urging my magic. It was something else, something I didn't know how to describe, fueled by her electrical current. The sense was overpowering, a white light intoxicating my body.

"Verena couldn't kill you herself, not in front of Societalists, not with a magic she must hide. It's my turn."

She reached forward, wrapping her hand around my neck. I tried to gasp in a breath. My own magic was choking me more than her hand was. She was playing mind-games, messing with my confidence, putting a stake into the emotional control I had over my power. For a fraction of a second, she broke our eye contact when she felt her thumb press against the scar in the middle of my neck. I caught a flash of recognition and confusion in her expressions before her anger only intensified.

She tilted her head at me. "You are so lucky that this is the magic I'm choosing to use on you right now."

"Why are you—"

I couldn't finish my sentence. Her grip tightened to stop me from speaking. It was almost as if I could feel her emotions throbbing through me. Fury, stronger than even my own anger, a resentment toward me that couldn't have been unfounded. Her anger reflected my own, enhancing the control I had over myself. My fingers curled into fists.

"I'll let you win this time, because I want to see you burn."

Her emotions flooded uncontrollably into my own from an ancient connection I couldn't identify, what felt like an exact connection of magic. I punched my fist toward her, and it all came roaring out. The darkness around me shattered as light exploded from my fist into the shape of a zodiac wheel. It blasted Narah backward before I could grab it with my other hand, careening her across the dock and into the river.

Chase's voice returned as all my power rushed out. I barely got a glimpse of the darkened clouds before my vision blackened, and I collapsed.

Chapter 15

The sway of a boat rocked my body awake. My skin felt as if it was vibrating, veins on fire, and I groaned as the night sky spun above my head. I was on a sailboat. Kaia had one glowing hand focused on the water before us as we sailed along the river, guided gently by the wind. I held my head, unable to shake the image of Narah's stare as dread filled my chest.

"Rieka?" Chase leaned over me, supporting me with a cautious hand as I coughed. "What happened back there?"

"I know her. How, I'm not sure, but I know her."

"You're definitely a Zodiac Turner, that's for sure," Avia interjected, then paused. "At least your assassin's hot. I didn't get the chance to say that the first time we saw her."

"Your priorities are so messed up, Avia," Chase grumbled. "She looks familiar to me, too. Like, her face does."

I lifted my hands and stared at them. "I couldn't control my magic."

"But you did blast her with a wheel into a river. That was pretty cool," Chase said as he kneeled next to me. "It gave us enough time to get out of there."

Horror rushed through me. "Oh, *shit,* did I—"

"Nah, she's alive." Avia laughed. "We saw her on the banks on the way out."

"It looked like she had a very similar magic in her veins," Chase said, motioning toward his arms.

"You think she's a Zodiac Turner?" Avia asked. "It looked more like weather magic to me."

"That electricity was way too powerful to just be weather magic. It was like there was a direct energetic attachment between them."

"Explain," I said. "What did it look like from the outside?"

"She touched your arm, and both of you froze. It was like she put you in a trance. It seemed dangerous to interfere with, so I stayed back. The light in both your veins grew brighter until I couldn't even look at it."

"I think we were in some sort of void or dimension. All I could see was the two of us and a lot of darkness." I looked up at Avia and Chase, attempting to make sense of anything that was happening to me. All I knew was the feeling of uneasiness and slight panic. "What if I accidentally change one of your signs? I had no control over what I did to her."

"Hey, hey." Chase put a hand on my shoulder. "Don't overthink it. You've only lost control twice, and both were with an enemy. You'll start to figure it out."

"How?"

All of us went quiet for a moment. Chase gave me a specific look before standing up, brushing himself off. He'd taught himself how to cope with an archpower, and I would do the same.

"We're surrounded by water," Avia said dramatically, laying down like a starfish on the deck. "I miss the Woods."

"Stop complaining, I'm tired of it," I snapped at her, barely recovered from fainting. I hugged my knees to my chest to stop my surroundings from spinning. "I want to go back to sleep."

"You weren't sleeping, don't do that. You were unconscious for an hour, and we couldn't get you awake. Eat something," Chase interrupted, gently tapping me with his boot to keep me awake. He dug through his bag, handing me a fresh apple and a flask of water. "The fruit will help you to rehydrate."

"Okay, doctor," I mumbled.

He rolled his eyes at me, then decided to distract himself by inching closer to the front of the boat. Kaia was steering it between a wheel that I assumed was attached to the sails and the control of her water magic to guide us along. Chase hovered back, obviously nervous to mess up her process. I had yet to see such a curious look on his face.

"The wheel's cool," he said, pointing at it. "I've never been on a boat before."

"Never?" She looked up at him with an amused smile. "And it's called a helm, not a wheel."

"Oh, sorry."

"I can tell you want to try it. Here, just don't make any sudden movements, it's touchy. We are heading straight toward the Nix Mountains, and this river leads us right there." Kaia carefully handed off the steering to Chase, who looked way too excited about having control over the boat. "You Convictionists wouldn't have made it far if I didn't catch you in Lyra."

"I was stuck in the middle of the continent in a cursed forest my entire life, do you blame me?" Chase said, his hands white from how tightly he was gripping the helm. "I'm having fun with this, though."

"At least you're making an effort to learn," Kaia said, looking over at Avia, who was uselessly basking in the Sun. Kaia reached over, gently readjusting the helm that Chase held. "Keep it here. Good luck."

She walked away from him, and his face flooded with panic when she sat down next to me. She pointed at her eyes, then to the front of the boat, and he quickly looked forward instead of over at us. Kaia watched him carefully, and I laughed at how incredibly easy he was to mess with.

With Chase distracted, I laid back down, closing my eyes. I struggled to focus on any kind of conversation when I was still half-awake and couldn't shake Narah's anger from my head. I skimmed every edge of my memory to conjure something, anything, that would explain her spite toward me.

"What's on your mind?" Kaia tapped my shoulder, snapping me back from the brink of falling asleep. She'd deliberately taken over Chase's job of monitoring my half-conscious state and let him have fun with the boat. She was shockingly fast at reading right through unspoken intentions. "You look concerned."

"She's been laying there questioning herself because of a pretty girl," Avia said.

"Excuse me?" I sat up.

"I said what I said. Am I wrong?"

"I—no." I paused, then bit my tongue at misspeaking. "Wait. Before you speak, that's not what I meant. She was trying to murder me, Avia."

"Yeah, and? I saw the look on your face. A pretty girl trying to murder me would fluster even me, and I'm not easily flustered."

"Leave her be, Avia," Chase said, his attention diligently fixed forward as he listened. "Forcing her into talking about things she's not ready to talk about won't help anything."

"Yeah, and what you just said doesn't help, either," I snapped at him. "God forbid I try to figure out the intentions of an assassin who hates me for unknown reasons."

"Right." Avia snorted. "Also, who gave you permission to tell me what to do, Chase?"

Chase turned to her with a glare. "I am trying to help."

Kaia snapped at him, pointing toward the river in front of us. He grimaced and put his hands back on the helm. Avia crossed her arms and pretended like she didn't hear Chase. I hadn't noticed the difference between them; Avia, who I personally associated with physical strength, looked small next to Chase. He had to be almost a foot taller than her, let alone muscular. Avia generally took pride in being the strongest of a group to make up for her shorter height—an insecurity I'd heard her bring up many times—but Chase outmatched her by a landslide in all aspects. It probably peeved her that he was older, too.

"She's *my* sister. I know what she can handle when I'm teasing her," Avia continued the argument. "*You* don't have a sister. Being a little bit mean is in the requirements. Makes her more tough."

"Have you actually asked her that?" Chase said, looking back at her again. "She's gone through a lot today. Give her a break for just a bit."

Kaia sighed, standing back up. She shooed Chase away from the steering.

"*Shit,* I'm sorry," he apologized profusely, guilt spread across his face as he stepped back. "I should've been focusing."

"She's irritating. I don't blame you." She gave him a smile in response. Chase's face lit up at her patience. "You'll discourage yourself if you're frustrated while learning. Go do your thing. Please diffuse."

"You." Avia took the opportunity to grab his cloak, pulling him down to her height. "Is there a reason you keep trying to boss me around?"

Chase grinned, entirely unintimidated by her. I couldn't comprehend his patience. He gently—almost effortlessly—pushed her hands away. I stepped away from them when I felt Avia's skin increase in temperature. I was not about to get in the middle of whatever was happening between them.

"Get that stupid smile off your face."

"Make me."

Kaia winced at their interaction and focused her hands on the helm of the ship. It was only then I noticed her fingers anxiously tapping against the polished wood, her gaze flicking up and down to the distant flashes of lightning. There was no stop anywhere in sight as the storm clouds drew closer, thunder rumbling in the distance. I moved next to her, attempting to drown out the banter that was happening behind me.

Kaia held out her hand to push the boat forward through the river. I observed the blue magic pull from her veins, giving her fingertips a starry hue, almost transparent, as she contorted the water. Over the edge of the boat, a soft bioluminescence followed our wake from the water her magic touched.

"Are they always like this?" Kaia asked.

"She's got a vendetta both against the fact that he's a Libra and that he's taller and stronger than she is." I sighed, crossing my arms with a shiver at the cooler mountain air. "She's so particular about who's in charge, and he's a natural mediator."

"I don't know who it was centuries ago that decided to put Aries and Libra in one Union, but I disagree with that decision."

"That decision was probably made for this reason." I nodded at Avia and Chase, who were still going back and forth about something that I didn't care to listen to. Chase remained *perfectly* calm. "We'd be a wreck without Libra."

"How long do you think it'll take before he loses his mind?" Her voice lifted with amusement. "That *cannot* be sustainable."

"I don't know. It's been sustainable for Conviction for as long as we can remember." I shrugged, narrowing my eyes at the storm clouds gathering above us. "You think the weather will be okay?"

"A mountain thunderstorm pales in comparison to the things I've sailed through," she said, stretching her arms out. "It's a river. It's not like we can lose direction. My older brothers are Sagittarians. I've been through much worse."

Yeah, Kaia intimidated me. She scowled, looking ahead at the murky water. Lightning flashed in the sky. There was no possible way to stop, and being so far north, the water couldn't be a comfortable temperature, especially with the melting snow around.

"Rieka," she said, "just in case we do hit a bad patch of the storm, you should rest in the cabin. Chase wants you awake because he's worried about you going unconscious, but I'll mitigate his panic. Your magic is the most important to tend to, out of all of ours, and you've had a long day."

I knew Chase's healing was far more important than my magic. I had no doubt about it. He could save our lives, but he hadn't been healing anyone—he wasn't magically exhausted. Avia's magic was useless when she was surrounded by water, and Kaia had to stay awake to use hers.

I stood still for a moment, closing my eyes and drowning out voices. I had to take a deep breath before walking toward the ship's cabin, opening the door, and lying down on a captain's bed.

Chapter 16

*I*n my rest, Conviction Woods fleshed out around me. The patterns of the trees and mosses contorted, swirling in an unconscious mess, my transparent spirit forming separately from my younger self. When I quickly recognized that I was experiencing the return of a true memory, I was pulled into my past self. My spirit and body merged as one.

    I gasped in a strained breath of humid air, my back pressed against a massive cedar giant. The bright summer Sun glared through the branches of the canopy, washing the Woods with green-tinted sunrays. My chest rapidly rose and fell as I recovered from the chase through the Hub. We'd barely made it beyond the boundaries of the Woods in time. I slid my back down the trunk of the tree to sit on the ground with an exhausted groan. Only a few feet away, a Scorpio Stellarium member stood in front of the border of the Woods, peering beyond the line of lanterns to understand where we'd escaped to.

His two spirit hounds circled him, pitch black dogs with claws and hungry chops, their massive shadowy shoulders as tall as his hips. Their Stellarium handler had summoned and commanded them to hunt us down when we'd tried to shove him into an alleyway. We couldn't have predicted his rare form of animal magic, one that allowed him to summon the spirits of deceased animals. Even with the magical commands controlling them, the hounds wouldn't dare to stray into the Woods. The Beasts would outmatch them in seconds. We were safe.

I lifted the mask shielding my identity and placed it in my lap. The face of a wooden wolf stared back at me, its abstract hand-carved shape paling from the amount of Sun it'd been receiving. With a sigh, I threw my head against the cedar. The adrenaline sprinting through me wouldn't ease up. I slipped my gray veil off my shoulders to cool down.

"If it wasn't for the damn hounds, we would've had 'em," Narah huffed as she stood next to me, shaking out her hands to dissipate the magic raging in her veins. She flipped him off, even though he couldn't see us. "Let's see how long it takes him to send the dogs back to the spirit world. Surely those monstrous things are sucking up his energy."

I glanced up with a smile at the rebellious tone that came from Narah. She removed her identical wolf mask and tossed it on the ground next to mine, uncovering white hair stuck to her sweaty forehead. She yanked out the tie holding her hair back to move the escaped strands away from her face. I watched as she removed her gray cloak, revealing her tight-fitting sleeveless black top, and, more importantly, her muscular shoulders and toned arms.

"Give me a second to recover before we go anywhere else," I said, my voice raspy from my dry throat. "I don't understand how you run faster than me without getting even slightly winded."

Narah grinned at me, flexing her arms before she lifted them above her head to stretch. The fabric of her shirt lifted to briefly expose her toned core, her pants resting low on the curve of her hips. She glanced down at me, and I looked away quickly when she'd caught me staring. Again.

She laughed at me. "Nice try."

"Shut up." I rolled my eyes. Her teasing would've been a lot worse if my face wasn't already flushed from running through the Hub. "Do you have any Pisces in you? At all?"

Narah shrugged. "Fuck if I know."

I smiled at her. My heart pounded so hard that I could feel its pulse in my fingertips. The blood rushing in my ears muffled the birdcalls of the Woods and the barking of the hounds. Every nerve in me was awake. I closed my eyes to calm it all down—the racing thoughts, the terror from moments before, the spinning vision.

"The hounds are moving," Narah reported, interrupting my few seconds of peace, and I opened one eye to look at her. Her expressions had become more serious as the dogs distanced themselves from us. Narah bent down to pick up her mask and refasten it on her face. "They're distracted by something."

The hounds were trotting toward an uninhabited house just outside of Conviction Woods. Amid my panic and adrenaline rush, I hadn't even noticed the abandoned cabin not too far away. It was close enough for me to see a shadow of movement through one of its shattered windows. Its roof was caved in, wood walls rotting away; I wasn't entirely sure how the structure was still standing. Both of the spirit hounds began sniffing around its structure, their tails wagging with excitement at the potential of a victim. The official followed behind them as he went to inspect what had attracted them.

"Goddammit," I grumbled while reaching for my gray veil. I brushed off the tiny hemlock cones it'd picked up from the forest floor, fastening it over my shoulders. "What the hell could they possibly be attracted to over there when they were sent after *us*?"

"Don't know, but it's got me curious." Narah quickly swiped my mask off the ground before I could put it back on. She dangled it in front of me. I tried to snatch it, and she moved it away to try to get me to jump to my feet. I glared at her instead. She tilted her head at me with one side of her mouth quirked up. "Fine. I'll help you, since you're so tired from running for, what, ten minutes?"

Narah offered me a hand, and I took it. She yanked me to my feet with a lot more force than I expected. I stumbled forward and fell into her as I lost my balance from her strength. She grabbed my side to stabilize me, even though I was *sure* that she deliberately pulled me up too fast to shove my face into her collarbone. She tilted her chin down to look at me, pale blue heterochromatic eyes staring through the eye sockets of the mask as she stepped forward with my mask in her hands. I didn't move, frozen as she bent closer to me, too nervous as to what she'd do. She carefully moved my raven hair over my shoulders to tie the back of the mask underneath it, her hands temporarily following my jawline as she readjusted it on my face.

A nearby yell resounded through the Woods. Both of us immediately turned our attention to the house with its front door wide open. The sound of the breaking wood and excited barking echoed—the spirits had found something. The official slowly approached the abandoned cab-

in, drawing a long blade from his belt. Narah and I hurried through the Woods, staying beyond the boundary. We paused next to the house.

A teenager in Scorpio colors crashed out of the front door, followed by a snapping spirit hound. The official lurched for him while another boy ran out, his shirt donning the Gemini glyph.

"Leave!" the Scorpio boy yelled at the Gemini, his voice splitting in agony as the official grabbed his arms and kicked the back of his legs to bring him to his knees on old, splintery wood. One of the hounds licked its lips, circling him. "Get out of here! *Run*, before the other one—"

The Gemini spun around as the second hound leapt through a half-broken window, shattering the remaining glass. Terror spread across his face as the hound stalked toward him, saliva flying from its mouth as it viciously barked. The Scorpio boy desperately fought with all the strength he had in him as the official held him down and the hound approached its victim.

Narah didn't wait another second, sprinting out of the Woods, her veins immediately illuminating with a pale blue light. I immediately ran after her. She grabbed the official by his shoulders and tore him away from his target, throwing his arm to the side. His blade clattered to the ground, and I grabbed it before he could, hurling it toward the hound targeting the Gemini. It struck the black-shadow dog in the hind leg. It spun to me as I became its target again. The other hound followed suit, their noses twitching as they took in my scent. Narah spun the official around, shoving him back toward the Woods with ease. Completely ambushed by our presence, he had no time to properly respond to Narah's brightening magic.

Both the hounds jumped for me. I ran for the Woods, breaking through the aura underneath the lanterns. I gripped the branches of a fallen trunk on the boundary and hoisted myself up the tree with only seconds to climb and find a part of the tree peeking through the boundary. The hounds needed to stay distracted. I carefully stepped to the edge of a thin branch, thankful for my weight as I tediously balanced a few feet above the snapping dogs. They snarled and jumped for the branch I stood on. I was far too high up for them to reach without following me into the Woods. They refused to turn away from me, set on my presence above them, as if the boys they were attacking moments before weren't even there.

Narah had forced the official to the line of lanterns guarding the Woods. She slammed her fist into his chest, blasting him into the Woods with a wheel of light before opening her hand to shove the wheel against him to keep him beyond the boundary. I stuck one foot beyond the lanterns so I could see both in and out of the Woods to keep an eye on Narah.

The Woods began to contort and shift, shadows looming over trees and fog drifting amongst the branches surrounding me. A rotting stench filled the air as a Beast of the Woods stalked toward the official. Narah forced her energy forward with a scream of pain as she froze him in place with her wheel of light. The Beast approached him, shadows following in its step as blood dripped from its tongue. It sunk its maw into the man's legs. He shrieked in agony as the Beast smothered him in a tar of shadows, blending the shape of monster and human into one. Smoke smoldered as yells disappeared into the depths of the Woods. Narah released the wheel, shoving her arm down to avoid throwing herself backward. An explosion of light followed as she collapsed.

Moments later, the hounds outside the Woods vanished, their magical attachment following their handler to the spirit realm. I almost fell feet below as I flung myself down the tree to where Narah laid motionless on the ground. I scraped my knees as I threw myself on the ground, hooking my arms underneath hers as I tugged her body closer to mine. Grasping her wrists, my magic immediately began flowing from my arms into hers. She gasped in a breath seconds later, jerking back awake as I gave her the excess energy from the sheer amount of adrenaline pumping through my bloodstream. Narah stabilized, the rise and fall of her chest evening out as we balanced the energy shared between two Zodiac Turners.

Narah stared at the empty space before us where the official stood moments before, horror flooding her face as she processed what she'd done. The Beast had feasted. We'd led the official to his death.

"*Fuck!*" Narah cursed as she trembled against me, her head against my shoulder. I wrapped my arms around her to provide her a sense of safety and comfort, and she shoved her back into my chest. Her heart pounded against me as she pulled herself close with one leg propped up on the ground. "I just killed someone, Kira."

"You had no choice. You did the right thing. *I promise,* Narah." My grip tightened around her shoulders underneath her cloak as I forced more of my magic into her own veins. Sheer, unbridled horror consumed her, flowing into my body, attempting to take over my own emotions. I fought it with everything I had in me to calm her down, focusing intensely on the heat of her body against mine, the comfort she found leaning into me. "The hounds would've killed them, and if the spirits were attracted to them after being attracted to us, I know for a fact that they did nothing wrong."

"But I told myself I'd never kill anyone. I don't want to be like them," she stumbled over her words, her entire body tense. "I *promised* myself."

"You also vowed to reverse that damn Code with me." I paused, looking over to the abandoned house where the two boys were. "And Narah? The first step to get there is recognizing that we're not alone in this fight, that we may have to sacrifice for others sharing our struggle."

The Scorpio boy laid on the ground, shivering with his eyes wide as he stared at Woods. To him, we were gone, the shimmering aura protecting the inside of the Woods being seen from the outside. The Gemini was standing directly in front of him in a defensive position, watching carefully for any sort of movement or threat following their attack. After he was met with silence, he whirled around and threw himself on top of the Scorpio, grasping both sides of his face. As both of them broke into sobs of relief at their survival, they desperately kissed, the Scorpio's arms hugging his partner's back in an indescribably tight embrace.

Narah slowly moved away from me. My hands fell away from her arms. With one look at each other, we made a mutual silent decision: they needed to know we survived. We wanted them to know we survived.

I gently helped Narah to her feet, keeping her close to me to ensure she was stable as we stepped out of the Woods. Both boys froze when we reappeared, their faces full of confusion as they tried to understand how we'd survived in the Woods.

"Is he coming back?" the Scorpio boy croaked, panic flooding his expressions. "He can't. He *can't*. I broke the Code."

"He's not coming back, I promise," Narah reassured him, though she refused to look back at the Woods. "The Stellarium won't know you broke the Code."

"Thank you." The Gemini gasped in air between sobs, tears streaking his face as he looked at us. "How did you—"

"Don't question it," Narah interrupted. "You didn't see us go in and out of the Woods. Got it?"

They nodded quickly. I slowly approached them, careful to respect their space. The Gemini barely moved aside to let me sit down next to the other Scorpio. I reached underneath my hair, lifting the mask off my face to place it at my side. Narah leaned over me and untied my gray cloak, sliding it off my shoulders to reveal my black undershirt with a tiny Scorpio glyph. Shock tore across the other Scorpio's expressions.

"You're not alone," I said.

Narah placed her hand on my shoulder. "You did nothing to deserve what just happened to you."

Through the terror of a shared traumatic event—Narah, who swore she'd never kill, and the Scorpio, who had seen his life flash before his eyes moments prior—we came to a mutual understanding. The Scorpio boy smiled at me, tears still flowing down his face, his emotions contorting as he took it all in. He lifted his hand toward mine, offering a handshake, an action forbidden to Scorpio. His face was full of sheer hope, more hope than I'd ever seen in another human before, hope for his future, hope for his love.

"Quinn," he introduced himself.

I shook his hand. "Rieka."

"Why are you over here?" he forced out, nodding once toward the house. "This is where we..."

"I understand," Narah said before he finished. "You don't need to explain yourselves. We use the Woods as a safe haven. The masks, they help us to get away with our method of taking the Stellarium down, one official at a time."

I glanced down at the wooden wolf mask, the gaping opening of its eyes staring back into my soul, waiting to don my heterochromatic irises. I had an incurable hunger to tear the Scorpio Stellarium apart one by one. Narah and I, we'd stalk them through the Hub, luring them to the hidden alleyways, illuminating the shadows between looming buildings with the light of our magic to change the fate of every Stellarium member we could; to allow them an escape from the government that used *them* to hurt *us*.

Chapter 17

Before the dream could continue, a crash woke me, followed by a scream.

I was thrown off the bed to the hard floor as the boat jerked. Springing to my feet, I threw my bag over my shoulders and touched my neck to make sure my necklace was still there. The boat shook again.

I bolted out of the cabin into pouring rain. Thunder roared and lightning flickered through the sky. Chase was standing up with trembling hands after falling down while Kaia held a desperate grip on the helm. Avia had her cloak thrown over her head, glaring at the downpour. The boat smacked against a wave again, throwing Avia onto the ground while Chase barely held himself up, and I threw myself against a wall to stop myself from falling.

Lightning snaked through the sky, and seconds later, thunder roared. Our boat lifted in the foaming, thrashing water, and then came down with another crash. Rain pelted the deck.

Avia rolled to where I was and I grabbed her arm. Chase reached Kaia, pulling his cloak hood over his head to shield his face from the rain. My sister and I could barely stumble to where they were, Avia protesting as I dragged her through the rain.

"Why the *hell* didn't any of you wake me up?" I screamed through the wind. I held onto Avia's arm to keep both of us on our feet.

"We *couldn't*, Rieka!" Avia screeched back. "We had to come out here to help—"

Kaia grimaced as she yanked the helm again, barely avoiding a near-invisible boulder in the river. The side of the boat clipped the protrusion, answering the tides with the sickening creak and crack of wood. Lightning flared, striking somewhere near the riverbank. Avia, Chase and I fell to our knees at the impact.

The helm spun out of control; Kaia's hands were forced off. The boat rocked back and forth as rain filled the deck. My stomach turned. Chase and Avia gripped their bags close to themselves on the ground while Kaia yelled something inaudible. She balanced herself at the front, holding her hands out. The rain bent around her as waves curled in front of us as she guided the ship with her own magic.

I pushed through the rain, closer to Kaia manipulating the waves, closer to the most dangerous part of the boat. Her hands trembled with the force of her glowing sapphire magic. She grimaced as she struggled to control the course of the waves, screaming at me to get back to the stern before I was thrown off. I couldn't leave her side, and I was no stranger to balancing myself through slippery mud in the Woods.

The storm clouds were lighter in the north. If we could get through the worst of the storm, we would be on-course to the Nix Mountains.

I narrowed my eyes at the difference in the river. From what I could see, the dark, foaming waters were eerily calm a few dozen feet in front of us. The mountains were startlingly close on the horizon. Kaia caught on to it at the same time I did, immediately pulling her arms back to slow the ship. It was too late. With only seconds to react, we were heading straight toward a cliff.

I craned my neck toward Avia and Chase, pointing wildly at the side of the boat. "Jump!"

"*What?*" Avia screamed back at me. Kaia whipped around.

"*Jump!*" Kaia and I yelled in unison.

Avia looked over at the ledge of the boat. She and Chase couldn't see what was ahead of us. Chase met my gaze wildly. It took a split second and a tiny nod for him to trust my judgment. He grabbed Avia and yanked her toward the edge as she gasped and tried to shove him away. I didn't have time to see what would happen to them as Kaia motioned toward the edge of the river ahead of us.

The boat would crush us if we didn't act. I gripped the railing, tightening my bag on my shoulders, and hoisted myself to the edge. Drawing in a deep breath, I threw myself overboard.

A cold shock pierced against my skin as Kaia's waves crashed against me. Water frothed angrily around us as we were hurled off the waterfall. Kaia twisted her body midair and faced her palms to the falls, summoning the water to wrap around us. Her eyes illuminated blue as we rode the wave down. I couldn't fathom the amount of strength she must've needed to hold so much control over her magic.

Kaia and I landed softly against what must've been a lake. I gasped for air, choking in water as I swam out of her wave. The winter freeze stabbed into my skin, instantly numbing my fingertips. Kaia guided both of us to shore. I was never more thankful to touch sand, desperately clawing for it as I gasped in breaths and coughed up water. Kaia collapsed with a groan. The ship was sinking behind us.

"Where are they?" I wheezed. "Did you see them jump?"

Kaia was unresponsive as she gripped the sand. The rain hindered our visibility. I scanned the lake for any sort of foreign color, but with each plank of wood and wave, an anomaly of a human was indistinguishable from the angry water. Fear coursed through my body as I stumbled to the lake. The sound of the pelting rain was deafening.

I waited, and waited, falling to my knees, trying to see anything but rushing water.

At last, a blur of golden light tore over the lake's surface. The aura ran with the waves, and once it touched Kaia's skin, she jumped to her feet. She gasped in a desperate breath, the light of healing quickly scanning her body.

I dove into the water as soon as Chase surfaced with Avia thrown over his shoulder. I had to divert my eyes at the blinding brightness of what only could've been described as instinctual magic powerful enough to spread through the waves. Lunging forward, I fought through the currents to reach them. Together, Chase and I dragged her to shore. A wave pummeled my body, knocking me over. Chase pushed me up underneath the water as we stumbled onto land, lowering Avia's body.

He immediately kneeled over her, his veins alight with magic. He was quick to flip her wrist over, pressing two fingers to her veins and bending his head close to her mouth to listen for breathing. Seconds later, he felt across her neck, shoulders, arms, ribs, down to her hips and legs, checking for injury. He then moved her onto her side, following her spine with his fingers before readjusting her into what I recognized as a recovery position.

Chase wrapped his hands around her wrists, focusing his attention on her face. Her body illuminated with the healing as it spread rapidly from his veins to her limbs. Golden magic enveloped both of them as it restored her purple-tinted skin and snapped bones back into place. Her heat returned, her eyes flaring open a minute later as she gulped in a breath of air. She coughed up water as Chase's healing continued to pulse through her, a heartbeat pumping through both of them, sourcing from the center of his chest where the light shone the brightest.

Leaning over her, Chase put a supportive hand on her back as she readjusted to breathing again. Avia laid on the sand, eyes wide as his healing slowly ebbed away. He pulled his hands away. Both of them stayed in the same position, Avia gasping for breath and Chase's eyes wide with shock.

"You're a healer?" she spluttered.

"Yeah, I am," he said, his voice utterly still. "It's a long story."

"Did you just save my life?"

"I'd hope so?" He shook his head in disbelief at her. "A thank you would be nice, Avia."

"Yeah, yeah, thanks." She paused. Chase was heaving breaths in, arms shaking from the weight of carrying her through the water. If he hadn't been a healer and withstood the impact to his body, neither of them would've survived.

"You're a Libran Healer," Kaia repeated, sitting next to me as she, too, recovered. Her voice was strained, her breaths long and desperate; I hadn't noticed the strain her water magic took on her. "Anything else I should know about the three of you?"

Avia squirmed away from Chase's hand on her back. He looked mildly insulted as she held her thighs on her knees, still clearly struggling to breathe. He monitored her carefully, inching closer to carefully reach for her wrist.

"Avia, please. Let me make sure you're not having heart issues."

She gave him a hesitant look but allowed him to press his fingers against her wrist again. He was too focused on checking her pulse to notice the way her eyes ran up and down his body, lingering on his drenched white shirt exposing his torso. I felt like I was interrupting something.

"I hate water." Avia's body shivered, something I'd never seen her do before. "Also, you're a Libran Healer?"

Chase unbuttoned his cloak and draped it over her shoulders. "Yeah. Not entirely sure how I healed you so well, though."

"It felt warm," she said. "I liked it."

"Was that a compliment? Maybe you need more healing. You must be ill."

"Shut your mouth," she snapped as Chase leaned down. "You ruined it."

I glanced over at Kaia, who met eye contact with me as we both cringed and turned our backs to them.

"Thanks for saving me."

"My pleasure."

"Personally, I am so glad you joined us," I said quietly, refusing to look at whatever was happening behind us. "I might've started to lose my mind about now."

"I am so surprised you haven't already." She laughed, shaking her head. "It's weird, I've never been able to perform water contortion so easily."

"I'm impressed," I said, following her gaze to the lake that was still rippling with gold and blue energies from the two activated magic systems. The light danced with the Moon's reflection, soothing the angry waters as parts of the boat sank.

Strangely, the crash into the valley felt somewhat comforting, as if I had a physical representation of my tumultuous emotions. A waterfall poured into a lake on the coast of a beach. Seeing a forest at the base of a mountain made me smile, rocky walls rising around us in somewhat of a circular formation. Knowing there was a forest nearby soothed me, reminding me of home, yet I had been home only minutes before when I stepped into a memory.

I let my eyes follow the gentle ebb and flow of the lake with its blue and gold light. The events of the memory came in waves. I traced my hand down the side of my face, trying to recall the way it felt when Narah adjusted the mask. It struck me—she'd used Zodiac Turning to keep the official in the Woods. When she collapsed, I understood how to hold her and connect my magic to hers, balancing our energy, aiding in her quick recovery. Back then, I'd known I was a Zodiac Turner, and I'd forgotten. Narah and I had some sort of strategy with the officials in the Hub, changing their signs to reduce the numbers of the Scorpio Stellarium.

The masks were Sun bleached. We were going after the Scorpio Code with everything we had in us. We'd revealed ourselves to the two boys for a reason, unafraid of showing our identities for solidarity.

"Kaia," I started, keeping my voice low so the other two wouldn't hear, "was your brother's name Quinn?"

She glanced over at me, her face outlined by the dominant golden light cumulating on the shores of the beach. "My Scorpio brother, yes."

I swallowed hard. While being dragged to his death in the Hub, he'd given me a forgiving smile. He'd known my name when I couldn't remember his. My heart strained, and I closed my eyes to stop myself from crying. The day I met Quinn, I finally knew how it felt to be seen; understood. I'd never been alone in my hatred toward the Code, nor my breakage of it.

The memory haunted me—the way that Quinn kissed his boyfriend after they'd survived an encounter with the Scorpio Stellarium, the hope in his eyes when he introduced himself, our forbidden handshake. Then it was Narah's lighthearted teasing as she pulled me into her, her hand on my neck as she adjusted a well-worn mask, the look of relief we'd exchanged after seeing the two boys break the Code.

"Are you crying?" Kaia asked quietly. I opened my eyes, quickly wiping my arm across my face. I met her deep blue eyes as her face twisted with emotion. "You remembered him."

"I don't know what, or who, caused me to forget, or why it's only coming back to me now."

"Rieka." Kaia's voice wavered. "I'm sorry, I have to say this for your sake, I really think someone might've taken her from you. Quinn told me the entire event, how he'd finally felt like he wasn't alone in the way he broke the Code."

I slowly nodded, my lips pursed. "There's no reason I would've forgotten on my own."

"And now she works for the Stellarium." Kaia's voice wavered. "When she approached you on the docks, she radiated so much anger."

"She's not angry on her own will." I breathed out slowly as my arms lit with a white light, beginning at my fingertips and slowly making its way through my veins up my arms. "She told me how she'd promised herself she'd never kill."

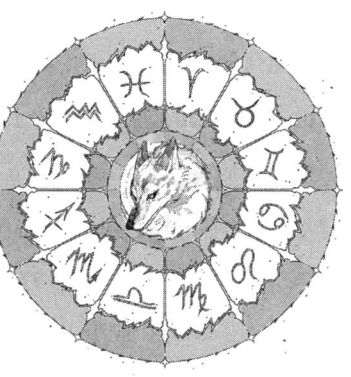
Zodiac Turning

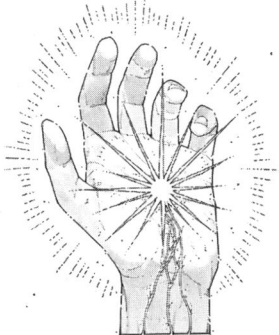
Libran Healing

Spirit Walking

CHAPTER 18

We left the conversation behind at the lake when Chase and Avia started looking for shelter in the rock walls surrounding us, eventually finding an entrance to a cavern. Avia didn't hesitate to step into it. When Chase didn't hear her scream or complain, he ducked down to follow her, Kaia and me after them. I held my necklace for comfort while observing the surroundings closely. I could hear Avia drying off her hands the best she could, and light sprang to life as she summoned a tiny flame in her palms.

The cave was no bigger than the boat cabin. With a sigh of relief at the dry area, we set our bags down and rested on the sandy floor. I slipped my cloak off my shoulders, wringing out my shirt while shapeshifting my cloak into a fluffy blanket, hissing at the sting in my arms. I wrapped it around myself, shivering, and ran my hands through my soaked hair a few times as Avia built a fire in the middle of the cavern.

Kaia was engulfed in thought. Chase settled next to the fire. He stared into the flames with an empty stare on his face, completely and entirely drenched with water. Kaia opened her backpack and spread a blanket in front of her. Miraculously, it wasn't wet—she must've had waterproof protections on her backpack, probably a good idea for a water mage. She offered a shirt to Avia, who denied it; hers was already drying from her abnormally warm body. When Kaia offered one to me, I instantly took it; I despised the feeling of the wet shirt clinging to my skin. Chase turned away as I put my back to the others and quickly changed. Avia nudged him when I was done.

"I'd give you a dry shirt, but I'm not sure if you could even get it over your shoulders," Kaia said to Chase, who gave her an amused smile. "Sorry."

"Is that not bothering you? The wet shirt?" I asked.

"Oh, it definitely is."

"Maybe just take it off?" I suggested, holding back a laugh. "If you're worried about coverage, I hate to break it to you, but a wet white shirt is not any better than no shirt."

"Thank god someone said it. I was worried I'd make someone uncomfortable." He immediately pulled it off. "I didn't want to be weird."

I shook my head with a laugh. "Trust me on this. It does not affect me."

"It definitely affects me," Avia said, and I wrinkled my nose at her. Kaia massaged her forehead. "You hide a lot under that cloak."

"Isn't physical strength frowned upon in Libra?" Kaia asked, who was refusing to look at him as she stared into the fire. "The whole thing with neutrality and anti-intimidation?"

"Yeah, exactly," he said, crossing his arms, as if trying to protect himself. "It's related to Libran Healing. There's nothing I can do about it.

I've always been like this."

"Speaking of." Avia tilted her head at him. "I've never felt healing like that before."

Kaia rested her back against the stone wall. "There's got to be more Healers and Turners out there."

"At least six Turners, according to Atlas," Chase repeated. "I don't know about Libran Healers, though."

I wondered if Narah was one of the Turners on Atlas's list of six. Surely, he'd know about the Scorpio Stellarium using a Zodiac Turner as an assassin. I tried to push the thought out of my head, watching the rain drum against the lake outside the cavern opening, my eyelids threatening to close on me. Even though I'd taken a nap on the boat, my body ached with exhaustion, a shiver traveling up my spine from the inescapable cold. I clutched my blanket closer to myself.

"Chase," Kaia started, catching my attention, "are you hurt?"

His hands dripped with blood, yet there were no cuts or abrasions on his palms. It seeped through his skin as he wrapped his hands with a cloth from his bag. His pattern of bandaging himself was in a specific ritual, in strokes of three, carefully attuned to the curvature of his palms. He looked up when he noticed we were watching him.

"Why are your hands bleeding out?" Avia asked.

"Ah, when I use too much magic, it does this." He tied the gauze off and set his hands in his lap. "My magic sources from my blood. Normal healers use water."

Kaia's face fell. "It looks painful."

"It is. A bit." He winced as his thumb massaged against the gauze. "I used more magic than I should've, but that's how it goes sometimes."

"Can I ask how it works?"

"Sure. I've been studying medical stuff since I was a kid. I have to understand an illness or injury to heal it," he explained, reaching over into his bag for tape to fasten the guard he'd created for his hands. "My healing is either activated emotionally or instinctually. If someone is hurt, my body reacts. It just knows what to do."

"You were *struggling* at the Balancing Ceremony when they tried to test you for Libran Healing," I recalled. "I remember you looked so incredibly focused. Your hands were shaking."

"Yeah, that's why I was two years delayed. I had to practice fighting my instinct. Dad made stuff up about my job making me too busy to attend."

"You're twenty?" Kaia asked. "I had my Ceremony two years ago on my eighteenth birthday so I could join the Cancer Stellarium as fast as possible. I'm twenty-one in July."

"You're only a few months older than me," Chase said to her. "Avia also delayed a year to protect Rieka from the Code."

"Nineteen," Avia added, then nodded at me. "But Rieka's still a baby."

"Hey." I crossed my arms with a glare at her. "That's not very nice."

"How'd you heal me this well? I've never had a healer repair me so effortlessly," Avia diverted the conversation. "Only my lungs burn, really."

"I mean, the magic was banished for being too powerful. And, also, easy, you had a pulse but weren't breathing," he explained. "I full body scanned you while you were unconscious and found that your ribs, hips, and legs were broken. I needed to clear your lungs and repair bones."

"Damn," Avia said simply, pulling her knees into her chest. "You're a lot smarter than you let on to."

"Thanks." He held his bandaged hands together to ease his pain. "The stronger my emotions are, the better I heal. No amount of emotion or instinct can make me invincible, and like anyone else, I feel the consequences of overuse of magic."

"I thought I burned you." Avia looked relieved. "You had strong enough emotions to do all of that?"

He looked up with a smile. "I try my best."

As soon as I fell asleep, I was yanked into someone else's dreamscape.

I stood upon a misty hill, grass brushing against ankles. The night sky spread above my head, the full Moon hiding the light of the Stars. I let my gaze wander to the stream in the near distance, where an angry red aura throbbed. It fought with what was meant to be a peaceful setting. I narrowed my eyes at the shape it surrounded. Someone was at the river, bent down, hands in the water. The furious glow pulsing around them made their shape unclear.

I carefully stepped toward the person, bare feet against dewy ground, watching as the aura throbbed harder the closer I neared. Foreign emotions soaked into me.

Fury. Betrayal. Hurt.

The emotions accumulated at the back of my throat, intensifying with each step I took. A distant memory flared through my head, blurry and confusing, painful when I tried to decipher the details. Someone screamed out. A child, torn away from their mother, ripped of innocence. A piercing pain struck my head, and with a hiss, I put my palm to my forehead.

My body heated with anger as I pushed closer. I stumbled backward as shock coursed through me.

Narah was before me, her long white hair draped over her shoulders in the water as she trembled. Her hands were buried in the creek, as if she was grasping for a sense of reality or aid. Through her armor and cloak, the red aura throbbed from her skin.

I turned my hand around as the red light shifted, blending into my fingers. A soothing blue energy sunk into the edges of the aura. Her shoulders relaxed as I pushed past the foreign anger. She turned her torso enough for me to see the outline of a round pendant resting on her neck, glowing fiercely with a blinding red light. I shied away, blinking to rid the floating glow left behind.

"Narah."

Her eyes snapped open. She stood up and whirled around to face me. The crimson aura returned with a shock through the air, reeking of decaying metal and smoldering skin, originating from the pendant. It knocked me backward and instantly absorbed into my skin. A look of pure confusion and shock tore across her expressions.

I knew intuitively that it was an anger I should've been feeling, a familiar madness. Toward someone. Someone we both knew, somehow, some way.

"Why are you here?" she demanded, fingers curling into fists. "Get out of my head!"

"Who is it?" I pushed past the fear and fury through all my willpower. "Who are you angry at?"

She narrowed her eyes at me, and without missing a beat, she said, "You."

I awoke with a gasp, scrambling to sit up while clawing at my blanket. A piercing pain tore through my head, and I fell back, my ears ringing as the light of day filtered through the cavern. Chase flinched and accidentally hit the back of his head against the wall. Kaia was already awake, looking at me with concern while Avia slept through it all with a snore.

Chase rubbed the back of his head. "Are you good? What was that all about?"

"It was her." I gripped my scalp, trying to ease the fury and anger still echoing through my limbs. "She's been hurt by someone, someone that I was hurt by, but I don't know why I was hurt or who it is, but it's a mutual, and—"

"Rieka." Chase leaned over and placed his hand on my shoulder. I didn't react.

"—I'm so confused. I don't know how she got into my dreams, and—"

"Rieka."

"Yeah?"

"Breathe. It was just a nightmare. She's an assassin the Scorpio Stellarium sent after you. Of course you're going to have nightmares about her."

"No, Chase, you don't get it. I was talking to Kaia about this last night. When I was asleep on the boat, I remembered how I saved her brother's life. Narah was with me." I stood up and started to pace. "I knew her for much longer. It was clear. There were a lot of things that were clear. Something is so wrong with her anger, and something is so wrong with the way I can't remember a damn thing."

"I—okay. Great, you know your assassin on a personal basis and can't remember why. You need some fresh air." Chase gently pushed me to the cave opening. He paused to nudge Avia. "You. Wake up."

"What the hell do you want?" she mumbled, turning over and covering her eyes.

Chase draped it over his shoulders, looking down at Avia. "Wake up, we need to leave before your sister loses her mind."

"What are you talking about? She lost it a long time ago."

I rolled my eyes and walked out of the cavern with Kaia.

The change of scenery in the valley we'd fallen into immediately grabbed my attention. It was magnificent in the rising Sun; fiery hues reflected on the steep, staggered rock walls and the tangerine-tinted lumbering firs. An eagle soared above the lake, swooping in and out of the mist from the waterfall, its feathers sparkling in the dawn's light. The crisp air was an aroma of fresh water and petrichor. The trees sparkled with dew and droplets while the sand glowed underneath the peeking Sun. Gentle lake waves caressed the shoreline as the water shifted with a tiny breeze. The valley sang with noise as the forest became a harmony of birdsong and humming, the waterfall crashing in the far distance. There wasn't snow on this part of the valley, perhaps at a lower elevation than surrounding peaks.

"Hey! Rieka, come look at this!"

Chase was pacing along the rocky wall when he stopped next to what looked to be another arch. I hurried over. Avia stared curiously at the cavern opening outlined by stones, holding a piece of rock in her hands. The arch was made of slabs inscribed in ancient Driksaal and Rurian—again. I looked over at Chase, who stepped forward to inspect the runic.

"Same thing as the arch on the East Trail," he said. "Restore and revive—"

"Chase," I interrupted him, "what did we learn last time about speaking ancient incantations?"

He nodded slowly, stepping back. "Yeah, you're right."

Kaia gave him a weird look. "Did you just read ancient Driksaal?"

"Mm, it's a Healer thing."

"Are you sure we should just approach foreign objects that quickly?" Kaia asked.

I shrugged. "Been doing it this whole time and we haven't died yet."

She pointed at Chase. "He is the *only* reason you guys are alive."

"Okay. So, do we go in here?" Avia asked.

"Do we have enough food and clothing to be able to survive for a few days?" Kaia said before Avia could rush in.

"Yeah, I checked last night. The freeze-dried packs didn't get wet. Also, I read a little bit in the book Atlas gave to us. There're underground rivers that run through these caves with fish," Chase said politely.

Without another word, Avia ducked under the archway into the tunnel in the rock wall. The rest of us followed suit.

Chapter 19

We began a trek through a cave system. The tunnels weren't uncomfortably small, and I found the cool temperature to be pleasant compared to the chill that had crept into my skin outside on the beach. Our walk was illuminated by a small flame Avia was careful to keep controlled in her hand as she marched forward. The air was damp and sticky with an underground humidity. The walls of the tunnel leading down into the cavern would touch my fingertips if I held both my hands out, the ceiling a couple of inches above Chase's head.

Besides the drumming of our footsteps against the slate floor, our travel was almost silent. Chase's heavy breathing was somewhat prominent alongside the distant crackling of Avia's tiny fire. The elevation in the mountains was taking a toll of my body. Time would only tell how long Avia could keep her magic strong until she exhausted herself, and we'd have to stop.

My veins burned again. I held my finger against my skin at the piercing sensation. My palms were itchy and dry, too, and it was almost as if I wanted to release all the built-up magic. There was no reason for me to, and I wasn't sure how to repress Zodiac Turning without blasting someone into the wall, or why I'd never struggled with the pain before.

In front of me, Chase reached out his arm, letting his fingertips brush against the slate walls. He rolled his shoulders and neck with a long breath in and out.

"These routes are special." My brain was itching with the history of the tunnels. "During the War of the Rebalancing, the Autarians carved escape routes for Zodiac Turners and Libran Healers in the mountains from pre-existing cave entries. Assidians discovered them and executed those traveling."

"There it is. I was waiting for you to start talking about something historical." Chase laughed at my sudden share of knowledge. He glanced back at Kaia. "She did this the entire way to Lyra."

"Rieka—how much do you know about all of this?" Kaia asked. "The Callexus, I mean."

"I was a training historian-in-training before all of this mess started." I pursed my lips. "I'm extremely familiar with mythology."

"Didn't Cancer play a role in that myth? It's been a while since I last heard someone talk about it."

"Kaia, *no*, you just asked the wrong person the wrong thing," Avia said with a deep sigh. "Please, no—"

"Yeah, Mathias was the guy who went on a mission from the God of the Sun to take immortality from Gardian and transfer it to the Callexus," I interrupted her. "His wife was a Cancer."

"I thought Mathias was supposed to be a Libran Healer." Chase asked. "Union Law?"

"He was. That's why they say that he became immortal as a punishment for breaking balance by marrying his wife. So, he became immortal, alongside the Callexus being created, and he later transferred his immortality to his son, Silas. Who is the author of the scroll we have."

Avia groaned. "Rieka—"

"Let her speak," Kaia snapped. "Silas is an immortal, and he wasn't just a myth, so he's still out there somewhere. Do we know his magic?"

"Nope. There's not much known about him in myth. He became immortal when he touched the Callexus and was punished with its immortality."

"What's the whole deal with immortality?"

"Imbalance," I continued. "Gardian turned into a mess when society revolved around the unchecked power behind immortality. Mathias was said to be instructed by the God of the Sun himself to rebalance Gardian by removing immortality with the Callexus. He performed some sort of holy ritual to transfer immortality from Gardian's magic system to the Callexus instead."

"I never fully believed in the three deities until recently." Chase glanced back at us. "Because what other explanation is there for that myth being real?"

"Oh, I've always believed," Kaia said quietly. "I've been drawn to the Moon my whole life. I feel like she watches over me. It's honestly comforting to know all of this."

"I still don't know about it," Avia added.

"What other explanation do you have for immortality being real?" I questioned her. "How would you explain the Callexus's existence in the first place without divine intervention? If immortality is real, the gods have to be."

"I don't know. I feel like we're missing something." She shrugged. "You tend to question everything, Rieka."

"Questioning everything is how I get answers," I said, staring off into the dark abyss.

"Well, we'll see if it's all true," Kaia paused in her walking as her fingers fell into grooves along the walls.

Avia turned her hand toward where Kaia was, illuminating the stone. Runic was painted like a mural, symbols blending into larger pictures of humans and magic. Chase paused to peer closer, Avia holding her hand next to him to provide him a light. Stories we didn't understand surrounded us, intricate paintings full of history and art that would take me years to decode.

Chase followed the writing with his index finger, narrowing his eyes while he walked forward. "Is that going to wear you down?"

All of us paused. I wasn't sure if he was talking to one of us, or the wall itself.

"Using your magic, Avia," he clarified. "What's your breaking point?"

"I don't really run out of energy," Avia said with another shrug.

"You will eventually. We should stop for the night," Chase insisted. "I'm concerned. You're still recovering from being thrown into a lake last night."

"You mean we should stop right here?" Kaia asked. "Kind of a strange resting point."

Chase looked over at Avia. "She's tired."

"I am *not*," Avia retorted.

"Your hands are trembling. I can barely read with your flame bouncing all over the place. Your non-flame hand is slick with sweat, considerable for someone who runs at a much higher temperature than all of us. You're also breathing heavily. You are most definitely tired, Avia."

"Okay, *doctor*," she said, and kept walking. "You're a healer, not a doctor. Let me remind you—doctors diagnose the problem, and you fix the diagnosed problem."

Chase hesitated. I exchanged a wary look with Kaia, and she opened her mouth as if she was going to say something. Chase reached forward, grabbing Avia's arms and spinning her around. I caught the look of shock on her face before the quick extinguishing of her flame. Darkness engulfed us.

"Listen, I'm sorry. This was the only way to get you to stop." Chase's voice echoed through the darkness. "We were *just* talking about the harms of invincibility. We all have weaknesses, including you and your fire. You *need* to rest, Avia. It's not an option. You know what's worse than admitting weakness? Passing out. And then you'll have me bleeding again."

The flame reignited in her hand. Chase held her arms tightly, unfazed by the sudden increase of heat in the tunnel. Her face was flushed red as she gave Chase a wild look, as if trying to discern what to do. He was right—Avia, who usually stepped all over him, needed a dose of her own medicine.

"Now," he said, "why don't you cast a stationary fire like you normally do, so you don't use up any more of your energy? Let me heal you."

Kaia leaned over to me. "She was read like a *book*."

"That's what he does," I quietly agreed. "He's pretty good at it."

Chase coaxed Avia to sit down, and she was silent as she faced her palm forward, sending a small, weaker-than-usual flame out into the open space for light and warmth. For the first time in a long time, Avia's vulnerability radiated in her flames as she listened to Chase. She reached into her bag and pulled her blanket out, draping it over herself. Chase sat next to her and helped with each action, while Kaia and I remained a distance away from them. Kaia gave me another look before she and I sat down a few feet from them.

Kaia messed with a water droplet between her hands. "Don't think I would like to be corrected by a healer."

"Me neither," I said, even though I most definitely had been attacked before by Chase's strong-willed health suggestions. Kaia drew a tiny stream of water from the humidity lingering on the ceiling above us. "Were you taught by anyone how to use your magic?"

She furrowed her brows. "Kind of. My older brothers were both Sagittarian fire mages, so I figured out a bunch of it on my own."

"Hold on, and your mom is the Libra Leader? With two Sagittarians, a Cancer, and a Scorpio? Where's your dad?"

"Get this, he's a Capricorn." She shook her head. "As far as I know, she's severed any connection to him. Quinn was a full sibling. The two Sagittarians are half-siblings. They're twins, eighteen years older than I am, and their dad was a Cancer. He died before I was born."

"I'm sorry, but how does the Libra Leader mess up *that* badly? She literally monitors the law; how did she get away with Capricorn and Cancer?"

"The Union Law makes it illegal to marry, not to fuck, and she's a Libra." Kaia paused, looking over at Chase to see if he was listening. She cleared her throat to get his attention. "They like to bang anyone who gives them the opportunity to do so."

She made aggressive eye contact with Chase. I lost it, wheezing with laughter. When he glared at her, she simply gave him an innocent smile.

"That was so personal," Chase said with a tone. "You barely know me."

"I know Libra." Kaia shrugged. "Just speaking the truth."

"Way to stereotype me."

"Yeah, okay." I snorted at Chase. He shook his head at me as he realized where I was about to go. "Robin was ripping into you about this exact thing."

He rolled his eyes at me and didn't respond.

I turned back to Kaia. "You're Cancer. You are nowhere near Conviction, let alone Capricorn. What happened?"

"I was cryptic. According to my brothers, she had no idea I existed until she was in labor. She's lucky I ended up as an Autarian and could be handed off to the Sagittarian twins."

I nodded. "I was also cryptic, I get it. Your other three siblings, though... why?"

"Quinn was supposed to be a Libra. She's the Libra Leader, and she has money, so I know damn well she had access to the right healers to induce an early birth with him. Or she could've straight up aborted any of the three of them. They weren't cryptic. But she didn't. Quinn was always trying to figure out the story behind that. It doesn't make sense."

"That's so strange." I bit the inside of my cheek. I didn't want to accidentally insult her or hurt her feelings. "Quinn was onto something, that sounds... intentional, does it not? Why would she willingly have a Scorpio and two Sagittarians?"

"Your best guess is mine. All I know is that all four of us were preventable, but for some reason, that fact was ignored."

"I'm sorry, Kaia."

She gave me a gentle smile. "It's okay. That's why I'm here. Maybe in the process of wrecking the Scorpio Stellarium, I can answer the questions he had about our mom's intentions."

I admired the sheer amount of patience she had. I could learn from her emotional maturity, her lack of reactivity. She'd lived with impulsive Sagittarians, and I grew up alongside an Aries with anger issues. Kaia understood the complexities of being out of place in a family unit.

I looked over at Chase in the middle of our conversation, half expecting him to join, but he was completely distracted with Avia. His hand rested on her skin, his golden magic drifting from his palm into her arm. The space was lit with a warm, sparkling golden light. Avia leaned back against the wall, relaxed by the sensation.

It wasn't until Chase hesitantly pulled his hand away from her that her eyes snapped open, and she shoved him away. She moved next to my side instead. Chase frowned, his eyes glinting with hurt. Kaia stood up and sat back down next to him, cheerfully greeting him so he would perk back up. We all spent a few minutes eating canned food in quiet conversation between Chase and Kaia. It wasn't much, but it was enough to feed us and ease my anxiety.

Chase and Kaia were the first to lie down and close their eyes. Chase's spaced-out breaths told me he was asleep, and Kaia's movement fell still between gentle breathing. Avia sat, wide awake, eyes focused on her fire. I rubbed at my skin as my magic's burning sensation returned.

Avia scooched closer to me. "Not good."

I raised a brow at her.

"I hate vulnerability," she said.

"That's surprising."

For the first time, I saw my sister cry. Guilt struck me, and I immediately swallowed my words. Tears welled up at the edges of her eyes, and she trembled, the heat surrounding her diminishing.

She closed her eyes, as if looking away from Chase would help. I would've never expected her to admit vulnerability so easily.

"It's okay," I finally said to Avia. "At least you're allowed to let those emotions out, legally."

"I wish it was easier than legality," Avia said.

"Everything I'm doing here is illegal. I'm one tenet away from breaking the entire Scorpio Code."

"Sounds like an accomplishment, if you ask me." My sister flashed me a half-smile. "But I guess you've never had any kind of romantic feelings toward anyone. As far as I know."

Yeah, as far as she knew. The emotion I'd felt when Narah's hand followed my jawline to adjust a mask said otherwise.

"One thing I've found, Rieka... love is encouraged among Aries. We don't fear heartbreak, we don't fear others," Avia continued when I didn't respond. I let her continue chattering away. I was used to the one-sided conversations with her. "You know, I've fallen in love before. It's kind of fun, and it hurts when it fails, but it's nothing to fear. The Aries guy I was in a relationship with last year, the one who shattered my heart. He was so pretty. Sometimes I still miss him."

"He really wasn't that pretty," I disagreed with a small laugh, shaking my head.

"Okay, Rieka. I can't think of a single time you've agreed with me about a man being attractive. I don't trust your word."

"Probably because I'm not attracted to them."

"What?" Avia's face lit up with surprise. "That was the first time you've admitted that so confidently."

I shrugged. "I have my reasons."

"Reasons related to the way you keep staring at someone who wants to kill you?"

"I don't think she actually wants to kill me," I corrected her. Avia did a double take at me when I failed to deny the accusation. "Did you hear any part of the conversation that Kaia and I had last night on the beach?"

"No, I was too distracted by him." Avia motioned with her head to Chase, who was knocked out on the floor. "If you want to explain anything, though, I'll listen."

I smiled. "I do, actually."

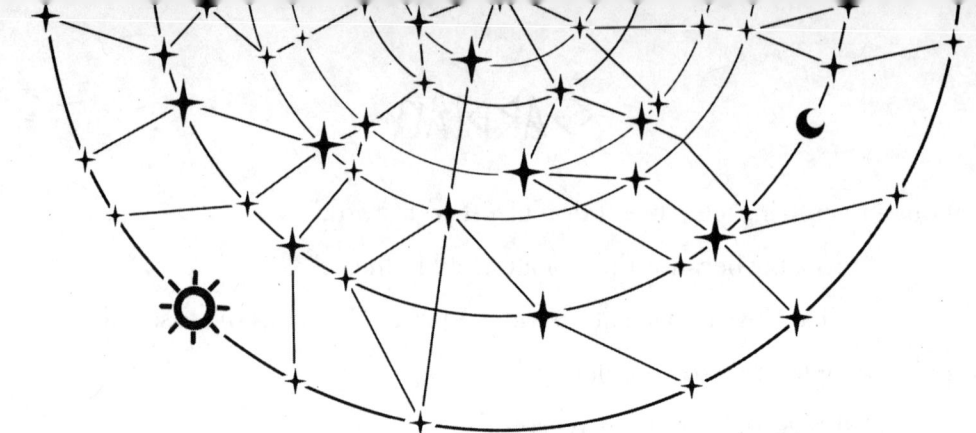

CHAPTER 20

After a long day of traveling through dark caverns with an ease of tension in the group, we stepped into a large cavern.

The cave was much larger than any chamber we'd yet entered. A small stream coursed through the middle of the floor, dividing the space in half. A few towering rock formations jutted from the wall, intruding upon the otherwise empty space. The ceiling was maybe a story high, rounded and curved, while some areas looked to be dipping down from the pressure of the earth above. The sound of distant rushing water echoed from where the stream disappeared into the walls. A cooler breeze caused goosebumps to rise on my skin.

"Finally," Avia said, heading straight toward the stream, "*real* food."

"I assume we're done traveling for today?" Kaia said, placing her pack down. "It looks safe enough to me."

"It's more comfortable than the tunnels," Chase pointed out, watching Avia as she dove her hands into the stream. "Thought you didn't like water?"

She was kneeling at the creek's edge when he approached. "I don't, but hunger triumphs over fear."

Kaia held her hands out to the creek. With the motion of her fingers, a glob of water with a fish plopped directly into Avia's hands. Avia didn't waste a minute to kill it.

Chase cringed and shielded his eyes. "God, do you have to *burn* it to death?"

She looked up with a cheeky smile, holding it out to him. "It's cooked now. You want it?"

I sat down on the slate ground next to them, resting my muscles. My limbs burned with the pent-up magic beginning to make its presence stronger in my body. It was progressively becoming more difficult to fall asleep at night with the annoying sensation caused by the overabundance of power.

Chase must've noticed my whitened grip on my arms. "Do you need help with that?"

I considered it.

"No," I decided, "I should learn how to manage it myself."

"Would it help you to shapeshift something?" Kaia suggested.

"I tried last night. Didn't help much."

Avia sat down next to us, placing the dead fish in front of her. She held out her palm, sparking a floating fire in front of us, much more vivid and alive with the full night's rest. I leaned toward the warmth, breathing in the homey smell of river fish and my sister's smoky magic. Chase rubbed his arms, as if hugging himself, protecting his own emotions. A stance I recognized far too well.

We ate in silence. My exhaustion was catching up to me as I laid down while the other three had a conversation I was too tired to listen to. I fell asleep, leaving my magic to ebb in my arms.

Dread consumed me as all my senses all slammed into me at once—the smell of musty walls in an older school building in the Hub, the voice of the monotonous Scorpio teacher who I hated, the sound of some other kid snoring in the back of a near-silent classroom. I so badly wanted it to be a nightmare, but I knew when the door flew open and two Scorpio officials stormed into the room, it was a forgotten memory.

I stood up instantly, expecting them to run toward me. I'd lost count of how many times I'd broken the Code, so often that I'd already prepared for the day the Stellarium would ambush me. Instead, they set their sights on Narah, who was sitting in front of the class. Before she had enough time to defend herself, one of the men grabbed her arms and forced them behind her back, his hand tightening around her wrists.

Fury struck me within seconds.

I threw my chair behind me. Both officials snapped their gazes toward me. They'd hurt me before, time after time again, but hurting her invoked a new level of anger I had no idea I was even capable of feeling.

My fingers curled into fists. "Let her *go*."

Furious magic surged through me in an instant, unfamiliar to the typical control I withheld over my Zodiac Turning. An ancient anger unleashed itself at the way her hands went pale from the Stellarium members cutting off her circulation at her wrists. My veins lit up with a white light. I didn't resist it, bristling at the officials as they watched me with expressionless faces.

"You have no idea what I am." I threw a foot onto my desk and stepped on top of it. I was done with their manipulation. I lived through their shit my whole life, but going after Narah? I'd made a promise to her. "I will fucking *destroy* you."

The entire class went silent in shock. I was losing it. Insane, like they always told me. Mom would murder me once she heard of my outburst, but I was too exhausted from cowering to care. Magic surged through me, stronger than it ever had before, brighter, viscous enough to wash my vision with a pale red glow. I broke into a coughing fit, as if the power was suffocating me.

"Rieka." Tears streamed down Narah's cheeks. "Stop."

I knew she would've defended me in the same way. I held up my hands. A white light consumed them, daring to burst through my fingertips. A primordial, primitive sensation of protection ran through me.

I jumped off the desk, and in a frenzy, charged the official holding Narah back. I instinctually rolled my fingers into a fist and aimed for the man's chest. A burst of light escaped from my fist in the form of a zodiac wheel, slamming into the man's chest and throwing him into the wall. The other official caught me, dragging me out of the room to the hallway. I fought back with everything I had left in me, kicking and screaming until my voice cracked and my throat went raw.

Narah bolted after us, trying to drag me back to the classroom. I caught the sheer desperation and panic reflecting in her eyes as she grasped my hand, mouthing something to me. She was afraid to say it out loud. Tears blurred my vision.

"Enough!" the man yelled, turning around to us.

I spat at him. "You think beating the shit out of me is something new to me? Get your hands off me, now."

"Do you think I am an idiot, child?" he snapped, dragging Narah and me to the office we'd first met in. He opened the door, shoving both of us in, and slammed it behind us. "You have always known the archpower, yes?"

I threw his hand off my arm. "Wouldn't you like to know?"

"Who taught you this?" he roared, slapping me across the face.

I retaliated, shoving my knee in between his legs. He buckled at the knees with a gasp at the unexpected backlash, and I grabbed the collar of his shirt, dragging him down to my level with a screech. I met his eyes, my magic roaring within my body in that same moment; the Stellarium had brewed the perfect storm within me.

"I won't be your echo. I won't be a mother to children you breed from us. I won't fall underneath the Stellarium's control, and *nothing* you can do will ever take that away from me," I snarled. "I won't be your bitch."

Though I was smaller than him, my anger fed my strength. I screamed as I threw him to the floor by the collar of his shirt. The Stellarium supervisor, who sat at the desk, usually unbothered by the way the officials treated me, jumped to his feet and grabbed both of my shoulders before I could go after him, too.

The official on the floor stared at me with the most vengeance I'd ever seen in another human's eyes. I kicked him again as the supervisor threw me against the wall. I shrank underneath his shadow as he inched his face closer to mine, his warm breath on my skin.

Narah, who I could see only out of the corner of my eye, hadn't said a word as she quivered with terror. She was frozen in place, too afraid to make the wrong move and agonize me as a consequence. She couldn't, so I would. I met the eyes of the supervisor with spite, hardening my gaze as I twisted my wrists to wrap my glowing fingers around his arm. He hissed at the sharp sting and quickly moved to pin me against the wall by my forearms instead.

"They are both Turners," the official said through gritted teeth.

"Are they now?" The supervisor tilted his head at me. "How peculiar."

"Additionally, Spring violated all three tenets of the Code," the official continued, scrambling to stand as he reached for Narah and held her in place. "She does not learn. I will leave her punishment to you."

He tilted his head at me in consideration. "Physical pain no longer aids in learning, does it?"

"Never has," I said through gritted teeth. "What are you gonna do, kill me?"

He smiled. It was the first time I'd seen someone from the Scorpio Stellarium express emotions.

"Perhaps." He glanced over at Narah, who tried to struggle again when he met her gaze. "But why would I do that, when I could watch you conform instead? A Pisces-Aries Turner could be of great use to us. I thank you for giving her to us."

My heart dropped. Horror rushed across Narah's expressions.

"You will not disobey," the supervisor started as he reached to his belt, unsheathing a lengthy blade, "if you cannot remember your reason to do so."

When I looked over at Narah, I wanted nothing more than to run to the Woods like we normally did, don our masks, and escape from the

Stellarium's wrath. I should've known—there was no true escape from a system we were forced to rely on. No matter how many times we thought we were safe in Conviction Woods, we'd always have to return to the Hub for sustenance, resources, education; the cycle would continue each time we ran away from it.

The supervisor shoved the tip of his blade up to my neck. I leaned my head back to avoid the pressure. It was the first time they'd involved knives in a punishment.

He looked to Narah. "Summon your magic."

The official holding Narah dug his grip into her sides, causing her to flinch with an outcry. Her entire body shivered as she gagged at the official's tightening grasp. She attempted to break free of her captor, screaming from the depths of her chest, but she was no match for a man double her size; we were only kids.

"Do it!" the supervisor yelled. I gasped as the tip of the knife poked my skin. "*Now*, or I'll kill her!"

Her Turning was already active in her veins from the panic. She sobbed as she shoved her fist out. The magic in her veins took seconds to form a wheel of light, making her writhe in pain from the forced Turning. An inhuman, agonized groan escaped her throat as the magic burned her hand from holding the wheel in front of her.

"Use it on yourself now," the supervisor commanded. "Gemini-Cancer."

"No, *please*, I can't do this," Narah begged them as she desperately maintained the wheel. "I can't hurt her."

"Very well."

The blade slowly pierced into my skin. I felt the warmth of blood slide down my neck. Narah screeched, immediately spinning the wheel to Gemini-Cancer. Narah was shoved forward by the official, throwing her in front of me while stepping on her back to keep her down. The supervisor pulled the tip of the blade out of my neck.

The supervisor tossed the blade in front of Narah as she was held with a boot close to the floor. Her eyes followed it as it clattered on the stone floor, sprinkling my blood on her face.

"I will force you to shove that blade into her throat if you do not summon the secondary magic."

She had no choice but to listen. They'd threatened my life to gain her as a weapon. An unfamiliar blue magic covered her skin in a wave of light. Both Stellarium members yanked her to her feet, twisting her arms as they each grasped a wrist activated with a raging sapphire glow.

"Kira," Narah forced out between sobs, "I'm so sorry, I love you."

The two officials pushed her hands to my arms before I could repeat it back to her.

The magic burned through me, as if the water in my body had been evaporated all at once, setting my organs on fire. I coughed wildly, tears gathering in the corners of my eyes at the immense agony and immediate fog consuming my thoughts. I held my anger at the top of it all, the indomitable spirit they were trying to take from me, and in that moment, I swore to myself I would never let them steal my emotions. I would devote my life to personally see the downfall of each and every single Scorpio Stellarium member who dared to try to silence me.

A blue-black light consumed each cell of my being. Somehow, despite the sinking darkness that washed over my body and stilled my body, my anger survived; thrived, even, from my Turning. It was fighting the erasure, saving a part of myself, a part of my fury to unlock later. I understood the love I couldn't describe nor forget, surging through my body as it triumphed over her magic stealing away my experiences. I promised myself I'd remember Narah, recognize her familiarity—they could not take my fury or my feelings.

Rage.

Rage, that was it. An anger so spiteful, ever consuming and furious; stronger than any magic that could ever touch me. I would bite the hand that chained me. I would snap the links until my hands were raw, until my fangs were stained with their blood. I would be the voice with my Zodiac Turning as some sort of blessing. I had the power and strength to *fight*. To ignore the call would be to hush the howl escaping from my lips, the hunger for justice that inherently existed within me through the balance my magic craved.

With balance came the chaos, and I would be its conduit.

CHAPTER 21

I snapped out of the memory and back into the cavern. Without even punching my fist out or sitting up, my arm released a burst of light into a zodiac wheel above my body. My hand slipped when I tried to send it to the ground beside me. In the process, I lost complete control as it spun, settling from Libra to Scorpio. The force of its energy slammed into me, leaving me struggling to take in my next few breaths. I shielded my face as electrical particles exploded around me. With each contact of light to skin, it felt as if a tiny needle stung me.

A yell echoed through the cavern. Chase, who had jumped up at my aggressive actions, was immediately knocked to the floor by the energy released from my body. The glow of my Turning surrounded his body, sinking into him.

I'd changed his sign.

Avia lunged forward. She placed two fingers on the back of his neck and bent down close to his face to feel if he was breathing. Pain spiraled up my hands, through my arms, into my core, like a poison from my own body. My breaths were raspy, my vision dotted with black spots as I tried to watch

Avia.

"Is he alive?" Panic rippled through Kaia's expressions as Avia failed to find a pulse on his neck. She leaned her head against his chest and placed two fingers on his wrist. A tense silence blanketed us. His eyes were shut, mouth slightly open as his chest shuddered with an attempt to breathe.

Avia finally yanked her head up. "He's alive. He's breathing and has a pulse."

The realization of the pain I'd put him through struck me. Tears welled up at the sides of my eyes as a cold terror washed over me. The scars from my past seared on my back as I breathed in and out, as if that would stop my instinct from controlling me. My hands trembled as I held them up, the same hands from when I was a child clawing at the ground for mercy. My emotions hurt someone I only wanted to protect. Chase was innocent, and just when I began to understand the storm of my emotions, I instead cast my pain upon him.

"Wake up," Avia said, bending over Chase. "I can't tell if you're in pain."

His head moved and his lips twitched before he went limp again. Avia threw a leg over him, grabbing his cloak to try to wake him up with the intensifying temperature from her fear. Chase finally groaned and moved his head to the side, fingers twitching as he began to regain his consciousness.

"You're too warm," he grunted, turning his head away from her. "Get off of me."

She moved to the side. Kaia summoned a splash of cool water in her palms and spread it across his forehead. His breaths were dramatic and spaced apart. As I tried to focus on him, reality drifted away from me. I stood still, staring at the tunnel we'd come from.

I should've been dead the day my memory was taken from me.

"Rieka," Kaia's weary voice cut through my realizations as I fought against my crying, and at last, found triumph in the numbness swallowing any reasoning left within me. "This isn't your fault. You don't know how to control it."

Chase groaned as Avia tried to help him sit up.

"It is," I said, my voice evenly toned. "It *is* my fault."

Kaia hurried over to me, placing a hand on my shoulder. I flinched as dizziness contorted my perceptions, my consciousness jumping between the cavern and the office. I lost sight of the distinction between the past and present.

"What caused this?" she asked gently. "Did you have a nightmare?"

"Get *away* from me!" I yelled. Shock spread across Kaia's face as she quickly stepped back. She was afraid of me. "They should've killed me that day. I was supposed to have a knife through my throat."

Chase hoisted himself up with one arm. "Rieka, stop. What's going on?"

I slowly stepped away from them, reaching for my throat to feel the scar on my neck. When I drew my hand away, there was no blood on my fingers; I was a year older. I could remember, so clearly, the hot stickiness of fresh blood against my skin.

"I'm okay, Rieka, and it really *isn't* your fault," Chase insisted. "Scorpio has taught you to repress emotions, and now they're manifesting through a magic system that you couldn't help being born with."

I shook my head, turning around to run for the tunnels. My ears rang as the world spun and contorted. The voices calling my name faded as

I forced myself up the one-way tunnel. When I was shrouded in complete darkness, safe from any sights or sounds, I allowed my shaking knees to give out, falling against the wall.

I was surrounded, protected, shielded by the familiar unknown. I couldn't hurt or be hurt. The scars on my back and neck were throbbing and torn apart, freshly opened with the emotions I'd tried so hard to repress.

I sobbed, my fingers tangling in my hair as I gasped in breaths like they were my last. My memory came alive again, vivid against the black canvas of the darkness, a hallucination haunting me of the splatters of my blood on Narah's face. The cavern air filled with the stench of the school, of lantern fire and old chalk. Then it was the supervisor's rancid breath on my face and Mom's floral perfume when she got close to scream at me.

I held my head at the thought of Mom. Mom, who would rant about the Scorpio Code, yet reprimanded me each time she learned I broke it at school. She didn't mind when I smiled and laughed with Dad and Avia but wouldn't talk to me for days after I was punished at school. Her energy toward me was that of indifference and displeasure, yet obligation and necessity.

I could see it in my father's eyes when he looked at Mom, the complexity of betrayal. He understood Mom treated me unfairly, but he had a drive to protect his family, enough to stay quiet about how she'd changed since he'd met her. Dad had always been my comfort, my defender. He'd kept his arms open for me, a solace from the cruel outside world, a constant against the bloody society I was forced into from birth.

My fingers scraped against my scalp as tears slid down my face. My entire body burst into a series of nervous shivers as my hands moved from my head to my arms. I dug my nails into my skin to try to feel anything, pressing my back into the wall.

Show no emotions; I wasn't supposed to be crying. Why was I crying? It was the reason they punished me. I was weak, exposing myself as a kid. I'd never learned my lesson, allowing my emotions to prevail over my strength. My whole life had been a fight for control that I'd never even gotten close to touching.

I curled myself into a ball, breathing slowly to ease my shivering. My exhaustion from panic and magic usage numbed me, lulling me to fall asleep in the darkness and silence.

In my rest, my wish came true. I was home again amongst the aroma of pine sap and the sound of footsteps against moss. As soon as I recognized the hyperrealism of the dream, I identified it as a memory.

At the boundaries of the Hub, the magic of Conviction Woods was alive. Fireflies buzzed around trees with a distant glow and hum of golden magic while particles like floating stars danced amongst the needles of the pines. The ground illuminated with every step I took, a reflection of the full Moon spreading its light amongst the aromatic forest. At my side was Narah, traveling with me through the thick of the Woods on a path we'd traveled numerous times. She must've been around fifteen, possibly younger, but I wasn't entirely sure.

"Are you sure he left for a couple of days?" I asked Narah, my voice riddled with concern. "I don't want him to hurt you.

"*Yes*, Kira, for the last time, that is why the bastard put a week-long curse on me to keep me in the damn Woods. I genuinely thought I was dying when I stepped out of the boundaries earlier to test it, couldn't see or hear a damn thing outside the Woods."

I huffed, shaking my head at her. "He's an asshole."

"At least he left me with food. I wasn't expecting that."

"I'll stay with you as much as possible while he's gone," I reassured her. "My family's used to me disappearing into the Woods. They know I'm safe. They won't question a thing."

"At least two days without him beating me up, and I get to be with you constantly?" she said with a broad smile. "That sounds like *torture*."

I laughed at her sarcasm. She stopped walking to grab my shoulders, and I froze at her touch. She reached her hand to my face, smiling. Her thumb gently brushed my cheek, and I leaned into the touch as a sprouting warmth. My magic jumped to life at the same time as Narah's, just like I'd trained it to do. The two of us were only getting better at the control we had over our Turning.

She took my hand, guiding me forward through the Woods until we found the clearing that we'd scouted out earlier in the week. Artifacts scattered around from ages prior, stones with etched ancient Driksaal creating a circle in the trees that we had stepped into. Though it was dark, I could see perfectly with the warm light of Conviction Woods buzzing around us, as if it was welcoming us into the space.

Narah let her bag slide off her shoulders and tilted it upside down to empty it of the numerous blankets she stuffed into the travel backpack. I threw mine down with a huff at its weight, unpacking it to add to her pile of cushion. Narah flopped down onto the pile while I stood above her with a smile. She reached up to grab my leg, pulling me down to her. I yelped as she caught me, my back falling against her chest as she wrapped her arms around me with a laugh. I lost my breath, and not because it was knocked out of me; it was taken from me.

"You could've given me a warning," I said as I tried to wiggle away. She held me in place. I already knew I had no chance of escaping. I'd lost to her strength many times before. "What's the plan?"

"I read something new the other day about magic in the Woods during the full Moon," she said, her voice vibrating against my back. "Figured this would be a good time to try it."

"Sure." I sat up when her grip loosened. "What about it?"

"Vascular connection allows for an attachment between two arch-powered individuals and opens a psychological connection." Narah crossed her legs as she got comfortable on the blankets. "It's enhanced in the Woods and let alone enhanced with the Moon. Couldn't entirely figure out why that was the case, though."

"Sounds cool." I offered my hands to her without hesitation. "Let's do it."

"Are you ready?" She asked as she straightened her back. She threw her hair over her shoulders. "Do you trust me?"

"As always, of course."

She held her hands upright on each of her knees, her palms illuminating with her Turning. It spread up her arms in a flash like blue lightning, striking through her body within seconds. I held my own hands out, allowing my light to run through my veins, slowly, gently, to prevent the feeling of setting my own body on fire. Narah reached her hands out, meeting my gaze with a smile. I returned her eye contact, and without hesitation, I set my palms over her own.

Our magic exploded in a furious buzz, aggressively illuminating both of our bodies in a screaming, energetic connection. Narah's fingers tightened around my hands, and the surroundings began to blur and darken, as if the magic was rapidly entrapping us in our own dimension. Yet, my body remained eerily calm as white light pulsated through my veins and hers, jumping to and from each of us as it balanced its flow between two souls. The air smelled of blood and smoke and flora, of a distant thunderstorm approaching and a searing forest fire. A harmonious hum emanated from our hands where the forces were centered.

As I looked at Narah, feelings arrived and departed in a flow of gentle waves. I would identify them to feel them fade into the light of our bodies. Any anxieties or worries washed away into the abyss surrounding us. If Narah had an emotion that arose, it was quietly echoed into my own spirit. In this space—our space—nothing else existed but the two of us, entrapped in the stream of ethereally calm magic and emotion, frozen in a moment of time.

As I focused on what we each felt, I caught a commonality in emotion: love itself as an essence, as a warmth, as a fire. It was the strength of the force behind each of us, fueling the magic we both harnessed, calling in the gentle temperance as we balanced on the line of chaos and power and peace.

My eyes settled on Narah's illuminated figure. Her white hair almost sparkled in the moonlight, her sharp facial features accented by the glow in her body. I was entranced, and it only sent another wave of magic exchange between us. She caught the surge, mirrored in herself. Her hands tightened around mine.

"If they catch us," I realized, "they can't take our magic, it'll remember our emotions."

"And that, Kira, is why they are so scared of it."

Narah's grip loosened on my hands, slowly letting them go. I pulled my own back. A release of magic sprinted through me, spilling out of our bodies in an aura of white light. A shockwave spread through the magical circle, lighting each and every runic stone. The hum in the trees enhanced, magic particles exploded in the circle as it throbbed with a balance of power. I felt the equilibrium settle within myself, as if the Woods *craved* the balance of magic between us. As if the Woods *needed* our magic.

I was far more connected to Conviction Woods than I had ever imagined; it granted me protection, and I granted it power. It was somehow deeply intertwined with magic, not only within Narah and me, but within Gardian as a whole. Conviction Woods was a sacred space desperate for balance, and I was a constituent of its balance.

Narah's power enhanced mine. It made my head turn, spin, as I brainstormed all the ways in which I could learn the secrets of Conviction Woods. I found my mind still with peace.

CHAPTER 22

"Rieka. Wake up."

I groaned as my limbs instantly burned. Sweat dripped down my forehead as I lurched away from a light, wincing in retaliation from the brightness.

Kaia kneeled, her hands on my shoulders as she shook me awake. "Hey, you."

"Rieka." Chase stood in front of me. "Look, you didn't hurt me."

I squinted at him, blinking slowly to let my eyes adjust to a white light illuminating in his body. To my relief, Avia was nowhere to be seen. Chase offered me a hand, and without hesitation, I took it. He pulled me up into his embrace, and I latched onto him instantly. Any previous fear surrounding physical contact with him vanished at my desperation for comfort.

"I'm so sorry," I whispered, trying to stop my body from bursting into a bout of shivering.

"Breathe, Rieka. I promise, I'm not mad at you. Things happen. Archpowers are hard to control, I get it," he spoke softly. "Let's sit down.

You're unstable on your feet."

As nervousness consumed me, Chase coaxed me to sit back down, Kaia shuffling to my side. My veins lit white from my fear, and at Chase's touch, they intensified. The electricity buzzing through me was racing through him, too, the same magic, an absence of his typical golden glow.

"So," he said carefully, "don't freak out when I tell you this, but you turned my sign to Scorpio."

"I know," I said, my voice hoarse. "I'll change it back. I just need a minute."

"There's absolutely no need to rush," he said. "We can take all day if needed. I can give you far more than just a minute."

I reached toward his glow, touching his skin lightly, but snapped my hand back when the energy instantly transferred from him to me. My fingertips stung with the magic absorbed. I looked up at Chase slowly as I realized what that meant.

He gave me a half-smile. "Well, I can't be a Libran Healer if I'm not a Libra, can I?"

I stared at him. "You've got to be kidding me."

"It started last night, but he recovered just fine," Kaia explained. "We made Avia stay back so she couldn't be loud and interrupt you. I can leave, too, if you want to be alone with Chase."

Meeting Kaia's eyes in the dim light, I wasn't sure how to express the appreciation I had for the two of them, their understanding and patience far beyond anything I'd ever experienced before. Without the pressure of my sister laughing at me for being uncomfortable with my own emotions, I felt a surge of trust with the two of them, and within me I found the courage to speak my weakness, because perhaps, just maybe, it meant that I was getting stronger.

"No, please stay," I said quietly, shrinking back into the wall. "Thank you."

"Of course." Kaia stretched her arms out. "You don't need to thank us. We were worried about you. None of this was your fault, really."

"It was, though."

"Stop telling yourself that. You had absolutely no control over that situation."

"I can't believe how many emotions you must feel all at once," Chase said, crossing his ankles. "As a Scorpio, I mean. Everything feels so much more intense."

"I'm sorry," I apologized again, "really, Chase—"

"Rieka." He tilted his chin down to consider me. "You don't need to keep apologizing. I'm totally fine. I know that you'll turn my sign back, yeah?"

"Yeah." My voice split as tears gathered in my eyes. "I'm so afraid of hurting you. What if I hurt you again getting you back to Libra?"

"That's why we're here. You don't need to be alone," Kaia reassured me. "We're going to stay right here, in this tunnel with you, for the rest of the day, or as long as you want us here. If we need to go sign by sign, we can do that. No obligations, no pressure. It's just us and the cave."

"We're not mad, Rieka. Friends would never be mad at what you're going through." Chase paused. "Also, I might be able to help you out to make it less painful."

He held out his arms, closing his eyes. The white light amplified in his body, first emanating from his chest, then slithering through his arms in one fluid motion. The magic smelled strongly of Conviction pine and smoke, not as metallic as his typical healing, and instead carrying aromatics closer to what filled the air after I used my magic.

"I haven't tested it by punching out my fist, and I don't have any intention to, but I'm fairly certain this might be Zodiac Turning." Chase pressed his palms together. I was in awe at his control over the magic that burned through my body. "I am a Scorpio right now, and if I carry the genetics for Libran Healing, I'm assuming there could've been a Zodiac Turner somewhere in my family. Quite honestly, I'm really starting to doubt everything my dad told me about my mother."

"But you've never felt Zodiac Turning before." I shook my head. "How are you in control of it?"

Chase shrugged. "Well, I've been regulating my healing for quite some time, so I am fairly familiar with keeping an archpower under control. It feels softer and less painful than my healing, actually."

Kaia rested a hand on my shoulder. "He's a Libra. Their whole thing is neutrality and balance."

Chase tilted his hand around, observing as the light throbbed in his veins, swiveling with his skin. There was no mistaking the obnoxiously bright light, especially in the sign of Scorpio, from someone who was born as a Libran Healer. He held his hand to me, and carefully, I set my palm on top of his. I flinched as the magic spread from his body to mine, wincing as I anticipated the typical pain, but instead found relief in the intensity.

I'd seen it happen in the memory: the ability for Zodiac Turners to balance each other, reaching for an equilibrium of magical exchange between two bodies. I closed my eyes to interpret the magic flowing from Chase—calm, *impressively* calm, and neutral. Instead of a strong positive or negative emotion, Chase held a neutral serenity.

"Was it a flashback?" Kaia asked.

I opened my eyes to look over at her, tilting my head. "What do you mean?"

"After you turned his sign, I could tell you weren't with us. You looked like you were distant and touched the scar on your neck," she explained. "I have them, too."

I absentmindedly reached to my neck again. "It was a memory."

"Ah, that's why we couldn't wake you up. We couldn't when you were on the boat reliving a memory, either." Chase's hand remained on mine in an exchange of magic, as if he and Kaia had planned how to approach me together, using Chase's new magic to keep me stabilized. "You were screaming in your sleep right before your Turning activated. We're here to listen."

"I had my memory erased." I swallowed hard, closing my eyes with a wince. The shared magic encouraged me. "I'm not sure when, or how, but they'd caught me breaking the Code."

"With..." Kaia trailed off, too afraid to suggest something that could trigger me again.

"They held a knife to my throat and threatened my life to force her to change her own sign. There was some sort of magic in Gemini-Cancer I didn't recognize. They put her hands on my arms, and then it was all gone."

I omitted Narah's last words to me, swallowing as I faced the truth of the fact. For the very first time, I felt what I immediately knew to be heartbreak.

Chase caught it within the shared magic. "Look at me."

I could barely look up at him, my body shaking.

"You don't need to tell us about all the details," Chase said. "Stop thinking about the thing that's bothering you. Let it go."

His chest rose and fell as he took a deep breath. I found myself doing the same at the wave of calm energy. The pain eased, the sense fading, and I was back into the moment. The magic between us amplified as I rebalanced my emotions back to his steady calm. He nodded confidently at the notion.

"You can't blame yourself for whatever happened," Kaia said. "I obviously don't know the extents of it all, but it sounds like there is absolutely nothing that you did to warrant the pain that the Stellarium put you through."

"We figured Avia might've not been super helpful in this situation," Chase said. "Had to force her to stay back."

My muscles relaxed. "Thank you."

"I wasn't exactly treated the nicest either," Kaia said calmly. "I'm the daughter of a Convictionist Leader. I was an outcast. I understand, Rieka, and I understand the vengeance in you to tear that damn Stellarium apart."

"What you went through your entire childhood was traumatic, Rieka," Chase added. "You are *bound* to struggle with your emotions. I don't want you to feel like you have to hide them from us. It'll only make your magic harder to control, yeah?"

I nodded.

"Besides, look what I learned from you turning my sign," Chase said, his eyes flickering back down to his hand and mine, still held together in the exchange of magic. "Is this helping at all?"

I nodded. "It's like an equilibrium. I can't feel anything intense."

"I understand with my whole heart, the terror you must be feeling with this," Chase continued. "When I first felt my healing, I was left confused and traumatized for weeks. Its onset burned me until I healed a dying animal in the Woods. When you turned my sign, I'll tell you this much—it didn't even come close to the pain from the onset of my healing, if that makes you feel any better."

I breathed out slowly, letting my shoulders ease.

"Are you comfortable trying to turn my sign?" Chase asked, and I met his gaze with confidence. "I can tell you're feeling balanced and relaxed. Now might be the time."

"We are *right* here for you, Rieka," Kaia reassured me.

After finding balance amongst the shared Zodiac Turning, I separated my hand from Chase's, letting my gaze fall upon him while my hand still lit up with magic. While sitting, I punched my fist out gently, and in return, a burst of energy shoved me against the wall. The immediate burning began, but Chase didn't even seem to react to the zodiac wheel illuminating in front of him. I quickly grabbed it with my other hand, and with all the strength I could muster, I twisted it from Scorpio to Sagittarius. Kaia's grasp on my shoulder tightened. I gasped in agony. I had to keep going.

With a sharp breath in, I twisted the wheel quickly, stopping it as it reached Libra. I slammed my hands down. The wheel exploded into light with a piercing screech. I shouted and ducked, holding my hands over my ears and protecting my vision as black spots dampened my eyesight. The breath was knocked out of me and I started to wildly cough to attempt to resolve the burning sensation in my chest. Chase wheezed, leaning back against the other wall. The tunnel's light diminished as particles danced. Kaia placed her other hand on my other shoulder, directly facing me.

"Look at me. Breathe, slowly," she said loudly as the ringing in my ears amplified. "You've got this. I promise."

I blinked rapidly to erase the darkness seeping through my consciousness, fighting the feeling of knives diving into my skin. Chase's arms immediately illuminated with his familiar golden magic. While still gasping in breaths and trembling, he reached forward toward me to stabilize my reaction. Kaia grabbed his arm to stop him before he knocked himself out trying to help me.

Both of them froze.

A ripple of a sapphire magic raced through her veins, spreading across the surface of her arm as a transparent aura of a night sky coated her skin. Light clouded her vision before she blinked it away. Stars flickered on a blue gradient second-skin, concentrated most where she grasped onto Chase's forearm. Their magic remained in an equilibrium at their physical contact. His healing brightened as it reversed back through his veins and up his arm, shrouding his own skin with a new pale golden glow.

A flash of light burst around the three of us, and my strained lungs opened up, the painful sensation of my magic instantly easing. A low, harmonious humming resonated through the space, and the air filled with the fragrance of a powerful, indescribable floral.

"Um," Chase started, too afraid to move his body. "Care to explain what's happening?"

She appeared to be just as shocked as he was. "I have no idea."

They looked over at me, as if I knew anything.

"Why the hell would I know?"

"You're the historian," Chase said quietly, as if his voice would disrupt the connection of power. "I know absolutely nothing about whatever this is. Kaia, you've never experienced this before?"

"No, I swear, this is new to me." She shook her head slowly, eyes wide. I could tell from the shock written across her face that she was being honest. "I'm a water mage."

"Yeah, I'm not so sure of that." Chase said, looking down at the blue magic, then back up at her. "I've done a shit ton of research on Libran Healing and, as far as I'm aware, other magic systems don't react to mine."

"That's obviously false." I inched closer to them. I inspected Kaia's arm closer, though didn't dare to touch and interrupt the flow of magic. "What is that? You've literally got the Stars on your skin."

"Rieka, you really, honestly think that I have any clue about this?" For the first time, she looked terrified. "Neither of you have ever read *anything* about Libran Healers and water mages?"

"Kaia, with all due respect, that is not water magic," Chase said, shaking his head. "And no, Libra Healing is an isolated magic system."

"By looking at your arm and mine, I can tell you that you might be wrong about that." Kaia slowly loosened her grip. Some of the magic dissipated in her arms. "Chase, keep it activated."

"Okay?"

Kaia pulled her hand away. The healing in Chase moved back into his palm, dripping onto the floor in liquid light. The magic in her arms stopped activating. She held her palm to the ceiling and drew a droplet of water from the dew. She flicked it aside, then returned her hand to his arm. The aura instantly rippled over her skin again, and his healing reversed up his veins.

"That is so incredibly weird," Chase said, watching his healing twist through his arm. "I've never seen it go backward, either. It feels a lot cooler than normal; it typically burns and aches. It's almost refreshing, for a lack of better words."

"Strange." Kaia lifted her hand again, diffusing the magic. They both sat back, then glanced over at me again. "Rieka?"

"I've got nothing."

Kaia crossed her arms. "What am I supposed to do with this information?"

"Not sure." Chase shrugged. "I guess watch for signs and symptoms for any changes in your normal magic."

"Best we can do." Kaia nodded toward the main cavern. "We're going to need to explain this to Avia, and it's going to take a bit to get her to actually believe us. Do we want to start heading back?"

I hesitated.

"Hey, if you don't want to just yet, we can stay here, too," Chase said. "Want to keep talking? It can be about anything in the world."

I smiled at Chase and Kaia, and there I found my fear slowly slipping into the dark, the fear of my own self—because as much as I feared myself, Chase and Kaia didn't fear me. Not like I'd been feared all my life, and with the most dangerous magic in Gardian, I was met with warm gazes and smiles, understanding and hearing.

A part of me was faltering; a facet of the Scorpio Code slipped away before my eyes into the darkness behind me, illuminating hope again in the light ahead, in the particles still shimmering on the floor, in Chase's remaining healing.

I vowed to never again follow the second law of the Scorpio Code.

Chapter 23

Sunlight filtered into the tunnel, beaming onto my face for the first time in days. As we walked out of the damp cavern, I breathed in the crisp air of the mountains. My adjusting eyes fell upon a small village ahead with buildings constructed of white reed and other lightly colored woods, blue cloth banners flapping with an alpine breeze donning Autarian symbols. It took me a moment to register that we were in Assidian territory, not Autarian—exactly what Atlas had told us us.

As I opened my mouth to say something to the others, a dark blue shape of a person materialized next to me. I yelped and ducked at the bright flash as a cloth was thrown over my head and body. A burst of magic smacked into the side of my head. I instantly went limp, my muscles weakened and dampened as a lethargic energy devoured me whole. I slumped as I was dragged across the ground, unable to control any of my body movements as the sounds of surprised villagers surrounded me. A door opened and closed.

The cloth was yanked away, my arms tied around my back as I failed to move my body. The other three were in the same position, laying on the ground or propped up against a wall with hands tied behind their backs. We had been placed in a wooden hut raised off the ground made of white reeds. The only light provided in the empty cell was sunlight leaking through the gaps of planks in the walls, otherwise an empty single-room trap.

Standing in front of the door was a woman with pale skin and braided blonde hair that was so light that I first thought it was white. A couple of red Aiksil—Autarian's out-of-use language—runic tattoos spread across her arms. She wore baggy layered tans and browns accented by a spectrum of greens. A long ombre cloak matching the outlines of her clothing draped over her shoulders, with the Leo-Virgo glyph and Assiduous Union emblem embroidered onto the face of the fabric. Her hand carefully rested on a blade on her hip. She looked to be in her mid-thirties, at most. She met my gaze with one brown eye and one hazel eye.

A man stood next to her, around the same age, who had colorfully beaded braided black hair and sepia-colored skin. He didn't wear a cloak but instead had thin navy-blue clothing covering him, outlining his muscular figure, with a separate hood and black pants. An intricate tattoo of a dragon swirled up his arm. He proudly wore a large Capricorn glyph across his entire torso—Assiduous.

"It is her," the man said, nodding toward me, his voice thick with a Rurian accent. "Scorpio."

"Is that so?" Unlike her counterpart, the woman spoke as if she'd lived in the Hub speaking Kaelin. She strode toward me without a stumble in her step. Her movement was flawlessly fluid and graceful as she lifted one of my limp hands.

The Capricorn man took a few cautious steps toward me. He began speaking to the woman in Rurian, to which she fluently responded. Their Assidian accents were far too strong for me to decipher or try to pry a word out of their conversation. They seemed to be arguing in a quiet, but calm, tone.

The woman kept an eye on me. "Release them from the spell."

The man's eyes widened. "Sora, they will bring this town to ash."

"They have an Autarian in their party." The woman—Sora?—nodded at Kaia. "I doubt they will try to retaliate."

I didn't understand the sudden switch to Kaelin. With a cautious look, the Capricorn carefully held his hands toward us, and four bursts of white light darted at each of us. At the stinging contact with my skin, I regained control of my own body and muscles, carefully flexing each of my fingers to make sure I could fully move them; I'd never seen or heard of a magic that could paralyze its receiver. When Avia immediately started to struggle, Chase gave her a sharp look, and she stopped. Kaia sighed at them, leaning her head back against the bamboo wall.

"Where are we? Avia pressed them.

"You are not aware?"

"I mean, we've been in the caves for a few days," Chase said to the man. "We were following coordinates."

"You are in the village of Rayka," Sora responded. Chase flinched at her response, and I wasn't entirely sure why; for a moment, he looked baffled but then shook his head at himself. "We have strict magical borders set up at the waterfall and around the valley to protect our town from outsiders. How did you venture past them?"

Avia shrugged before I could answer. "Dunno. We were thrown

off a waterfall, went through a cave system, and here we are. Why are there Autarians in the middle of Assidian territory?"

"*You will be shocked at the truths lying dormant in these mountains,*" Sora spoke in fluent Driksaal tongue, and Avia gasped. Kaia's lip curled in confusion as she tried to understand the foreign language.

"*You speak both Driksaal and Rurian?*" Avia responded to her in Driksaal. "And Kaelin?"

Sora smiled at her, and responded in two phrases, one in a completely unfamiliar language—presumably Aiksil—and the other in Tyak. Kaia tilted her head at the Aiksil. Avia shut her mouth in shock.

"We're no harm, I promise," Chase interrupted the conversations. "Rieka barely knows how to use her own magic. We're trying to find the Callexus."

"You may be no harm," the Capricorn warned, "but the Stellarium will follow a Scorpio who has broken the Code, and—"

"We know about the Callexus," Sora interrupted him.

"Guess we're ignoring the question about having an Autarian town in Assiduous territory and whatever the hell is going on with you speaking five languages," Avia grumbled.

"The Callexus." I leaned forward. "Where is it?"

Sora moved closer to the man as a cold breeze seeped into the hut. "It lies underneath Rayka in a tunnel system. Since it was returned to its cavern, the caves beneath us have killed anyone who has attempted to locate it."

"You believe in its existence?" Chase asked hopefully.

"Of course I do," Sora said. "Our village has been here since the Callexus was returned to the caves to protect the artifact and uphold the true history of the War. We have since placed magical barriers to protect outsiders from entering Rayka."

"And yet, the Aries Arctura knows this town exists," Chase said. "He literally told us to come here."

"I am aware." The corner of Sora's mouth quirked up. "Fulbright is a good friend of mine."

Kaia had her concentration locked on Sora. Without even knowing that I was watching her, Kaia deliberately wiggled her hand behind her back to grab my attention. I caught sight of her veins that were barely visible with the deep blue light she'd activated the prior night. Whatever the new magic was, she was utilizing it in some sort of way.

"Nothing surprises me at this point." Avia laughed, interrupting Kaia's focus. "Listen. We either die to the hands of the Scorpio Stellarium, or we die going into those caves taking the chance. Also, my god, can someone tell me why we are in an Autarian town?"

Sora sighed at her insistence. "We were a sanctuary for Autarians during the War. We are home to both Autarians and Assidians here, an allied town remaining in secrecy." Her gaze darkened. "You could summon the wrath of the Scorpio Stellarium to this village."

"You said you had magical barriers up, right?"

Sora paused to consider my sister's words.

"It is too dangerous," the Capricorn insisted. "We cannot allow them."

"*If* they find the Callexus—and they made it through our shields—they have enough evidence and power against Scorpio to abolish the Code," Sora said. "You understand as well as I do that the Scorpio Stellarium has not known of us for centuries. This village is the last place the Scorpio Stellarium would suspect, especially if Fulbright instructed these young ones to find us."

"Sorry, I don't want to interrupt, but just to make this clear, Atlas Fulbright is protecting this village from the Scorpio Stellarium?" Chase asked. "He knows, but the Scorpio Stellarium doesn't, and he's a friend of yours?"

"Correct. Fulbright has been on our side for a very long time."

"Sora, outsiders are forbidden." The man shook his head and began pacing. I caught a glimpse of his upper arm on the arm without a tattoo, and it almost looked as if there were scales on his shoulder.

She continued the conversation with him in Rurian. Their words jumbled in my head, between his intense Assidian accent, Sora's vagueness, and my sheer exhaustion. I was further than physically tired, emotionally drained after the previous night. Our two captors burst into another bout of debate in Rurian, surely to decide whether to let us stay or cast us out.

"Sora, I apologize for interrupting," Kaia interjected, halting the argument between the two Assidians. "My name is Kaia Moku, Cancer. I'm with the Autarian Stellarium. My mother is Rhea Moku, Libra Leader."

Kaia paused, as if debating on further explanation. She decided to continue.

In fluent Aiksil.

Sora smiled at her. Avia flinched and Chase shook his head quickly, as if he'd taken a shot. I wanted to understand so badly what she and Sora were exchanging in the ancient language. It seemed serious, concentrated, then focused on me and Chase.

"Pause." Avia stopped their conversation. "Kaia. Why can you also speak a forgotten language?"

"Hush," Sora scolded Avia, her focus still on Kaia. She was beaming with a newfound trust in Kaia. "You must be a Spirit Walker."

"I must be a what?"

"Which means—" Sora pointed at Chase, "—you're a Libran Healer."

"Kaia, you know Aiksil?" Chase questioned, then did a double take when he processed Sora's words. "Hold on, yeah, *what?*"

"I never learned Aiksil. I didn't think I could speak it, and I..." Kaia stopped in the middle of what she was going to say to Chase. "For the record, I didn't tell her that you're a Healer."

"Spirit Walking, the third archpower," Sora informed her. "Documentation of Spirit Walking was forcefully removed in the past three centuries. Libran Healers were killed in the War because Spirit Walkers cannot access their magic unless they come in contact with a Libran Healer. Spirit Walkers were our connection to the astral realm, and when you are a Stellarium enforcing a fabricated law meant to be from the gods, you do not want individuals communicating with those same divinities."

"I can't do this anymore," Chase said with a groan. "So, we weren't just murdered because our magic was too close to immortality?"

"The strength of Libran Healing was part of the reasoning, but the highest motivation was to remove Spirit Walkers."

"There's a third archpower?" I followed up.

Sora looked amused. "*You* are the third archpower. Libran Healing and Spirit Walking were the first two archpowers."

"Sorry, I accidentally told her." Kaia cringed at me at the mention of my archpower.

I shrugged. Hiding my Zodiac Turning had become a lost cause after I blasted a Scorpio official into a wall in the middle of Lyra.

"Spirit Walkers inherently understand Aiksil. It became outdated at the loss of Spirit Walking," Sora continued. "I can assume he is a Libran Healer, because you had to be in proximity to one to know you're a Spirit Walker."

"Okay, yeah, the speaking Aiksil makes sense, because I can read ancient Driksaal," Chase said, stumbling over his words as he tried to understand. "But, just... why? For any of this?"

"In the vascular system, Libran Healing is a blood-based magic that converts to magical energy. Spirit Walking is a water-based magic that converts to magical energy. They are highly interconnected magic systems in the human body and co-evolved as the earliest forms of magic."

"That's actually so cool," I said, looking over at them. I struggled to understand how they weren't more fascinated with the entirely new magic system we'd been exposed to. "We have all three archpowers."

"Yeah, I feel left out," Avia grumbled.

I rolled my eyes at her. "At least you don't have to worry about being chased around by the Stellarium for something you can't control."

"We can teach you more," Sora reassured Kaia before turning to her companion. "Instruct the protectors to increase our invisibility at the waterfall and borders."

The Capricorn shook his head, pulling his hood over his face. "Do not make me regret, Sora."

She met his gaze. "Trust me. I will find them a warm place to stay."

The Capricorn finally nodded, and without a word, walked out and shut the door behind him. Sora pulled her blade from her belt, leaning over Chase to cut the rope off him. He sighed in relief and stretched his wrists, standing up to twist his back and neck. Sora individually released each of us from the ropes.

"It is frigid this time of the year," Sora warned us while we prepared to follow her. "We can fit you in better suited clothing for the duration of your stay, snow is expected."

"We have a material shapeshifter." Chase gestured to me. "If it's too much of a hassle, she can just change our clothes, too."

"She's a shit shapeshifter, Chase," Avia said. "As if we want her wasting her energy on that."

I sighed at her. Kaia rubbed her forehead. Sora opened the door for us, holding her arm out. Avia marched right on through the exit, undaunted by what the village would present. Chase sighed and followed her while Kaia and I stuck together, close to Sora.

Underneath the setting Sun, the village was alight with the mountain spirit. Twisted black and white pines surrounded the village, their trunks bent toward us, as if protecting the town from harsh alpine windstorms. Evergreen forests spread on the outskirts of the valley walls, cloaked in a thin mountain mist towering into the clouds. Walkways of pebbles and gravel paved the village, and despite the midwinter's curse, the grass was remarkably vibrant and alive. Winter alpine blue and white flowers sprouted in the open spaces and between cracks, blending in with the cloth colors of Autarians. Banners next to predominantly white-wood homes and businesses flapped in the orange sunlight. Not too far from where we stood appeared to be a traditional Autarian temple. Water sources of fountains and wells covered the village between stone pathways, perhaps meant for water mages to easily access a source of magic. Jagged and snowy peaks soared from the tops of clouds, waterfalls and greenery pooling over the edges of rocky cliffs.

The village, despite being hidden amongst the mountains, was alive and thriving during a bitter alpine winter.

Sora waved to the townsfolk as she walked down a path heading north toward the temple. As we traveled, locals clothed in thick white fur and blue fabric met us with looks of unrest. Most of the women wore their hair braided, men with lengthy, uncut hair. A duo of two tall men glared at us as we passed, and I clutched my cloak closer to myself.

The thin, clean mountain air carried the scents of flowers, damp wood, and freshly baked bread. The sound of trickling water was omnipresent no matter where in the village we stood, a small creek following each and every path. A larger river laced through the middle of the village, where a couple of children playing in the water were being scolded for soaking themselves on the cool eve.

"We're almost there," Sora reassured us. "This house, right here. There is a bathroom and a couple of rooms. It should fit your group well."

"Why do you have spare houses lying around when you're protected from outsiders?" Chase asked.

"We have two, and we typically find them useful to house injured or ill members of our village. We thankfully haven't had an injury or illness in a few months now," she explained. "Find yourselves a comfortable space here. I will be at the temple tomorrow at 3 if you wish to talk."

With that, she bowed her head and hurried off while the four of us headed into the small house.

Chapter 24

Once we were settled, I savored the feeling of resting in a real bed for the first time in days. To my exhausted dismay, I woke back up in an overly realistic dream, though it didn't carry the same feeling as one of my memories returning.

I stood in the same dreamscape where I first saw Narah by the creek. The wind whipped my hair around my face. Black storm clouds rumbled above me, and lightning slithered through the sky as a storm threatened the atmosphere. The nearby river roared and rushed, misting my ankles with its force.

"Rieka."

I spun around at the mention of my name. My breath caught in my throat.

Narah stood in front of me. In the midst of the incoming storm, she was spared her grace by the sharp winds. It curved around her as she moved toward me, her step unbroken. She was disturbingly elegant as she paused before me. For a moment, I could've sworn her smile was genuine.

I opened my mouth to search for words. I had no idea where I'd even start. The anger that emanated from her was smoldering. She so clearly wanted to avoid hurting me the last time we'd known each other; there was nothing I'd done toward her to make her so furious.

I panicked instead. "How are you Dreamseeking me?"

Her expressions didn't change. "I have access in Aquarius-Pisces."

"What have they done to you?" I forced out. "I've just started remembering—"

"Where are you, Rieka?" she interrupted me, her gaze hardening.

"Wouldn't you like to know?" I attempted a sharper tone to see if she'd react. Her anger didn't change. I fiercely met her eyes. "Do you remember me?"

She grabbed my shoulders. I yelled and tried to struggle against her, but with her strength, she easily shoved me to the ground. I had no idea how I was supposed to react as I laid on the ground underneath her, my face rapidly heating. It was one hell of a way to disarm me, that was for sure.

"Of course I fucking remember you," she snapped, shaking her head as if she was fighting against her own thoughts. "I will *kill* you for what you did to me."

"Go ahead and try." I let her hold me down, narrowing my eyes. I'd trusted her, without hesitation, to place my hand upon hers in the Woods to activate a magical connection. I had every reason to believe she'd resist killing me. "Tell me what I did to you, then."

Her nails dug into my shoulders as she leaned closer to me, her face dangerously close to mine. "You have no idea how much pain you've put me through. Where are you?"

I defiantly met her gaze. "I don't need to tell you anything."

Her breath grazed across my skin. "I *will* find you, Spring, and I'll destroy everything in my path until I can tear you apart."

She pushed down on me with such a force that a sickening crack came from my right shoulder. I yelled as a slicing pain tore through me. Agony pierced my upper body, leaving me recoiling underneath her. She lurched back. Her chest rose and fell rapidly as she wildly stared at her trembling hands, shock covering her face.

"*Rieka.* Fuck." A blur of emotion consumed her expressions, and a faint red glow emanated from underneath her shirt. Her wide eyes darted, pupils dilated as she took in rapid breaths, looking at me with sheer terror. "*No!* I didn't mean…"

Her voice trailed off, her shoulders tensing. The anger returned to her face.

"You'll understand soon," she said hoarsely, her voice splitting, "why I am doing this, and it'll *break* you more than anything ever has. Ask yourself who you are."

In my terror, my magic sparked to life in my hands, and I gritted my teeth. I spread my fingers apart to avoid accidentally turning someone's sign in my sleep.

"Fight it," I pushed my words between the pain in my shoulder. "Fight whatever you're under right now. I am beginning to remember you and everything you were to me."

The dream ended abruptly as rain poured from the sky, blurring everything around me in the dream.

I woke up with a gasp. A sharp pain struck my right shoulder. Kaia sat up at the exact same moment as I did, grabbing the couch she was sleeping on as she was thrown back to her senses. My light illuminated the room, though not strong enough to spill out of my hands.

"Are you alright? Holy shit, I just felt your fear, and it woke me up." Kaia urgently peeled her blanket away. She stumbled to her feet, holding her hand to her chest. "Rieka, oh my god, your emotions."

I couldn't process or understand what she was trying to say. She offered me a hand. I slipped out of bed and let her guide me to the couch, where she carefully helped me remove my tank top. Kaia's fingers traced over the protruding bump on my shoulder. Her cool hands, slippery with water, provided a soothing ease to my angry red skin. She moved her hand from my back to my forehead, carefully touching her palm to my temple. I relaxed at the sensation.

"Since when does water magic calm?" I asked, my vision swaying. "I mean, forcefully, like you can force someone to relax?"

"Since I touched Chase's arm, apparently," she said, standing up and gently pushing me along while wrapping a blanket around my torso. "Come on, be gentle with yourself."

I followed her to the room adjacent to ours where Chase slept. Kaia quietly knocked on the door moments before she opened it softly as she could. Despite being almost silent, Chase instantly sat up. He relaxed when he recognized our shapes in the doorway, then flinched and looked away. It didn't register with me why; pain blurred my senses.

"Avia's out cold and did not wake up despite any of this." Kaia guided me to him. "Dislocated shoulder. I think. I'm not a healer. I'm sorry about how she is."

"She's…"

"Rieka, turn."

Almost mechanically, I did as she said, protecting my torso with the blanket I'd been given while sitting down on the bed. Chase leaned forward, placing his palm against my inflamed skin. I groaned at the burst of agony that spread through my upper body while he tried to navigate the injury.

"Kaia, can you do me a favor and grab the notepad from my backpack? If you wouldn't mind recording her vitals for me. It's in the burlap sack with other med supplies," Chase said quietly. Kaia listened, hurrying over to his bag resting next to the door. "Rieka, permission to make sure you don't have any further injury?"

I nodded.

"Let me know if there's any pain." He gently grasped my arms, moving across my body while checking his hands every few moments for blood. "How'd you mess yourself up this bad in your sleep?"

"Narah," I said. He cringed at the answer. Kaia sat back down next to me with the notepad in hand, observing Chase's intricate process. He held my arm, pressing two fingers to my wrist. "She Dreamsought me and then shoved me into the ground."

"Kaia, 100 beats per minute, 46 breaths per minute, accelerated heart and respiratory rates."

"No one gives you enough credit." Kaia shook her head while scribbling on his notebook. "Have you been recording these things the whole time?"

"Yeah. I memorize the vitals and write them down later. Helps for future reference if it continues to be a problem." His voice was utterly calm, despite the severity of the injury. "Rieka, do you know why she hurt you?"

"No," I answered Chase, tears daring to spill across my cheeks again. I began my fight against my own childhood memories with a tremble. "She was confused, too, like she didn't have control, and I think she's being manipulated by the Stellarium—"

"Breathe." Chase tested the joint of my elbow before moving to the injury. I flinched away from him when he felt around the shoulder. He pushed on my collarbone, and I retaliated, shoving him away with my functional arm. He was completely unfazed. "You've definitely got a dislocated shoulder. Inflamed, swollen skin, so I suspect your clavicle is also broken."

"How did she hurt you? To my understanding, Dreamseekers can't inflict pain during sleep," Kaia asked as she tried to keep up with what Chase was telling her.

"I don't know," I murmured. "She panicked when she heard the crack in my shoulder."

"Ready for this?" Chase looked over at Kaia to make sure she was alert. She confidently nodded. "Pupils dilated, pale, clammy skin. Shivering, disoriented, confused. Chief complaint is shoulder pain with a suspected posterior dislocation and fractured clavicle. Low to moderate trauma-induced shock, or potentially a post-traumatic response from unknown origin."

Kaia glanced up while finishing his notes. "*Damn*, Chase."

He paused when he noticed Kaia's skin rippling with the new soothing blue luminance emanating a quiet hum, like a far-off whisper of a choir's melody. She set down his notepad as stars sparkled across the surface of her skin, constellations connecting between the blood vessels in her arms. I couldn't comprehend how unbelievably calm and indifferent she was to the entirely new magic she was experiencing.

"That's so cool. It looks like you have clusters of stars outlining where your muscles sit." Chase curiously tilted his head at her magic. "Do you know what's inducing that?"

"Her emotions woke me up. I can feel them. It's a little bit overwhelming."

"I understand," he said. "It's uncontrollable when someone's in distress. Your body wants to fix it."

"Exactly. This is going to sound crazy, but it's like I can see the emotions around her. Same thing happened earlier with Sora."

"It's not crazy at all." Chase smiled at her. "What do emotions look like?"

"Like a faint aura," she said. "Rieka has a bright red around her. I can tell that's panic or anxiety. Gray might be dissociation or confusion. Those are what's standing out. There's a lot I can't recognize."

"That's helpful. You can work with me here." He adjusted where his hand sat on my collarbone despite speaking to her, dually focused. "Kaia. I want you to follow your instinct and act on what it tells you to do. Don't hesitate. I trust whatever you're experiencing right now."

She sat next to me on the bed and nudged my non-injured side as I rattled in raspy breaths. The world spun. I couldn't stop my body from shivering as my heart felt as if it would pound out of my chest. I started to worry I would pass out on top of Chase.

Chase's magic lit on my shoulder, the warmth of his healing absorbing into my shoulder. Kaia took both of my hands, allowing the light in her veins to expand into mine. At the instant contact of the blue and gold magic in my veins, I went completely numb. I was the middle source to an equilibrium, neither warmed nor cooled, as if I laid weightless on a pool of water. Both of their calm demeanors carefully drew me back to the present. My breathing slowed, my muscles relaxed; emotions rushed back into my senses, and suddenly I couldn't stop myself from bursting into tears.

"You've got it," Kaia said gently.

I stared at the wall. "I'm so confused."

"About what?" Kaia asked. She kept her grip on my hands, and when I met her eyes, I was pulled into a serene trance. Kaia felt like she had stepped into the emotional realm of my mind, walking another dimension of the subconscious, simultaneously human and spirit.

"About the memories I haven't remembered yet, or why I'm even remembering any at all," I said, holding my head as Chase finished healing me. "I know, though, that they forced Narah to make me forget her because I broke the full Code."

The two of them immediately exchanged a look, as if trying to figure out how to respond to what I'd just admitted to them.

"I'm sorry." Kaia's expressions mirrored my sorrow. "They sent someone you loved to kill you."

"Oh my god." Chase shook his head. "And they sent her to kill you because you're trying to change the law..."

"That made this happen in the first place, yeah," I said, my voice splitting with both pain and spite. "I will do *anything* to tear the Stellarium apart for what they stole from me."

Kaia reached forward to wipe a tear off my cheek. "They took someone I loved, too."

"I feel like I'm going insane."

"I promise, you're not. That's just what you've been told all your life," Kaia comforted me. "It's not insane to want revenge and justice against a system that took your humanity from you. So be angry, and be scared, because that is exactly how you've made it this far."

I glanced over at the door. A nervous shiver through me.

"She's not awake." Kaia read my mind, placing a hand on my shoulder. "Don't listen to your sister when she says those things about you. She needs to watch her words more."

"That's what Aries does. They rip into each other to make themselves tougher," Chase added. "She's been trained to react with aggression and anger."

"I know she doesn't mean it, though. It's her way of communication."

Kaia sighed at the way I defended her. "Right, but that doesn't change the fact that it reinforces what you've been told by authority all your life."

"And Rieka?" Chase started. "This can stay between the three of us. If we know she'll just antagonize you about Narah, then she doesn't need to know the full story."

Kaia pointed at him. "He's right. Don't let your sister step all over you or try to tell you that she deserves to know these things about you."

"*How* do you see right through people like that?" Chase touched the back of his neck. "We're not gonna be able to hide a thing from you, are we?"

"That's a problem for you," I teased him with a small smile, and he rolled his eyes with a laugh. I rubbed my healed shoulder. "Thanks for Dreamseeking my shoulder."

Chapter 25

"Is it 3 already?" I asked in disbelief, readjusting my new scarlet winter coat. I tucked its white fur interior around my neck. Earlier in the day, Kaia had run off to get us new warm clothing. "How long did I sleep?"

"For as long as you needed," Kaia insisted as we approached the temple. She seemed perfectly happy in her new coat. It was an ocean blue with ornate wave designs hand-painted across its surface, accented by the same luxurious white fur hood. Her tie was a deep blue, matching her pants and fuzzy boots. Her thick hair was braided back in a single braid, embellished with beads in an array of shades of blue. "Chase beat us out here hours ago. He left early this morning to explore."

"He mentioned something about a library." Avia shrugged. She wore a thick, pale yellow winter coat with white fur on its edges, a satin tie around her waist, and fleece-lined snow pants. "Willing to bet he's been here for a minute."

From the outside, I would've had no idea the building was a temple with its unassuming half-dome structure made of white and gray stone, less than two stories high. An open archway for a door beckoned us in. We walked inside, met with a wave of warmth from the enclosed space.

Inside the sacred space was a massive statue of a woman with crossed legs, each of her hands resting on each knee in a meditative pose. Water trickled from the ceiling upon her eroded and mossy head, rippling down her body into a reservoir of water she sat in. The source of the water was unclear, likely magical, pouring from the middle of a vibrant, hand-painted intricate mural that spanned across every inch of the walls, from the sandy floor to the apex of the dome. Lanterns lined the walls, flickering flames making shadows dance amongst the scenes of a story told in art; a tale of bloodshed and healing, of community and war, of love and hate.

In front of the statue, Chase sat across from Sora. He was leaning forward, entirely invested in whatever story Sora was telling him, so much so that he hadn't noticed us walk in. Sora's expressions were full of an indescribably warm joy as she spoke. She smiled through her words, talking with her hands, her face glowing with pride and hope.

When Chase finally noticed us walk in, his eyes brightened. "Look who finally decided to show up."

"Welcome," Sora said, dipping her head as a greeting. "Did you rest well?"

"More than I should've."

"Good." Chase turned his attention to Avia as we approached. "You look good in that."

She looked down at her outfit, then back at him. "You think so? It's kinda hot and itchy."

"I think so." He flashed her a warm smile. "It's something different. I like it a lot."

I admired Chase's social ability to know exactly what someone needed to hear at that moment. Part of me wondered if it was in his nature as a Healer—a healer of not only the physical, but the emotional. Another part of me figured his intuition to feelings was his conditioning to recognize a dispute between two and an urge for him to solve it.

"How beautiful," Kaia said as she gazed up at the mural. "I cannot fathom how many years this must've taken to paint."

"No kidding," Avia agreed, looking over at Sora. "Who's the artist?"

Sora smiled. "I am."

"*You?*" Kaia gasped, her eyes widening. "You look so young to be capable of a project with such intricate detail and skill. I grew up around art and murals in Autarchic, but I've never seen anything near this level of mastery."

"Are you serious?" Avia asked her. Sora nodded. "Really?"

"How long did this take?" I couldn't comprehend the skill necessary to accomplish such a feat. "This is incredible, Sora."

"Thank you." Her voice was even and still as her eyes followed the art like brush strokes. "Time is a craft secret. I have my ways."

"It's so much to take in," Chase said. "I don't even know where to start when I look at this."

"Good. That is how it is meant to be." Sora stood up, leaning over the fountain. She glanced back at us, her hand glowing with a faint lavender magic. "I suggest you find yourself a comfortable position."

I didn't hesitate to listen, pulling off my coat to fold it and use it as a pillow. Laying down on the floor of the temple, I sunk into the warmth of the sand as I stared at the mural above. A lavender aura rippled over the painting. Its scenes jumped to life.

"This story begins 300 years ago, when immortality began to disrupt the flow of life and death within Gardian, dictating who was in power. Mathias went in search of our sacred Callexus to take immortality from Gardian."

Upon the canvas of stone, the Callexus struck a stone deep within a cavern underneath Rayka. On its left and right were symbols of the Sun and Moon, morphing into two ghostly shapes. Together, a hand from each deity of the Sun and Moon rested on the ornate handle of the Callexus, sending an aura of red over the weapon's surface, marking its immortality.

With a flash of a purple aura to reset the image, and a man's figure rose from the blank stone, his hands glowing gold with Libran Healing. Materializing in front of Mathais was the God of the Sun, and with an extension of each of his hands, a blend of a blindingly bright divine blessing seeped into Mathias's heart through his golden veins. The Sun leaned over to whisper in his ear, and an image of the Callexus reappeared above his head.

A new picture was painted of Mathias Merek in a cave with his wife, Mari Merek, a Cancer. The Callexus lodged in the ground before the two of them, shadowed by a hellbent beast, a slender, scaly creature contorting in the mist, its features not completely clear in the magical illustration. Mathias wrought the Callexus free from stone, and the images repainted themselves to depict the beast with the Callexus through its chest. The red aura, representing immortality, was sucked from the land, instead sinking into Mathias and the Callexus.

"*After the Callexus's return to the caves, immortality could only be gained by an infliction from the Callexus. The Mereks would go down in history as heroes. Mathias and Mari sought to pass their legacy to the next generation.*"

The images cleared again, resetting to a picture of Mari and Mathias's arms wrapped around two young boys, each with a glowing symbol over their heads. The taller boy with dark umber hair wore a black cloak with a red Scorpio glyph, while his younger brother with lighter brown hair wore orange as he stood underneath the Aries glyph. Mari bent down to her knees in a meadow to face her two sons, and both of the children reached a hand forward, and the zodiac wheel lit for them in each of their respective signs. The two Zodiac Turner brothers pressed their hands to the wheel.

At their touch to their magic, a burst of color reshaped the story. Between an old growth forest and the sea, a small village sat on the cliffs of the southernmost point of the Conviction-Autarchic border. There, the Merek brothers trained a new character, a young Scorpio man with long gray hair, who harnessed the zodiac wheel as a Scorpio—Blaine, a childhood friend of the brothers. In a picture off to the side, Blaine's persona stood underneath a Scorpio woman with a crown, the Scorpio Leader. The group of three became four as they were joined by a blonde Aries woman, a child of the Aries Leader. Scenes of the four mages growing up together rapidly morphed on stone. They were kids of political powers, heirs to thrones.

The stone canvas reset to depict a throbbing red heart. First to appear from its pulse was an image of Blaine and the Aries woman as a couple, laughing together in the shade of Conviction Woods. Blaine was replaced by Silas, one of the Merek brothers, a moment later. Silas and the Aries woman faced each other, fingers reaching to each other before their energies merged into each other in a violent, crashing spectacle of color and light. In the shadow of a Conviction Woods pine, they laid together in warm sunlight, their lips pressing together.

The image of the beating heart washed the water canvas in blood. From it, rose Blaine's furious expression. He stood underneath a shadow cast by Mathias, Blaine's passion and love smothered by the Gardian's admiration for the Mereks. Blaine rotted in jealousy while his heterochromatic eyes fixated on the embracing bodies of Silas Merek and the Aries woman.

"During Conviction's political tensions between the Mereks and Blaine, a group of Scorpio Zodiac Turners—a troop commanded by Silas—and Gemini border guards were found dead in the Hub."

A wave of blood washed upon the mural to reset it. In the streets of the Hub, two Gemini men donning Stellarium glyphs killed two prestigious Scorpio Turners. The Scorpio Leader's image towered over the scene, and in her scream of fury at the murder of her people, she sent a blast of light with her own Zodiac Turning to curse the Gemini Leader. A painting emerged of the Gemini Leader's funeral, who was killed by the Scorpio Leader herself. For the first time, Gardian felt anger against Scorpio and the Conviction Stellarium at the loss of the Gemini Leader.

The image of Blaine triumphed over the chaos of Gardian's anger. Each yell sunk into Blaine's body, his society's fury against his own Scorpio Leader mother seeping and pouring into him. His face contorted in emotion, quickening his temper, hardening tired eyes from a world that betrayed him and his family.

"Blaine's resentment toward Silas only grew when Silas married the Aries woman. In his blinding anger, Blaine tried to murder her to stop her from becoming an Aries heir. Silas set a curse to force Blaine away from the Aries woman, killing Blaine's mother."

Silas Merek, the son of a hero, killed the Scorpio Leader with his Zodiac Turning. Gardian began to despise Zodiac Turners for their power.

Blaine's body caught on fire with a raging inferno of fury and vengeance as he devised a plan against Silas. He punched his fist out, summoning his Zodiac Turning, and with one swift movement, Blaine changed his sign to Leo to hide his own Zodiac Turning. A wicked smile spread across his face as he chose betrayal against his own people; Blaine spoke to Gardian about the death of his mother, killed by Silas Merek, a Zodiac Turner far too powerful.

As Blaine delivered a speech on the extreme danger behind Zodiac Turning, society was painted with fearful faces underneath the symbol of Zodiac Turning. The image of the Zodiac Turner only darkened as the War progressed, creating themselves a horrific image while defending themselves in battle. In a massive castle sitting within the Hub, a meeting took place where the Council of Leaders debated on the threat of Zodiac Turning. Societal's Stellarium ordered for the erasure of all Zodiac Turners to protect the safety of Gardian's people, agreed upon by the majority of Leaders. Assidian and Societalist armies set out to ensure the eradication of all Zodiac Turners in all Unions. The large majority were Scorpio Zodiac Turners.

"Blaine advocated for eradicating Libran Healers and Spirit Walkers. He claimed that Libran Healing, like immortality, would be used to gain power in the government."

It would be an age of reformation and attempt to restore balance. The Mereks reappeared on the reset stone canvas again, cowering underneath society's screams of their abuse of power. The Healers fell to the gravesites they were meant to prevent as Blaine looked to the Stars with a smile. Without Healers, the same Stars were torn from the hands and hearts of Cancer. Defeated cries echoed through the air, trembling the canvas of stone with their uproar. Mathias's figure became contorted with red and black smoke, a shameful Libran Healer with two Zodiac Turner sons who caused thousands of deaths in a gruesome war.

The Callexus, in all its shimmering crimson glory, returned to the scene. A group of Gemini attacked Silas. On the verge of death, he was saved by his father, who passed his immortality to Silas. The other Merek brother pressed his hand to the blade of the Callexus, his body shimmering with a red hue as he took immortality to remain at his brother's side. Next, it was Blaine who stole immortality from the Callexus. The Merek brothers and their shimmering-red shapes melted into the shadows of the canvas, lost in the whispers of history.

A sinking despair crept over the canvas in another wave of black smoke, creating a reflection of Blaine's figure, bent over a desk in the dimly lit Scorpio Archive, scribbling on paper with a quill. As Blaine lifted the text to read his work, the scene transformed to his hand grasping the paper. His mouth opened in a yell. Below him, there were thousands of individuals clothed in black. Blaine lied of a holy law he said to have discovered in the Scorpio Archive, hidden by his Scorpio Leader mother; a Code of which the Sun and Moon gave to Scorpio, one to prevent a war from ever happening again; a promise to protect Gardian's delicate balance.

Scorpio enthusiastically cheered for the introduction of the fabricated holy law, marking the end of the War of the Rebalancing. The mural reset to its original state, a combination of all the pictures that had animated.

"Silas returned to Rayka 300 years ago. He placed the Callexus back to its original location. Rayka devoted to protecting the Callexus and upholding the truth of Gardian's history."

"History in the rest of Gardian teaches Zodiac Turners to be exactly what Blaine painted them as—cruel, vicious people who only called for death. The truth? The conflict was a deeply complex fight between love, hate, and legacy."

"Zodiac Turning needed regulation, not eradication. The damage remains. We have accepted that this cannot be reversed by the village but set right only by someone meant to break this curse."

Chapter 26

The story finished Sora's last sentence, breaking me out of my concentration on the brilliant presentation of history. Sora was staring directly into my eyes, a smile on her face. She knew. She had answered each and every question I'd had about Gardian's history, the shielded truth I'd been straining to find in the Woods for all those years; the suspicions confirmed, I had been right all those years—the War of the Rebalancing had been reduced down to part myth, part manipulated truth.

Yet I wasn't comprehending why the burden of Zodiac Turning and reversing a major historical belief had been placed on me. I didn't understand; something wasn't adding up, and I felt as if I was missing a horribly obvious answer.

"What we were taught, it doesn't make much sense now that I think about it." Chase shook his head as he refused to look away from the ceiling.

"They protect our kind," I quietly said to Chase", who nodded at me with relief spread across his face. "If you look close enough, you can begin to bring blurs of history into clarity."

"Rieka."

I stiffened at the mentioning of my name to sit up and look at Sora.

"Thank you for such a striking presentation," I bowed my head respectfully. "Your artistry is so admirable."

"Welcome to Rayka," she said. "Thank you for allowing me to show you my project."

"Where could you have possibly learned all of this from?" Kaia asked, scooching closer to us, her face bright with fascination. "You're an excellent storyteller, too."

"Rayka keeps a well-preserved archive of unaltered documents," Sora explained. "It is just a story that feels personally significant to me."

"Your passion is clear. You tell the story like you were there," Chase said. "How moving for those of us that are so impacted by the inaccuracies in everyone else's version."

"There are forests surrounding the village if you wish for time alone to process. They are peaceful. Perhaps they would remind you of home." Sora walked toward the door with a smile. "Otherwise, I will leave you alone to take it in."

She exited the temple without another word.

"I might do just that." I glanced over to Chase and met his eyes, who must've been as equally shocked as I was about his place in our world. He gave me a tiny smile. We needed to talk about what our magic meant, privately, just between the two of us. "Chase?"

"Are you sure it's safe?" Kaia interrupted.

Chase narrowed his eyes. "Are you feeling that it's not?"

"Not necessarily." She held the side of her arm, glancing over at me. "I think I'm just worried about..."

She trailed off, avoiding speaking out loud that she was concerned about my broken shoulder from the night before. Avia had no clue what happened to me in the middle of the night.

"I'll go with her," Chase reassured Kaia. "Avia, could you stay and make dinner so Rieka and I can talk about this?"

Avia paused, looking in between us. Finally, she gave me a nod and a smile. She trusted Chase. Chase trusted me.

"Don't let her get hurt, alright?" Avia warned him. "You also need to be careful."

"You, caring about me?" Chase joked.

She pushed him back with her hand to his chest. "Shut up."

"Rest assured, I'll be careful," he said.

By the time we'd exited the temple, snow had flurried from a canopy of clouds hiding the jagged mountain peaks. Chase and I were silent as we followed the village paths accumulating with fluffy snow toward the forest on the east of the village, allowing our bodies to adjust to the new freeze. We stepped into the forest with spruce and fir, far more rugged and rocky than the humid climate of Conviction Woods. Chase and I first followed a path woven into the ground, but it was quickly lost by snow and distance. I could sense shared excitement between us; the forest felt like home.

"You trust we'll find our way back?" I asked Chase.

"The trees are unique enough to follow. This isn't too big of a forest, and both of us are pretty solid at navigating, yeah?"

"I suppose. I miss Conviction Woods." I sighed. "I miss *home*."

"Conviction Woods, that reminds me—I have to ask. The dream

with Narah. What did she say?"

"She kept going on about her anger and how she has to kill me." I kicked a small build-up of snow. "I know damn well it's not true."

"You know, I get the same sense that I know her from somewhere, too. It's strange." He tucked his hands behind his back. "I'd never admit that around your sister, though. She'd say we both lost our minds."

"Would she be wrong?"

Chase laughed as we continued our walk through the woods. The snow fell heavier, though not nearly enough to be indicative of a blizzard. We'd learned our lesson once before about the danger of snow. The snow was serene as it silenced the creaking of trees in a soundproof white blanket. The new type of subalpine forest, silent and safe in the mountains, was soothing in an entirely different way than Conviction Woods.

Yet, something seemed off. I couldn't pinpoint what it was. Perhaps it was almost *too* quiet; there wasn't a sign of a single creature in sight, no hushed brushing of feathered wings, no movement except the two of us. The Sun was heading toward the horizon, casting a few shadows to stretch from the slender white tree trunks, but still bright enough for us to have another hour or two of light.

Chase suddenly stopped in his tracks. "Did you hear that?"

"Hear what?" I said, peering around. The forest was eerily still. Chase's uneasy look confirmed my suspicions—it was too quiet without a sign of life besides our two human presences.

Chase narrowed his eyes at a nearby tree, running his fingers along its soft bark. Gash marks were etched into the trunk, carved by claws of a creature large enough to scare animals away. Chase slowly turned to me. My body went cold as Chase slowly turned to me.

"It's not safe," he said quietly, as if his life depended on the noise level of every word he spoke.

"Would the village lie to us?"

"Would they know if it's something that just got here?" His fingers pressed deeper into the trunk, and when he withdrew them, his fingers were sticky with fresh sap. I inched closer to him. The tree's open cambium was still moist from the claw marks.

My body went rigid. "It's fresh."

He met my eyes. I drew my sword.

A blur of white movement flared in the corner of my eye. Chase and I spun around at the same time. In the near distance, a pair of pale, icy blue eyes stared at us from behind a tree. I held my sword in front of me while Chase inched closer to me with the knife he'd pulled off his belt. We'd been through the same situation before; Chase didn't have offensive magic.

The shape began to transform and split as it lumbered from behind a tree. One still-white paw first, and then the next. Spirals of black smoke spat from each step as its shape materialized from a mirrored monochromatic shadow. Icy blue eyes opened above its snout, and any courage I had escaped my body—it was transforming like a beast of Conviction Woods, making itself the worst version it could be to terrorize the two of us. A pink, forked tongue exposed itself as the creature opened its half-canine, half-draconic mouth. Its fur popped and sizzled as its shape couldn't decide on scales or fur. One of its back legs was a talon, horns curling out of its head, its tail a terrible concoction of patches of fur and slithering, scaly length. As it approached, its claws grew into razor-sharp talons cutting through the accumulating snow.

I couldn't bring myself to call the beast a dragon. I'd heard rumors of them prowling through forests in Assidian territory, but this thing was more of a demented, rotting body of a wolf transforming into a pearly white dragon to blend in with its surroundings, too big to be a dog but too small to be a full dragon. The hungry glint in its eyes accented its vicious, curling snarl and furrowed muzzle. It reeked of rotting flesh and organs left in the Sun on a summer day.

It *smiled* at me, and while Chase opened his mouth to say something, it stood on two legs. Its shadow swallowed my body as I stood in its wake with its blue gaze sinking into my skin with an inhuman dread and despair.

I blinked once.

The setting screamed into a blur of color and action. The beast let out a ferocious battle screech, returning to its four legs with a thump as it pounded through the snow. Chase rolled to the side as it lunged at us, and I yelled so loudly my voice split as I charged toward it. I threw my sword onto a patch of its fur in between scales. Aqua blood spewed from the monster's side onto the snow. It roared, rearing back, and thrashed its tail at me. I collapsed at the impact.

Chase shouted and waved it to the side when I was down. It yanked away from me and granted me enough time to bolt to my feet, pulling my sword back up to charge it again. It reached out a paw and talon to swipe Chase, but before it touched him, my blade made contact with its fuzzy leg. Blood spilled as it spun around and slammed its talons onto my shoulders. I was paralyzed. Chase's frantic yells to pull its attention away failed as it stared directly at me, its nose wrinkled in a snarl as it bent its head close to my face. Slitted blue eyes stared into my soul, a foul breath wafting across my face. Beads of acid and bubbling saliva dangled on its pink tongue, its teeth shining with scarlet stains.

"It will devour you, the metaphysical before the physical." The words echoed from the beast as it laughed at me, mocking my own description of the Beasts of Conviction Woods.

"But child, I am not your greatest nightmare." It bent closer, a drop of its saliva stinging against my cheek. "*You are your own greatest nightmare, and with the passing of time, I am allowing you a blessing; your death will inevitably grant life to those you love.*"

I couldn't fight it anymore, sinking into its hypnotic words. My grip fell loose on my sword as my fingers brushed against its handle. My breath caught in my throat as it blinked with another laugh.

"*You fool. How dare you try to save your people when the cause of their peril exists in your own blood?*"

Claws tore into my shirt and sank into my skin. I gasped as my vision spun with dark spots as talons ripped into me, swipe by swipe. Red splattered against the pure white snow and the taste of metallic blood bubbled in my throat. Shock numbed the pain. I turned my head to the side as Chase threw himself at the beast, attempting to drag it away from me.

The monster craned its neck to Chase. A single dagger pierced into it.

Without even a spasm, the beast went completely limp, crashing to the ground next to me, its tail smacking across my legs. Chase's voice was barely distant in the background as he ran to me, unharmed. His hands immediately pressed to my open stomach, healing and absorbing into me. A new person entered the duel, his golden magic fluttered uselessly across the snow, and he was torn away from me. Chase retaliated, fighting to reach me.

 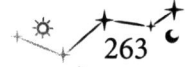

He yelled out again as a hand touched his arm, and just like the dragon, Chase's body folded as his eyes rolled backward. A foot rested on his arm as he tried to struggle.

Narah stood above him.

CHAPTER 27

"She is going to *die* if you don't let me heal her."

The first sensation to return was a searing pain through my torso. When I ran my hand along the wound, I gagged at the feeling of crusty, dry blood smeared across my body. The air got caught in my throat as I leaned over to cough up blood. I clawed at my legs, paralyzed. My body burst into a bout of shivers as I released a low groan.

Reality returned to me in snippets of context. I was in a cave again. The light in the cavern was low and dim from a small torch on the wall. Chase leaned against a wall with his hands tied behind his back. Narah stood in front of him.

"*Listen*, Narah," Chase threatened, "I know you don't want her to die."

Her gaze didn't budge.

"Narah," he repeated, his face twisted in a fury of emotions. I'd *never* heard his voice so sharp and aggressive. He glared at her with such an angry desperation that I had to look away. "Let me heal her so you can at least speak with her before she dies."

Narah leaned over to cut the rope behind his hands. Without a second of hesitation, he sprang to his feet and threw himself to the ground to hold my arm. All his medical training was abandoned. Golden light smeared across my skin before his hand settled and the light ebbed into my arm and torso. At last, I was brave enough to look at my shredded body.

Claw marks had opened my shirt and skin. Huge, reddened gashes leaking blood spread across my core to my chest, partially healed from earlier. Chase's magic throbbed through me as he entered a trance, all his attention focused on healing me.

"Could you be more desperate to save a life?" Narah said, leaning against the wall.

"I promised her sister I'd protect her, and I've already failed."

"What a surprise."

My wounds were barely beginning to heal. Chase lifted his hands with a yell, and he winced when his hands bled from healing, holding his shaking wrists as he glared at Narah.

"How did you bypass this town's protections?" Chase demanded.

"Rayka's magical shields have used the same enchantment since they were cast 300 years ago. They're designed to allow certain bloodlines into the village, and all three of us—" she paused with a smile, "—happen to be part of those."

Chase almost lost his aggressive demeanor at the sudden information. I propped myself off the ground with one arm so I could see both their faces clearly. Chase gave me a side-eye.

I gripped my torso as sharp pains spread up my body. "What the hell are you talking about?"

"Stop spitting out nonsense," Chase added.

"*Listen!*" Narah yelled suddenly. "I am telling the truth."

Both of us went silent.

Narah sighed and reached to Chase's forehead instead, touching her illuminated palm to it. A shock jolted through him. He instantly passed out. She wrapped her arms underneath his, dragging him away around a corner with ease.

"He's fine," she said as she came back into view. "He'll be out cold for a few hours, won't remember what just happened."

A feeling of intense vulnerability washed over me as I processed how alone I was, the utter lack of control I held. Narah sat down in front of me, leaning against a rock jutting out of the floor. I didn't move; I couldn't. Chase was maybe a quarter way through healing me before he run out of strength.

"How did you do that?" I rasped.

"Cusp Zodiac Turning mimics a storm." She held out her hand. A fizz of electricity buzzed between her pointer finger and thumb. "It's an electrical current."

"What were you talking about? The bloodlines?"

"He's my brother." She laughed at me, shaking her head, as if her answer was a casual piece of information. The blood drained from my face. It made sense; her tone of voice, slightly sharp facial features, strong jawline—it was all vaguely familiar to him.

"That's nice." I tilted my head back to keep my world from spinning. I wasn't sure how to react or what else to say. "You could've killed me."

"I know," she said, her voice still cold. "Why do you think you're a Zodiac Turner?"

"What does that have to do with anything?"

"Answer the question."

"Maybe my dad? I don't know." I shrugged. "Atlas did say there were at least six Zodiac Turners. My mom refuses to talk to me about my biological father."

"*Fulbright.* Fulbright is helping you. Of *course* he led you to the scroll his brother wrote." Her tone of voice suddenly sharpened, the anger on her face intensifying. "Chase and I—our father is Silas Merek."

My world spun as the breath escaped my chest. The arm I was propping myself up with collapsed. I trembled. I stared at the rock ceiling as I tried to process the information. Chase got his healing from Mathias Merek.

"Silas and Atlas, both immortals. Fulbright is the forgotten brother, omitted from the myths our family was made into. Our mother is an immortal, too, Sora Merek. And—" Narah leaned forward with a smile, "—all three of them are Zodiac Turners."

"I have a scroll written by Silas about the Code's lies, and they're fucking using his daughter as a weapon against me?"

She met my eyes. "I must stop you before you instigate another uprising."

"That is *not* what you said a year ago." I laughed at her out of sheer astonishment. "Narah, we—you and I—were trying to reverse the law that was partially created to damage your family. How are they controlling you like this?"

"You will start another war. Let Scorpio keep their power, and Gardian stays at peace."

"Your father's scroll warns of the opposite, that the Scorpio Code will upset the gods and cause an imbalance in Gardian's magic system."

"You don't understand." She leaned closer to me. "I wasn't raised by Silas, barely by Sora. Our parents were forced to separate because of a curse Blaine put on them. If Silas and Sora are near each other, Chase and I will feel the consequences."

"Then who were you raised by?"

The details of the memory in the Woods at night—she'd made mentions of how much she hated the man she lived with, how she was surprised that he even left her food when he disappeared for a few days, the curse he put on her to trap her in the Woods while he was gone.

"Chase and I were raised together until he was 5, I was 3. He's two years older than me. Neither of us remembers that part of our childhood. Blaine found our parents in a town on the Conviction-Autarchic border and put the curse on them when he learned they had children. Silas believed Chase shouldn't know about our family's history and raised him in Conviction Woods. Sora wanted me to know. I was raised by her and Fulbright for thirteen years before Blaine finally got ahold of me."

"Pause," I stopped her. "Where did Sora and Atlas raise you?"

"The same town we were born in. Blaine kidnapped me when I was 13 and cursed them away from me."

Though anger clearly consumed each word she spat out of her mouth, growing with each mention of her family, she looked like she was on the verge of tears. As if she had been waiting for a long time to tell me the truth. Her eyes darted when she told her story, her body switching between bouts of shivers and angry explanations—she was only partially in control.

That was the thing about the Mereks; they were never in control.

Mereks made up four of the six Zodiac Turners: Narah, Atlas, Silas, and Sora. There were only two Turners left on the list; one was me, and the other was an immortal man who manipulated history.

Narah smiled. "Your father, Blaine, created the Scorpio Code."

CHAPTER 28

"You fool. How dare you try to save your people when the cause of their peril exists in your own blood?"

My body went cold.

I stared blankly at Narah as I attempted to digest what I inherently knew to be the truth. My vision went fuzzy from tears, the blood rushing in my ears. My magic spurred, and I pressed my hands to my legs before my light could escape from my hands in the intense shock.

"He is a monster," I choked out, shaking my head. "I cannot be related to him."

"Quite honestly, I'm shocked you didn't even consider it."

I wanted to tear open my own skin and let my blood pour. The man who had caused each and every problem I was to fix was my own father, my own blood. It all made sense; why I was a Zodiac Turner, why my mother refused to speak of him, why she despised the existence of her own daughter. Each revelation stung me in a different place, as if I was being turned inside out from my organs to my skin, a sickly dread thick on my skin with the cold dew of the cave.

Reversing the Code doubled in complexity when it was my own father who created it; I would have to prove not only its legitimacy but myself, too.

"My father couldn't stop yours," Narah said, moving closer to me. My breath lodged in my throat as I choked down my emotions. "Now it's my turn to stop you."

My body swayed. Narah noticed me on the verge of passing out, leaning over and touching her fingers to my arm. I gasped and sat up, rigid as pain screeched through my chest at the abrupt movement. I yelled out as my fingernails dug into my torso. My heart pounded faster, my magic throbbed, and my blood rushed as her hand slowly lifted from my arm.

Uncontrollable tears slid down my cheeks, exhausted from fighting against my own emotions. I was only the next-generation child of war.

"It's why the village's shields failed," Narah continued. Anger rushed through me at the sound of her voice. "Our two families. We are the only bloodlines to walk out of those caverns alive."

"If you're planning on killing me, why haven't you already?" I snapped back. "End my life. End your problems."

Narah didn't answer.

I shook my head as tears slid down my face. I was dramatic, over-emotional, everything I'd been taught to not become. My magic was from the same man whose anger induced a war. My heritage was tainted. The Stellarium had every right to repress me; I was a threat, a living weapon of generational vengeance.

My thoughts blurred. My breathing shuddered. I drew my legs

closer to myself with a wheeze, wrapping my arms around them. There was no one to punish me for embarrassing myself. I choked on air, clawing at my thighs as the world collapsed on top of me. It was my fault. Everything. Chase was knocked out somewhere around the corner. My body was torn and scarred forever.

Narah struggled to respond to any of my actions. I tried to stop breathing, so I'd faint. I silently begged her to kill me, to get it over with. Perhaps my death would give justice to history in itself. My purpose served metaphorically through the end of my story.

"Why don't you do it?" I snarled. Narah flinched at my sudden outburst, her eyes filling with anger again. "Kill me."

Tears streaked my cheeks; my nails dove deeper into my bloody leg. For the first time, I enjoyed my pain as a punishment. My ears rang, my vision shaking from fury.

"Do it!" I yelled. "Kill me right now, if that's what you want!"

For a split second, there was a flash of empathy across Narah's face. A red glow emanated from her chest underneath her shirt.

"A year ago, the Stellarium held a knife to my throat and forced you to take my memories of you." I stood up in a flash, ignoring the tearing open of my skin. "In front of everything we were afraid of, you told me you loved me."

Horror flashed across her expressions. The same horror I saw on her face when the blade pierced my skin. The recognition of how it was supposed to be between us.

Her face contorted with fury. She pulled a blade from her belt, grabbing my shoulders to drag me to the ground. She pinned me down with one leg and shoved her knife to my throat. I leaned back from the blade as she held it against my skin.

"I wouldn't have been tortured by the Stellarium," she hissed, her face inches from mine, "if I hadn't loved you."

I met her gaze fiercely as her pale hair shielded her face. "But you knew the risk, what the Stellarium was capable of, and you still chose to love me."

She pressed the knife closer to me. There it was again—behind the fury spread across her face—a desperation, a plea for help. Her fingers almost slipped off the dagger's handle.

"You are being used as a weapon against a person you loved. Wake up, Narah, before you become the reason we lose our second chance."

She kept me pinned, pressing her leg into my scars. I didn't flinch. I leaned my head back as she readied to cut open my neck, my magic flaring to life again as she held me down. Narah bent closer to me, her thumb squeezing the knife. I struggled to stay awake at the sheer agony. Light bolted through my veins as I stopped resisting my magic. The blade didn't move. Narah gasped in breaths full of anger, and then her eyes darted away from mine, looking down at her knife on my throat. It aligned with the scar on the middle of my neck.

She hissed with agony as the red glow on her chest burned brighter and the air thickened with the stench of burning skin. Narah yanked the blade away from my skin, hurling it toward the wall with her full force. It clattered against stone. She screamed out in pain, her palm slamming against her chest.

She leaned down to cough up blood, and with agonized tears streaming down her face, she sparked a light between her fingers to press to my forehead.

    The bright daylight in Conviction Woods was a drastic change to the darkness of the cave. I was thrown into a memory where the mossy earth cushioned me as I sat in the Sun. In the forest clearing, wildflowers grew around us in pastels of pink, yellow, and blue. The Sun beamed against my bare shoulders as Narah moved my hair away from my back. Though I wore black shorts, my shirt was neatly folded next to me. Narah's hand carefully moved down my spine. I winced at the burning sensation following the ghost of her touch as her fingers skipped over the gauze tightly wrapped around the middle of my back and over my chest.

    "Why'd they hurt you this much?" she said quietly, inspecting the open wounds on my back. "It's so much worse than what they normally do to you."

    "Stood up for a Libra getting beat up by a group of Aries boys right outside the school this morning." I shook my head slowly. "I didn't even show emotions, and it wasn't like I was automatically friends with the Libra. All I did was warn them to back off."

    Narah sighed. "Kira."

    "What was I supposed to do? Walk away?"

    "I understand, but this is horrific, and I don't like to see you hurt." The cadence of Narah's tone and gentle pattern of her speech soothed me. I could've listened to her voice for hours. "Did your mom find out about this yet?"

    "No, she's not home tonight."

"Thank god." Narah breathed out slowly. "What about Rowan?"

"He comes home tonight." I smiled at the thought. "I'll tell him you helped to heal it."

"Good." Her hand centered on the gauze as she found the medical tape keeping it together. "May I?"

I nodded, holding my breath as she peeled back the bloody wrap. We'd planned earlier in the week that today was a good day to explore the Woods together, and I knew as soon as I was shoved into the school office that Narah would finally get the healing practice in Libra-Scorpio she'd been wanting. I'd mentally prepared throughout the day, the nervousness only growing up until the moment she finished unraveling the gauze in circles around my body. I was left completely vulnerable with my back to her.

"It's so much worse than I thought," she said quietly. "Take a deep breath in and out."

I did as she said, grimacing as she slowly pressed her palm to the open gashes from the damn whip. Moments after the agonizing sting of the touch, warmth passed over me in a wave, beginning on the wound and spreading to my heart. It circulated to every part of my body, tracing through my veins as a shimmering gold energy. I could feel how much Narah cared, how badly she wanted to ease my pain. It was the most soothing sensation I'd ever experienced, the gentle mending of the torn skin on my back, the emotion carrying from her heart to mine in the light of the blood she gave to me. I felt her nervousness, yearning, possession; underneath it all was a fierce desire to be my shield.

As the golden light faded, Narah's hands slowly followed my sides, lingering on my hips. Her grasp barely tightened before she hesitantly drew her hands away. I immediately missed her touch. She slipped my shirt back over my head, and I lost my breath as she wrapped her arms around my ribs to pull me closer. With her chest against my back, she pressed her lips to the slope between my shoulder and neck.

I couldn't handle the tension any longer.

I turned toward Narah. Her legs were folded neatly, her white button-up shirt partially astray, no longer tucked into her dark blue slacks. When I'd first seen her that day, her hair had been partially braided back, but now strands escaped and drifted with the spring breeze. Her legs draped one over the other, as if grace was natural to her, despite her headstrong and confident demeanor. I was entranced, observing every tiny detail and etching them into my memory. Her blue eyes, and the way her skin almost sparkled in a patch of sunlight dancing through cedar branches. She was the very balance of gentle and fierce, of water and fire, of vitality and eloquence.

I met her eyes. My body reacted before my mind could. I reached forward, tracing her jawline with my hand, and she tangled her fingers in my hair as she pulled me closer. In the summer heat, we kissed with the intensity of a connection I could barely fathom as possible.

Seconds later, I moved my face away from hers but couldn't bring myself to undo the touch of our bodies. "I'm so sorry."

"Kira, what could you possibly be apologizing for?" she said as she brushed strands of hair out of my face. "Look at me and tell me what you feel."

"I'd be killed for this," I said, "but I think I love you."

"You think? I know I love you."

She tilted my head up to meet her eyes, and my jaw trembled, my eyes darting to her lips. I'd never seen so much warmth in someone else's expressions, her gentle smile telling a story of us that I wanted to know every detail of again. I was at the mercy of the way it felt when her hand grasped my side, paralyzed at her thumb brushing over my lips. I could not help but be blinded by her bright smile and soft grin in that moment, in those green woods surrounded by sword ferns and cedars and pines, a feeling so reflective of the home I found in the Woods itself.

"The next time someone lays a hand on you," she said, leaning toward me, "I will tear them apart with my bare hands."

Chapter 29

A small jolt of energy woke me up. My eyes flew open, and I sucked in a breath of moist cavern air, another pang of pain spreading through my chest. A few of my barely healed wounds had been opened up again. A wet cloth was placed on my forehead while my body burned with a fever. The heavy and harsh breaths I fought to take in sent beads of sweat rolling down my body. Hunger gnawed at my stomach and thirst dried my mouth.

"She's awake."

I jumped at Chase's voice resonating from across the cavern. He was in sight again.

I did *not* have enough time to recover from the memory before I realized that Narah was at arm's length with me. I could've sworn I could still feel the warmth of her hand against my back, the taste of her mouth. She was messing with something in her hands, sitting against the rock across from me. Standing up without a word, she leaned over me to flip the cloth on my forehead, then winced as she turned away. My eyes followed her. She'd shed her long pants and heavy clothing, sitting in black base-layer shorts and a white tank top. On her chest was a pendant that looked as if it had welded to her swollen and red skin. The air still stank of skin on fire, an unfortunately familiar smell.

"You could let me heal her if you don't want her to die," Chase said.

Narah reached over to grab a flask of water, handing it to me. I tipped the water into my mouth and drank it hesitantly. When it didn't taste abnormal, I desperately inhaled the rest. I leaned against the ground, too exhausted to fight. Chase sent me a sympathetic look, his hands tied behind his back again.

Narah stared at me with her back to Chase. I fiercely returned her gaze. There were so many emotions hidden behind her eyes. She walked over to Chase, reaching down to cut the ropes off his hands. Chase looked at her wildly, backing up against the wall. His eyes darted to her pendant.

She motioned to me with her head. "Heal her."

Chase hurried to me. He leaned over, lifting the washcloth off my forehead while pressing the back of his hand to my skin. His other lay on my arm, and he closed his eyes. I breathed out slowly as the golden light pooled into me again. It felt smooth. Clean. Gentle, happy. It wasn't nearly as abrupt and staggered as before.

"I talked to Avia, Dreamsought her," Chase leaned closer so Narah wouldn't overhear him. "She knows we're alive."

When he healed as much as he could manage, he lifted his bloody hand. The tension in my chest had loosened, and I gasped in a full breath of air. The wounds on my torso were no longer trickling blood. With a shaking hand, Chase helped me to sit up while glaring at Narah.

She sat against the rock across from us. The cave was brighter, two torches lit instead of one. Narah leaned over and rummaged through a backpack, sliding two bags of freeze-dried food to us.

"You took care of her while I was passed out?"

Narah stared at him in response.

"Are you alright?" Chase asked me, ignoring Narah's presence when she didn't respond. I opened the bag of dried food. It was an assortment of meats, fruit, and vegetables. I stuffed it in my mouth with a trembling hand, disregarding how disgusting the mix was.

I was still so far out of it from the memory. "That's a really complex question for me right now."

"Narah," Chase started, shifting his attention to her. "What were you talking about before you knocked me out? Someone is related?"

She sighed. "You didn't forget?"

"What? You walked up to me, pressed your fingers to my forehead, and I was out cold."

Narah stood up, walking over to him. She rubbed her index finger and thumb together, creating a spark of energy. Chase ducked away from her as he realized what was about to happen, but it was already too late. She grabbed his arm and shocked him. He went limp.

"Listen. He can't know." Narah met my eyes. The pendant grew brighter, and she sucked in a pained breath. She was losing her aggressive demeanor. "I can't explain why."

She hissed through her gritted teeth as she leaned her head back, gasping in a breath of agony. She refused to look over at me, leaving us both in a temporary silence.

"Narah," I pushed, "I just remembered when you healed my back."

"Rieka, I can't—" Her voice split with pain as her fingers tore into her thighs at the agony. "Help."

A drop of blood traced down her lip. Her body was trembling as she fought against her overwhelming anger, and I was watching it kill her. The pendant on her chest brightened.

In my delirium, I found a sort of superhuman strength, pushing myself to my feet. Anger rushed over Narah's face as she attempted to push me back weakly. I grabbed her arms, shoving her against the rock. She released a guttural, furious cry. I threw my legs around her side to ground her.

I wasn't sure what I was about to do or how I was going to do it. The fear in Narah's eyes was overwhelming enough to spark an adrenaline so intense that my veins exploded with light. Electricity ran hot through me, and I gasped to alleviate the pain. I shoved my palm into the burning pendant on her chest, allowing my light to fall out of my hands and surround the object. The red-hot metal was welded into her skin, and at the touch of my light, it frosted over, so intensely cold that it seared my hand. I dug my fingers into the burn, and as fast as I could manage, I ripped it from her chest and snapped the chain on her neck.

She writhed in pain underneath me as I yelled at the freezing cold sensation sizzling against my hand. I hurled the pendant to the nearest wall with the last of my force. Blood immediately burst from where it had previously melted into her, and I unraveled a cloth off my healed arm, pressing it against her wound. She groaned as her head fell back, her hands grasping my injured sides for support. She rattled in rapid breaths, grimacing as her pain eased and the fog in her eyes cleared.

Silence spread between both of us. Her hand fell atop the cloth I held against her, and I let go, leaning back. Her other hand lingered on my waist, falling away as I backed up. I had no idea how to act around her.

"I'm so sorry." Her voice split as she leaned her head back, staring at the ceiling. "I could only feel anger. The pendant, it was an artifact from the War, cursed to weaponize one soldier to kill the other."

"How did I release you from that?" I stumbled over my words.

"You wanted to save my life. Zodiac Turners can reverse curses if they use their magic with the opposite intention."

"Narah, my memory." My body shook at the release of magic. The lingering sensation of her hand on my waist distracted me. Her face contorted with grief and guilt. "What happened?"

"We knew each other for five years," she answered hoarsely. "I'm a Spirit Walker in Gemini-Cancer. Spirit Walkers can manipulate memory with fear. They forced my hands on you when I was terrified, and it cleared your memory of me. Verena, she knows I knew you, but I was the only member of the Stellarium who could follow you into Rayka and kill you. They want me to retrieve the Callexus."

I knew the truth in the matter when I caught her solemn and regretful emotions seemingly blending into my own. The infectious anger was only but a scar on the outside of her chest. I ached for the pain she must've endured, and as much as she'd hurt me, she was no stranger to being a victim to the Scorpio Stellarium.

"If they find out I've told you any of this," she said, "they'll kill me. Or, worse, they'll take my memory, and I won't be able to stop them from using me to take your life."

"I'd rather live."

"And I'd rather not kill you." She choked the words out. "How much do you remember?"

"Not much, if it was five years." I shook my head, shivering with nervousness. "I don't know why I'm only remembering now. I don't understand."

Her brows furrowed. "The only people who can restore or remove memories are Spirit Walkers."

"I had no contact with a Spirit Walker prior to meeting Kaia, though." I shook my head. The first memory I recovered was in the Woods at Chase's house, weeks before I met Kaia. "How do you know these things about Spirit Walking? It was wiped from historical records, according to Sora. Or, sorry, your mom, I guess."

"I'm not sure how you're getting your memories back," she said quietly. She swallowed hard, unable to look me in the eyes. "You were not the only Scorpio they forced me to use Spirit Walking on."

"Oh." My heart dropped. "How long did they make you do that?"

"Up until they realized they could use my Zodiac Turning for much worse and started training me as an assassin." She held her arms closer to herself. "You have no idea what they've put me through."

I couldn't fathom the horrors that the Scorpio Stellarium must've done to her, but I knew it hurt so badly to see her pain. I reached forward, placing my hands over hers and forcing her gaze to mine. She could've shoved me away or knocked me out with her magic, and I expected her to do so. Instead, she met my eyes with a level of emotional intensity that reverberated through my body and chest.

"They hurt both of us, Narah," I said. "I don't want to be my father. I am going to continue to do what is right for my people, and I am going to reverse the Scorpio Code, even if it kills me."

"They told me they'd take my memory if I didn't bring back the

Callexus." Narah blinked tears away. "If you get the Callexus, the Code is at risk. If they get it, they'll never have to worry about the Code being threatened again."

"The Stellarium is sick for using you as a weapon. You never should've been put in this position. We're not supposed to be enemies."

"I know that. I had one motive with that damned pendant, and it was to fight against everything you willed," she said, and then paused. She held something back.

"Narah."

"I need to let you leave."

Hope soared through me. "Do you know how to get out of this cave?"

"Yes."

"There's no exit?"

"There is. But I'll only let you out under one condition."

I perked up.

"Don't tell Chase." She pressed her hands together. "There is a reason Fulbright and Sora haven't told him. It's... it'll make sense later. It's for his sake."

I didn't question it; if Atlas and Sora had willingly withheld the information from him, it had gravity that I could not comprehend.

Narah led us through a tunnel to the surface underneath one of the rocks she had leaned against. We emerged in the forest.

"The hell?" Chase said, rubbing his eyes. Narah had woken him up only to release us. "Did you drag us in there or something?"

Narah shrugged. "I have my ways."

When she was ahead of us, Chase pointed at her with wide eyes, shuffling through the snow next to me. He motioned toward his neck, as if it was being cut open, then to his upper chest to mimic the pendant.

"I'll explain later," I whispered as we followed Narah through the woods. We would've never navigated it by ourselves. Narah weaved through the trees as if she'd walked the path many times. Her movements, fluid and graceful, were completely opposite to Chase as he tripped over buried branches. I couldn't blame myself for not catching their similarities faster.

When we reached the village, Narah stopped at the tree line. I paused, holding my sore burning torso.

Narah nodded at the village. "You're welcome."

"You're welcome?" I repeated, my heart sinking as Chase and I stepped toward the Rayka. "Narah, you should come with us. You'd be safer."

She looked over at Chase, then grabbed my arm to pull me closer to her so he wouldn't hear. "I'll repeat myself, Blaine cursed Sora and Fulbright away from me. Sora is in that village."

"Narah—"

"Listen to me." She stepped forward, grabbing my arm. I was wordless for a moment, sucking in a breath as she inched closer to me. Despite the cold air, my face was burning up. I had no idea what the hell was going on. "You need to go. I'll tell the Stellarium I didn't find you in the village."

"Narah, please," I said again, my heart lodged in my throat as I forced each word out. She'd already started to turn around. "Wait—"

I was cut off as she let go of my arm and tore away from me. She didn't give me time to convince her, slipping back into the woods and disappearing from my sight. Chase touched his hand to my shoulder. I jumped.

"What just happened?"

"Honestly? I'm not sure," I said quietly, still focused on where she left. "She didn't want to kill me. I was right. She had a curse set on her by the Stellarium that made her angry."

"Why'd she just run off? Did you not..." Chase said, attempting to find the right words to avoid making me uncomfortable. "Okay, I don't know the full story, but I thought you said you broke the third tenet of the Code with her."

I barely laughed. "Oh, I definitely did."

"And you just removed a curse. So why is she not coming with us?"

"It's complicated."

I tore my eyes away from where she disappeared to and swallowed my frustration. She would've followed us in, if it weren't for Sora's presence. Narah hadn't even told me the full extent of the curse.

"I'm sorry, Rieka," Chase said solemnly as we started to walk back to the village. "If she's in the area, maybe she'll come around."

I would've appreciated his optimism if it wasn't for the fact that I knew she couldn't come back around. I'd never seen Chase in such a terrible, distraught condition—his hair was strangely parted in three directions, greasy and oily with sweat. Red stains covered his shirt as blood dripped from his hands.

"Excuse me?" I motioned with my hand toward his palms as we returned to the village. "You could've hurt yourself, too."

"Being forcefully zapped to unconsciousness a bunch of times is not true rest. I didn't have time to recover."

"And you still healed me?" I said. "You can't do that to yourself. Now what if you get sick?"

"I'd say the same to you. We can rest before even attempting anything with the Callexus."

The mention of the Callexus reminded me of what Narah revealed to me about who my father was. My stomach turned again at the thought of being related to someone so horrible. I shut my mouth and tried not to think about it, but I couldn't stop the curse of my own family from dangling over my shoulders. I had to fix a lot, somehow responsible for the deaths and mess Blaine had caused over centuries-worth of time.

"Rieka?"

I hadn't realized I stopped walking. We were close to the house, and I'd halted right in my tracks in the middle of the path. Chase raised a brow at me as I opened my mouth to say something but couldn't force a word out. Dipping my head, I hurried after him again as we approached the house.

I could barely muster a smile as Chase knocked on the door, faltering at the hovering pressure. I wasn't sure if my emotions would ever stop smothering me under the guilt flowing through my own blood.

Chapter 30

Avia practically tackled me.

"Careful!" Chase scolded her as she jumped on me. I wheezed and flinched at her tight hug. One of the wounds on my stomach felt like it was dampening. "Avia!"

"I'm so glad you're alive." Avia didn't loosen her grip, despite Chase's warning. When he gently tapped her shoulder, she stepped back from me and smacked him on the arm. I winced. I knew how hard she could hit. "You almost got her killed."

"I am aware," Chase said, shaking out his arm while she glared at him. "I'll talk to you about it later."

She nodded at him, unlatching herself from me. They must've spoken about the situation when Chase Dreamsought her; otherwise, Avia wouldn't have been on speaking terms with him.

"We were about to set out to search for you," Kaia said, beckoning us in. Chase and I collapsed on the couch while Avia sat on the floor, Kaia leaning against the wall. "You're both a mess."

"You should probably get washed up, Rieka," Avia interrupted my thoughts. For a moment, I was annoyed at her for messing up my concentration, but I was lost in my own head again. "You're soaked in blood. We'll talk to Chase about this while you're in the shower."

"We got invited to a dinner with Sora, by the way," Kaia added. "Tonight. She wanted to talk to us about the caves, history, that kinda stuff."

I glanced up quickly and looked over at Chase. Sora—his mother. An immortal. An immortal Zodiac Turner, the wife of Silas Merek, who had a war blamed on who she fell in love with. The entire time, the living proof that the Mereks weren't a myth was traveling with me.

"Rieka, go shower, shoo." Avia huffed and rolled her eyes. I grumbled and stood up. "Chase also clearly needs a nap."

Chase crossed his arms. "No, I don't."

"Yes, you do." Kaia added. "Your hands are bloody. You're not fooling anyone, tough guy."

He sighed. "What time should we be out of here?"

"Chase, look at me," Kaia said. He still tried to avoid eye contact until she stepped directly in front of him. "You need rest. We can tell someone we need extra time so you can take a nap."

Both of us nodded in defeat, and I headed to the bathroom, my thoughts still cloudy. I felt raw and split open, emotionally and physically.

The Sun was setting by the time we were ready. All of us stood at the door while Chase attempted to make sure we were all in one piece, despite being all over the place himself. He wore the garb given to him by the village; a simple white tunic, furred at the edges with a golden outline, and slacks designed more or less the same. Kaia had taken my clothing to a material shapeshifter somewhere in the village for repair while I showered and rested, assumably to a material shapeshifter somewhere in the village.

"Everyone ready?" Chase said, straightening himself.

"Are you sure you'd like to join us tonight, Rieka?" Kaia said, gesturing to my torso. "That wound can't feel good."

"She'll be alright," Chase answered for me. "I'm monitoring her. I can always heal her if something happens."

"I think you've done enough healing," Avia said, pushing him out the door. "Stop being a doctor. Let's go."

He grumbled at her but let her push him outside. Pressed snow and ice sheeted the stone streets. Avia took the lead, melting the path so the rest of us didn't slip.

We arrived at a restaurant, though it was more of a hut. A blue door was placed in the center of the wooden building, two windows cracked open. Steam drifted from within the restaurant, carrying the savory smell of noodles and meat. Kaia led us in. Chase had to duck to not hit his head on the low ceiling.

Inside was a one-room dining area and a singular door to a kitchen. A raised slab of pinewood sat in the middle of the space, outlined with mats. The table was set with a particular order to it with a napkin, plate, bowl, and a glass of water at each spot. A few round paper lanterns hung from the ceiling in gold, blue, and orange, softly buzzing with a form of light magic. Fairy lights draped along the ceiling, and melted candles fused wax with wood on windowsills.

The back door to the kitchen flung open. Sora hurried in, and I tried not to stare, but it was difficult when I noticed the traits that her two children inherited. Narah had her pale hair, both of them with her defined jawline, and skin tone a perfect match. Sora's eyes were deceiving, the green and brown heterochromia matching whatever magic she possessed in Leo-Virgo. Sora caught my stare, and I looked away quickly.

"Welcome," she said softly, dipping her head. "Please, have a seat. Your platters are being prepared in the back."

I made sure to sit across from Chase to watch his reactions, placing myself the closest I could to Sora, while Avia sat next to Chase, and Kaia on my left. I crossed my legs on the mat, clasping my hands together to avoid revealing my nervousness.

"Good evening," Sora said. "I am pleased to welcome you to supper."

"Just you?" Chase echoed warily.

"Just me." She smiled at him but turned her attention in seconds. Her eyes didn't linger on him for too long. She leaned over to remove her dark brown and green jacket.

"I'm sorry we've been out for a day," Chase apologized. "We went into the woods and a monster attacked us. Long story short..."

He trailed off, internally debating if he should tell her about Narah. I mentally willed him to. I wanted to see Sora's reaction.

"...we were too unwell to be out in public."

"As Avia kindly informed me," Sora said. Chase's face flooded with relief at his unquestioned lie. "We have not seen a dragon in those woods for ages. Capricorn typically keeps them much farther north. I'm relieved to hear of your swift recovery. The healers in our village would've found pride in assisting with your treatment, too."

It was the way she said it. Sora met my eyes with an intensity I couldn't have prepared for. She knew. A tiny smile rested on her face, unreadable to anyone else, a smile that told me she didn't believe Chase's lie for a second.

"I was disappointed at your departure, though I am pleased you have returned. I hope you connected well."

It was astounding how she could communicate that she knew what had happened, without giving it away to another soul. Her excellence with language and vocabulary was indicative of an immortal's knowledge. I was completely dumbfounded as to how she'd found out the truth of the matter in the first place.

"Connected?" Kaia echoed.

"Oh, I do apologize." She cleared her throat. "'Connected' is a medical term we use in Rayka. It is poorly translated from the Rurian word for 'heal.' I should have assumed your unfamiliarity with ancient terminology foreign to the majority of Gardian."

"Does that mean you've been outside this village?" Chase asked.

"Dion and I hold the role as the traveling folk of Rayka," she explained. "Our job is to ensure our town's security."

"He's the Capricorn, isn't he?" Kaia asked, leaning forward. "What about Gardian's fear toward Capricorn?"

"He travels north, I travel south," Sora answered her simply. "Most of Assiduous resides north of Rayka."

Chase nodded in approval. "Cool."

"Rieka, you are a Zodiac Turner. You understand that our village, of all the communities in Gardian, believes Zodiac Turners to be a symbol of balance?"

"It's been comforting," I said, letting my shoulders relax at the warm, inviting look on her face. I had so many questions for her. I was the child of the man who caused her centuries-worth of pain and struggle. I was from her family's enemy. I struggled to understand why she looked at me so lovingly.

"Have you trained to mitigate the harm of your magic?" she asked as our food was brought out by a server. A bowl of noodles was set in front of each of us.

"Uh," I stammered, "no. I mean, I can create the wheel, I recently accidentally turned Chase's sign. I haven't really talked to many Zodiac Turners."

She frowned as she finished eating a spoonful. "Zodiac Turning is immensely dangerous when the handler has not been properly trained."

I sighed. "I know."

"Try to avoid shame. Many centuries ago, we protected Zodiac Turners during the War of the Rebalancing," Sora said. "There is a training arena here, in Rayka, where they'd practice their magic."

"Really?" I perked up. "Where?"

"Patience. I suggest you enjoy your meal. I would be honored to show you to the temple tonight."

"Yes, please." I smiled at Sora again, leaning down to eat some of the noodles. I ate much faster than I expected myself to, still ravenously hungry from the days in the cave.

"While you were gone, Sora was telling me about Spirit Walking.

She's very informative about magic systems," Kaia brought up, nodding at her. Sora bowed her head. "There're many different skills that are far past my current level of ability. Spirit Walkers are capable of memory alteration and astral travel. I need to begin studying the stories of the Stars."

"Yes, Spirit Walkers begin with limited skill because of the magic's easy onset. Kaia has many years of practice in her future," Sora added. "Chase, your Libran Healing—how did it show up for you?"

He tilted his head. "It was agonizing. I was 10, I think. It burned through me, like the Sun itself existed in my body, and didn't ease up until I healed a wounded animal in the Woods. I didn't know what I was doing."

"Right. Though you began with powerful and painful magic, you needed to accrue medical knowledge to refine your skills. A Spirit Walker's magic begins with low strength with emotional sensing but advances into more branches of magic." Sora turned to me. "Rieka. The onset of your Zodiac Turning?"

I wasn't sure how to answer, because I didn't know. I'd discovered it before my memory was taken. So I answered her question about what happened in Lyra.

"I was so angry that it woke up."

"Correct. Zodiac Turning is entirely dependent on emotional control. While Libran Healing centers itself in the body and blood, Spirit Walking is the realm of mind and water. Zodiac Turning draws its power from emotion, converting feelings into usable energy. Each represent... never mind, excuse me for a moment."

Sora stood up, hurrying into the back kitchen to go grab something.

Kaia's eyes flickered between Chase and me. "Did either of you know anything about that?"

I shook my head. Chase shrugged.

Sora reentered the room, placing a paper in the middle of the table with a quill and ink in her hands. She leaned over to draw three circles, labeling each one with body, mind, and magic, and then Libran Healing, Spirit Walking, and Zodiac Turning. She pulled a line through all three circles.

"Libran Healing, the Sun, physicality," she said, sitting back down. "With a lack of Libran Healers, we have experienced increased illness, a decrease in the overall number of healers."

"Is having more Libran Healers in Gardian the only way to repair that imbalance?" Chase asked hesitantly. "Maybe you don't know the answer to this, but I'm not the only modern-day Libran Healer... right?"

Avia wheezed at him, sitting back with a laugh. "No, Chase, you're the last of a dying system of magic, and Gardian's depending on you to have Libran Healer children. Hope you can plan well."

"Can you stop?" He glared at her before looking over at Sora. "I was asking seriously. I'd really like to know if I'm not alone."

Sora had a tiny, amused smile on her face. "No, you are not the only Libran Healer, and there may be other ways to return the magic system to Gardian. I can speak to you about it another time."

"Thank you, Sora," Chase said respectfully. I could've sworn there was a flash in Sora's eyes of regret, sadness, when he spoke her name. It couldn't have been easy, watching her son fail to recognize his mother.

"Rieka." Sora turned to me again. "Zodiac Turning, magic, emotion. You are a living representation of the balance in magic systems in all 12 signs. Since the lack of Zodiac Turners, Gardian has experienced a decrease in functionality in all powers, and a heightened tendency for political and emotional imbalances in society."

"I never would've thought," Avia said, looking over at me. "It put Gardian into an imbalance that much?"

"Far more than people realize. The archpowers were established for a reason. They are critically necessary. It has resulted in hundreds of thousands of deaths since the War of Rebalancing, between increased illness and decreased magic performance."

"How ironic, It was meant to be the War of the Rebalancing, not the War of the Debalancing," Avia said. Chase shook his head at her dry joke. Kaia sighed loudly, putting her face in her palms. Avia crossed her arms at them. "I thought it was funny."

"Is it getting worse?" I asked Sora, ignoring my sister.

"Imbalance takes years to worsen," Sora pointed out. "When it happens over a period of three centuries, it is difficult to notice change. If Libran Healing and Zodiac Turning returned to Gardian, we'd restore much of our strength as a society, let alone regain connection with the divinities through Spirit Walkers."

"That's what happens when you let men make decisions," Kaia sniped, and I laughed. "Wasn't all this bullshit started by two men that were angry at each other?"

"Correct," Sora said, her voice faltering. I could see the guilt on her face. Sora was the spark for that anger, and I couldn't even begin to comprehend how it felt to have all of that upon her own shoulders. "It was far more complex than that, but at most, a cause of ignorance to nature and increased ego and revenge in... some individuals."

"Sorry, are there any texts I could read to help me better understand?" I asked carefully. "Rayka preserves that history, and that's where you're drawing your information from, yes?"

"No need to apologize, love. There are scripts in the temple I'll show you to. History and ancient magic coincide. Zodiac Turning is a power few have ever come close to perfecting. It is equally as dangerous as it is powerful, the great dance of balance in your own body, like in time and society."

Chapter 31

The Sun hadn't even begun to rise. I grunted with frustration as I struggled to slip my boots on without untying them. Sora hadn't said much after dinner while she showed me to the temple, instead instructing me to return once I'd rested. I had so many questions for her.

"You're up early." Chase strolled into the living room with a cup of tea in his hand. "Your sister was just telling me yesterday about how you like to sneak out before dawn breaks."

"I'm going to meet Sora at the temple she was showing me last night." I reached over and grabbed a long shoelace, sticking it in my mouth as I tried to re-lace the tangled boot. "What's your excuse?"

"Kaia was showing me some books from the library about Spirit Walking. She told me to check out the stuff they have for Libran Healing. I'm getting a head start on my homework," Chase said with a smile. "You should really take a minute to let your body wake. You look like you got up five minutes ago."

"That's because I got up five minutes ago."

"Rieka. Come on now."

"Where's Avia?"

"Still sleeping in the same room as you? Did you not see her when you woke up?"

I looked down at my shoes as I finally untangled them, slipping them on. "Yeah, I guess I did."

"She's your sister. You should probably check to make sure she didn't wander off in the middle of the night."

"Why would she do that?"

"Maybe it runs in the family."

I stood up quickly. When I rose, Chase blocked the door with his arms crossed. I glared at him, but he silently pointed toward the couch. Defeated, I sat down reluctantly as he settled in the chair across from me.

"You need some patience." He took a sip of his tea. "Have you had anything to eat?"

"No. I'm not hungry."

"Water?"

"I drank water, yes." I closed my eyes and fidgeted against the couch. "Can I leave now?"

"Are you going to listen to me if I say no?"

"Nope."

"Rieka." He gave me a look of pure disappointment. "Breathe. You're pushing yourself. I don't want you to get sick after you just recovered from being torn to shreds by a monster."

As he reached over to set his tea on the side table next to him, I caught sight of the bandage wrapped around his upper arm underneath his sleeve.

"What's up with that?"

"With what?"

I gestured toward my arm. "Did you hurt yourself on something?"

"Oh." His gaze cast aside. "No, just... scratched it on something in the cavern."

"I didn't notice, but I was pretty distracted. Are you being honest?"

"Yeah, don't worry about it." He leaned back and stared at the ceiling. "Pretty distracted, or distracted by pretty?"

"Both."

"Thought so. Don't you think you should wait until your sister gets up so you can spend some time with her? She was upset about your disappearance."

"Nah, I'll leave her to you." I shrugged at him, hurrying to the door. "You're all over her right now, anyway. I'm out. If you need me, I'll be at the old training arena on the western side of the village."

"Whatever you say." Chase sighed at me. "Don't get yourself into trouble."

"No promises."

I grinned at him, running out of the house before he could try to stop me again. I barely stayed on my feet as I navigated the shadowed, icy streets of Rayka. By the time the triangular-shaped temple was in sight, the dawn's chill had invigorated my body and mind. I slowed as I approached it. When I didn't see Sora, I started to inspect its log wall sides, decorated in unreadable ancient runic that I hadn't noticed in the dark. I traced my finger alongside a couple of the old Aiksil inscriptions.

"Good morning, Rieka."

I stepped back quickly at the sound of Sora's voice, tucking my hands behind my back. She stood in front of the door to the temple, opening it and beckoning me inside. I bowed my head at her as I hurried into the building. My feet shifted on top of sand, and in the dim morning light, I could barely see the unlit torches lining the walls.

Sora reached over to a rope hanging from the wall and twisted it. I flinched when the flame to my left flared to life, each of the torches catching fire one by one. A few crackled as they struggled to activate an old magic. The arena was mostly empty, with a sandy clearing covering the floor across the space. Despite the walls looking poorly insulated, the room was perfectly warm and comfortable.

"Now, Rieka." Sora made sure the door was locked before stepping onto the sand. She beckoned me to sit in front of her. "Tell me what really happened."

"How'd you know?"

"When you are nearing 300-years-old, you tend to understand the unspoken." She held out her hand to me. "I suppose I should properly introduce myself. Sora Merek, Zodiac Turner."

I shook her hand. She sat back, crossing her legs and straightening her back. She breathed in deeply, holding her hands out in front of herself. A controlled pale blue light slithered through her veins. She slowly faced her palm out as a zodiac wheel formed before her. She took her other hand, reaching it to push the wheel back onto her chest. With two fingers, she carefully twisted the wheel through the cusps, landing on Gemini-Cancer. As her hands lowered, the wheel quietly dissipated into a sparkly burst of light. She looked at me, holding her hand out to show me the deep blue light that coursed through her veins, mimicking the magic I'd seen in Kaia.

"I could sense that my daughter was nearby. What happened?"

"We were attacked by the dragon-monster... thing? Narah took us into a cave." I gestured to my torso with three fingers to represent claws. Sora winced at her daughter's name. "I had to remove a cursed pendant they put on her to make her want to take my life."

My mind clouded as I struggled to finish my thoughts. A powerful wave of emotions washed over me, and I shut my eyes tightly. Sora placed both of her hands on top of my own. My tension eased as a calm energy rippled over me.

"It's a shame how these events unfolded." Sora considered me. "Rieka, do not be afraid to open up to me. I will not judge."

Sora exuded an energy of such stability and strength that I inherently knew she was a trustworthy individual. I could see it in her considerate eyes, in her gentle smile, the way she looked at her son; she had truly pure intentions, an understanding from the centuries she'd lived through.

"They made her a weapon against me, because of me." The words fell from my mouth. I quickly swept away a tear sliding down my cheek.

"Sorry."

"I understand," Sora said when I struggled to finish my thoughts. "You do not need to explain yourself if you do not wish to do so."

I sat in silence, my shoulders shaking as I broke down again. With each heavy and mourning breath, a pain struck my core. I gritted my teeth and tried to shield my face from Sora.

"Rieka."

I looked up as I fought through my breakdown. Sora reached to my face, curling her palm around my cheek. I sank into the touch, shocked with myself as to how much I inherently trusted her.

"Be gentle with yourself," she comforted me. "You are safe here. I am no stranger to misunderstanding and judgment."

The emotion across her face struck me. She wasn't angry, nor upset, at how I was expressing my emotions. She beamed at me, truthfully, authentically, not with some fake smile to make me feel better. All my life, I'd searched for a glimpse of understanding, and I would've never predicted it to resonate with my best friend's immortal mother.

"May I remind you, for hundreds of years, a war between two men was blamed on me; instead of recognizing the vicious pattern of abuse and manipulation from Blaine, I was considered the cause of thousands of deaths."

"And history doesn't even know your name."

"Yes, I was lost with time when I became misunderstood. We are both misunderstood; I understand your struggles."

I trembled with a sudden rush of emotion that manifested itself in a sob.

"You are allowed to express emotions," Sora said softly, her other thumb rubbing against the back of my hand. "The core of our magic relies on the balance of our feelings."

Chapter 32

"Observe the space between my feet."

Sora stood in front of me, and adjusted her position so her feet were planted in the sand of the arena.

I did as she said, digging my heels into the sand and spacing my legs out. Sora straightened her back, and I immediately copied her action. She closed her eyes to focus and fine-tune her breathing, spacing out her careful breaths.

"Focus is required for harm reduction," she said, her eyes still closed. "You must be tunneled on both your emotions and your target. Without focus, you risk impacting someone you weren't intending to strike. Becoming inattentive to your emotions will cause pain and exhaustion."

"Do I focus on only one emotion?"

"For now, yes. Too many emotions may confuse your intention or drain your energy. When your skills are more advanced, you may experiment with two at once to understand how it strengthens and amplifies your Turning. Right now, you must focus on safety."

I frowned. "I feel so many emotions at once."

"You are human. We will work through it." With her back straight, she punched out a fist in a fluid motion. "The rest of my body does not move. It remains planted in the ground. Your fist moves directly outward from your shoulder, in line with your eyesight. Your arm should be parallel to the ground."

I repeated her motion. To my relief, no zodiac wheel appeared before me. She paused in her stance to lean forward, touching her hand to my back to straighten my posture. She adjusted the position of my shoulders and touched her index finger to my chin.

"Keep your head up. Your body must be steady. Bad posture will lash you backward. I could tell you many century-old stories that demonstrate the consequences of a lack of confidence." She walked around me, then held my other arm, lifting it to the same height as my fist. "When you turn someone's sign, you want to firmly grasp the wheel. Never pull backward, say from Scorpio to Libra instead of Scorpio to Sagittarius."

"Got it."

"Remember to keep your feet planted. I do not want to watch you fly."

I nodded, mentally noting the delicately stabilized position.

For the next few hours, Sora drilled me in repeating the initial motion until I was convinced I would find the same stance in my sleep. Sweat dripped from my forehead. Sora corrected me if my arms even slipped an inch. My delts quickly became sore from holding my arms up. I flopped onto the sand when I couldn't handle it any longer, leaning over to cough from the tightness in my lungs.

    Sora stood above me with a smile. "It will become easier over time."

    "You mean 300 years' worth of time?"

    "Not necessarily." She considered me. "Mastering Zodiac Turning is not a matter of length of years. It is understanding who you are and how you emotionally respond to the stimuli around you."

    "Sounds like something that's difficult to practice."

    "Yes." She began to walk to the door of the arena. "Come with me."

    I jumped to my feet, as if I hadn't been tired in the first place and hurried after her into the streets of Rayka. As she followed the curves and winds of the gravel pathways, I struggled to comprehend how she moved with such grace, steady as she walked over each path of ice on the trails, and in sandals, at that. Resistance to temperature must've been a benefit of immortality. She guided me to the side of the village where we'd initially entered, a less-trodden path to the rocky walls nestling Rayka in the valley. The trail seemed to reach a dead end as it led directly into the face of the mountain.

    "Do not use this as an example." She punched out her fist without warning or preparation, immediately activating her magic to form a wheel of light. She pushed it back to her chest, quickly switching herself to Pisces-Aries before dismissing the wheel with ease. "For someone married to a man for three centuries, it is easy to gain a vast amount of emotional control and patience. Do not use that as an example, either."

    "That's not a concern for me," I said quietly, mostly to myself, then processed that she used her Zodiac Turning for what seemed like no reason. "Why'd you switch to Pisces-Aries?"

"I was born as Pisces-Aries." Sora kneeled down; her magic still activated in her hand as she pressed her palm to the ground. A magical circle illuminated with a flash of light, revealing a wooden door in the mountain's side where the trail ended. She opened it, holding her arm out to invite me in. "I prefer Leo-Virgo, but in this space, we embrace what we are given at birth."

I bowed my head as I walked past her into the small cave, immediately hit with a wave of serenity. Upon entrance, torches of all colors flashed alive on the stone walls. Specks of light dotted the dark space of the ceiling, mimicking a clear night sky above a perfectly preserved pond that refracted the Stars above. Two white pines curved toward the ceiling while a waterfall trickled from a rock formation covering the back wall. Grass blanketed the floor, as if it had been growing in broad daylight.

Sora removed her sandals as she carefully stepped into the patch of earth, gesturing for me toward a spot where the grass was slightly worn away. I repeated her action to sit down beside her at the pond's edge, breathing in and out, focusing on the pond's presence to try to calm my racing thoughts.

I peered into the water. Flowers gathered at the bottom of the pool in groups of shimmering color. I was mesmerized by their fluid motions. Each flower was dispersed in a balance of color, stirring as if they were trying to communicate with me. In the middle sat a red lily blossoming under the reflection of my one red eye blinking at me. The flower's petals sparkled as if they were made of a thousand tiny rubies.

"Go ahead," Sora coaxed me, "you may take it."

I reached into the warm water. A soothing sensation spread through my body, putting my nerves to rest. I grasped the crimson lily and gently picked it out of the pond. Though a few other flowers twitched, the still waters remained almost entirely undisturbed. I tilted the flower in the light, observing its shimmering petals.

"Each Zodiac Turner to step into this divine space has picked a flower," Sora said. "Hundreds of years ago, Silas picked a black dahlia, representing betrayal, and I found alyssum, worth beyond beauty. You will understand your flower's meaning with time and knowledge."

She pulled her hair behind her ears, drawing attention to the earrings she wore, each with a tiny, preserved cluster of lavender-colored flowers suspended in glass. Her thumb traced over one of the earrings, a sorrow flashing through her expressions.

I carefully set the lily beside me, crossing my legs. I mourned for Sora, a woman so innocent and graceful despite all the pain she'd incurred from a War that seemed to drag on for 300 years longer than agreed upon.

"Why don't you hate me? I'm the daughter of the man who caused hundreds of years of your pain. Don't I remind you of him?"

"You are not your father, Rieka. We have all suffered at the hands of Blaine's abuse."

"I don't look like him, do I?" My voice shook. "I don't want to look like him."

"You do not resemble him much, no. I would not have recognized you as his daughter if I had not known your story." Sora tilted her head, examining my face. "In fact, you remind me of Rowan."

I set my eyes upon the pool of flowers and relaxed at the soothing sound of trickling water. "Both you and Atlas know Rowan's name."

"Yes, and for good reason." Sora gazed at me with compassion.

"Rowan is a long-standing friend of our family; he and I, we grew up together as Autarians in a town on the southernmost point of the Conviction-Autarchic border, with Silas, Fulbright, and Blaine."

"Rowan's an immortal?"

"Correct. He obtained immortality through sacrifice for a good deed, but I will allow him to tell you his own story."

I blinked tears away as all my emotions flowed together, interconnected in the serene space. "He encouraged me to study history because he lived through it. He knew the truth about the Code, that I was fighting against what my biological father created."

"Though it may seem upsetting," Sora began, "what good would it have done to tell you?"

I knew she was right; if Dad had given away the answers, I wouldn't have found interest in solving the puzzles that gave me my spark. I could trace my fascination with history back as early as I could remember. I was born with my passion and energy, the drive for change, the hunger to know more about the mysteries surrounding me in the Woods. Dad celebrated my victories with me as I fit together each piece of Gardian's fragmented historical record. He stood beside me through each answer I found, just as excited as I was. I understood that his intention was never to hide who I was from me, but to let me find it on my own; he'd done the right thing.

"Rowan knew you were more than your heritage. Your heritage doesn't define you; you define yourself by your choices," she said, "and you have chosen to be a force of fighting and fury and fire, rebelling against painful retellings of history, before ever knowing your biological father."

I blinked a few times. But then it sank in—she was right. I couldn't change my family, but it was entirely plausible for me to amend their wrongs and define myself.

"He is so proud of you, Rieka. He speaks fondly of you. We have always admired how deeply Rowan cares about those he loves."

"You're saying that you still communicate with him," I said aloud to process the information. "Atlas, too. Right before we left the Hub, Atlas gave me a compass he said was a gift from my father."

Sora perked up. "Do you have it with you?"

"Yeah, I've had it on me the whole time. The last time I spoke with Dad was in a dream right after Chase and I found the scroll. He said the same thing, how proud he was of me, but he was losing energy the longer he was in the dream. Told me not to worry about him dying, which makes more sense now." I leaned over to pull the compass out of my pocket, carefully handing it over to Sora. She tilted it in the light, watching the blue shimmer ripple across its surface. "Not sure what he enchanted it with."

"I do." She handed it back to me with a smile. "How are those memories treating you?"

I froze. I'd never mentioned to her that I'd lost memory, only that Narah had been turned against me. "How'd you know that?"

"I have a couple of reasons. Though Fulbright and I were cursed away from Narah—we are no longer, Fulbright finally succeeded in reversing it a month ago—we still had eyes on her," she explained. My heart fell at the mention of the reversal of the curse; if Narah had known, she would've followed me into Rayka. "You also told Rowan of Narah, and he would update us. Rowan is a Spirit Walker, they can restore or remove memories. He gifted that enchanted compass to you to aid you in recovering your memories of her."

"That's how he can be both a water mage and Dreamseeker." It clicked. "And, yeah, now that I think about it, I mentioned in one of the memories that I'd tell Dad about Narah healing some wounds I got from the Stellarium. That makes sense for me."

"The memories you've dreamed about, they are the ones that Rowan was told of. Though most memory alteration is a person-to-person ritual between a Spirit Walker and their receiving party, it is possible to enchant objects with specific memories."

"As in... he had to know the full details?"

"No. If you confided in him about being healed by Narah, Rowan enchants with only the knowledge that the memory exists, as it triggers your mind to recall the full memory." Sora looked amused. I was getting the feeling that I didn't have much to hide. "If he was exhausted while Dreamseeking you, he expended his energy when enchanting that compass."

"Why didn't he restore my memory earlier?"

"Using Narah to erase your memories was the Scorpio Stellarium's final attempt at forcing you to conform. If you were to remember her and rebel again, they would have considered killing you." She tilted her head at me. "When the Stellarium sent Narah to assassinate you, Fulbright knew. He told Rowan, who decided it was the right time to return the memories you'd mentioned to him."

I stared at my lap to avoid eye contact. "I'm sorry. How much do all of you know about this?"

"We know what Rowan knows. Rowan, rightfully so, kept me informed of what was happening between my daughter and my enemy's daughter. We could not see the two of you alone, but Rowan gave Fulbright and me a general understanding of what was happening."

As I opened my mouth to come up with any kind of response, the door to the space flew open. I covered my ears as it cracked against the stone wall. Sora sat up quickly, alert at the sudden new presence. I shielded my eyes from the sudden burst of sunlight beaming into the dim space.

"I heard my name." Atlas casually walked in, flinging his orange cloak away from himself. "Hope you're saying good things about me, Sora."

CHAPTER 33

I blinked hard a few times to see if I was in some sort of dream where the Aries Arctura suddenly appeared. But he did not disappear, and instead waltzed in as he kicked the door shut. Sora winced at the slamming, leaning over to look past Atlas at the door, ensuring it was still intact. I quietly laughed at the fact that Sora wasn't even remotely surprised at his abrupt entrance. She cared more about the door being in one piece than Atlas's presence.

"Must I remind you this is a sacred space for us?" Sora sighed deeply, holding the bridge of her nose. "How long have you been in Rayka?"

"As of five minutes ago, I transported." Atlas glanced at his wrist. He didn't have a watch on. He looked back up, pointing at me. "You. Don't question the transportation. Arcturas get special privileges."

Sora gave him a wary look. "Why are you here?"

"The Stellarium found out that your daughter's a terrible assassin. Who would've thought?" Atlas pulled a leather sword holster off his back, holding it out to his side to drop it on the grass. "She's on her way."

Sora jumped to her feet. "Elaborate, Fulbright."

"They sent her back after the Callexus. She'll be in Rayka by tonight."

"Rieka broke her curse." Sora's face twisted with horror. "What did they do to her?"

Atlas avoided eye contact. "You're not going to like what I'm about to say."

"Atlas," I said quietly, "now."

"They threatened to involve Blaine," he said quickly.

"Involve him how?" I demanded.

"Blaine has no idea that you were close to Narah." Sora shoved her sandals back on, her voice suddenly spiked with aggression. "His goddamn ego thinks that Narah's finally doing something to make him proud."

"Narah pretended like she willingly joined the Stellarium as a Zodiac Turner. She made a deal with the Stellarium that she'd willingly erase the memories of other targets so Verena wouldn't tell Blaine about her involvement with you," Atlas explained. "Blaine thinks that Narah genuinely wants to murder you. You're absolutely fucked if he finds out that's not true, trust us on this one."

Sora opened the door. "She is going to do anything and everything to avoid involving Blaine, even if that means giving them the Callexus."

"He does not fuck around with cursing people. Blaine finding out would mean torture-till-death for both of you." Atlas pushed the sword holster toward me with his foot. "That's yours now. Hope you're ready."

I picked up the leather guard as Sora placed her hand on my back to guide me out of the cave. "Sora, I thought you said the caverns were too dangerous to enter without preparation?"

"It is extremely unwise to rush into them," Sora said, "but if Narah finds the Callexus before you, she cannot escape the Stellarium, and any hope of reversing the Code is lost."

"Chase looks identical to the guy that put the sword down there in the first place. They'll be fine," Atlas said, waving his hand at Sora as we hurried back into the village. He glanced over his shoulder at me. "Tell him to activate his healing when you see the beast. It'll think he's Mathias and leave you alone. The real threat at hand is Narah."

"Shouldn't he know about... any of this?"

"*No*," Atlas and Sora both said at the same time.

"Okay, why? Narah told me the same thing. It seems a bit relevant that he might want to know who his family is, if it was his own grandfather who put the Callexus down there."

"Silas messed up real bad," Atlas said. "If Chase questions why Silas lied to him his entire childhood, we can't answer."

"It is complicated." Sora shook her head, grabbing Atlas's arm when he almost slipped and crashed on a patch of ice. "Silas made a mistake, and Silas needs to own up to the mistake. He has hidden numerous things from Chase that will break him. It is Silas's responsibility to explain them."

"But you're his mother. He's waited a long time to meet you."

"Rieka, you have no idea." Atlas sighed. "Silas completely changed the entire course of Chase's life, and it wasn't for a good reason. I'm not elaborating."

"*Fulbright.* Hush." Sora smacked his arm. He shoved her back as we hurried toward the library, and she flattened her gaze on the path ahead. It was the first time I'd seen her annoyed. "I am so tired of existing with you."

"And whose fault is that? You married my brother."

"I thought Fulbright was your alias," I asked Atlas. "You told Chase and me to call you Atlas. Narah also called you Fulbright. Do you not use Merek?"

"I'm a Merek when I feel like it," he emphasized with a smile as we neared the library. "Fulbright was my late husband's surname. Met him 57,505 days ago. Sora started to call me Fulbright before I married him and never dropped the habit. Narah picked it up from her. Sora and I raised Narah for the first thirteen years of her life."

The more I spoke with Atlas, the more curious I got about his story. He and Sora both struck me as extremely old, but each had aged in completely different ways. It was fascinating to me.

"Atlas?"

Atlas jumped when Chase almost ran directly into him as they both turned a corner at the same time. Kaia stepped to the side to quickly avoid any collision, almost stepping into the creek next to the pathway. She did a double take at Atlas while Chase stared at him in confusion.

"Hi again," Atlas said, holding out his hand to Chase, who hesitantly shook it. "Bad news. You need to be underneath Rayka in less than an hour."

"What? For the Callexus, you mean?"

"The Stellarium is forcing Narah to go for it. We need to get there before she does," I explained quickly.

"I thought you removed whatever curse they had on her?"

"I did." I bit my tongue. "No time to explain. Where's Avia?"

He shrugged. "That's what we were trying to figure out."

"You must be Rhea's daughter," Atlas said to Kaia, holding out his hand to her next. Kaia was far more confident in accepting the handshake. "She's a good friend of mine. Pleasure to meet you."

"I've heard a lot about you," Kaia said with a smile. "Why are you here?"

"Don't ask questions—pause." Atlas took a step back to look between Kaia and Chase, who both clearly had no idea how to react. "Are you a Spirit Walker?"

"I didn't know until last week, but yeah?" Kaia answered, narrowing her eyes. "How do you know what Spirit Walking is?"

"I told you, don't ask questions," Atlas repeated with a laugh at Chase and Kaia. "That'll be fun. Gardian hasn't had a Spirit Walker and Libran Healer working together since Mathias and Mari. Good luck."

Sora had her arms crossed as she death-stared Atlas. He smiled innocently at her. Chase and Kaia exchanged a look.

"Good luck?" Chase echoed.

"Oh, you have no idea," Atlas said as he walked away, waving for us to follow him. "Let's go. I rather the Scorpio Stellarium not stay in power because Narah gets to the sword. Move it."

The four of us stayed where we were for a moment. Chase and Kaia watched Atlas walk away, both of them incredibly confused. Sora sighed, holding her forehead.

"He just gets more confusing," Chase said after a moment of silence.

Kaia nodded, looking over at Sora. "What was that about?"

The corner of Sora's mouth twitched in a tiny smile. "I told you; he's a good friend of mine."

CHAPTER 34

I could've sworn a whisper echoed from the depths of the entrance to the tunnels, luring us in, inviting us to walk ourselves to our fates.

By the time we'd found Avia in the village—who'd been taking a nap at the house the entire time we'd searched a good portion of Rayka for her—we were forced to run to make up for lost time. Chase stumbled to a halt at the opening in the mountain face with a groan while I paused to catch my breath. Kaia leaned down to hold her knees with a wheeze. Avia did not pause, entering the tunnels without a second thought.

"Are you serious?" Kaia held out a hand. "Pausing for the rest of us would've been a little bit more considerate."

"Considerate isn't in her vocabulary," I said.

"I have to make sure she doesn't kill herself right away," Chase grumbled, trailing after her. "To be fair, Atlas did tell us to be fast."

Kaia and I followed them down. I tried to ignore my pounding heart as we descended a rockier and less-trodden path than the cave system we'd traveled through to find Rayka. The tunnel was too narrow for any of us to stand next to each other. I carefully stepped down ancient, dilapidated steps, a pathway that surely hadn't seen travelers for a good amount of time. The sound of our footsteps and breathing became a song to march with as Avia's flame guided our way. Her smoky warmth smothered the smell of musty water and old earth in the tiny space.

The air grew heavier with each step we took down. Though I tried to ignore the weight in my chest, the shift in energy made us all go quiet. My heart felt as if it was being pulled down to the Earth's core with each step I took. An undeniable, pressuring heat was seeping into the moist rock walls. I could've sworn I caught a glimpse of a red shimmer rippling across the walkway.

"So, hypothetically Rieka's ex-girlfriend catches up," Avia broke the silence, "would she be behind us?"

"*Avia,*" I snapped, "stop it."

"Why? Am I wrong? I haven't actually met this girl. The only true interaction I've had with her was when she shocked me by the arch. I don't feel like I'm on a first-name basis."

"You don't want to be on a first-name basis with her. She kept shocking me asleep when the dragon thing attacked Rieka and me," Chase said.

Avia laughed. "If I could shock people, I'd shock you, too."

Chase groaned.

"You know I'm kidding." She turned to flash him a grin. "I can compliment you, too. You are very gentle and kind."

"Oh, good, you've been practicing."

Kaia sighed behind me. I glanced back and nodded at her.

"I was seriously asking, though. If that was the only entrance, and she's trying to beat us down here, she could easily destroy us from behind."

"Okay, then shut your mouth and move faster," I said. "You're the person in the lead. Go."

Avia listened, maybe a bit too well. I couldn't tell if it was the increasing underground pressure, or my lungs burning from how fast we were moving, but an intense sense of dread seeped into me. The tunnel became winding as it flattened out, making me dizzier with each sharp turn. The wider the path became, the more our movements echoed. Chase, in front of me, flinched at each sound of a clattering rock or drip of water. I shivered at the strange energy the underground passage evoked.

I almost crashed into Chase when he stopped in front of me. His height had blocked me from seeing that we'd entered a larger chamber. Avia's flame was barely enough to see the ceiling expanding above us where stalactites reached down toward us. As she walked the space to evaluate the situation, the light of her fire revealed another tunnel opening across from us. Then another, next to it. A third. By the time she'd reached where she started, I'd counted six tunnels in total, all identical.

Chase stared forward with a horrified look as we stood in the middle of a maze. I averted my gaze from him. With a facial structure so hauntingly similar to Narah's, his expression of horror reminded me of how she looked at me when the Stellarium shoved a blade to my throat.

"Chase, stop hiding and come here," Kaia said as she examined the ground in front of a tunnel to our left. "Can you read any of this? Looks like a form of Driksaal to me."

Chase hesitantly stepped further into the cavern. I hadn't even noticed how he was lingering close to the tunnel where we'd come from. Avia moved the flame closer to the ground, revealing ancient etchings covering the floor of the cavern. Chase kneeled to trace the runic with his finger.

"**Restore and revive, by the balance of the blood, call upon the cause of the Callexus.**"

The runic illuminated gold with the familiar incantation, magic weaving through inscriptions upon stone in every direction. The space filled with the smell of pine and metallic blood. A pulsing glow mimicked a heartbeat. As the magic coursed the floor in an intricate spiral, it settled with a bright aura in the tunnel directly across from us.

"Ha." Avia headed off into the golden tunnel. Chase sighed and hurried after her. "Bet the ex-girlfriend won't get that one."

"She will. She's a Libran Healer. Keep moving," I urged them. Kaia raised her brows at me as we followed them into the tunnel again. I tapped the outline of the veins on my forearm. "Zodiac Turning, she's got it in Libra-Scorpio."

"I was looking at you like that because you didn't refute your sister that time," Kaia said. "I have no doubt about the Zodiac Turning."

"She's a Libran Healer?" Chase butted in. "As in, you have a memory of her healing you?"

"Yeah, and she's a strong Healer, at that. She was—probably still is—actively building her skill in Libran Healing."

"If she's a Libran Healer, even in a different sign, that means she had the genetics for Libran Healing."

I immediately shut my mouth. I held my breath, hoping with everything in me that he wouldn't make the connection I'd accidentally given away.

"She's got both Zodiac Turning and Libran Healing in her family," he continued. "When you accidentally turned my sign, I had Zodiac Turning in Scorpio."

Shit. He was fast. I bit the inside of my cheek as I accepted the fact that there was no way I'd stop the line of logic coming from a Libra.

"I've said multiple times now how I think she looks familiar. Rieka recognized her because she was forced to forget Narah. But my memory is perfectly fine." Chase looked back at me. For the first time in my life, I was thankful for the Code teaching me how to hide my emotions. I swallowed my panic. "She also survived in the Woods."

"Are you saying she might be related to you?" Avia asked. "I think that might be a little bit of a stretch, Chase."

"I don't, considering Rieka just resorted to hiding her emotions when I would've expected her to have a reaction." He turned around to stop in front of me, looking down to meet my eyes. I'd forgotten how intimidating he could be. "Do you know something I don't?"

"No," I lied, because I had no idea what else I should've done. "I—"

"My dad also kept the knowledge of my mother from me," he interrupted me. "There's something here you're not aware of, Rieka. I have sworn for years that one of my earliest memories is playing by the ocean with whom I thought to be my sister. My dad constantly denied it and insisted it was my imagination. I've never fully believed him. Narah's Pisces-Aries, the ocean would've made sense."

Chase was five when he was separated from her. He definitely could've remembered. Guilt swallowed me alive. Narah, Atlas, and Sora all had warned me away from telling him. Atlas had specifically mentioned that whatever the Mereks were hiding from him, it would break him. That terrified me; I did *not* want to be the reason he hurt. Chase, Avia, and Kaia's gazes all tore into me, expecting me to say something. I hated the situation I'd accidentally put myself into.

"Actually, you might be right about this." Avia stared up at Chase. "I did say that she was hot, and I think you are, too. That tracks. I didn't notice before how you had a similar face to her."

"Rieka," Chase said, refusing to break eye contact with me. "Tell me the truth."

"I'm sorry, I don't know."

"You absolutely do," Kaia said, and I froze. I'd remembered too late how she'd mentioned that she was beginning to see the emotions around others as part of her Spirit Walking. "You are burning up with guilt and panic."

"I'm going to give you one more chance to answer this honestly," Chase said loudly, pulling my attention back to him, "is Narah my sister?"

"Yeah, she is," I gave in to the pressure. With a heavy exhale, I took a step back from him. Equal amounts of terror and relief flooded me. "I'm so sorry, I didn't... I couldn't—"

"She didn't hide that from you on her own will," Kaia said to Chase, and I snapped my gaze over to her with my mouth open to protest being called out. "I'm trying to help your case here, Rieka. There is no part of you that wanted to deliberately hide that from him. You weren't afraid of him, you were afraid for him."

"Thank you for telling me the truth," Chase said to me, his demeanor softening when he realized I didn't have control. "I'm guessing she told you this while I was asleep in the cave?"

I nodded, internally begging that he wouldn't question any further, willing Kaia to stay quiet if she noticed I was still nervous.

"Your ex-girlfriend is his sister?" Avia laughed so hard that she started coughing. Chase set a hand on her back to steady her. "That's hilarious. We have the same taste, just different genders."

He removed his hand with a sigh. "Great, you made it weird."

"Stop being dramatic. It's not that weird," Avia insisted. "I'm not even kidding. If she didn't have the white hair and blue eyes, you could pass as twins. Face, height, muscles, there's a list here I could make. She must be a full sister."

"Did she tell you anything else?" Chase carefully considered me. "Considering I now know my dad lied to me about always living in the Woods and gaslit me into thinking that I was crazy for saying I had a memory of a sister."

I was absolutely no match for how fast he was with following clues.

"What else did he hide from me, and why?"

Before I had the chance to make something up again, a faint white light quickly flashed down the tunnel from the direction of the middle chamber we'd exited.

"Speaking of, that's Zodiac Turning. Run."

Chapter 35

There was no way Narah hadn't heard us take off running down the tunnel.

We gave up any hope of stealth as we sprinted from the chamber, the illuminated golden runic following us as we flew down the open space of the pathway to the Callexus. I wasn't sure how many minutes passed as adrenaline blurred my senses, my heartbeat thundering and lungs burning as I pushed my body to its limits. The red shimmer of the walls became more frequent the further we got from the split in the tunnels. I could've sworn there was a distant hum of a heavy magic occupying the space.

We slowed when we were greeted with a low, red-tinted mist, hiding the entrance to the main chamber of a cave. The sound of a crashing river beckoned us to advance to a room in which we'd become merely echoes of our bloodlines, evolved ghosts of our families. The energy floating from the opening was not threatening, nor welcoming, but instead thick with intensity.

Chase bent down to pick something up. He turned toward us slowly, holding a bone in his hand.

Gash marks carved into its surface. It had to have been ages old, yellowed and moldy from underground humidity. Teeth marks were gnawed into the ends of what once must've been an arm or leg. Fragments of bone scattered at Chase's feet, a shattered skeleton of a human body. Someone had died running from whatever was before us.

Narah must've been close behind. Pushing past Chase and Avia, I tore my necklace off to transform it into my longsword. I held it in front of me to cut through the fog as I stalked forward, blinded by some sort of bravery that couldn't have been my own. Chase, Avia, and Kaia hesitantly trailed behind me. A crimson mist surrounded me as I stepped into the cavern. My knuckles whitened from my desperate grip on my sword, as if that would swallow any last crippling fears whispering in the back of my thoughts.

The low mist dissipated, swarming into the raging, frothing stream in the middle of the space. The rock ceiling expanded dozens of feet above our heads, and I silently willed the massive space to not indicate the home of something much larger than us. A few stepping stones in the stream were slicked with foam, leading across the river where a flat rock top shadowed a protruding stone.

A hole underneath it indicated the absence of a sword—a sword that now sat at the bottom of the rock.

We'd beat Narah to it.

Avia walked to the stream and beckoned Kaia over, who took far more caution with her steps. Kaia stole glances around the cave, anticipating a danger much greater than initially visible. She held her palms out to the stepping stones, barely moving her fingers. The waters parted around the stones, enough to make the slick surfaces slightly less treacherous.

Chase gave me a look, and the two of us approached the new path.

I kept my own sword in front of my body, my eyes scanning the veil of darkness behind the sword. The rest of the cavern, excluding the shadows, was lit with a bioluminescent blue, green, and pink, spotting the ceiling in an array of dazzling crystals.

"It's almost too easy," Chase murmured as we strode across the drying rocks. "The Callexus is literally *right* there. For anyone to try to pick up."

The two of us carefully approached the Callexus laid across stone. With a hesitant nod at each other, we bent down to examine the weapon.

The Callexus consisted of a long steel blade, devoid of fingerprints and inscribed with ancient runes. When I shifted my weight from one knee to the other, a dim crimson color shimmered across the weapon, signifying the enchantment bestowed upon its creation. Its handle was a dyed scarlet leather, accented with gold filigree streams of light magic shimmering and darting, alive. I narrowed my eyes at a tiny inscription of contemporary runic at the base of the blade: *Silas/Atlas Merek. SAFE TO TOUCH.*

I laughed to myself, wondering which one of them had to write on the handle of the Callexus that it was, in fact, safe to hold.

"This is it." Avia asked. She reached toward the handle of the sword.

Chase quickly grabbed her wrists. "Let Rieka do that."

"Why?"

"She started this whole thing, yeah? It should be her honor."

Avia, with a huff, retreated her hands. I flicked my own sword back into my necklace, draping it over my neck to empty my hands. With trembling fingers, I reached for the handle of the Callexus. I closed my eyes, my hand lingering over it. If I were to accidentally brush its blade and draw blood, I'd be stuck as an immortal for at least 300 years.

I held my breath as I lowered my hand to the handle, wincing and leaning away as my palm made contact with leather. Nothing happened.

I closed an eye with anticipation of a living hell as I lifted the Callexus, significantly heavier than my personal sword. The leather rested in my hands and fit in the grooves of my fingers as if it was meant to be held by me. I tilted the weapon in the ethereal crystal light, watching a crimson aura shimmer across the metal of the sword.

A screeching scrape against stone shattered the silence. Something shifted in the darkness.

More scrapes pierced the air; claws. A sickening slithering noise of rippling scales echoed from the shadows. A shape of darkness twitched. Chase took a step closer to Avia, Kaia backing up toward the stream. With a loose, shaking grip on the Callexus, I stood my ground and held it in front of me.

A pair of slitted, scarlet eyes blinked open.

Two footsteps shook the floors of the cavern, two lion-like arms forming out of the darkness like a Beast of Conviction Woods. Talons stuck out of fuzzy paws as if ripped from an eagle and sewn into a lion's paws. Its arms grappled the rock where the Callexus once sat. Two back legs contorted with three-pronged anisodactyl feet, connecting to a snake-like body with rippling scales. A lengthy neck sulked over the edge of the rock as the monster stood, three times larger than the creature in Rayka's woods, five times more intimidating than a beast of Conviction Woods. Pitch black horns curled from the head, matching the raven-colored scales spanning its body. A slitted tongue flicked in and out of its mouth with a warm hiss. A tint of a crimson aura flared across its scales as it moved in the light, matching the

Callexus.

It was immortal.

I no longer held control over my body's actions as I stepped back twice. Its once-pearly white eagle's talons were bloodstained from those who came before us. Its putrid stench of rotting flesh seeped into the surroundings, causing Chase to cough and wheeze behind me. The scraping of its claws shrieked against my ears as it climbed over the boulder.

It paused directly before me, dipping its head to mine. I froze in its hypnotic gaze. It pulled its lips back in a ferocious, bone-chilling snarl.

The monster reached out its massive claw toward me, and Avia reacted before I could. She sprinted forward with a battle cry, her hands red-hot, one hand holding a dagger on the verge of melting. She threw one hand to the paw of the creature to singe its fur and dove her blade into its leg, hoisting herself up with one arm as the creature roared out. I hurled the Callexus to the side while withdrawing my own sword to open a gash where Avia burned away fur. Kaia drew water from the stream and yanked it at the face of the wyvern.

It screeched, whipping its neck around as I sliced open another part of its leg. Blood spurted on my clothing and face, blinding me for a second before I wiped it away with the back of my arm. It effortlessly shook off Avia and her blade, slamming her into the ground and knocking her out instantly. Her side was open with a gash. Chase threw himself over her, gripping her body and dragging her away before the monster could strike again. The dragon shook me off just as easily as it threw Avia to the ground. It snarled at Kaia next, standing on its hind legs while shaking itself out. The damage Avia had done must've felt no more than a paper cut to the beast. With a flick of its leg, the fur Avia burned off and the gashes I made disappeared, mutating a stronger muscle upon its paw. It shook its head, refocusing, and though we were covered in its blood, it had healed to its pre-attack state.

"Back up!" Chase yelled at me as it opened its jaws in another massive, deafening roar. I buckled down to a knee, covering my ears as its shriek bounced off stone walls. "Rieka, *now!*"

I listened to him, stumbling backward. He was still bent over Avia, healing her side wound. In seconds, she was back on her feet, gasping in air as a spark glowed in her hands. Smoke billowed out of her mouth as she heaved in a breath. Chase, still on the ground, grabbed her leg before she could attempt to run at it again.

"It'll kill us the second we try to run to the tunnel," I said breathlessly.

"There's got to be another way to get this thing to fuck off," Avia hissed, digging her feet as she prepared to rush at it again. Chase held onto her, and she glared at him. "A weak spot, maybe its mouth. Kaia! Distract it!"

"Avia, wait—" Chase started, but it was too late. His grip slipped away from her.

The beast swung a leg toward Avia, and she drove her blade into it again to climb up the creature. It thrashed, reaching its other leg toward me. I barely rolled away from its massive claws. Kaia gathered a burst of water in her hands and struck the dragon on its other side, causing it to yank its head toward her. Avia grabbed its neck, dragging herself across its back. It unhinged its jaw, and Avia shoved her hand into its mouth. I threw my sword against a paw that was preparing to crash down on me, cutting it off as I scrambled away from it. It regrew its missing foot within moments.

A burst of flames exploded in the beast's mouth, and it reared, thrashing Avia to the ground as a fire roared. Its jaws snapped down, almost costing Avia her hand as she flung herself off its head seconds before disaster. She fell unconscious at the sickening strike to her body, the crack of her fall echoing in my head. I threw myself over her as the wyvern smashed its talons on my back, opening a gash as I dragged Avia away from it.

Pain spiraled up my back. Avia was out cold but appeared to be breathing and alive. Chase helped me pull her out of the way and held onto my arm, his magic spreading through me instantly to heal my back. I gasped, the wound still open as he pulled his hand away to instead heal Avia.

The wyvern paused. It tilted its head, its nostrils flaring as Chase healed its victim. Atlas had instructed me that Chase needed to use his magic, but it wasn't helping us in any sort of way.

Chase looked over at me. "Can you use your Zodiac Turning on *just* humans?"

I stared at the dragon. Terror caused my magic to spur, and I stood up with the open wound still pouring blood on my back. The adrenaline numbed any pain I could've felt from the wound.

"I'm about to find out."

"*Careful*, Rieka!" Kaia screamed as she slammed the wyvern with another burst of water. The fire in its mouth was still raging as it swiped its paw over its nose, as if that would extinguish the flames searing its gums. There was enough time while it was distracted.

I breathed in deeply, then out. I planted my feet in the ground, evening my arms out, and closed my eyes to let my magic take control.

Fear; determination; anger. A trio of prominent emotions, followed by a throb of light in my veins. I looked upon an amalgamation of a monster composed of many beasts, a protector of an ancient weapon my father had abused. Fear was a delicate balance; without it, I would be unaware of my danger and powerless, and with it, I trembled at the foot of a beast much larger than any human fears I'd ever comprehended.

And there I was, a shadow of my biological father. Though I was not born to reverse that damned Code, I had instead found truth within my own self and exploration of history. I had never known his name, never known his relationship to me, and I still fought with everything I had to reverse it. I would not be eaten alive by my fear, or the dragon, or the cavern—I was stronger, stronger than my father was, and nothing would stop me from taking that sword back with me.

Blaine Spring.

My blood boiled, the third part to the trilogy of emotions, and a roar bubbled in my throat. Light sprinted through me, magic alive with my anger, thrashing like a flood on fire meant to burn and drown all in its path. I had never met the man, and somehow, my anger accumulated into an eruption of a storm inside of me, one that forced my mouth open in a scream.

A relearned anger seared through me. I wanted to tear my skin open with my teeth of a beast of my own self, let myself cry until I bled a new color. I had been trained in a militaristic fashion to survive, to take the arrow and rise again, to yell and scream until I was heard. A promise was made—I would reinvent myself until I was heard, until my muzzle became agape with a howl that could not be ignored.

I was ready for a new color of blood, ready to tear each part of myself out until I became a blank canvas, ready to grow my new claws.

I unleashed the storm, punching my fist out. The magic snapped out of me in a furious rush, bright enough to cause Chase to gasp and look away from me. A zodiac wheel began to twist and spin before me, first flowing easily, but as I pushed it toward the beast, the pain striking my body began. I winced, gritting my teeth and fighting the blood gurgling in the back of my throat. Piercing pain, like a thousand knives embedding themselves in my arm, then my chest, then my legs. The wheel grew in size, numbing the cavern with a deafening buzzing sound. I was on fire with a flame inside my own body. The wyvern stood on two legs, looming over me as a zodiac wheel illuminated atop its chest.

I shoved it forward with a final guttural yell, throwing my right arm down to spin the wheel with all the force I had.

A blinding light consumed the cave. All the pain sunk into me at once, like a spear through the heart, emotional and physical pain aligned. I couldn't see what sign landed atop the wyvern, as my vision blackened, and I fell to my knees in the abyss of white. The wyvern's shape disappeared, The pain both began and faded away. I let my body collapse, blood pouring from my mouth and hands.

Somewhere in the delusion of death, I returned to Conviction Woods. Though I wasn't sure if I was dead yet or on the verge of an afterlife, a low glow illuminated from between two trees. I stumbled toward it in the soft summer soil. Reflections of my childhood danced around me, and the ghosts of the past swiveled in a low mist cloaking the trees. Visions of Avia and me running through the pines drifted through the firefly glow, mirrors of all my memories.

Before me, a warm white glow throbbed, a solace beckoning me forward. As I looked down at my hands, a black mark had scorched up my arm from what looked to be a combination of lightning and magic. My skin had a surreal ethereal glow, unlike anything I'd seen with any kind of light magic, or even my own. There was a feathery sensation to my hands, a comforting lightness.

And as I stepped toward the light, a branch cracked behind me. I whirled around, my gaze yanked away from the light. The shadow of the Woods was behind me, a looming, familiar darkness, pines scented of death and despair to outsiders. Though I was accustomed to its perils, the Woods were warm to me, my home, and they had always been my home.

The presence of another creature was looming thick in the forest air.

According to the myths, the wolves of Conviction Woods could transcend planes. Dad had told me when I was a child—their devouring darkness would transport you to a limbo, an in-between of the dark and light. In one bite, you'd be swallowed whole. The Woods itself was a blend of dark and light, a duality our world couldn't quite understand, shutting off outsiders.

In the corner of my eye, a reflection of my father, yet not quite my father, flashed by me.

It was me and Dad, sitting by a fire near the patio. I was young, maybe five or six, peering up to him with wide eyes as I gripped his arms. From his mouth sprouted a wild myth of the wolves when transformed into Beasts, and their shadows, gaping maws, arched, spiky backs like the cliffs of the southern Conviction bluffs. I cried and curled up closer to him, and somewhere in the distance, Mom scolded him for terrifying me.

Dad grinned, looking down at me while his story convoluted into a tale of a wolf, a savior wolf, protecting me, looking over me. The Wolf of the Woods, the one we knew and understood, the creature otherwise misunderstood.

GARDIAN

He told me that this wolf was fierce, and brave, and that I'd grow into those same attributes over the years—he knew it from the heart. His wolf was well-groomed, amber and blue eyes of warmth, no more than naturally wild, and a faint magic in its gentle heart to protect. This wolf, he said, would watch over me. It would protect me from the Beasts or comfort me when I was scared; a guardian Dad had seen with his very eyes for many years, a constant force behind each of my journeys, a soft whisper in the back of my mind, a ghost shrouding over my body in a protective spirit. I saw myself in the wolf— I always had.

"When I was a child, it was there for me," he said, holding me to his chest. "When I was afraid that the Woods would turn against me, it would guide me through the shadows. I have faith that, some day, when you truly need it, the Wolf of the Woods will guide you, too."

And as I turned toward the looming darkness, there was a pair of glowing eyes—one amber, one blue. The wolf emerged from the swallowing darkness. It padded toward me, gently, quietly. I kneeled down, welcoming it with open arms.

It paused in front of me, a low golden glow illuminating right beneath its neck where its heart must have been. In those wild eyes, there was something of purity and warmth, but not the drowning purity that erased all sin. No, this wolf had flaws, too, a few scratches across its forehead, a nicked ear, a crooked tooth. A misunderstood creature made into a monster when all it had done its whole life was defend itself and its home.

There is a balance in our world, a balance that cannot be disrupted by the removal of one link to the chain. The Zodiac Turners, a blend of the humanity force itself handing life and death at their hands, were feared creatures, stolen away by the likes of history, war, and misunderstanding.

But to balance this world, there comes an understanding that not all is good, and not all is bad—to call the wolf a beast without looking past its balance to the forest, a disruption is caused to the ecosystem. To take the Zodiac Turner and our emotions from us distorts our own perceptions of the good and bad, to deny that we must learn to balance our power and morality alike, to learn that our emotions do not dilapidate us, but drive us forward to become better at the magic we wield to better ourselves and the societies around us.

I welcomed the wolf—him—forward.

He rested his muzzle on my shoulder, and I lifted one arm to his scruff, burying my hands in prickly fur. It smelled of fir and cedar, a sweet evergreen aroma, and the rock and dirt of the earth.

You,

he said,

have much to do in this vast world before the light's ancient trance enchants you.

With a surge of golden light, everything around me instantly snapped back to reality.

Healing was running through me. Chase's soothing healing. I groaned. I sat up quickly, Chase flinching as I leaned down to spit up traces of blood.

Silence. The wyvern was on the ground.

But then its claws twitched. Another red shimmer spread across its body, lighting its scales with a combination of my own white light and its immortal shine. It blinked its eyes open, and with an earth-shaking growl, it rose to stalk toward me. Its talons struck the ground. It lowered its head in a cruel snarl, narrowing its eyes at me. My light still throbbed through my own body, as well as the wyvern's conductive scales.

It was examining who I was. The wyvern smiled. And then reared to crash upon me, to pulp my being into a mess of organs and bones and blood.

A light flared in my left peripheral, so bright that it could only be discerned as a light from the clouds and sky itself. The wyvern paused before it sent its body weight crashing upon me.

Narah grabbed my shoulders and shoved me out of the way as the dragon's jaws clamped shut on thin air. Its body fell to the cave floor, sending all of us stumbling for our balance. Time slowed; Narah had run in with barely enough time to deceive the beast with her Zodiac Turning. The air was knocked out of me as her grip sent both of our balances awry, my body slamming on rock as she pinned me down.

"Why didn't it recognize Chase as Mathias?" she said quietly, and I stared back at her, unsure of how to answer. She glanced over at Chase, who had his arms around Avia, healing her while she leaned against him. "Never mind. Got it. That's why."

She stood up, placing herself directly in between me and the wyvern. Her hand illuminated with a golden light as she held it up to the creature. It didn't immediately attack Narah, tilting its head as it inspected the new stranger. It froze, hypnotized by the healing, as she waved her hand in its face. Once the wyvern was still, Narah sprinted to where Chase and Avia sat, heaving Chase off the ground with one arm. He protested, struggling against Narah as she dragged him to Kaia, next to me. Narah was—somehow—stronger than her brother.

"What the *hell* are you doing?" he yelled, struggling against Narah's forceful grasp.

"I need you to trust me, even if this is the last time you ever trust me." Narah pushed him forward. "Draw your blade, *now*."

Kaia's hands fell to her sides as she stopped distracting the wyvern. Avia's eyes blinked open, and she propped herself up with one arm to watch Narah place Chase in front of Kaia. Chase shoved Narah's hand away and spun around to face her, equally as furious as he was terrified. The shape of the wyvern stood on two legs, casting a shadow over the three of them.

"Chase," Narah said calmly, "draw your blade before it snaps out of its trance."

He listened, sliding the knife from the holster on his belt, barely holding it steady in his trembling hand.

"Both of you, cut a deep slit in your hands, hold them together."

Chase gave her a wild look, but still did as she said, opening a wound in his hand before Kaia repeated his action. Narah quickly stepped back, grabbing my arm to yank me away from them as they pressed their palms together.

Upon contact, their magic was instantly activated, stronger than I'd ever seen it before in either of them, entrapping them in a trance. A golden luminescence beamed through Chase's veins, concentrated in the middle of his chest as the light in his eyes blinded him. A blue aura covered Kaia's body, Stars dotting across her arms and face. Blood seeped through their hands, a singular drop falling upon the cavern floor.

A burst of light exploded around them, sending out a shockwave. Its energy slammed into me, sending me stumbling backward. I ducked, holding my arm in front of my face to shield me from the glare of the blue and gold aura. It spread across every surface of the cavern, weaving like rivers in the cracks of the rocks, washing over the crystals, tracing every shape in the chamber. The light raced through ancient runic inscribed to the center of the ceiling, brightening and dimming with the force of a heartbeat, humming with every throb. A sweet floral smell overtook the cave, as if the space had been created for the two archpowers.

The wyvern, its face reflecting with blue and gold light, bowed its head to them. Kaia and Chase snapped out of their trance, gasping as if they'd stop breathing entirely. The beast above them reached for the Callexus with a single claw, pulling it across the floor before it bent down and nudged it toward Chase. His hand fell away from Kaia's as he lifted the ancient weapon. The wyvern kneeled to Chase as he held the sword.

Fear paralyzed Chase. "Thank you?"

Kaia looked over at me and Narah. "Explain."

"Mathias, a Libran Healer, brought the Callexus into this cave," Narah started, her voice shaking, "and Mari, a Spirit Walker, not a fire mage, accompanied him."

"It's bowing to Chase." An epiphany visibly struck Kaia. "Avia threw it off. It couldn't fully recognize him as Mathias until it saw that he was working with a Spirit Walker."

Narah's face was full of a somber truth. "Yes. Chase is a spitting image of Mathias, our grandfather."

CHAPTER 36

Chase's gaze tore to Narah. "You're telling me I was raised by Silas Merek?"

"That's a funny thing to ask when you're holding the Callexus." Avia laughed at him, shaking her head. "You know, the weapon that made Silas an immortal."

"I'm not supposed to be telling you any of this," Narah said with a heavy exhale, "but, yes, Silas raised you. Our mother is Sora."

Chase set the Callexus down slowly, carefully, pushing it away from himself, as if the weight of the sword was suddenly a burden from his family.

"Silas owes you a lot of truths he withheld from you. Our parents didn't have a choice. They were cursed away from each other. If they're within proximity of each other, we're in pain."

Narah's voice was pleading, but Chase didn't appear to have the energy or strength to respond negatively. His full body shook in bouts and waves of shivers, his palms bleeding from an overuse of magic.

"Do you want to tell him?" Narah asked me. I opened my mouth, trying to form words, but I was equally as lost as Chase.

Avia, confused and exhausted, let her arm fall as she laid back down and stopped watching the situation. She rubbed her face, covering her ears, as if she couldn't take any more information at once. Her battles didn't typically involve family drama.

"Rieka is the daughter of Blaine," Narah explained before I could give her a true answer. "The six Zodiac Turners that Fulbright told you about—himself, me, Sora, Silas, Blaine, and Rieka."

"Who's Atlas related to in that group?"

"Brother to Silas; he's our uncle."

"That makes so much more sense." Chase held the bridge of his nose. Realization struck him. "Oh my god. The eyes. You all have two different colored eyes."

"Yeah, Zodiac Turners have heterochromia," Narah said. "That fact was wiped from history to protect Blaine, and evidently the rest of us, too."

Chase looked over at me. "Did you have that figured out, with the eyes?"

I stared back at him in response. I was so far in shock that it didn't surprise me whatsoever, and in fact, I felt a little bit stupid for not catching it before Chase did.

"What?" Avia leaned forward but was clearly on the brink of unconsciousness as smoke escaped her lips. Kaia sat down next to her, offering her a glowing hand. Avia laid back down, grumbling and relaxing at the sensation of her Spirit Walking. "Too much at once."

I swallowed hard, as if that would wash down the anger building in me from her nonchalant attitude toward a piece of knowledge with such gravity. She wasn't entangled in the mess of a family conflict like Chase, Narah, and I were.

Movement out of the corner of my eye caught my attention. Narah had tensed when she spoke Blaine's name. She touched her shoulder, wincing as if she was remembering her pain. Tears welled in the corners of her eyes.

"Let me get this straight. Our mother is Sora Merek, in Rayka, and our father is Silas Merek, a Zodiac Turner. Both are immortals from the War of the Rebalancing. You are my full sister. I am a Libran Healer because Mathias Merek is my grandfather."

"Yes," Narah said. Her face contorted with a fury of emotions. "You were damn lucky that you grew up blissfully unaware of this goddamn family. I wasn't protected like you were."

Chase frowned at her, and then at me. His stance swayed from a dizziness that must've been eating him alive as he tried to process the wealth of information. "Rieka, I'm so sorry you're related to—"

"She is *not* him," Narah interrupted, and I flinched at her sudden shift to defend me. Something wasn't right. Her back-and-forth morality was becoming more and more obvious each time she spoke. "These families are beyond fucked up, and the trauma has spread to us."

I stood up in a flash, stumbling from my dizziness as I hurried to where Chase and Narah stood. I took a moment to regain my composure and placed my hand on Narah's shoulder. Her stance wavered, her gaze tearing over to me with a tiny glint of terror in her eyes. She looked down at the sword, then back up to me.

I'd almost forgotten that we were racing to the Callexus.

Both of us dove for it. I held my breath as I went for the handle, gasping in a sharp breath as the blade barely avoided my body, a wave of fear crashing over me. Chase yelled and jumped back to avoid being in the middle of a fight over the Callexus. Narah's hands quickly fell on top of mine on the handle, and for a moment, she tried to pull it toward herself before she realized that was a terrible idea. She fiercely met my eyes as both of us stood our ground, the Callexus acting as the only separation between us, barely avoiding both her skin and mine.

"Narah." I kept my voice firm as I planted my feet on the ground in case she decided to pull again. The warmth of Narah's hands was both terrifying and humanizing. "What are you doing?"

"They'll tell Blaine." An unfathomable fear consumed and controlled her eyes. One that was taking hold of her body, of her muscles, of her mind—a fear so great built upon years and years of manipulation. "We're both fucked if he finds out. Can't you see what he's done to my family?"

"Do you really think the Stellarium values you for anything more than the Callexus? He will find out, no matter what."

She didn't respond. Her fingers tightened around my own. I braced my shoulders in case I needed to pull again, but Narah was much taller and stronger than I was—it was a losing battle for me if she decided to switch it to strength.

"Do you believe they'd prioritize the requests of Silas Merek's daughter?"

Her fingers twitched. She didn't break my gaze. I could see the wars within herself crashing in her eyes, an ocean of tumultuous emotions and a storm equally as vengeful. It was wrecking her head and body, day by day, and I could feel her slowly winning it with the tiniest release of tension in her hands.

I was never meant to be an enemy in her wars.

"If you take this sword to the Scorpio Stellarium, you will betray your family." I tightened my own fingers around the leather handle. "Your father would wish for you to let go of the weapon that made your family a myth."

Her eyes narrowed. "I am not my family."

"You *are* your family, and I am mine. Act like it." I didn't move, didn't dare allow a single muscle in my body to twitch. "You will break every promise you made to me. You told me that you'd tear anyone apart who laid their hands on me. You fought the Code with me. For me."

"I already broke the promises I made to you. I couldn't protect you. I will only keep failing you, so why would I promise you again only to hurt you more?"

"Because I'm not afraid of being hurt. I accepted a long time ago that loving you would agonize me in ways I couldn't fathom. I knew I'd have to fight for a life with you, and I cannot fight without the pain that gave me my will to prevail over all I've been taught my entire life."

Narah shut her mouth. Out of the corner of my eye, I could see Chase quickly look away from us. Avia laughed. Kaia was face-down on the floor with her cloak over her head to avoid our emotions.

"You understand as well as I do that the Callexus does not belong to either of us, nor our families, nor the Stellarium." I stepped toward Narah, dangerously close with the blade between us; one more step, and we'd both be doomed to centuries more. "It is meant to fulfill its purpose, to balance, to act as proof to reverse the Code."

The Callexus lingered between us, a physical representation of the generational tension between us, her hand atop mine; a weapon so fated to belong to neither of us, yet so intricately intertwined with the stories of both of our families. Two families who spent centuries racing to kill each other's bloodline, fighting to curse one over another, and somehow, Narah and I existed without a curse in between us.

"You didn't deserve what they did to you, Narah, and you don't deserve what they'll do to you after they're finished using you. We will both drop this sword, and both of us will step away. Do you understand?"

I saw the change in her expressions, the storm of emotions, finally letting go and giving in. Her shoulders eased; her gaze softened. I had to trust her, and she had to know I trusted her. Her grasp faltered; her gaze softened. With an earthquake in my palms, I stepped back, letting my arms fall and my fingers loosen.

I was learning to trust, to lose trust, to mend trust. And with that trust came Narah's hands sliding away and the sound of metal rattling against stone. Each of us took one step away from the Callexus.

When it had settled against the floor of the cave, Narah launched forward at the same time I did. She wrapped her arms around me, and I held her as if she'd die if I let her go. She broke into tears, dragging both of us to our knees. Her hands gripped the sides of my torso as she sobbed, gasping in breaths of air. Chase and Avia stood at a distance, unsure of how to act or what to do. Chase reached his foot forward to gently pull the Callexus away from us, carefully sheathing it in its holster.

"Thank you for trusting me," I said quietly, focusing on Narah again. The others disappeared as my world confined itself to the two of us. A blend of her magic and mine interacted at our touch to dissolve our surroundings into a cloud of the unknown, isolating us in a space only we could experience. "You're safe, I promise."

"I missed you so much," she said in between her sobs. "I just wanted to go home. You're home."

"You won't need to miss me ever again."

"I'm tired of fighting." The exhaustion in her voice rang clearly. I held her tighter, and her shoulders eased, as if she'd been waiting for this moment—her moment of final release, of giving into the unknown, of taking the leap of faith within herself. "I want to rest, Kira."

Her use of the nickname—I'd heard it a few times in the memories but hearing her say it out loud felt so much more real. Though I didn't know where it came from, or why, I recognized the comfort in me evoked from hearing her say it.

"I'm sorry," she choked out, her fingers grasping my back so tightly they pinched my skin. "I don't know what to do for you to forgive me."

"Narah." I leaned back to look her in the eyes. "You don't need to apologize. None of this was your fault. I don't need to forgive you in the first place. You did everything you could to keep yourself safe, and keep me safe. What they made you do is not what you wanted to do."

"I don't want to lose you again."

"And you won't." I rested my forehead against hers. "Welcome home."

As the fog between us cleared, my eyes drifted to the wyvern, watching the five of us.

"Sorry, can I interrupt?" Chase took a hesitant step toward us. I moved back from her with a nod at him. "I feel like I should let you know that I've got your back, too. No vendettas, promise. You're just as subject to the Stellarium's wrath as we are."

"I'm sorry if I hurt you in any way. I don't remember much from when I was under the curse, but I know I hated you," she said, looking up at him. "They forced me against my own family, the same family I wanted to meet, I—"

"Narah." Chase knelt down before she could continue. "First of all, you don't need to explain yourself. I'm not mad at you. I don't know what you've been through, but I'm sure it was hell. Second of all, nice to meet you. Third of all, relax."

I smiled at Chase. He smiled back at me and placed his hand on my shoulder as a show of trust.

Narah hesitated, but let her shoulders ease as she peered up at her brother. "Thank you."

"Are we gonna do anything about the wyvern?" Avia asked, still on the ground. "This is sweet and all, but there's currently a massive scaly thing watching us."

"It doesn't care what we do as long as it thinks Chase is Mathias," Narah corrected her. "Its job is to protect the Callexus from causing a spread of immortality, and Mathias held the same responsibility."

"Got it." Chase helped Narah to her feet. "Slowly, you're in shock. Don't want you passing out."

Narah didn't respond to him as he put his hand on her back and directed her to the river. Kaia extended a hand to Avia and helped her off the ground. Narah held a blank stare at the cavern exit, her eyes darting back to the dragon as it retreated to its hiding spot among the shadows. Chase lifted the Callexus and strapped its holster over his shoulder. He let Kaia and Avia walk first, and he seemed to make a point of stepping in front of me to force Narah to stay aside me.

Narah kept her arms crossed, hesitantly following my steps as I trailed behind everyone else. I allowed some distance between the group as we started back down the tunnel. Chase looked back at us once to make sure we'd be alright, Avia promptly distracting him by a touch to his arm. Narah and I fell behind with enough distance between us and the others to prevent them from overhearing our conversations.

"So," I said, "it wasn't a goodbye, was it?"

"I'm still cursed away from Atlas and Sora."

"Nope. You're not. Sora told me that Atlas reversed the curse Blaine put on the three of you. Atlas is in Rayka. He transported in earlier to warn us you were going for the Callexus."

She stumbled a step when she looked over at me quickly. "You're being honest?"

"Why would I lie to you about that?"

"You have no idea how long I've waited to see them." Tears gathered in her eyes again. "Before Blaine took me from them, Sora and Atlas raised me for thirteen years in the village they'd grown up in, on the southernmost point of the Conviction-Autarchic border."

"Can I ask what happened?"

"It was my fault." Narah's face twisted with agony. "The village was protected against Blaine centuries ago. He'd betrayed the entire town in the War. Sora and Atlas constantly warned me I couldn't step out of its boundaries, and I defied them when I was thirteen."

"That is *not* your fault, what?" I shook my head. "You're blaming yourself for wanting to know the world past the town you were trapped in, and being kidnapped by a creep who's been obsessed with your family for 300 years? Do you realize how ridiculous that sounds?"

"If I had listened to Sora and Atlas, I wouldn't have been separated from them."

"*Any* child would've done what you did. The fact that you listened to their warning for thirteen years is impressive on its own."

She shook her head. "I don't know."

"It's the truth. He's a manipulative bitch who brainwashed you into thinking that everything you did was wrong."

Narah barely laughed. "You haven't changed at all."

"Good to hear." I smiled at her. "Do you know where the fuckhead is now?"

"I don't know," she admitted, "but I do know that Verena is his puppet."

"I am not at all surprised."

She went silent again. I shut my mouth, staring at the ground, questioning why I brought it up again when the conversation was about to turn. We were too far for the others to hear us, but I could see the gold light following them in the distance. They'd wait for us in the next chamber.

"The newest memory I had was when you were healing my back in the Woods. How much time was there between that and the Stellarium..." I trailed off. I didn't want to trigger anything again.

"That was when we were sixteen. We had a year after that."

Both of us stopped again. I breathed in the tension, soaking in the weight of her eyes reminiscent of a warmth I'd seen when I was younger. I felt as if each step I took risked scaring her away.

"Just so you're completely aware," I started carefully, "Avia's been calling you my ex-girlfriend, I don't want you to be surprised, especially if that isn't actually—"

Narah interrupted me with a laugh, gently pushing my shoulder as she walked forward while shaking her head. I stood in place, watching her, trying to get any kind of read on her reaction. I hurried after her a moment later.

"What's that supposed to mean?"

She glanced back at me with a smile. "She's not even close to wrong."

Chapter 37

As I climbed the last steps out of the mountain, the Callexus on my back, I first caught two distinct voices in harmony with a shaft of intense sunlight leaking into the end and beginning of the tunnel.

Sora and Atlas sat on a rock nearby, chatting amongst themselves. They both went silent when they saw me. A proud smile spread across Sora's face. She hurried to her feet, and I moved to the side as the rest of the group exited the tunnel behind me. Meeting Sora's eyes, I flashed her a tiny motion with my hand to behind me where Chase and Narah were.

Chase froze at the sight of his mother. Narah stood next to him. Though I couldn't decipher Narah's face, shock and realization filled Chase's eyes as he processed Sora and Atlas's presence.

Chase stumbled forward as tears welled in the corners of his eyes. Sora was still as she waited for her children to approach on their own. Narah was rooted in her place, her shoulders and back rigid with tension. Avia slowly stepped back from behind them and quietly moved to my side to allow them their moment, while Kaia waved at Atlas before doing the same.

"Mom?"

With the split in Chase's tone, he ran forward and embraced his mother. I saw Sora say something to him, too quiet for the rest of us to hear, something that seemed to make Chase's knees weak with nervousness. His body trembled with his vulnerability as he searched for the right words, while Sora seemed to know exactly how to respond to him; as if she had contemplated the very moment for years upon years. My heart strained with what they must've been experiencing emotionally.

For the first time since I'd met him, I saw Chase cry, shaking with emotion. He held his mother tightly. Sora, who I'd thought to be tall and fit, looked small while being held by her own son. Chase's intimidating persona fell apart as he gently reached a hand toward his mother, careful to not hurt her in his hug, despite knowing of her immortality.

"I missed you so much."

"Chase, look at me." Sora tilted his chin up toward her with blurred tears in her own eyes. I wondered at that moment how many times she'd cried in her vast lifetime, and how it must've felt to meet her son for the first time since she had lost him as a child. "I am so proud of you. From this point on, I'll be here for every one of your accomplishments and stories."

Sora brushed her thumb against her son's cheek before he pulled away from her. Chase extended his hand toward Narah, who had slowly moved behind me, almost as if she was seeking my protection, though that was tough with her height. I nodded at Sora, and instead of Narah approaching her mother, Sora carefully approached her daughter, pausing before Narah.

"I am so sorry, Narah." Sora finally wrapped her arms around Narah and welcomed her into her embrace. Narah didn't fight it. "You did not deserve any of it. Fulbright and I fought so hard to remove the curse. I wanted to raise you, love. The entire village mourned the loss of your presence."

Narah's face contorted with anguish, her fingers gripping so tightly to her mother's arm that both her fingers and Sora's skin were white with pressure. "Why didn't you fight harder?"

Tears streamed down Narah's face. She was completely beaten down to a shell of the facade she'd held against us all, but even amidst her despair, she held a love for her mother that became evident in the way she held her as if she would lose Sora at any given moment.

I could've sworn my heart tore open with Narah's pain.

"We fought until we were raw, Fulbright and I," Sora said. "You deserve so much more than all the pain you've endured, and I trust now that relief is falling into your life. I will be here for you, every step of the way, while you heal. You were only protecting yourself and your life."

"I never wanted to hurt anyone." Narah's voice split into what could only be described as a whimper. "I don't like my own story."

"You are far from finished with it. There is ample time to build yourself into all you've ever wanted to be," Sora said, pulling from Narah to hold her in front of herself. "And if I know the same girl Fulbright and I raised, I know that you are the strongest person I have met in all these years of my life. You and Chase, you are both stronger than Silas and I, and I will not allow you to carry our burden any longer."

Each word served as a spear into some part of Narah's dying self, beautifully painted in the picture of emotions lingering in her eyes full of relief and despair, and in that moment, I knew Narah had made her decision to fight for her sense of self again.

"If only your father wasn't cursed away from me." Sora reached a hand to Chase and pulled him next to his sister, gazing at both of them together. "Chase, Narah, if you would like, we'll have dinner together tonight, the three of us. I can explain everything."

Chase looked down at Narah, who looked up at him with a smile. I could practically feel the relief in her demeanor, the sense of safety in numbers amongst a family she was ripped from.

"And I don't get to say hi?" Atlas said, walking up to Sora and placing a hand on her shoulder. "If I do believe... these two are my niece and nephew."

Chase gave him a small laugh and Atlas held a hand to him. Chase took it, and Atlas pulled him into a hug with a pat on the back and broad smile, despite obviously being drastically weaker and much shorter than Chase.

"Nice to meet you—again," Atlas said. "Things starting to make more sense now?"

Chase nodded with another laugh. "Yeah, I get it."

"You." Atlas pointed at Narah. "Come here."

"Hi, Atlas, it's—" Narah didn't have time to finish as Atlas greeted her with a hug like he did to Chase, much to the shock in Narah's eyes. "It's been a while."

"I've missed you, kid," Atlas said with a smile. "I was keeping track of you while trying to reverse the curse. I watched your progress with Rieka on pissing off the Scorpio Stellarium."

"You all should rest and wash off," Sora interrupted them when Narah pulled away from her uncle.

"We'll talk in a bit, all of us, and figure out what the next steps are," Atlas said. "For now, she's right—go home and shower. You all stink. Sora and I will be there in an hour or two."

No one fought Atlas's opinion.

I stepped into the living room after I'd finished with my shower, a robe around me and hair still soaked. Narah had gone into the bathroom after me. The other three sat on the couch in the living room. I stopped in front of Avia, who was probably cleaner than she'd ever been before with her long shower. All four of us waited to say a word until the bathroom door clicked and the shower turned on.

Kaia pointed to the bathroom. "Someone explain."

"She's with us now," I said. "We need to make sure she feels safe and protected. Right now, she's terrified of the Scorpio Stellarium finding out she changed sides."

"To review," Avia said, leaning forward, "Narah is Chase's sister, their parents are Sora and Silas, their uncle is Atlas, I do not feel personally involved in the mess that is the Mereks, we have the Callexus now, and somehow, Rieka's assassin—sorry, no, ex-girlfriend—is in the same house as we are."

I was done with getting pushed around by her. "What about it?"

"Now that she's with us, I'll say that I'm a little bit pissed that you didn't tell me when we were younger," Avia said. "How long have you known her?"

"Since we were thirteen. And, I don't know, maybe it makes a bit of sense to hide a relationship that could've killed me when you run your mouth?"

"I could've helped to protect you if you'd just trusted me for once in your life."

"That's it, I'm done with you," Kaia jumped in, standing up to face Avia. "I *know* you're not using her trauma to guilt her into thinking you could've saved her. Don't you dare hold this over her head because you want to be perceived as stronger than her."

"Excuse me?" Avia tilted her head as a threat. "She's my sister, and you have no idea what it was like to grow up with the threat of the Scorpio Stellarium. They hate that shit when they need people to reproduce for their cult. I could've protected her better if I'd known that she was more at risk to the Code. I would've helped to prevent this if she trusted me more."

"So your protection for your own sister is conditional, based upon how much she trusts you?"

"*Enough*," Chase warned them. Kaia took a couple of steps back at his raised voice. "This is an unnecessary argument. Rieka can speak for herself."

Kaia shot him a glare. "You should feel ashamed for not standing up for her, Chase."

"Avia, do me a favor and think about why I didn't tell you about this." I met her gaze. A look of surprise spread across her face. "I've already seen Narah sacrifice everything to protect me, so I'm giving you the warning now that I'm not going to tolerate it if I see you try to push her around because you feel threatened by her presence."

Kaia gave me a satisfied nod before sitting back down. "Good for you."

"Be gentle with Narah," Chase advised Avia. "She's got a tough persona, but it sounds like she's been downright tortured in the past five years."

"Tortured is an understatement," I confirmed.

"I can already tell you that she's skilled at going numb when she feels like she can't handle her emotions." Kaia crossed her legs and adjusted her freshly washed fur vest. "No wonder she's so good at keeping her Zodiac Turning in check."

Chase shook his head slowly. "Listen. I'm going to dinner with her and Sora—sorry, my mom, I guess—and I'm sure I'll get more answers there."

"Where's she sleeping?" Avia asked. "Kaia is already on the couch in our room."

"I'll sleep out here, on this couch," Kaia volunteered. "That way, she can't try to run away in the middle of the night if she's in the room with you two. I'm a light sleeper. I'd hear her get up. She'll feel safer around Rieka anyway, right?"

"Definitely."

"What's the plan when we get to the Hub?" Avia asked. "Are we going to the Hub next, anyway?"

Chase put a hand up to her. "Not right now. Wait for Narah."

Avia yawned at his answer. "Fine."

"Maybe you guys should leave for a bit to give Narah some space to process what she's going through," I suggested. "I know better than to mess with heightened emotions and Zodiac Turning."

Avia narrowed her eyes again. "What if she attacks you while the rest of us are gone?"

Kaia held out her hand toward Avia. "And you're accusing Rieka of trust issues?"

"She won't attack. She obviously doesn't want to," Chase said loudly to stop them from arguing again. "Stop worrying about it. Let it be."

Avia grumbled. "Or Rieka wants alone time with her."

"I wish you'd actually think before you let things come out of your mouth." Chase stood up. "Let's go."

"Make me shut my mouth, then." Avia stood and crossed her arms at him. She threw her cloak over her shoulders when Chase responded to her with an annoyed stare. "See, you can't even do that."

"Oh, I absolutely can. I'm just choosing to not encourage you."

"Can I stay?" Kaia looked at me. "Please."

"Yes," I answered immediately. I was not about to leave Kaia to deal with them. "Just don't be in sight when Narah's done showering, so she isn't overwhelmed."

Avia laughed at me. "Terrible excuse."

"I need to go talk to someone civilized." Chase threw on his shoes at the door while they prepared to leave. "Avia, door. Come on."

"Let me know if you find anyone who's even slightly normal within a 500-foot radius." Avia backed up, motioning toward Kaia. "Have fun being in the house while they're all over each other."

"Anything is better than being around your aggressive flirting. Please go figure out a way to resolve the tension you're subjecting the rest of us to," Kaia snapped back. I covered my mouth to hide my amused smile. Chase opened his mouth to argue, but then realized it was pointless when Kaia gave him a look. "Leave. Shoo. Get out."

I pointed at Chase. "Behave."

"Bye," Kaia said with a wave as they walked out the door. "Practice safe sex."

"*Kaia.*" He spun around. "That was uncalled for."

"No it wasn't." Kaia stood up, kicking the door shut in his face. She locked it with a huff and flopped back down on the couch again. Pulling her hair back, she glanced over at me. "I couldn't deal with it any longer, sorry."

"No, they needed to hear that." I sat down on the couch, drying my hair off with the towel. I sank down into the cushion of the fluffy black robe I wore. My body was still damp from my shower, but my skin was free of the sweat and must from the caverns. "I appreciate you so much."

"My pleasure," Kaia said with a respectful nod. When she heard the shower turn off, she stood up quickly and walked toward Chase's room. "I'm taking a nap on the couch in here. Don't tell him."

She shut the door, and I breathed out heavily. Narah walked out of the bathroom a moment later wearing a white tank top and gray shorts she must've found in the cabinets. Her hair, dry and smooth, was brushed back. The tank top and dim afternoon light shadowed her broad shoulders.

"How is your hair dry?"

I wasn't sure of what else to say. It was the first thing that came to mind. Maybe not the first, but it was definitely the first thought I could say out loud without making a fool of myself.

Narah sparked her electricity between her fingertips. "A little trick. Zodiac Turning warms your hands and veins enough to work out moisture."

"Oh."

"You should try it," Narah said, walking over to me. "You'll freeze the second you step out there with wet hair."

I held my bruised palms up to her. "There's no way."

"I can dry it for you." She carefully ran her hands through my hair, working the water out. I almost forgot how to breathe when she draped my hair over my shoulder.

"We made the other two leave. Kaia's over in Chase's room," I said, standing up and holding my robe against myself. "She sabotaged their plans."

"She's striking me as the only reason that you have a barely-put-together team."

"We would've been dead weeks ago." I walked away. "I'll be right back."

She looked amused as I opened the door to the bedroom, shutting it behind me and leaving Narah in the living room alone. I immediately leaned against the door with a long breath out, closing my eyes. I hadn't noticed how hard my heart was beating until then.

With shaking hands, I threw a clean black shirt over my head, almost losing my balance when I slipped into my sweatpants. I pulled myself together before heading into the quiet living room again.

Narah sat in the corner of the couch with her knees up, glancing over at me when I made an appearance. "What's the plan?"

"Killing time before your family heads this way," I said, leaning over the back of the couch next to her. "Enjoying the lack of Chase and Avia's presence? Kaia's taking a nap in his room."

"So we've got time." She gave me a small smile. "We have a lot to catch up on."

"Yeah? Like what?"

"You used to tell me every update about the things you'd find in the Woods," she said. "I'm willing to guess that you might've made some progress, considering the Callexus is in my brother's room right now."

"No wonder I was all over you." I circled the couch, sitting down next to her. I tried to pretend like my blood wasn't rushing in my ears, like I couldn't feel the warmth in my veins. The bright glow of activated magic gave my nervousness away. "How the hell did I deal with this back then?"

Narah stretched her legs across the couch before she reached forward, her arms wrapping around my torso. I lost control as she pulled me into her embrace. I couldn't breathe, couldn't move, narrowed in on the way that it felt to lean my head back on her shoulder. It was all familiar; the shared warmth between two bodies, the steady rise and fall of her chest against my back, her hands resting on each of my arms. My magic hushed when it interacted with hers, rebalancing to a quiet hum in my body.

"Have you ever thought about the amount of times partnerships between Zodiac Turners are mentioned in some of the things you read?" she asked, her voice soft next to my ear. She held a quietly confident demeanor that told me she knew what I liked. She'd listened to my heart before. "Compatibility matters in the magical realm."

"Sounds like you took a particular interest in this subject."

"It's recorded most among the archpowers," she continued, then looked over toward Chase's room. "And, to be entirely honest, I'm a little bit surprised."

I opened my mouth to ask her what she meant, but I was silenced when her hand rested on the side of my face, her thumb resting against my cheek. I followed my instinct as my muscles relaxed against her, losing my rigidity as I fell into the sensation of safety. The back of my head settled in the crook of her neck, breathing steadily as I embraced the comfort of her heartbeat echoing mine. Closing my eyes, I took it all in.

She brushed a strand of my hair away from my face. "Tell me about what you've found in the Woods."

CHAPTER 38

The sound of the front door unlocking woke me up. I lurched back from Narah and sat up quickly, holding my forehead. I hadn't felt myself fall asleep after talking to her for at least an hour. She smiled at me, confidently throwing her arm over the back of the couch and glancing toward the door. As I gathered my composure, I caught sight of Kaia already sitting in the chair with a book. When I met eye contact with her, she simply gave me a shrug and gentle smile. At least someone wasn't judgmental.

Thankfully, it was Atlas who walked in first. He'd definitely caught our embrace but made an attempt to shield us by standing in front of the couch to block Avia's view. Kaia threw her head back with a sigh as Avia and Chase walked in, talking loudly. Sora shut the door behind herself.

"Where's the Callexus?" Atlas interrupted Chase and Avia's loud talking, nudging Chase in the leg.

"My room?" Chase said.

"Go get it."

Chase listened to Atlas without hesitation, hurrying into his room. He reappeared seconds later, holding the Callexus in its satchel far away from himself. Atlas took it from his hands. He pulled it from its holster, revealing its crimson blade. Chase stared at him with wide eyes as he handled the Callexus without any form of grace or caution.

"Haven't seen this thing for a minute." Atlas rested the blade on his palm. His skin shimmered red, matching the aura of the sword. The tension eased in Chase's shoulders as Atlas's hands settled on the handle instead. He held the weapon in front of himself.

Without warning, he swung it at Sora. Chase jumped while Avia ducked behind him, avoiding Atlas's reckless movement. The blade struck Sora's side, but didn't even cause her to stumble—instead, her side shimmered red as she didn't react to the brunt force of the attack. She hadn't even been startled, staring forward blankly with the most annoyed look I'd ever seen on someone's face before.

"God," Chase gasped, "did you have to be that aggressive with it?"

Atlas swung the sword in front of him again, patting it. "Just wanted to make sure she's still immortal."

Sora stifled her sigh. "I did not need a reminder."

"Why doesn't it affect you?" Chase asked.

"It won't, for a few more years," Atlas clarified. Sora sent him a look of warning. "We're stuck like this for at least 300 years. Your dad gets to explain that to you."

"We are here for a reason," Sora quickly changed the topic. "Talk us through what your plan is once you return to the Hub."

"Rewrite history," Avia said. "Get rid of the Scorpio Code."

"Who do you plan to show the scroll and Callexus to?" Atlas interrupted.

"That's... a good question," Avia trailed off.

Atlas pressed his palms together. "Great. Mission accomplished. Next?"

I searched for words. Atlas had seen the Callexus; now we were to take it into the Hub to reverse the Code. But I hadn't the slightest idea of how to do that.

"Well, we have an Arctura to back us. What about my mom?" Kaia pointed out. "The Libra Leader?"

Atlas narrowed his eyes. "She's already in."

"She knows? About all of this?" Kaia echoed, her voice faltering.

Atlas considered her. A moment later, he handed the Callexus to Sora and opened the front door to check outside and then shut it. He leaned against it while holding the doorknob.

"Atlas," Kaia said quietly, her face falling, "what wasn't I told?"

Atlas took a step away from Sora with his arm stretched to keep his grasp on the knob. "Rhea, the Libra Leader—she's a Libran Healer. Immortal. She's been the Libra Leader for over 100 years. I've developed my skill as a cosmetic shapeshifter in Gemini. She did the same thing I did, with shapeshifting to a child's form and growing up to become a Leader under... our own royalty, I guess? Rhea and I have our ways."

Sora leaned over to smack him in the arm. *"Fulbright."*

"She's a *what?*" Chase threw his hands against the wall to stabilize his body so he wouldn't collapse. Avia put a hand on his back to encourage his balance.

Kaia's eyes were wide, her mouth agape as she searched for a response to Atlas—anything to make sense of all the backstory. Narah nudged my shoulder, and I looked over at her. She nodded once toward Kaia, and I understood. I'd fought through the same revelations that my parents were immortals deeply intertwined with Gardian's history.

Sora drew in a deep breath. "I apologize, Kaia. He was supposed to tell you that later."

"I had to rip the bandage off," Atlas said. He walked to where Kaia was sitting in her chair, offering her a hand. She took it as tears gathered in her eyes; she must've found solace in Atlas's kind gesture. He was another Convictionist Leader. "She didn't want to force you into this mess."

"She agreed with how Silas raised Chase, hiding your history from you," Sora said. "I am so sorry, baby."

"Why didn't I learn about this the second I stepped into Rayka?" Chase pressed his mom. "And in what situation would lying about immortality and archpowers to archpowered children be a good idea?"

"Chase..." Sora trailed off, holding her hand over her mouth as she tried to decide what was safe to say.

"Stop, Sora. That is Silas's responsibility, and you know it." Atlas shook his head, focusing back on Kaia. "Rhea protected you. Completely different reason than my idiot of a brother. I'll talk to you tonight about this. Is that okay? Your mom gave me permission."

Kaia nodded as Atlas comforted her, helping her work through the shock.

"What are you not telling me?" Chase gave Sora an uneasy stare. "Why are you making my dad explain it?"

"It is not worth it to concern yourself over this. Just understand that Silas is the person who owes you an explanation," she answered simply.

"So, Rhea knows about this all. She's preparing," Atlas switched the conversation around again. "Rieka. What are you doing with the Callexus?"

I shrugged. "I guess presenting the information we found to the public and electing a new Scorpio Leader."

"How do you anticipate Verena to step away from her power when she's Blaine's puppet? He'll just find a new puppet like he has for centuries." Atlas stood up and returned to his spot next to Sora when Kaia calmed. He rested a hand on Sora's shoulder again, gently rubbing it as Sora seemed to fight her tears. "You're okay, Sora."

She nodded quietly, swallowing hard. It was the mention of Blaine that set her off.

"Scorpio would have to be knocked out of power," I realized. "Blaine will just take the next in line."

"Exactly. A democratic change in leadership has not been observed in decades. Scorpio elects the same family into the Arctura position, only following the death of a prior Leader, and even if they didn't, Blaine would find a way to get control over whoever sits in the throne. Rhea and I haven't been able to touch the Scorpio Stellarium for centuries."

That's where Atlas caught my confidence.

"So, trying to dismantle the Scorpio Stellarium is useless." My heart fell again. "Can the Scorpio Code be reversed by just the Scorpio Stellarium? Or can the other Leaders have a say in the laws?"

"Atta girl." Atlas grinned at me. "That's why we have a Council of Leaders. The 12 of us coordinate for federal lawmaking, but if a sign's lower Stellarium of officials proposes a change or law that the Leader disagrees with, it goes to the Council. We have 16 votes total. Verena holds a weighted vote by 3, Rhea and I hold 2—Libra always holds an extra, the second

Arctura holds an extra. You need a majority of 12 out of 16 votes to overturn a law in a sign whose Leader disagrees with said law."

"Okay, so encourage rebellion in Scorpio with the Callexus, so the lower Scorpio Stellarium proposes to reverse the Scorpio Code," Chase said, and Avia looked over at how quick he caught on. "Then it'll go up to the Council, right? 12 votes are then needed from the Leaders."

"That's right." Atlas rubbed his chin with amusement. "You just showed me that Rhea's doing a great job teaching Libra youth."

"What would the vote look like right now?" Narah asked.

"Ready for this?" Atlas pulled a notepad out of his pocket, flipping it open. "Rhea and I already give 4 votes total. Scorpio demands a lot from Taurus and Gemini with agriculture and light enchantment. Those guys will do anything they can to pull down Scorpio's power. As a baseline, you've got 6 to overturn the Code."

"So, six more." Avia groaned and tilted her head back. "That's so many."

"There are neutral stances of which can be easily turned against Verena," Sora added. "You have a Cancer and Pisces with you. Those two Stellariums will instantly be angry at Scorpio for punishing their people because of the Code."

"I work for the Conviction Stellarium," Narah said.

"The Scorpio Stellarium illegally hired you for your magic. You are not a Scorpio," Sora pointed out. "The Autarian Stellarium could have hired you. They will be angry that Scorpio took a potential asset from them."

Narah didn't respond, drifting off into her thoughts.

"Here's the problem." Atlas sat on the floor next to Kaia's chair.

"Sagittarius has been missing for ages. Capricorn doesn't interact with the Council. We've had two votes missing for, what, at least 100 years? They're out of the picture."

"So, Aquarius, Virgo, Leo..." Chase trailed off. "Well, shit."

"You're going to need to track down Sagittarius," Atlas finished for him. "Rhea and I can get Cancer and Leo on board. Rhea's daughter is the Cancer in question, Leo's just... Leo's just easy to convince, honestly. You'll need to speak with Pisces, Virgo, and Aquarius. Narah will have to meet with Pisces because of her Zodiac Turning, Virgo runs historical documentation and will not believe you unless you take the Callexus to their door, Aquarius runs magical advancement and will also not believe you unless you take the Callexus to their door."

"Alright. Sagittarius, Pisces, Virgo, Aquarius." Chase looked defeated. "That's so much land coverage."

"It's not all land. Autarchic is all reached by sea. The Pisces Stellarium resides at Vela-Cetus, and I've got a lead with Sagittarius with my brothers," Kaia interjected. She paused to think. "And, if I recall correctly, most of Aquarius also resides on an island?"

"You got it. The Center for Magical Advancement is west of Autarian and Societal territory. Virgo is north of us with the Lepus Archives. I suggest that as your starting point."

"However—do not rush from Rayka. Rest. Let this ease in your minds." Sora flicked Atlas in the arm before looking back at us. "Chase, Narah, would the two of you accompany me to dinner?"

"Sure." Chase smiled at her, looking over at his sister. "Narah?"

"I'll go," Narah agreed hesitantly, glancing at me as if I had a say in her decision.

Sora gestured toward. "Shall we head out now?"

"I'll follow you out," I offered, and in the corner of my eye, I saw Narah's tension ease. "Thank you."

"I have faith in the five of you," Atlas said with a proud smile.

Chapter 39

While Narah had dinner with Chase and Sora, I waited patiently on a bench across from the restaurant. The growing flurries of snow were gentle and fluffy, though it wasn't too cold, and I was plenty cozy with my thick cloak. The setting Sun tinted the village with a snowy pink hue as it fell behind the drifting clouds. I breathed out slowly, watching my breath puff into the frosty air.

Atlas had stopped me from going home and told me to wait for Narah. He'd said Sora thought it would be best for me to greet Narah after dinner, and I was happy to oblige. At last, the door to the restaurant opened, with Sora first emerging. Narah followed behind her. Sora's eyes lit with relief at the sight of me, and she placed one hand on Narah's back, as if reassuring her. Narah didn't push it away, let alone flinch. Chase followed behind them, talking with his mother for a moment before leaving for the house without a word to me—only slightly strange.

"Rieka," Sora addressed me, dipping her head, "thank you for waiting. How long have you been out in the snow, dear?"

"Oh, half an hour or so," I lied. "I don't mind the snow."

"I will see you tomorrow, Narah." Sora turned to her daughter, a mimic in their mannerisms as they both looked at each other at the same time. Both of them moved with grace and an air of silent strength. Sora waved and headed off toward the temple, leaving Narah behind.

I stood up and faced Narah, meeting her eyes. An intensity filled the space between us, an intensity amplified more than it had been for reasons I couldn't put my finger on. I tried to stop myself from staring—Narah wore a navy-blue coat with white fur and gold accents, village clothing that Sora must've gifted to her at dinner. The dark blue seemed to sharpen the shadows and accents of her facial features.

"Do you trust me?" she asked.

I didn't hesitate. "Of course."

I wish I knew *why* I trusted her with how little I knew about our full story. There was a glimmer of an emotion in her eyes that she hadn't had before. Sora must've said something to cause a change in her demeanor and attitude toward me.

"Come with me." Narah beckoned with her hand, leading me to a path in the southern part of Rayka. I hurried after her through the snow with a smile once she turned away from me. I tucked my hands behind my back, quietly following at her side as she led me through the village.

She was silent as she strode along the streets, veering to the west toward the rocky mountain wall. A path I hadn't noticed before weaved up the mountain side. Before beginning the trail, Narah pulled chains out of her bag to strap onto our boots for traction. She grabbed an icy rock with a gloved hand, hoisting herself up. I carefully followed her actions.

I was equally as curious as I was terrified for my life. My heart reverberated in every part of my body as I followed her up the village mountainside, barely stable on the icy slopes. I ducked underneath a pine tree to follow her after almost losing my footing on a rock. She glanced back at me to make sure I hadn't fallen before continuing her ascent.

In an environmentally precarious situation with a girl who was formerly my assassin, I felt safe. Narah extended a hand to me to help me up a rock bigger than I was. With my fingers trembling, I took her hand, she pulled me toward the sky with one arm. Stars peeked in between wisps of clouds, sparkles amongst dimming pink and orange cotton. I drew a deep breath in the crisp mountain air.

"Where does this go?" I finally asked as Narah effortlessly conquered the mountainside.

"I knew you'd say something."

"I'm sorry."

"It's not a bad thing, Kira. That's how you've always been." She turned to smile at me. My heart jumped. "Sora suggested it to me. She said it was a good spot to clear the mind."

"Do you want to clear your mind right now?" I said, half-paying attention to what I was talking about as I navigated the icy pebbles. I looked back at the distance we'd already covered. Rayka, far below us, flickered and flared with lantern light.

"Maybe," she responded simply. I forgot what I'd asked.

"What did Sora talk to you about?"

"Family stuff." Narah held a slim tree trunk and pulled herself up. I could barely reach it, and she grasped my arm to help me follow her.

"You're going to stay with us, aren't you?" I asked again as we neared the peak. "I'm sorry to ask. I know I ask a lot of questions. I'm working on it."

She held her hand to me again instead of responding. I took it, and she helped me to the top of the trail. I paused to catch my breath, a breeze cooling my face. The Moon was steadily rising as it glimpsed at us through the break in clouds. The flurries were at last dying off, the ground already blanketed in snow. Though I knew the path back would be treacherous, it wasn't the first time I'd navigated in the snow, and certainly not the most dangerous.

I gazed out to the land on the opposite side of Rayka. Mountains towered for as long as I could see, a vast Assidian evergreen forest spread below. The Stars seemed closer than they'd ever been, almost as if I could reach out and hold one. When I was a child, isolated in the temperate Conviction Woods, I dreamed of mountains that spanned all I could see. I wanted to know what it felt like to look upon the land I'd traveled from a higher viewpoint. My breath caught in my throat as the breeze brushed my raven hair astray. The Stellarium would never stop me from the fire of curiosity I had to learn; to explore.

"When you were younger," Narah said, breaking me out of my daze, "you would tell me how you wanted to explore the mountains, to live in Gardian without worrying about the Code; the Woods were safe, but you wanted more."

"Of course I did." Tears gathered in my eyes. "Narah, the Woods—"

"The archpowers," she answered before I finished the sentence. "Turning, Healing, Walking; we're immune to the Woods. It also protects those they love, their families. The magic of the Woods is centered in balance, and balance is often achieved through love itself."

"And we allowed the Woods to thrive—Narah," I started, "why did you bring me up here?"

"I made a lot of promises to you, and one of them was to experience this world with you."

"Is this supposed to be an apology of some sort?"

She looked to the horizon. "No, it's the start of a new promise."

That's when it hit me again.

She was beautiful in the light of the full Moon. Her white hair was slightly astray, with a couple of new braids tied into the side of her head, perhaps a gift from her mother. My eyes traced the curvature of her jaw and caught on the faint glimmer and glow in her skin, as if she was meant to be viewed in the moment, in the moonlight. Her blue eyes, resembling a lightning storm, watched the horizon as she carried a new softness. Her natural beauty reminded me of everything I'd been chasing; the feeling of the mountaintop, the passion, the warmth in an otherwise unforgiving, cold night. It all mimicked her.

"I want to remember everything." The words tumbled out of my mouth. "I'll get to experience our memories twice."

"I still remember everything." She glanced over at me. "I'll tell you all of our stories."

Emotions swelled in me. Her gaze was soft, *understanding*. All this time, I'd begged for understanding, and it was only the beginning of a journey of learning and remembering. Understanding others and understanding myself. I was understanding how to understand and be understood.

"Can I ask you about something I forgot?"

"You don't need permission."

"You call me 'Kira' when you speak directly to me. I really like it. Where did that come from?"

"I came up with that. We were fourteen." Narah barely laughed, shaking her head, reminiscing on the specific moment. "You were talking about how it bothered you when I said your full name. It reminded you of your mother reprimanding you for breaking the Code, which was uncomfortable when you were breaking the Code with me. I rearranged the letters in your name to 'Kira' so you'd feel better when I referred to you, and it became a special thing. You mentioned once that it made you feel like yourself, because you were yourself with me."

"Thank you," I said, holding back tears. "I don't think you realize how much that means to me."

"Do you want me to keep using it?"

"Of course I do. Makes me wish I had something for you."

"You've got time to come up with something." She smiled without looking over at me. "I don't plan on leaving your side."

"Right before I forgot you, Narah, you said you loved me. I wanted to say it back, but I didn't have enough time." I drew in a deep breath to prevail over my nerves. "I love you, Narah."

She grabbed the rims of my cloak and pulled me into her embrace. I gripped her side, our energies magnetic to each other. She pressed her lips to mine and my entire body went limp with a release of tension. I sank into the surge of the sensation. Waves of heat and warmth rushed over me, all at once, a spiraling feeling of bliss, and desperation, and adrenaline. I couldn't breathe anymore, soaking in every bit of her, my fingers tightening around her as she stumbled backward, her hand caressing my jaw to tilt it up. I returned her intensity; neither of us could stop.

Electricity traveled between our bodies. My magic surged in my veins, yet I wasn't afraid of it. I was set on fire with every limb on my body sparked from her touch as I tried to memorize the way she held me on top of the mountain. When she finally took a breath, her lips remained inches from mine. One of Narah's arms was around my back, holding me up, while her other hand cusped my jaw. I hadn't realized how tightly I was grasping onto her.

Narah pushed me to the ground, catching my weight as we collapsed into the dry snow with her hands on my upper back, shifting to my shoulders. Everything in me was screaming out, yearning for her to kiss me again.

"Did you ever fall out of love?" she asked, leaning her face closer to mine. "Or are you falling in love a second time?"

"A little bit of both, I think."

"I'd say the same." She whisked my hair away from my face. "We are going to do *everything* we can to reverse that damn Code."

She kissed me a second time.

My magic jumped to life underneath the moonlight, illuminating her body and my own in an ancient dance of blood and storm, of balance and unity, of the equal forces of change and fate. Within me stirred the calling of stories old and new to glow as if there were stars hidden in every part of my skin. I was made of a universal truth of love and war.

And I knew, with this force of *fighting and fury and fire,* nothing would stop me from tearing the Scorpio Code apart with my bare hands and sharpened claws.

THE WORLD OF GARDIAN

✦ GOVERNMENT SYSTEM ✦

STELLARIUM

ARCTURA
EXECUTIVE
→ SCORPIO/ARIES LEADERS
TWO SIGN LEADERS WITH THE LARGEST LOWER SIGN STELLARIUMS

COUNCIL OF 12 LEADERS
EXECUTIVE
→ ONE ELECTED LEADER PER SIGN

UNIONS
FEDERAL
→ CONVICTION ASSIDUOUS AUTARCHIC SOCIETAL

LOWER SIGN STELLARIUM
STATE
→ ELECTED OR APPOINTED OFFICIALS REPRESENTING EACH SIGN'S INDIVIDUAL GOVERNMENT

CAPITALS
LOCAL
→ LYRA (SOCIETAL)
VELA-CETUS (AUTARCHIC)
FORNAX (CONVICTION)
LEPUS (ASSIDUOUS)

TOWN/CITY
LOCAL
→ INDIVIDUAL TOWNS ACROSS GARDIAN WITH LOCAL RULES AND REGULATIONS

GLOSSARY TERMS

AIKSIL: Autarchic's runic language

ARCHIVE: Twelve highly classified storage rooms for sensitive documents and artifacts specific to each sign

ARCHPOWER: The three original magic systems of which all other forms of magic evolved from; primary powers that allow the user to access one or more additional magic systems

ASSIDUOUS: Northeast quadrant Union with Taurus, Virgo, and Capricorn; its individuals typically work in primary production or apothecary supply (Taurus), education or history (Virgo), and world protection (Capricorn)

AUTARCHIC: Southwest quadrant Union with Cancer, Pisces, and Sagittarius; its individuals typically work in water systems or supply (Cancer), healing or textiles (Pisces), and marine transportation or fishing (Sagittarius)

CALLEXUS: Sword of myth with the ability to make an individual immortal upon an infliction from its blade

CONVICTION: Southeast quadrant Union with Scorpio, Aries, and Libra; its individuals typically work in politics or economics (Scorpio), fire/heat enchantment or blacksmithing (Aries), and mediation or lawmaking (Libra)

GLOSSARY TERMS

DREAMSEEKING: The magic to facilitate live communication with another individual at any distance through visiting or sharing a dream

DRIKSAAL: Conviction's runic language

KAELIN: Universal runic language taught to all individuals in Gardian

LIBRAN HEALING: The archpower to heal illnesses, injuries, or ailments via a conversion of blood to magical energy, vascularly transferred from the Healer to the target

RURIAN: Assiduous's runic language

SPIRIT WALKING: The archpower to astral travel amongst non-physical realms, communicate with divinities/spirits, and alter memory or emotion via a conversion of water to magical energy, vascularly transferred from the Walker to the target

SOCIETAL: Northwest quadrant Union with Aquarius, Gemini, and Leo; its individuals typically work in magical advancement or alchemy (Aquarius), light magic enchantment or the arts (Gemini), and ranching or familiar work (Leo)

TYAK: Societal's runic language

ZODIAC TURNING: The archpower to reassign oneself or another to a new zodiac sign by energetically changing the individual's zodiac-associated magic system

SPECIAL THANKS

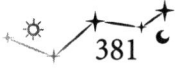

It would be wrong for me not to first thank my family: Karen and Christopher Prather, who have always encouraged me to chase my dreams as an author, and Aidan Prather, my little brother who has watched Gardian grow with me. I am also deeply grateful for my roommate and closest friend, Magnolia Baroli, for putting up with me complaining about the Mereks for 3 years straight.

Thank you to the wonderful team behind the World of Gardian: developmental editor Lisa Edwards, copy editor Fiona McLaren, and my 15 artists, Mandy, Elrose, Joe, Karen, Ikram, Brian, Sauli, Bug, Martín, Mikayla, Marti, Yama, Daniel, Dalton, and Iury. My local café (you know who you are) also deserves a special shoutout for cheering me on and giving me a workspace for the many long days I spent writing and revising this book.

After dedicating 10 years to the World of Gardian, I could write a novel's worth of acknowledgements for the many individuals who have inspired, motivated, and encouraged me. Writing professors, publishing experts, beta readers, fans, English teachers, old friends, extended family, you name it—the unwavering support I've received over the years has kept me strong throughout the many challenges I've faced as a writer, author, and human. Thank you to all who have helped to make this story come alive by believing in me.